End
Of
Dreams

End of Dreams

A Tale of Love, Marriage, Divorce, and New Beginnings

D.C. Douglass

Stratum Publishing

Stratum Publishing
P.O. Box 251278
Woodbury, MN 55125

ISBN 0-9724508-0-7

Library of Congress Control Number: 2002112340

First Printing, November, 2002

This title is available at special quantity discounts for bulk purchases for sales promotions, premiums, fund raising, and educational or institutional use.

Printed in the United States of America

1

Club Choices

December 8, 2000

CAMRON DICKERSON WAS SPEEDING through the crisp, chilled, night air, heading west on Interstate 94 toward Minneapolis, Minnesota. The sweet smooth sounds of a Mint Condition greatest hits CD were seeping from his car speakers.

> *It came unannounced,*
> *this feeling I feel for you....*

As he crossed the Mississippi River, just off to his right the downtown skyline of the city was plainly visible. The numerous skyscrapers—moderate in height but architecturally stunning—were well lit. From steam stacks, white fogs of frozen water stretched lazily upward, forming small clouds against the panorama of buildings and dark open sky. As he absorbed the scenic view, he wondered what the city had in store for him this night.

It was a clear, calm, Friday evening. And with an outside air temperature of fifteen degrees Fahrenheit, it was also quite cold.

Camron looked at the glowing blue face of his radio-CD player and saw that it was nearly 10:30. *Where should I go?* he thought. The Riverview, the most prominent—if not only—Black-owned club in Minneapolis, was one option. On Fridays, the Riverview, or 'View as it was called by many of its customers, would start the evening with a live band performing vintage songs by Marvin Gaye; Al Green; Earth, Wind & Fire; and the like. But the band usually wrapped up its show around 11 P.M., after which many of the old-school music lovers in the audience would excuse themselves and call it a night. A DJ would then take over, and the hip-hop crowd would make their way into the club soon after. From time to time they'd get rowdy, especially near 1 A.M. It was around that hour that many of the thugs in attendance felt they had got their ten dollars worth of partying, and were then ready to start or settle a beef. In fact, there had been a shooting at the club a couple of weekends earlier. Some knucklehead had been thrown out of the establishment, only to return to its outside doors minutes later with a gun retrieved from the trunk of his car. Ended up shooting three bodyguards and a patron. Miraculously, no one was seriously injured. Camron had been at the club earlier that evening, but had already left by the time those violent histrionics took place. *It's too cold to be dodging bullets tonight,* Camron thought. He decided instead to go to South Beach, a small but decorative nightclub located in the heart of the city.

Glancing over his right shoulder, he quickly veered into the far right lane because the 5th Street exit he wanted was fast approaching. Moments after completing that maneuver, he exited the interstate, and the downward curving slope of the off-ramp literally dropped him into downtown.

He hooked around the Metrodome, where the Minnesota Vikings and the University of Minnesota football teams—and professional baseball's Minnesota Twins—staged their home contests. Stokely, Mint Condition's lead singer, was grooving hard now.

> *Our love is here forever.*
> *I can see it in your eyes, a-eye-eyeeees....*

Damn that brotha can sang, Camron thought. *I don't know why they didn't blow up any bigger than they did.*

As the song faded, he switched from his compact disc player to Z-96 FM, the new Black radio station in town. A female accompanying the rapper Ja Rule was purring.

> *Every little thing that we do,*
> *Should be between me and you....*

Continuing down 5th Street, traffic slowed as he approached Hennepin Avenue. This was typical, as most of downtown Minneapolis's nightlife began at Hennepin and carried on for the next three streets—1st, 2nd, and 3rd Avenues North. Those streets, particularly 1st Avenue, were now teaming with scores of people sprightly making their way to a variety of restaurants, bars, and nightspots.

Camron turned right at 2nd Avenue, and a block later made a quick left into a parking garage. He had thought about taking advantage of the valet parking offered in front of South Beach, but that would have cost him five dollars, plus tip, instead of the three-something the garage would charge. Besides that, the wait to get one's car from valet after the party could sometimes be a long one. Indeed, one busy night last summer, he had waited forty-five minutes for the parking attendant to retrieve his vehicle.

Camron drove five levels up to where there were fewer cars, and spaces closer to the elevators, then quickly parked. After turning off his engine and removing the car key from the key ring, he glanced at his rich, smooth, brown skin in the rearview mirror. At least that was one thing he and Denzel had in common, he thought.

He locked the car door, dropped the key into his pocket, and walked toward the three elevators that serviced the 2nd Avenue end of the parking deck. Just as he was pressing the down button, he wondered if he had a pen. Patting his pants pockets through the black trench coat he was wearing, he realized he didn't, and immediately headed back to his vehicle. *Can't be caught up in the club without a pen,* he thought. *Never know when you'll stumble up on someone whose phone number is worth remembering.*

He returned to his car, a black '98 Dodge Intrepid. Rambling through the compartment between the front seats, he quickly found a suitable pen. He again locked the door, and dropped the single key back into his pocket. He didn't like carrying his full key ring with him while clubbing because that big mass of metal messed with the flow of his pants. He also checked to see if he had some business cards. He took out his wallet and saw that he had three. *That should be enough.*

By the time he got back to the elevators, a group of White people was waiting—three females and two males, all mid-to-late twenty-somethings—busily debating their plans for the evening. The doors of the elevator closest to Camron opened first, and they all got on together. He positioned himself directly behind the elevator buttons, and pressed "1."

"Which floor?" Camron asked, directing his question at no one in the group in particular.

"One," came the reply from one of the men, who then rejoined his friends in conversation. The confines of the closed elevator made their exchanges—punctuated by occasional bursts of laughter—even more boisterous and loud.

After reaching the ground level, Camron stepped off the elevator into the bright lights of the lobby, and made a broad U-turn, his black shoes clumping across the light brown, stone-tiled floor. After no more than ten steps, he passed through double-glass doors, walked onto the corner of 4th Street and 2nd Avenue, and into the cold night air. He came to a stop almost immediately and waited, along with his elevator companions, for a traffic light to switch in his favor. He stuffed his hands into the pockets of his coat, and, with the change of the light, crossed 2nd Avenue. South Beach was just a block away.

2

South Beach

UPON RETURNING TO THE SIDEWALK, Camron stepped gingerly across the remnants of two-day-old snow, his 6'1" frame slightly bowed as he looked down occasionally to survey his path. In addition to maintaining his footing on the slippery surface, he also had to dodge several people heading in and out of a smattering of colorful bars and restaurants that covered most of the first half of the block. The remainder of it was consumed by a parking lot.

South Beach was kitty-corner of his approach to 4th Street and 1st Avenue, and, as Camron neared that intersection, he noticed a line of a dozen-and-some-odd people under the two tan awnings at the nightclub entrance.

Damn, he thought as he watched his breath condense in the freezing air. *Gotta stand out in this cold.*

At the intersection, instead of crossing, Camron turned left and walked down the street a few paces until he was almost directly across from the end of the queue of people waiting to get into South Beach. He then jaywalked across 1st Avenue. That way he was able to avoid the probing stares he always seemed to garner when he walked beside the line of folk from front to back. He took his place behind the last person in line, a dark brown complexioned brotha dressed in baggy denim blue jeans, a dark gray pullover sweater, and a black hip-length leather coat. The young brothaman couldn't have been much more than twenty-five years old, typical of the age of the crowd Camron knew he would find inside. Sometimes Camron, who himself would be thirty-seven on Valentine's Day, felt self-conscious amongst the hip-hop Generation Xers at the clubs he frequented. He took solace, though—and some pride as well—in the fact that he could pass for thirty or younger. From time to time, he would reassure himself of this by asking a female he'd bought a drink or danced with to guess his age. Almost always they would say thirty-two or thirty or twenty-nine. Two weeks earlier, a sistah he was gabbing with at the Riverview (on the same night as the shooting) had even guessed twenty-eight. Maybe, since he had just bought her a drink, she was flattering him. If so, he didn't mind.

Camron looked at his wristwatch, which was always ten minutes fast. It showed 10:58. He turned to face the back of the line, in the process stealing a glimpse of his form in the smoky glass windows that covered the west face of the club. Five more people had lined up behind him and others were approaching.

One person walking up the sidewalk caught his eye, as she was familiar to him. Once she got to within twenty feet, she noticed Camron too. She smiled and so did he.

"Hi," she said.

"Hey," Camron responded. "How are you?"

He struggled to remember her name, but quickly gave up. This had happened on more than one occasion with this lady, so he knew it was no use trying to recall. He'd met her years ago, in '94. They had even went out once.

"I'm doing fine. How 'bout you?" she asked.

"Everything's lovely. Be nice to get inside where it's warm though."

"You got that right. Which I'm about to do as soon as I find my membership," she said as she looked down and began rummaging through her purse.

She had on gray snakeskin pleather pants and a matching, full-length, open coat with black boots. The shimmering black top she was sporting revealed a two-inch sliver of her torso. Given the temperature, Camron wondered how she could stand walking around with her midsection exposed like that.

He wasn't sure of her ethnicity. Perhaps a mix of Black and Asian. What was that term the golfer Tiger Woods had come up with? Cablanasian? Whatever the case, she was strikingly beautiful. And she was always sweet and charming to Camron whenever he saw her out at this or that club. She never failed to give him a smile, even if she was with a male. That genuineness was something Camron appreciated about her.

As she was pulling out her membership card, she said, "Why don't you come in with me."

Camron was flattered. "That would be real cool. Thanks."

He followed her to the head of the line. She flashed her card to the security guard, a barrel-chested, stone-faced brotha of moderate height, dressed in black. She then gave him her photo ID, which he looked over carefully.

It always irritated Camron how security guards checking identification changed their demeanor once a line formed outside the club. They suddenly became more deliberate, looking first at your ID, then you, then back at your ID again, reveling in the power they felt they now held over the increasing number of patrons wishing to enter the party.

Er'body see you, man, Camron thought as he surrendered his driver's license to the big Black sentry. *She's obviously over 21 and so am I, so let's minimize the dramatics.*

The security guard went through his routine, returned Camron's ID, then let them both pass behind him. They walked parallel to the street along a section of the sidewalk cordoned by a few feet of black velvet rope, and into the club entrance.

The loud, pulsating groove of hip-hop artist Jay-Z's spin on a Rick James lyric hit them in the face as they walked inside.

> *(Give it to me)*
> *Gimme that funk, that sweet,*
> *that nasty, that gushy stuff....*

They passed separately through a metal detector, and immediately found themselves in front of a wraparound podium, four feet in height, behind which sat a stern, heavyset sistah with a nutmeg complexion and blond short-cut natural. She was collecting the ten-dollar admission charge.

Camron's nameless friend showed the lady her membership card, and, looking back at him, said loud enough so the big-boned sistah could hear her over the music, "He's with me." The blond-haired attendant nodded.

Another security guard, a brotha bigger than the first sentinel, was standing to the right of the podium. He took a quick look inside Camron's stranger-friend's purse. Camron then stepped up to him to be patted down. Camron unbuttoned his coat, revealing the black dress pants and tan turtleneck knit sweater he was wearing underneath. In a macho reflex, Camron tensed his entire body slightly and raised his arms just a bit as the security guard shuffled his hands quickly along the length of his frame.

"Check your coat downstairs, sir," he reminded Camron.

With no more gatekeepers to contend with, Camron was anxious to show some gratitude toward his Cablanasian companion.

"Hey, thank you, sweetie. 'Preciate it," Camron said, most thankful for the ten-dollar cover charge she had just saved him. "Let me buy you a drink. What would you like?"

"Ahmm ... a Cosmopolitan," she said.

So much for the ten dollars, he thought.

They glided to the front bar, one end of which was no more than six feet from the last security guard they had just passed. It was one of two bars on the main level.

"A Cosmopolitan and an MGD," Camron said to the bartender, then handed him a charge card. "Keep it open." The MGD was a beer, Miller Genuine Draft, Camron's drink of choice when clubbing or socializing.

He looked back at his friend. She was checking out the clubbers, and unaware of his gaze in her direction. *This girl is fine,* he thought. He wondered if they shouldn't have went further than their one date years earlier. But a week or two after they went out, he met Lauren, a light-skinned cutie that stole his heart for a minute. Besides, his Cablanasian friend's life seemed too stressed for Camron's tastes. She had three kids, and her former boyfriend was prone to violent behavior. Once during an argument, the boyfriend stabbed her. When she told Camron that, he could only shake his head and wonder why any man would want to physically harm so sweet a woman. And why would she want to keep company with such an idiot? At any rate, it seemed at the time like a situation in which he didn't want to get involved. So after that one date, he didn't bother to call, and neither did she.

"Here's your drink," Camron said to her as the bartender placed a long-stemmed martini glass and a bottle of beer on the bar counter.

"Thanks," she said, and took a sip from the martini glass. "Well, I'm going to look for some friends of mine."

That was a standard line used in the clubs by both men and women when one or the other wanted some space and the opportunity to mingle. And, if mingling was her intent, that was cool with Camron because he was ready to do the same.

"All right," he replied with a smile. "Enjoy your evening."

"You too."

As she walked away, Camron made a quick scan of the club's

main level. The small front bar at which he was standing wound about itself. Only a mirrored partition, with glass shelves that held many of the liquors, prevented it from completing a full 360 degrees. As one walked around it, the floor surface went from worn hardwood to carpet that featured large, autumn-colored, fallen leaves. The carpeted section had a few waist-high tables and chairs, which, besides a little private section at the far east end of the club, served as the only seating on the main level.

Twenty-five feet away, diagonal to the front bar and nestled along the south wall, was the back bar. Behind the bar was a large, bright, fish tank. Eight feet overhead of each bar counter, a strand of neon light snaked along their perimeters.

The dance floor was east of the front bar, north of the back bar. It was small: a sunken rectangle measuring fifteen feet in one direction, twenty-four in the other. A narrow stage, three feet high, ran along its north and east sides. The portion of the north wall adjacent to the dance floor was covered with a mural of the shoreline and skyline of Miami, home to the club's namesake.

No one was yet dancing, and no more than fifty people were scattered about the main level, several of whom were looking at a Minnesota Timberwolves game on one of four 13" TVs located high in various corners. But it was still relatively early, and Camron knew, within forty-five minutes, the club would be packed.

He grabbed his beer from the counter—no glass because he pre-ferred to drink it straight from the bottle—and walked several paces to a flight of stairs that led to the lower level. That was where the coat check and a set of restrooms were located. He quickly de-scended along the carpeted surface of the steps, paid a dollar-fifty to check his coat, and went to the men's restroom.

He examined himself in the mirror. His caramel brown skin was even and clear, and, thanks to an oiliness he had inherited from his father, had a healthy glow. Even so, he unrolled some tissue from one of the restroom stalls, and dabbed his face to reduce some of the shine.

His black natural hair was short and neatly cut. The top was brushed back and displaying a few waves, the results of hair gel and a soft brush wetted with warm water. The sides and back were cut closer than the top, giving him an ever-so-slight high-top fade. His modest mustache was well trimmed.

Was he a good-looking man? Camron didn't think himself to be the best looking brotha in whatever nightclub he happened to be. But he did feel his features—full lips, strong nose, and gentle brown eyes—made him handsome in the eyes of many.

He moved closer to the mirror to take one last look at himself. A sudden surge of confidence and hopefulness that always accompanied the early part of his evening excursions swept over him.

Camron made his way back up to the main level. Shaggy's "It Wasn't Me" was blaring through the sound system, but still no dancers. He lingered near the stairs he'd just climbed for a minute, standing virtually equidistant between the two bars.

He noticed a young sistah with paper bag brown skin wearing tan leather pants. Her pants were skintight and provided a delicious view of her ample behind. And that was Camron's Achilles' heel: a big, shapely bottom. His and ninety percent of the brothas that would be up in there tonight.

She had a nice face—soft brown eyes guarded by full eyebrows, a small roundish nose, and thin lips. If he found a fault, it would have to be with her slightly extended jaw line. Not quite Jay Leno-ish in its proportions, he thought, but noticeable nonetheless. And her pulled-back hairstyle highlighted that part of her look even more. But *Mmm ... that bottom,* Camron whispered to himself.

She was standing next to a woman, dressed in black jeans and a black sheer top, that Camron sensed was her sister. The female in black was talking, on and off, with a balding, pudgy brotha. Neither seemed too excited about the other's presence. Perhaps they were girlfriend-boyfriend, Camron thought. The couple soon drifted toward the back bar, leaving the sistah in the tight tan pants in relative isolation. Camron, recognizing his opportunity, walked over to her.

"Can I tell you something?" he said to her, raising his voice so as to be heard over the thumping bass of the music. "You know, you're a very lovely lady, and I wanted to offer to buy you a drink."

She seemed hesitant. Confused even, her eyes looking in this direction and that. She moved her mouth as if she was about to speak, but then stopped, offering only a look of disinterest.

Camron's immediate sense was that he'd made a mistake. *Uh oh. This girl may be goofy,* he thought. Nevertheless, he decided to play it out.

"Walk with me over to the bar," he said, hoping that suggestion, and his own movement toward the counter where he had just left his charge card, would stimulate her to follow.

She did, but slowly. Camron had already reached the bar and was leaning on it with one elbow. To further encourage her, he angled his body partially in her direction and gave her a welcoming gaze. Her slow pace, though, made it seem as if she was umbilicaled to her sister-girlfriend.

What a silly-ass, Camron said to himself. *This was definitely a mistake.*

She got to within six feet of him, stopped, then turned and looked in the direction of her girlfriend and her girlfriend's companion.

Is this girl on drugs? Or just naturally inconsiderate and rude.

Camron turned his back to her to face the bar, and was considering placing an order. He realized, however, that she hadn't said a word, much less indicated a drink preference. For a fraction of a second, he thought about walking back up to her to ask what she would like to have. But then his pride kicked in.

Forget this shit. One of those I-wanna-drink-but-I-don't-wanna-talk-with-you babes.

Camron turned quickly and headed upstairs. A year or two ago he may have indulged her ridiculous behavior further. But now he didn't have the patience for that kind of immature silliness.

She ain't all that no way.

The stairs leading to the upper level of South Beach were above and parallel to those he had taken down to the coat-check and restroom areas. As Camron climbed them, he thought, *Note to self: tonight, leave the project babes alone.*

Over the years, Camron had learned to let brushes like that roll off him like water off a duck's back. So by the time he reached the top step, he had nearly forgot the incident. When it came to women, he found that skill—the ability to quickly forget unpleasant experiences—to be a useful one.

The floor on the main level was mostly hardwood, but the upper level was primarily carpet. Also, the main level had an art deco feel, while the upper level was more elegant in design.

The upper level was divided into four sections. The southeast and northwest sections each contained a traditional bar. The southwest and northeast sections were lounging areas in which green leather sofas and booths provided cozy sites for intimate conversations. Seven televisions, like the small ones downstairs, were strewn in different corners of the ceiling, and a glass-enclosed natural gas fireplace, located in the northeast section, made one feel warmer just by looking into its flames.

Between the northern portions was a square hole in the floor, fifteen feet in length along each side, and surrounded by gold-colored railing. It was directly above the dance floor, some twenty feet below. This was a favorite spot of the upstairs customers, as it allowed one a bird's-eye view of the dance action.

Camron made his way to the bar closest to the stairs, the one in the southeast section. The few chairs that were in front of it were all occupied, the last three by a group of sistahs. He went to the very end, sat what was left of his beer on the counter, and positioned himself no more than two feet from the nearest of the three ladies. He could feel the heat of their presence, but, because he wasn't quite yet in the mood to make another attempt at striking up a conversation, ignored them by pretending to watch the basketball game on one of the TVs.

After ten minutes of feigned interest in the game, Camron ordered another beer. He paid with cash since he'd left his card downstairs. He took a big swig, then walked to the square hole in the floor and looked down onto the dance area. A pair of Black females and two White couples were now dancing. He proceeded to watch from that location, where, over the course of three more songs, the number of dancers grew to thirty.

Restless again, Camron bought another beer at the other bar, then walked back downstairs. As he came down, he saw some of the people he had briefly stood with in the outside line who were now inside. Glancing through the smoky pane windows by the club's entrance, he also saw that those now waiting to get in were in an even longer line that stretched beyond the last of the windows' edges.

Moments after reaching the main level, Camron noticed a light-skinned sistah talking with two other females. She was dressed conservatively in a paisley wrap dress and knee-high black boots. But the roundness and size of her bottom could not be hidden. Just like that, his atomic-dog juices were flowing again.

He hesitated for a moment though. He normally didn't break in on a conversation amongst women, because, in that circumstance, one was almost certain to get turned away. But this was too much. *Too much ass,* he thought, *to be ignored.*

He approached her. Her back was to him, so he had yet to fully see her face. But he wasn't too concerned about that right now. His focus was elsewhere.

As he arrived in her space, he touched her lightly on her elbow. She turned her head toward him, and he saw that she was quite attractive.

"You know, I had to tell you what a beautiful lady I think you are, and wanted to offer to buy you a drink," Camron said, a slight variation on the line he'd used earlier.

"Thank you," she said, a smile on her lips.

Motioning to the front bar, Camron said, "My tab is at this bar right here."

She turned to her friends, said something to them, then walked with him to the bar.

"So what would you like?" he asked.

"Just a soda. A Sprite," she replied. "What's your name?"

This was already going much better than his first encounter.

Wow. Someone who's actually bringing some energy, he thought.

"My name's Camron. And yours?"

"Freda."

The bartender was leaning toward them, looking at Camron in anticipation of his order.

Camron leaned in too, getting close enough so that he could be heard over the incessant beats of DMX.

> *Y'all gon' make me lose my mind,*
> *Up in here, up in here....*

"A Sprite," Camron half-shouted to the bartender. Returning to the healthy lady beside him, he asked, "So are you enjoying yourself tonight, Freda?"

"So far so good. And what about you, Camron?" she said, a tinge of playfulness in her voice.

"It's cool. Looks like the DJ's got the party flowin'."

"Yeah. I've got to get out there soon," she said, looking toward the dance floor.

"We can do that right now."

"Nooo. It's too early," she said. "Me and my girlfriends just got here."

Camron had heard the I-just-got-here excuse so many times he thought that it must be a rule in the Sistahs' Handbook: *No dancing*

*until you and your girls have had two drinks, or have been in the
club for thirty minutes or more, whichever comes first.*

The bartender sat the pop on the counter. Camron told him, "Put
it on my tab," and gave Freda her Sprite.

"I do like gettin' my groove on though," she declared. "Can we
do it later?"

"Yes we can," Camron said with a smile.

She smiled too. "Okay. Thanks for the drink."

"You're quite welcome."

Camron took a sip of his beer, then said to her, "Listen, let me
give you my card in case we miss each other when it gets crowded."

"All right," she said.

He pulled his wallet from his back pocket, reached into the compartment holding the three business cards, and struggled briefly to
separate one from the other two. Once he did, he placed the card on
the counter of the bar, extracted his pen, and wrote on the back of it:

Freda,

*Luv your smile. Hope u'll share it with me again soon over din-
ner, lunch, breakfast ... a may'naise samich. Whatever.*

Call me.

Camron

He also wrote his home phone number in the upper-right corner
of the card, then handed it to her. She read his note and chuckled.

Happy that she was feeling his corny sense of humor, he said,
"So, now that you have *my* number, we should make it a fair trade,
and you can give me yours too."

"Maybe. We'll see," she said.

"All right, sweetie," he responded. "I'll find you later."

"Okay."

She took a draw of her pop through a thin red straw, then sauntered back to the spot where her two girlfriends were, that colossal
ass of hers in tow. Camron watched it as it went away.

What a phat ass, he said to himself, shaking his head ever so
slightly.

As Camron looked around at the new faces that had arrived
within the last few minutes, he removed the remaining two business
cards from his wallet and put them in his front pants pocket. That
way the next time he needed one he wouldn't have to wrestle it out

of his wallet.

The crowd was much thicker now. Suddenly curious as to what the atmosphere was like at the back bar, Camron maneuvered his way in that direction through the increasing throng of people. As he approached the counter, he found himself staring at the exotic fish trapped in the vibrantly lit tank, alertly, lazily swimming back and forth. He speculated as to whether they were enjoying the thumping music.

Just as he gulped the last bit of his latest MGD, Camron noticed another familiar face standing near the bar, facing the dance floor. A tall female with a slim, toned build. She was wearing shiny blue pants with a matching short-sleeve top, and had a mixed look of melancholy and bemusement on her auburn-colored face as she watched the dancers. Her curly hair was cut short, and her chiseled facial features gave her a regal beauty. He had met her at Second Saturday—a monthly soirée for the Black professional set—in November. They had danced and conversed. For quite a while too. Thirty minutes maybe. He had given her his numbers, work and home, but she never called. That was no big deal to him because women seldom did. The thing that stood out, though, was the sincere way in which she had promised she *would*. "I promise. I promise I'll call," she had said. And for that one moment, Camron had believed her.

He moved closer, leaned in toward her ear, and said, "So you promised you'd call."

She turned to him. The melancholy portion of her look gave way to a smile, and her eyes widened slightly with recognition.

"I didn't," she acknowledged. "I had meant to, but things got busy."

"Oh. Okay," Camron said with a few nods, a smirk, and a hint of facetiousness. "Anyway, how are you doing this evening?"

"Fine. I'm here with my sister. She's in here somewhere."

"Good luck finding her," he said, looking around at the swell of people. "You want something to drink?" he asked, again utilizing what seemed to be this night's expensive excuse to extend a conversation.

"No. Thank you."

He paused, then said, "Now tell me your name again."

"Paris," she responded.

"And I'm Camron."

"That's right," she said with recognition in her voice.

"So you're a busy lady."

"Yeah. You could say that."

"And what keeps you so busy?"

She considered the question for a second or two, then said, "Work. Life. The usual."

"Mmm. So busy you lost my card?" Camron asked.

"No, I still got it," she said with a grin. "It's at home. Somewhere."

"Somewhere? I know what that means. Done lost a brotha's card already."

She laughed and shook her head.

In the background, the pintsized rapper Lil' Bow Wow was blazing the dance floor.

> *All I wanna do is see ya'*
> *(Bounce Wit' Me, Bounce Wit' Me)....*

"So, Paris. Let's get this dance," Camron suggested.

He was becoming more and more anxious to join the party. Besides the flirting, he did enjoy dancing once or twice while in the clubs. Ever since he was a child, contorting in the living room with his two older sisters to the sounds of Motown and Stax artists, he'd always liked to move to the infectious grooves that Black people created. R & B, funk, hip-hop; whatever the genre of the day happened to be didn't matter. As long as the rhythm, the drum, the pulsating beats that were so much a part of Black culture were there, the urge to move was inescapable.

"No, thanks," Paris said. "Not right now."

"All right. Well maybe a li'l bit later," Camron said, hiding his mild disappointment behind a scant smile.

He turned his head away from her, and looked at the many faces and bodies that were feeling and feeding the energy. The crowd was as he expected it would be: mostly Black, mostly early-to-late twenties. There were a few White females, a half-dozen White males, and some Asian ladies as well. About four hundred bodies. Not many people, but the club wasn't that large, so it was becoming difficult to take even a small step without running up on somebody's heel.

Camron looked back in Paris's direction, and simultaneously, almost impulsively, reached into his pocket, removed one of his two remaining business cards, and offered it to her.

"So. Don't lose this one," he said as she took it from his hand.

She looked at it as if she were seeing it for the first time.

"I'm gonna circulate a li'l bit," Camron said, poising himself to move on. "Hear from you soon?"

"Yeah," she said with a nod of her head.

Camron smoothly stepped away, slid through the drove of people, and back in the direction of the front bar.

Damn. Why in the hell did I give her another card?

Given that she hadn't called the first time, he knew chances were slim to none she'd utilize his digits this time around. So he didn't have a good answer to his own question, other than the fact that it was part of the game. A reflex reaction when in the company of an attractive female. Yet he couldn't help but think, *A wasted card. Now I just got one left.*

No sooner than he'd reached the other bar and ordered a beer, another face that he recognized greeted him. It was a girl named Latoya. A wide, warm grin was spread across her cocoa brown face.

"Hey. I had a feeling I'd see you in here," she said as she gave him a soft hug.

Facially, Latoya looked like a darker skin version of Sanaa Lathan, the lead actress in *Love and Basketball* and *Disappearing Acts*. She was short—five foot three at most—and wore her hair natural and twisted. And she was fine, ridiculously so, Camron thought: toned upper body with small perky breasts, flat stomach, and of course the big booty. Yes, some of the other women he'd met so far that evening were phat, but Latoya had an ass like he'd never seen before.

On profile, her rump formed the letter "C." A head-on view of it revealed a beautiful roundness. Her thighs were lusciously thick, and her legs were slightly bowed, which enhanced the entire effect. If, some five hundred years earlier, Michelangelo had seen her ass, Camron had no doubt the artist would have painted it on the Sistine Chapel.

They had met at this same nightspot a few months earlier. It was a Sunday night, the day before Labor Day. She liked his jokes and intelligence. And (besides her backside) he fancied her smile and a maturity that seemed well beyond her twenty-three years. They went out to dinner the following Friday. She was funny, silly even, at times reminding him that she was twenty-three after all. But he liked her flow, her Bohemian hip-hop style. After that first date, he drove

her home to her tiny one-bedroom apartment with a front door that
went directly from the sidewalk through the side of a two-story brick
building. They sat down on her small orange couch and talked, a
near-silent TV running in the background. The vibe was comfortable.
So comfortable that, at the end of that evening, he didn't hesitate to
kiss her good night. It was a long, slow kiss. The kind of kiss that
suggested something special could be just around the corner.

Afterward, he'd call her, but her line was busy a lot, or would
turn over to her answering machine. And when they did talk on the
phone, her mood was often erratic, quickly going from funny and
vibrant, to distance and disinterested. Then later she canceled a
couple of their dates on the D-O: the Day Of. That was something
Camron always found irritating—a female calling just a few hours,
or minutes, before a date to break it.

In spite of that, they went out again two weeks after that first
date. They took in the earthy rap stylings of The Roots at a dreary,
but energetic Minneapolis nightclub made famous by Prince in
Purple Rain. Most of the time during the show, she seemed to want
to be alone, and often wandered away from him. They stopped
calling each other soon after, and, by early October, the spark and
warmth of that first kiss was nothing but a distant memory.

"And why would you think you'd see me here?" Camron asked
her.

"Because you're always here," she said.

"And how would you know that?"

"Because I see you."

"That must mean you're always here too then," Camron replied.

"Maybe," she said, with a light, coy laugh.

The DJ spun the maniacal rapper Mystikal into the mix.

> *Shake Ya' Ass,*
> *Watch Ya'self....*

"Let's dance," Camron suggested.

"Okay," she said, then strode toward the dance floor so quickly
that she momentarily left him standing in place.

Her progress was stymied, however, by the wall of people between the bar and dance area. Camron moved in front of her, took
her hand, and led the way. Stepping down onto the floor, they slid
sideways through the crush of people to a spot with some elbowroom, and staked their claim on it.

Finally can get my groove on, Camron thought as he let his body fall into the rhythm.

Now at the epicenter of the party, soon they were both consumed by the beat. Occasionally Latoya would turn her backside to Camron and back toward him ever so slightly. He responded to her subtle invitation by placing his hand lightly on her hip and echoing her movements.

The narrow L-shaped stage that bordered the dance floor was filled with dancers as well. The partiers, especially the scantily clad hoochies, liked to dance up there, high above the crowd, where they could garner maximum notice. Many of them there now were gleefully shaking what their momma gave 'em: a caramel brown sistah wearing a metallic gold miniskirt with matching top, and sporting long, straight, dark brown hair with light brown highlights (most likely bought earlier that week); another in tight tiger pants, jiggling her butt to and fro double time to the beat; and one other in a dark blue, suede body suit, thrusting her behind in and out to the beat, and bent so deep at the knees it looked as if she was about to take a shit right there on the stage.

They danced through two songs before Latoya turned to him and said something he couldn't decipher. She then moved briskly in the direction of where they had first come onto the floor.

Camron, a little confused, caught up with her as she was stepping up and back into the zone of the front bar, and touched her on her shoulder. Looking over the other, she explained, "I gotta go find my girl."

"All right. I'll catch up with you later," Camron said. Typical Latoya, he thought.

She disappeared into the crowd, and Camron turned his attention back to the dance floor. Freda, the conservatively dressed, big-booty, light-skinned sistah he had met earlier, was out there now, stepping it off with a brotha her same complexion.

In full control of the festivities, the DJ was ripping up the dance floor with an oldie but goodie from Biggie Smalls.

> *I'm going going*
> *back back*
> *to Cali Cali....*

Streams of blue, red, and white lights raced back and forth, and spun around the dance floor. The energy of the writhing crowd was reaching a fever pitch. Camron, though, was calm, content just observing the action. Dancing with Latoya had allowed him to get the groove out of his system, and, for the moment, he was satisfied.

Suddenly, he heard an almost pleading voice to his right: "Dance with me?"

He turned to see a slim, somewhat petite White woman—a brunette, perhaps in her early thirties—her outstretched arm and hand extended toward him. Well, he thought, he wasn't putting much of a fire under the sistahs tonight, so why not take a spin with a "sistah" of the fairer persuasion? Besides, Camron always took it as a compliment when any woman asked him to dance. So he accepted her invitation, and they stepped onto the floor.

She was wearing a black short skirt that terminated at midthigh. A purple loose-fitting sweater, shear black hose, and flat patent leather shoes completed her outfit. As they searched for some space to dance, Camron noticed her nice legs. She smiled at him as they danced; he smiled back. By the middle of the song, her arms were around his neck. By the middle of the next song, her hands were on his ass.

"So what's your name?" Camron asked, directing the question in her ear.

"Sheri," she said.

"You having a good time tonight, Sheri?"

"I am now."

Her flattery, simple though it was, brought a grin to Camron's face.

They danced through one more song before walking off the floor. He followed her past the front bar to one of the tall tables near the smoky glass windows. A chubby girl with sandy blonde hair and a pasty white complexion was sitting there, guarding three pocketbooks lined up along the windowsill behind their table. The windows themselves were fogged now, made so as the warm moist air created by the crowd collided with the frightfully frigid surface of the glass.

He stole another glimpse of Sheri's shapely legs as she occupied herself with climbing into one of the high chairs. She introduced him to her pasty-white girlfriend, one of two, she said, that was there with her celebrating a birthday. She told him she was a teacher: sixth grade. He told her he was an engineer: mechanical. After a few more minutes of small talk, Camron glanced at his watch and calculated that it was 12:40 A.M. He'd better get his coat soon, he thought, because once they stopped serving alcohol in ten minutes, a line would begin forming at the coat check area.

"Well, Sheri, I think I'm gonna get ready to get outta here."

"Oh, okay. It was nice meeting you."

"Nice meeting you too," he said. "You should consider giving me a call sometime."

By the time she responded, "Yeah, I can do that," Camron's hand was already in his pocket, searching for his last business card.

As he gave her the card, he advised, "If I'm not there, just leave a message."

"Okay."

"Listen, you drive careful, and hopefully we'll talk soon," he told her.

"Yeah. All right. You too," she said. "Good night."

"Good night."

Camron darted to the other side of the front bar and ordered another MGD.

His encounter with Sheri reminded him that there were options besides the sistahs. That was especially true of the Twin Cities of Minneapolis and St. Paul, which he'd once heard someone refer to as the Jungle Fever Capital of America. And there were certainly quite a few brothas in the Cities—and some sistahs too—who preferred White only when it came to dating.

Camron's preference, though, was Black women. He loved the way they moved, the way they talked, their infinite shades of beauty. But from his own experiences, he could understand why some brothas chose to date White women almost exclusively.

After he got his beer, he told the bartender, "Close out my tab," writing in air to emphasize his point as he spoke. "I'll pick it up in ten minutes."

How many beers had he drank, he wondered. Five? Six? Whatever the number, he could feel the slight tingle in his extremities and the mellow, relaxing haze in his head that followed steady alcohol consumption.

Taking his beer with him, he moved toward the stairs that led down to coat check. He hurried down the steps; walked past an ATM (that charged $4.50 to withdraw a twenty) and two pay phones (one of which was being screamed into by a Black girl in a blue dress); around a corner; and to the end of the queue that led to coat check.

The line was short: just six people. Within a minute or two, Camron reached the split door—the top half open, the bottom closed—that served as a gate to the coat check storage area. He gave his ticket to one of the two White girls behind the door, and she soon returned with his long black coat. He threw it over his arm and went back upstairs.

Upon reaching the front bar, he motioned to the barman, who in short order placed two copies of Camron's receipt—one for his signature and one for him to keep—on the counter. The bartender also positioned a small burning candle by the paper to provide some light. Camron always felt that was a nice touch, despite any ulterior motives on the barman's part. He added a four-dollar tip to his twenty-one-dollar tab, placed his charge card in his wallet, his pen in his pocket, and put on his coat.

Camron leaned against the bar and observed the still festive crowd as he worked on his last beer. The party would continue until near 2 A.M. But Camron liked to avoid the crush of people leaving the club, so he always left well before closing. He took one last gulp of beer and placed the bottle, with a sip remaining, on the bar counter. He then walked out of the club, past an off-duty policeman, and onto the sidewalk.

3

Home

CAMRON COULD STILL FEEL THE THROB of the beat from
South Beach as he buttoned his coat and took the first steps of the
walk back to his car. It seemed colder now. Eight, nine degrees he
reckoned. That frigid dry air was now filling his lungs. He found it
refreshing.

Approaching the 4th Street establishments he'd passed earlier,
Camron looked across the street at a red neon sign that read "Pizza
Lucé." They served some of the best pizza he'd ever tasted, and, for
a moment, he considered going in for a slice. However, he could see
through its large glass windows that the line was long, forming a
backward "L" as the two-dozen-plus people in it wrapped around the
main counter. So he continued walking, crossing 2nd Avenue and
into the lobby of the parking garage, which provided a brief respite
from the arctic temperatures. He got on the elevator, paused while
trying to recall which floor he'd parked on, then pressed "5."
Reaching his level, he stepped across the lobby, then through a glass
door and back into the cold pure arms of Minnesota in December.

Walking toward his car, he thought it looked lonely, as there
were now no other vehicles for several spaces on either side of it. He
retrieved the solitary key from his pocket, unlocked the door, and
slid behind the wheel, his backside thankful that the seats were
covered in velvet instead of cold leather. The engine whirred to life,
and Camron backed out of his parking lane. He switched on the CD
player and fell back into Mint Condition.

> *What kind of man would I be*
> *If I live unfaithfully?...*

Following the exit signs, he made his way to the vortex-like cement road that twirled him downward and to the payment booth. He
gave the Ethiopian brotha manning the booth three dollars and fifty

cents, and the red- and white-striped wooden arm blocking his path swung up. Coming out of the garage and back onto 2nd Avenue, he made a left. Two blocks later, he turned right on Washington Avenue.

As he cruised down Washington, Camron thought about the females he'd conversed with that evening: Freda, Paris, Latoya, and Sheri. He would later jot "Freda" and "Sheri" into his electronic organizer (Latoya and Paris were already there). They would be stored in dated fashion under the memo heading "Club Females," just in case one of them happened to call, or they ran into each other again.

But he seldom put any effort into memorizing names. For one, it was impractical. Over the last month, he'd been in full-out player mode, and had met over twenty women at numerous nightspots during that time. How many of those had he spoken with since? Three, maybe four. So why, he reasoned, memorize all those names when he'd talk again with only a fraction of them?

Also, Camron felt remembering the name of a woman he had met at a club, or wherever, was, in some ways, the start of an emotional investment in that person. But like all investments, there was a price to be paid, whether small or large, if things didn't pan out. And the currency to cover an emotional investment that provided nothing in return was pain. Mental pain. But his recent divorce from his wife of two years had already given him enough of that.

His thoughts were abruptly interrupted by a loud, piercing, high-pitched sound: *Whoop!* The interior of his car was suddenly awash in flashing red, blue, and white lights. Camron's calm demeanor was instantly replaced by startled surprise.

Damn, he thought, jolting forward and stiffening as he looked in the rearview mirror. *The police? What the hell?*

He hadn't even noticed that there was a cop behind him. Was he speeding? *Maybe he's after somebody in front of me.*

Camron slowed and hugged the curb, hoping that was indeed the case, and that the officer would go around him. But the squad car slowed as he did, and closed to within a few feet of his bumper, its lights continuing to blare. Clear now it was him the cop wanted, Camron searched for an opportunity to halt. He made a right onto a narrow side street, then a quick left into the parking lot of what appeared to be a high-rise apartment building.

He came to a stop; shifted his car into neutral; pulled up his hand brake; turned off his headlights, CD player, and engine; and sat motionless—disappointed, disgusted, and a bit frightened with the situation in which he now found himself. Camron racked his brain, trying to again remember how many beers he'd had. Two long minutes passed before the police officer approached, carrying a blinding flashlight that was soon shining right in Camron's face. Camron lowered his power window, and the freezing air allowed his nervous breath to be seen.

"Driver's license and registration please," the officer politely demanded.

Camron, moving deliberately, reached into his back pocket and removed his wallet. He took out his driver's license and gave it to the policeman.

"My registration is in the dashboard," Camron said, then leaned slowly toward the dash. The officer followed Camron's hands with his flashlight as he opened the compartment and snatched a handful of papers—mostly receipts for oil changes and repairs—and scattered them on the passenger seat. Fumbling through them, Camron found his car's registration quicker than he thought he would, and surrendered that as well.

After cursory glances at Camron's license and registration, the policeman asked, "Do you know why I stopped you, Mr. Dickerson?"

"No sir, officer, I don't," Camron replied, shaking his head while gazing at the policeman and trying to look slightly pitiful.

"Your taillight on the passenger side is out."

"Oh. I didn't realize that."

"Have you had anything to drink tonight, Mr. Dickerson?" the officer asked, now shining his flashlight directly into Camron's eyes. Camron blinked at the sudden burst of light into his pupils.

"I had a couple of beers earlier this evening," he lied.

The policeman leaned in closer, and, with clenched brows, looked into Camron's eyes.

"Mr. Dickerson, could you do me a favor and follow my finger?"

"All right."

The officer put his index finger about two inches from Camron's right eye, and slowly moved it across his face until it was just to the left of his left eye. He moved it back just beyond Camron's right eye, then repeated the movement two more times. Camron followed the policeman's long, off-white finger as best he could, but twice his eyes almost crossed.

"Yeah, you've had a few," the officer mumbled.

Camron, searching for a defense, said, "Officer, I wear contact lens, and my prescription doesn't allow me to see very clearly close up."

The policeman sighed, and a look of focused contemplation came over his face. "Mr. Dickerson, I see that you live in Maplewood," he said, referring to Camron's suburban hometown, fifteen miles from Minneapolis, seven miles from St. Paul, and east of both. "I'm going to let you go this time. But be certain that you drive straight home. Can you do that?"

"Yes, sir, that's not a problem at all," Camron responded quickly.

"All right then. Drive safely."

"I will. Thank you very much. I appreciate it."

Camron didn't hesitate in cranking his car, pulling out of the parking lot, and back onto the main street. He breathed a sigh of relief and said out loud, "Thank God. A DWI is the last thing I need."

He put his music back on, and moments later turned onto I-94. He set his cruise control to sixty miles per hour, and sliced smoothly along the freeway, passing in and out of shadows created by intermittent street lamps. He raced through a sleepy St. Paul, the conservative cousin to Minneapolis, and exited on Maplewood Avenue. A mile-and-a-half south on Maplewood, then two lefts later, he reached the quiet subdivision that housed his personal piece of suburbia. He slipped stealthily past a number of middle- and upper-middle-class homes before pulling into the driveway of his own. He reached overhead, tapped the up button on his garage door opener, and pulled into the garage.

Thankful to be home, he hopped out of his car, unlocked the door to his house, hit the button on the wall of his garage to shut its door, and stepped inside. He kicked off his shoes, then removed his coat and threw it over the short oak column at the end of the banister. He was in his living room: a fifteen- by thirty-foot space with a thirteen-foot ceiling (which made the room appear larger than it actually was). In the center of the far wall was a fireplace, flanked on both sides by tall windows.

Before he'd left earlier that evening, Camron had adjusted the dimmer controlling the chandelier lights to a low setting. He liked being greeted by the soft ambiance the dark lighting provided.

He climbed a short set of stairs and walked into his bedroom, one of two on the upper level. Camron dropped his pants to the floor, then pulled his sweater over his head. He draped it over a wicker trunk that was full of fresh towels and against the same wall as the headboard of his bed. He picked up the remote from his king-size, waveless waterbed, and put BET on the 19" color television tucked in the corner. A Black woman with a fake Jamaican accent was trying to convince people to call for a free tarot card reading.

Now wearing nothing but black socks and black athletic briefs, Camron plodded toward the bathroom. He flipped the light switch as he entered, and the eight vanity bulbs above the large mirror responded with an almost blinding brightness. He passed some water, then looked in the mirror and briefly admired his body—muscled legs and arms, toned chest, flat stomach. A body that was, as far as Camron was concerned, just a dozen aerobic sessions away from perfection. The thing about his physique that puzzled him most, though, was his hairy upper body. *Where the hell had that come from?* he'd sometimes wonder. His father had a sprinkling of hair between his pectorals, but that was all, so it wasn't from him. Anyway, it wasn't excessive, so he guessed he shouldn't complain. None of the ladies ever did.

He moved closer to the mirror and looked at his eyes. A slight redness was present.

"Shit, I ain't drunk," he said aloud, wondering what the police officer could have been thinking. "Just good-lookin' that's all."

Too tired to take a shower, he brushed his teeth, removed his extended-wear contact lenses, and grabbed his thick glasses from one of the sink drawers. He turned off the bathroom lights, then ran downstairs and turned off the chandelier. Returning to his bedroom, he slammed the door behind him, and pulled back the covers on the side of the bed closest to the television, furthest from the bathroom. He took off his socks and fell into bed, pulling the sheet and comforter over his shoulders. He looked up at the blades of the ceiling fan, which were reverse-spinning slowly overhead, then turned over on his stomach and let out a long sigh, releasing all the air he had in his lungs. The bed felt good. In fact, short of having a desirable woman there with him, Camron couldn't remember his bed ever feeling so good.

He closed his eyes. *Rest 'em for just a minute,* he thought. Afterward, he figured, he'd check out a movie, or whatever else he might find interesting on television.

I'm really not drunk. Tipsy maybe, but not drunk.

He knew he was lucky too. Lucky he didn't get arrested for a DWI. And happy to be home in his big cozy bed.

Within ten minutes he was sound asleep, snoring comfortably, his glasses and the TV still on.

4

Mara

ASLEEP FLAT ON HIS STOMACH, Camron's slumber was interrupted by the garbled double-ring of his phone. A second double-ring brought him to full consciousness. Without raising his head from the pillow, he looked across his left shoulder, and squinted to see the time on the cable box that sat atop the TV.

8:37.

Too early for calls on a Saturday morning as far as he was concerned.

By the end of the third double-ring, he had lifted the black and silver cordless phone from its base. The caller-ID panel displayed "ECHOLS J.D." with a 612 area code below it. A Minneapolis number most likely, but he didn't recognize the name. Camron pressed the "ON" button.

"Hello," he said in a heavy, sleepy tone.

A male voice, almost as deep as his own, was at the other end. "Yeah ah ... is Tamika there?" it said.

"You got the wrong number," Camron told him, and hung up without waiting for a reply.

Moments later it struck him that the call he'd just received may not have been by accident.

Probably got my number from some chickenhead female I met at a club.

He knew that was one of the games some of the "ladies" at nightclubs and bars liked to play: Blow off Guy #1 by taking his number, but not giving him hers. Blow off Guy #2 by giving him Guy #1's number under the pretense it was her own. And for good measure, include a bogus name with the bogus number.

If Camron's suspicions were correct, then, in this instance, he was Guy #1, and the brotha who just called was Guy #2.

That was why he preferred giving a woman his number, rather than the other way around. If she was interested enough, she'd call. That way he didn't have to run the risk of being okie-doked like the brotha with whom he'd just spoken.

Now, of course, he would still take a woman's number. But only if she gave it willingly, with little or no coercion on his part.

Camron pulled the covers back over himself and reveled in the quiet and tranquillity of the moment. Saturday mornings were always such nice, easy, lazy slices of time.

He considered going back to sleep, but, after the phone call, was no longer sleepy. He grabbed the remote from the headboard and turned on the television, which he vaguely remembered turning off earlier that morning. He searched for his glasses and discovered them on the other side of his big bed. *How'd they get there?* he wondered. *Must have fell asleep with 'em on.*

As he was flipping through the channels, he thought about being stopped by the cop earlier that morning. Looking back on that incident from the comfort of his bed, he could chuckle inside, but it wasn't funny at the time.

After twenty minutes of alternating between music and movie channels, Camron walked into his bedroom closet and pulled a long, dark blue, silk robe from a hanger. He put it on, pushed his feet into some soft leather slippers, went downstairs into the kitchen, washed a dirty frying pan that was in the sink, and placed it on top of one of the stove eyes. He turned the heat setting to just below medium, then put four slices of bacon in the pan.

He opened the three horizontal blinds that covered the bay windows of his kitchen. It was a cold but sunny day, so the room was instantly filled with natural light, giving it a bright, warm feel.

His kitchen was not very large. He could cover its white vinyl floor with five giant steps in one direction, four in the other. But it was more than ample for his needs. The natural wood cabinets and light tan countertops, appliances, and blinds gave it a contemporary feel. However, the brown, wood kitchen table and four matching chairs—a set he'd purchased in 1988 while a graduate student at North Carolina A&T State University—were older than the house itself, and seemed out of place.

Camron put some dishwashing powder in the dishwasher, which was already loaded with dirty dishes, and turned it on. He then went back upstairs to his bedroom, where it was warmer, and did some more channel surfing.

Within a few minutes, the smell of the frying bacon persuaded him back downstairs. He turned the slices over, then grabbed an eighteen-count box of jumbo eggs from the refrigerator. He cracked three of the nine remaining eggs into a bowl, dropping the shells down the sink and into the mouth of the disposal. After adding a dash of salt and milk, he mixed it all together. He removed the bacon from the pan, now nice and crisp, and onto a folded paper towel spread on the counter. He turned the stove eye to a higher setting, then rinsed the pan with water. The grease sizzled violently as the disparate temperatures of the hot grease and cool water intermingled. Camron wiped the pan with a paper towel, slapped a hunk of butter into it, and put it back on the hot stove eye. Once the butter began to bubble, he poured the egg mixture into the pan. As he stirred the eggs, he thought about his mother and smiled. Dead now for five-and-a-half years, she had taught him how to scramble eggs when he was eight years old. That simple lesson was still serving him well some twenty-eight years later.

As he was putting the last few scrambles on the eggs—now yellow and fluffy, just the way he liked them—the phone rang again. He emptied the eggs onto a plate, placed the pan in the sink, and ran up the steps and into his bedroom. The phone had just started its fifth ring by the time Camron picked it up. He thought maybe it was too late, that it had turned over to his answering service. So when he blurted "Hello" into the receiver, he expected the reply to be a dial tone.

Instead he heard, "Hi, Dickerson."

He recognized the sultry alto voice immediately. It was Mara, his ex-wife. Even if he hadn't been able to identify the voice, the greeting was the giveaway. She was the only woman on earth that called him by his last name as if it was his first.

"Hi, Mara," Camron said, trying to suppress any surprise that might have crept into his tone. "To what do I owe the pleasure?"

"Just called to say hello. See how things are in Minnesota these days."

"Things are cold in Minnesota."

"I'm sure of that."

"And how's Charlotte?" he asked.

"Nice and sunny. It should get into the 50s today."

"We got the sunny part here too," Camron said. "But we don't have the 50s. It might be 20, if that."

"That's one part of Minnesota I definitely don't miss," she said, referring to the bone-chilling temperatures that blanketed the region in winter.

Camron knew there had to be more to her call than just chatting about the weather. It had been ten weeks since they had last talked. He had called Mara then to let her know their divorce papers would be filed the next month, and that she should expect her copy of them in the mail soon after.

"So what's up?" Camron asked, anxious to get to the gist of what her call was about.

"Nothing. Oh, I did want to ask you if you wanted these tags back," Mara said as if suddenly remembering her motive for calling.

"Tags? What tags?"

"The tags that were on my car," Mara said. "The Minnesota license plates."

She was talking about the blue 1996 Hyundai Excel he had bought for her two months after their February '98 marriage. While driving the car she'd previously owned, a red '92 Geo Metro, home from a nearby Target store, it began spewing gray-black smoke. By the time she got it home, the engine was pretty much shot. Camron managed to get $200 for its parts. Neither of them had much money saved at the time, but with both of them working, they each needed a car. So he bought the Hyundai three weeks later, financing it with a home equity line of credit.

"My car"? Camron thought. *I paid for that car.*

"I've got North Carolina plates now," she said, "and I didn't know if you needed to turn these Minnesota plates in somewhere."

"Naw, I don't think so. But go ahead and drop 'em in the mail anyway though."

"Okay. I'll do that next week."

Changing the subject, Mara asked, "Are you coming down this way to see your family over the holidays?"

"No. I'll stay here in the cold. You got any big plans?"

"Not really. Just going to Momma's house."

Mara's mother lived in Raleigh, one hundred sixty-eight miles north and east of Charlotte.

"Everybody will probably be there," she added, a reference to her three brothers, two sisters, and their families.

"That should be nice."

"Yeah," Mara said, "it should."

There was a brief pause before Camron said, "So. You married yet?" He knew somebody had to start digging. Might as well be him.

"Camron, we've just been divorced for two months. Why would I be married? You so silly."

"Divorced for two months, true. But we've been separated ... for what? A year? And you've been in Charlotte since July. Plenty of time to find yourself a good Southern gentleman."

"Enough time to find a boyfriend maybe. But not a husband," Mara told him. "Anyway, I have a friend, if that's what you're asking."

I have a friend. Those were some of the most dreaded words a man could hear from a woman he loved, or used to love. "I have a friend." The translation of that phrase, as far as Camron was concerned, was, "I'm fucking the shit out of somebody *every night*, and it isn't you."

"Well that's good," he replied. "Glad you're happy."

Another pause, more palpable this time.

"Do you miss me, Dickerson?" she asked with a saccharine tone.

"Sometimes," Camron said. "Why? Do you miss me?"

"Sometimes."

Here we go, he thought. *Back to the quaint little mind games.*

"Of course I miss you, Camron," Mara decided to admit. "You're my baby. Always will be. You know?"

"Yeah. Miss you too," he said, able to concede now that she had.

"But ... guess it wasn't meant to be," Mara added.

Camron sighed, then almost whispered into the phone, "Guess not."

A few minutes after his conversation with Mara, Camron was rambling through a kitchen cabinet. Her call had reminded him that she had some mail there that he had been meaning to forward to her. He soon found a handful of envelopes with her name and his address on them, none of which appeared to be of much importance.

As he reached back into the recesses of the top shelf of the cabinet to be sure he had retrieved all of the envelopes, his hand came upon something that felt like a small box. Pulling it from the cabinet, he saw that was precisely what it was—a tiny, white, cardboard box. He lifted the top from the box and observed that it contained another box, this one covered in soft, light gray felt, which he recognized right away. It was the box that had once held Mara's engagement ring. Camron turned the cardboard box upside down and let the ring box fall into his hand. He rubbed his fingers across the smooth felt. He walked into the living room, staring at the little case as he went. He sat down on the living room couch, then reclined onto his back. All the while, his eyes never left the ring box. Holding it above him, he lifted its lid, touched the pillowy softness of the area around the slit where the ring had once been firmly tucked, and a flood of memories came gushing to the forefront of his mind.

5

Beginnings

I MET MARA IN THE FALL OF 1996 at a wedding reception. It was a mild, sunny, Saturday afternoon in September. A co-worker of mine, Patrice, had just gotten married to Donnell, a brotha she'd known for all of six months. I was sitting at a table trying not to choke on the dry chicken breast I was eating, and listening to Marcus and Dwight, two other co-workers, giving their prospects for the marriage.

Marcus was sounding off. "They met six months ago, right? Well that's how long I give the marriage. Six months."

"I give it nine," Dwight piped up. "Six months to get to know the real Patrice, and three mo' to realize he can't take it."

We laughed. Marcus's girlfriend, Stephanie—a light brown-skinned cutie in her late twenties—said, "Y'all oughta stop." Then she laughed too.

"Patrice *can* be difficult at times," I said. "Dwight, you remember when we were at that National Society of African American Engineers conference in New York? When was that? '92 I believe. Anyway, seven or eight of us from Bidell were at a restaurant in Harlem. Patrice got her food, complained immediately, and sent it back. They brought her another plate. She didn't like *it*, sent *it* back. By the time they had finally satisfied her, the rest of us had finished eating and were ready to go."

"Guess that means he better not try and cook for her," Marcus said. "He'd be in the kitchen all night tryin' to get it right."

We all cracked up again. Just as I was finishing my laugh, I noticed an alluring brown-skinned woman walking across the floor towards the table at which the bride and groom were seated. She was dressed in a black formfitting dress. It displayed her hourglass figure perfectly, and gave her a look that was conservatively sensual. I momentarily stopped chewing my food as my eyes followed her across the room. *Who's that?* I asked myself.

Patrice stood and greeted this lovely stranger as she approached their table. They smiled and hugged, then Patrice's attractive friend hugged the groom. Even though I was seated some fifty feet away from where they were, I could see she had a beautiful smile. She and Patrice talked some more and laughed before she walked back across the banquet hall, and seated herself at one of the tables. She sat down beside a light-skinned brotha with a small, unkempt Afro who appeared to be in his early thirties. They exchanged smiles and conversed a bit, which caused me to speculate as to whether he was her boyfriend. If so, that was cool, but, one way or another, I knew I had to talk to her.

As late afternoon turned to early evening, and a DJ began playing music and many of the sixty or so guests yet in attendance started to dance, I thought I had my chance. The object of my scrutiny was at her table chitchatting with some ladies. The brotha with the weak-ass Afro who had been sitting beside her was nowhere to be seen. I began stepping towards her table, intent on asking her for a dance. When I was within a few feet, the DJ put on "The Electric Slide," which threw a monkey wrench in my plan because you can't dance with a woman, certainly not for the first time, on no 'Lectric Slide. The best you can do is dance in front, beside, and behind her, looking like a fool in the process. So I had to play it off and kept walking like I was going to the bar, which I did and got me an MGD.

An opportunity to get close to her came again minutes later. The beautiful stranger in the tight black dress, and two of the ladies from her table, had gotten up to do the Slide. As the song ended, they paused on the floor, and seemed indecisive as to whether they wanted to keep dancing or sit down.

I was at the dance floor's edge and decided to make a second move. I put what was left of my bottle of beer on a table, and sauntered up to her. "Would you like a partner?" I asked with a smile.

"Sure," she said with enthusiasm, and a smile of her own so radiant I could feel the heat.

Her facial features were exquisite—high cheekbones with just a hint of dimple in her left cheek when she smiled, deliciously full lips, a J-shaped nose that flared with determination, and dark brown, feline eyes highlighted by perfectly arched eyebrows. Her relaxed, jet hair was swept up and layered in wide tresses over the top and back of her head. And her buttery brown complexion reminded me of a Sugar Daddy—that old-school rectangular caramel candy on a stick that, as a kid, I used to love to lick.

I was suddenly glad I had come alone. If the reception had been the week before or after, Kimma, a cute Liberian girl I had been dating since late spring, would have been with me. But that particular weekend she was in Washington, D.C., visiting relatives.

"So what's your name?" I asked her over the opening bass thumps of Lakeside's "Fantastic Voyage."

"Mara," she said as she began to sway in time to the music.

"Hi, Mara. I'm Camron," I said as I mimicked her movements. "So are you a friend of the bride or the groom?"

"A friend of the bride's."

"Were you at the wedding?"

"No," she said.

"I didn't think you were. I definitely would have noticed you because you're a very lovely lady."

"Thank you," she responded with a sincere, blushing smile. "I would have loved to have attended the wedding, but I had to work this morning."

"Work on a Saturday? What do you do?"

"I'm a flight attendant with NorWest. We flew in this morning from Miami, in time for me to at least make it to the reception."

"I'm glad you made it," I said. "Not only for the reception, but for this dance."

She flashed her dazzling smile again. The kind of smile a man could stand to look at for a long time.

After our dance, I followed her back to her table and, without asking permission, sat down beside her in the seat the light-skinned brotha with the fucked-up Afro had occupied earlier.

"Thank you for the dance, Mara."

"You're quite welcome."

I paused to absorb her beauty, then asked, "Would you like something to drink?"

"No, I'm fine."

Indeed you are, I thought to myself.

"So, tell me this: how is it we never met before?" I asked.

"I don't know. We must hang out at different places."

"Well, the Twin Cities is a small place when it comes to Black folk. Which means you must keep a low profile."

"I guess you could say that," she said with a sly grin.

"Where are you from?" I asked. "I know you're not from here."

"Why do you say that?"

"I'm not sensing a native Minnesotan vibe. I would guess you're from the South."

"Yes I am. North Carolina."

Astonished, I said, "You're kidding." Actually, screaming, "Get out!" while simultaneously pushing her hard in the chest the way Elaine used to do Kramer on *Seinfeld* may have been more expressive of my surprise.

"Why would I kid about that?" Mara asked.

"Not that you would, it's just that I'm from North Carolina too."

"Really?" she said. "Where from?"

"I was raised in a small town called Spivey's Corner. I lived in Greensboro for six years, and Durham for three. What about you?"

"Before I moved up here, I was living in Charlotte, but my hometown is Raleigh," she told me, then offered the old cliché, "What a small world."

"Yes. Small indeed."

Having discovered that none-too-insignificant bit of commonality, we talked for the next fifteen minutes, each of us answering the same questions: How long have you been here? What made you decide to move to the Twin Cities? When you lived in North Carolina, did you make it to Raleigh/Charlotte/Durham/Greensboro often? Do you have family here?

She was divorced and had moved to the Twin Cities just over two years earlier, after NorWest Airlines had declared it her home base. She wasn't happy about it at the time, but had made the move during the summer, which, in Minnesota, is often warm, beautiful, and void of serious humidity.

I told her I had lived in the Land of Ten Thousand Lakes since 1991, after having accepted a job offer from the Bidell Corporation. I also told her I had never been married. Her own marriage had lasted five years.

"So is it something you think you'll ever try again?" I asked.

"Marriage? Yeah, someday. Marriage can be nice. You know … if the right two people are involved."

I started to ask her what brought on the divorce, but thought that might be too personal at that stage of the game. So I asked her for another dance instead.

We soon found ourselves grooving beside the bride and groom. Patrice—with brown skin a shade lighter than Mara's and accentuated by the décolletage of her long, ivory wedding gown—looked gorgeous. She hugged Mara again as the both of them giggled, and exchanged glances as if they were harboring some feminine secret to which men could never be privy.

I shook the groom's hand, a short, dark-skinned brotha who reminded me of Wesley Snipes.

"How you feeling, man?" I asked.

"Fine, man, fine," Donnell answered with a weak smile. He seemed dazed and somewhat tired.

"The honeymoon is in Hawaii, right?" I asked. I couldn't help but still notice Patrice and Mara, grinning and whispering, and looking more like they were dancing with each other than Donnell and me. What the hell were they talking about anyway?

"Yeah," Donnell said.

"When y'all heading out?"

"Tomorrow morning around ten. Right, baby?" He directed the question in Patrice's direction.

Patrice—who, in her heels, was as tall as her husband—pulled away from her conversation with Mara. "Say what, honey?"

"We leave at ten tomorrow, right?"

"Mm-hmm. Which means we've got to be at the airport no later than quarter to nine."

I made a playful suggestion. "Well since y'all have to get up so early, you better take it easy tonight then."

"No we ain't taking nothing easy tonight," Patrice said as she grabbed both her husband's hands, leaned in and kissed him sweetly on his lips, then naughtily licked them as she pulled away.

"Aw sha' now," I said, hauling out one of my Dirty South expressions.

"Save it! Save it for tonight, girl," Mara chimed in.

"So, Patrice, why didn't you introduce me to this lovely friend of yours earlier?" I said, motioning in Mara's direction.

"Because she ain't interested in no players, Camron," she grinned and kidded. Or at least I thought she was kidding.

"You got that right," Mara responded, giving Patrice a high-five of approval.

I shook my head and gave them both a smirky grin.

Later Mara and I slow danced. As I put my arms around her small waist, I realized she was a petite woman. No more than five-feet-four-inches tall. But the body was slammin'. A few dirty thoughts of me positioning and tossing her small frame with ease this way and that ran through my mind.

"You know, Mara, I've really enjoyed meeting you," I told her during our slow wind.

"I've enjoyed meeting you too, Camron."

"I think we should get together again real soon," I suggested.

"You think so? I don't know. Especially after what Patrice said about you being a playa'," she said with a smile on her lips.

"Patrice was just trying to be funny," I said, a smidgen of joshful disgust in my voice.

"You don't have a friend?" she asked.

"No. Not really. Do you?"

"What does 'not really' mean?"

"Well you know, I'm just sayin'. There's no one special in my life at the moment."

"So a handsome man like yourself isn't involved with anyone right now?"

"No," I told her. "Why is that so surprising?" I didn't feel like I was exactly lying because the word "involved" could be parsed a number of ways. "But you didn't answer *my* question," I said, looking to divert her attention from my situation.

"And what was that?"

"Do *you* have a friend?"

"No, I don't," Mara said. "Kind of like you I guess."

"Then that should make getting together again no problem," I declared. "How about dinner next week?"

She pondered my question for a few moments before saying, "Dinner would be fine. It would have to be late next week though because I'll be traveling early in the week."

"Well, how about this," I said. "I'll call you tomorrow, and we'll pick a time that works."

"Sounds like a plan."

After we completed our slow drag, we went back to her table, and I wrote her number on a napkin as she recited it to me. I grabbed another napkin from the table and was about to write my work number on it for her, but then decided to write my home number instead, despite any potential complications that might come of it, because this was a *home-phone-number kind of woman.*

Just as I finished, somebody with the DJ's microphone was exhorting the single men to come up for the removal and tossing of the bride's garter. A group of fifteen men, myself included, meandered to the dance floor, while many of the remaining guests gathered about its perimeter. Patrice took a seat in a chair near the middle of the floor and put on a pretense of shyness as Donnell raised her full-length, silk wedding dress just enough to expose her stockinged calf. People whooped, whistled, and catcalled as he worked his way up to Patrice's generous and sexy thigh. With his hands, he pulled the garter to her knee, then grabbed it with his teeth and worked it down to the middle of her calf before taking it in his hands again, and removing it from her leg. We single men got into a tighter group as the groom prepared to make the toss. Donnell threw the garter high in the air and towards us. Our testosterone-laced competitive juices kicked in as we all leapt skyward and strained to catch that strip of cloth. I got a hand on it, but another brotha banged into me. I lost my balance for a second, but spun out of the group without, in my opinion, losing any cool points in the eyes of the ladies present. The dude who had bumped into me came away with it.

Shit, he can have it, I thought. *I'm not breaking my leg for a garter.*

The single women were up next for the bouquet toss, and were even more intense than the men had been. About twenty of them formed a loose pack fifteen feet in front of Patrice, who was facing and laughing at them as they jostled for position. She then turned her back and faked two throws, giggling after each. But that only served to make them more anxious, and a couple mad. When she did throw the bouquet, it was the wildest scramble I'd ever seen by such a well-dressed group of ladies. It reminded me of times when I had watched my grandpa feed his chickens. He'd throw out that first handful of chicken feed, and the chickens would swoop and fly towards those morsels of grain without concern for life or limb.

Several hands touched the bouquet as it came down into the gaggle of females, but no one could grab it. Two women, who were not as mindful as they should have been of the fact that they were wearing high heels, just flat out fell on their asses. The bouquet ended up on the floor right in front of Mara, who, up until that point, hadn't been trying too hard because she was one of the smallest ones out there. However, recognizing her opportunity, she reached down and grabbed the bundle of flowers, and ran off the floor laughing before circling back. Some of the women gave her hugs of congratulation.

"So it looks like you'll be next," I told her as she walked off the floor.

"I don't know about that," she said with a quizzical smile.

6

Kimma

MARA AND I TALKED THE NEXT MORNING, Sunday, and made plans for dinner the coming Thursday. A few hours later Kimma called.

"Hi, honey," she said in her cute, little girl tone.

"Hey, you. Welcome back," I said. She had been gone since Tuesday, and, other than a brief conversation Thursday night, we hadn't talked. So I was glad to hear her voice. "How was D.C.?"

"My cousins are so crazy," she said. "We really had a good time. How was your week?" I loved the lyrical nature of her West African accent. It wasn't a thick accent because she had spent the last ten of her twenty-five years in America, but yet quite pleasant to my ear.

"It was cool," I said. "Pretty relaxed."

"Oh!" Kimma exclaimed. "How was the wedding?"

"The wedding?" A twinge of guilt tightened my throat. "It was nice. The bride and groom are probably arriving in Hawaii as we speak."

"That's where they're doing their honeymoon? They should love that."

"I'm sure they will."

"Have you ever been there?" she asked.

"No. You?"

"No. But I'd love to go," Kimma admitted, then with a smile in her voice asked, "You wanna come with me?"

"Yeah. There's another flight heading that way tomorrow morning. Think you can be packed by then?"

"Seriously. I think it could be a fun trip. Especially in the winter."

"I agree."

"So we should go in January. Or February would be even better.

We could celebrate your birthday in Hawaii!"

"All right. We'll look into it," I said, hoping that would satisfy Kimma for the time being. "What are you doing tonight?"

"Nothing. Just a load or two of laundry. Other than that, just getting myself mentally prepared to go back to work tomorrow."

"I'll come help you."

"Wash clothes?"

"No. Get mentally prepared for work. I have some techniques that'll help you to relax."

"You do, huh?"

"Yes."

"You'll have to show me some of those techniques," Kimma said.

"Gladly," I told her with a chuckle.

"I brought you something from D.C.," she said.

"What?"

"It's a surprise. I'll show you when you get here."

"How's seven o'clock?" I asked. "Think you'll be through with laundry by then?"

"Should be."

"Well I'll see you then," I said.

"Okay."

"Bye."

"Bye, honey," she bid.

Kimma was so sweet. I almost wanted to call Mara back and cancel our date. Almost. I didn't see any need to do that, though, because it was only a date. Besides, we'd probably go out a time or two, decide it wasn't all that, then go our separate ways. At least those were my thoughts at the time.

I left my house around six-thirty to go see Kimma. She lived on the south side of Minneapolis in a small split-level complex of eight apartments on a quiet, tree-lined street populated by an eclectic mix of brown people.

I found a parking spot within a half-block of her building, then walked up to the entrance and pushed the button beside her name on the intercom system.

"Yes?" Her voice was distorted by the cheap speaker, like the kind you find at the menu boards of fast food drive-throughs.

"It's me," I blurted.

She buzzed me in and I climbed the short set of stairs to her level in three giant steps. I walked through a door that led into the hallway of the upper-level apartments. Kimma's was the first one on the left. I was about to rap on her door when it opened. Standing behind it was Kimma, a welcoming smile spread across her lovely, dark brown face, looking cool and relaxed in a white sweater and tight, well-worn jeans.

Kimma was a pretty girl. Not a beautiful pretty, but—with her big, sleepy brown eyes, pug nose, smooth cheeks, and pouty lips—a cute, precocious, chocolate-baby-doll kind of pretty. And, at five-feet-seven-inches tall and just under one hundred thirty pounds, her figure was quite nice too.

"Heeey," she cooed as she wrapped her arms around my neck and gave me a gentle kiss. I put my arms around her waist and pulled her body tight against mine, then parted her lips with my tongue. She gave me hers, and murmured "Mmm" as we smooched in her doorway.

She pulled away before I was ready for her to and said, "I guess you *did* miss me."

"You could say that," I told her as I smiled into her eyes. "I like your hair."

Kimma usually wore her shoulder-length black hair straight with the ends flipped. But now it was in thick braids that were angled across and down her head.

"Thanks. My cousin did it for me. You hungry?" Kimma asked as she turned and stepped quickly towards the short hallway that led to the bathroom and bedroom.

"Li'l bit. What you got?"

She looked back at me over her shoulder and said, "Look on the stove!" then disappeared into her bedroom, shutting the door behind her.

I walked into the apartment, then closed and locked the door. Just a few steps inside, a kitchen and small dining area were to my right, the living room to my left.

I looked over at the stove and saw a lone, covered pot sitting on one of the eyes. Speculating on what was in it, I said *Rice and something* to myself. Rice was a staple, I had learned, of the Liberian diet, and, as best I could tell, Kimma ate it most everyday. I lifted the lid of the pot, and sure enough, it was half-filled with fluffy white rice. Mixed with it were broiled chicken pieces and spinach. I scooped several big spoonfuls of the rice and spinach, along with a leg and a breast, into a bowl, put it in a small white microwave that was on the kitchen counter, and set the timer for two minutes. I then walked into the living room, found the TV remote, turned on the television, and began flipping through the channels.

Besides the living room, kitchen, and small dining area, her bedroom and the meager bathroom were all there was to her small apartment. The decorum was simple and she kept it neat and clean, which gave it a comfortable feel. The 27" color television, supported by a wide slat of wood painted black and resting on four cinder blocks (also painted black), was perhaps the most extravagant item present.

"Kimma, what are you doing?" I bellowed in the direction of her bedroom.

"Getting your surprise," came her faint reply from behind the closed bedroom door.

Ten minutes later I was savoring the food I had heated and checking out replay action from the day's NFL games, when Kimma walked into the living room.

"Sur-pri-ise," she sang as she stepped between me and the TV and twirled.

She was wearing a red camisole, red panties, sheer red stockings that ended just above the middle of her thighs, and red high-heel shoes. The stockings were held in place by a garter belt, red as well, that was around her waist.

All I could do was smile at her. And it was quite clear to me that the time for eating food was over, so I put my bowl of rice and chicken and spinach down on the coffee table.

"Ooh, baby," I said.

Kimma was grinning big. I lifted myself from her dark blue couch and stepped to her. She shimmied into my arms and we kissed deeply. As I let my hands drop from her waist to her soft shapely behind, I could feel the heat gathering in various zones of my body.

I unlocked my mouth from hers, and pulled the black, long-sleeve pullover sweater I was wearing over my head. I threw it over the back of the couch as Kimma rubbed the hair on my chest and asked, "So you like my surprise?"

"I love it, sweetie," I said, then kissed her again.

I swung her around 180 degrees and pushed her down onto the couch. She undid my belt and the top button of my jeans, and planted a wet kiss just below my navel. I kneeled between her legs. She leaned back; I leaned in, and traced my tongue from the side of her neck to the middle of her chest. I pulled the straps of her camisole from her shoulders, then pulled it down on one side to reveal one of her small, doughy-soft breasts. I wrapped my mouth around it, then teased her nipple with my tongue. Kimma moaned her approval. She flexed her top lip into a thin line and sucked air in between clenched teeth, making a sensually charged hissing sound. The skin between her brows rippled as she concentrated on the pleasures her body was experiencing.

I rose to my feet and reached for her hands. She opened her eyes, saw me towering over her with outstretched arms, and placed her hands in mine.

"This couch is too small," I complained. "Let's go in your room."

"Okay," she whispered, thinned her top lip again, and inhaled another hiss as I lifted her from the sofa.

Kimma was already a fairly tall woman, so the two inches added by her high heels made her seem even taller, her legs even more long and sexy.

She headed towards her bedroom, and reached her hand back for me. I was a giant step behind, though, too far to reach her. I was lagging intentionally so that I could further admire her feminine form and the contrast of her beautiful chocolate skin against the deep red of her lingerie. Her outfit was nice. Real nice. But it would have to go soon.

We stepped into her bedroom. The white horizontal blinds, accented by thin yellow curtains, were closed. However, the last vestiges of a setting sun were seeping in, which gave the room an auburn haze.

Kimma reached her bed, sat down, and gave me a sexy-cute come-hither look. I dropped my baggy blue jeans to my ankles with dramatic flair, revealing black boxers with vertical white stripes. Kimma laughed as I kicked off my shoes, stepped out of my pants, and took off my socks. By the time I got to the bed, she had already removed her camisole and was reclined. With the cream-colored sheets of her bed as a backdrop, she looked scrumptious—like a delectable work of art painted on a lightly hued canvass.

There were more deep kisses, and in short order her shoes, garter belt, and panties, as well as my boxers, were relegated to the carpet. I caressed and explored and made love to her body with my tongue and mouth. Spurred by her passion, she did the same to me without hesitation, with vigor and gusto. Our bodies entwined. I entered her, raised her legs high, her red pantyhose still covering them, and gave her all of me. I found my rhythm and leverage as she periodically twisted, pulled, and pumped beneath me. The pressures of our lust intensified until, with nowhere to go, they exploded. First she, then me.

The purity, calm, and exhaustion of sexual satisfaction washed over us. Our bodies remained as one as my member pulsed inside of her.

"Aah," Kimma exhaled. "I need a cigarette."

I laughed at that statement because she knew she didn't smoke. I also took it as a compliment, an indication that I had satisfied her to the point of silliness.

"Mmm," I moaned softly in her ear, then kissed her on her cheek. "That was good."

"Damn good," Kimma concurred. A few seconds later she was exhorting, "Up up up," as she patted me softly on my naked rump.

She hated for me to stay on top of her after we made love. I guess a limp, spent two hundred and five pounds *could* get a little heavy. I raised up, pulled myself out of her, rolled to one side, then gathered her into my arms.

We laid there—cuddled, silent, eyes closed, and completely re-laxed—for what seemed a long time.

Then Kimma tilted her head up towards me and softly touched her lips to mine.

"Thank you for coming to see me," she said. "I missed you."

Again I looked into her big, pretty brown eyes—eyes that told me she was ready to love me—and kissed her on her forehead.

"I missed you too," I whispered.

7

Phone Calls

December 13, 2000

I T WAS TWENTY-TWO MINUTES AFTER NOON on Wednesday, hump day. Camron, sitting behind his computer, was finishing off the last of two cheeseburgers included in his #2 Value Meal. He was also checking the latest news online. If nothing else, he thought, the Internet was good for killing some time.

Bob, an upper-middle-aged, hearty Norwegian who served as a technician for Camron and one other engineer in their group, stuck his head in Camron's small office.

"Cam, that setup you wanted is ready to go," he said.

"Okay, thanks. I'll take a look at it in a few minutes," Camron told him.

Bob's head disappeared from the doorway, then immediately reappeared. "Oh. Got a joke for ya'." Bob was always telling jokes, most of them bad. "What do you call a lesbian dinosaur?"

Camron knew there was no use resisting. "I don't know. What *do* you call a lesbian dinosaur?" he asked with an assumed look of inquisitiveness on his face.

"A Lic-a-lot-a-puss."

Camron cackled, shaking his head. "When are you gonna get the help you need, man?"

"My medical insurance can't afford to give me the help I need," Bob replied, then disappeared again.

Still amused, Camron laughed once more at Bob's joke. It was actually one of his funnier ones.

Rrring.

Camron picked up his phone, an arm's length away, before the second ring.

"FPC, Camron Dickerson," he said dryly. The acronym stood for Fluid Processing Center, and was the department within Bidell's Twin Cities headquarters at which he'd worked for the last three years.

"Camron?"

It was a female voice. Soft.

"This is he."

"Hi. This is Paris."

Who the hell is Paris? he thought. The name sounded familiar. A club babe he suspected. But, at the moment, he couldn't connect a face or personality with the name.

Then she quickly, graciously, jogged his memory. "We met last Friday at South Beach. Or I should say, met again. Remember?"

"Hi, Paris," he said, thankful for her reminder. "I remember you perfectly. So how are you?"

"Fine."

"You at work?"

"Yes," she said. "I'm a nurse at Abbott Hospital."

She had a seductive voice, Camron thought. Smooth, relaxed, and mixed with just a touch of sensuality.

"Yeah, I remember you telling me that when we were talking at Second Saturday," Camron said. "How do you like that career?"

"I don't. Not anymore. Too much work. Hours are sometimes terrible. And they just seem to want more and more for less and less."

"Yeah, I know what you mean," he said.

To be truthful, he didn't know what she meant because he wasn't a nurse, his days were strictly Monday through Friday, and rarely did he work beyond eight hours on any of them. Nevertheless, the empathy seemed appropriate.

"Now is Abbott in St. Paul?" he asked.

"No, Minneapolis. I live in downtown St. Paul, so it's not too bad of a drive."

As she was speaking, Camron was trying to think of a way to suavely fashion a face-to-face hookup. Nothing came to him, so he stalled for more time.

"Did you enjoy yourself at South Beach?" he asked.

"No, not really. It's not necessarily my kind of atmosphere. I don't even know why I go sometimes."

"Let me guess. To avoid boredom."

"That's probably as good an excuse as any," she said.

"Did you ever find your sister?"

"Yeah. We left early though. Before twelve-thirty. It was getting too crowded in there. We got our money back too."

"How'd you manage that?"

"My crazy sister running game. On our way out, she told the guy at the door it was too crowded, and that we wanted our money back. Of course he told us no. Then she pulled out her cell phone and threatened to call the fire marshal and ask him to come check and see if the club was overcrowded. And you know there's a fire station right around the corner from South Beach, right? They couldn't give us our twenty dollars back fast enough."

They both laughed.

"That was clever," Camron said. "Devious … but clever. I might have to use that one myself sometime."

"Just be sure and have your cell phone with you," Paris said, laughing more.

"Exactly," he said. Camron now had a first-date idea in mind. "You know, given that you're right there in St. Paul, and I'm not too far from you, we should get together for dinner one day after work."

"Yeah. We can do that."

"What time do you normally get off?" he asked.

"I'm on days for the next two weeks, so I get off at three."

Camron's workday typically ended between 5:00 and 5:30. But he could come in early or skip lunch so he could meet her a little sooner. As far as a day was concerned, he was about to suggest the coming Friday, but thought that might strike her as too soon, too anxious on his part. He opted for the following week instead. "How does next Tuesday look for you?"

"Tuesday? That should be okay," Paris said.

"Cool. Do you know where the Wild Onion is?"

"Grand Avenue, right?"

"Yes."

Grand Avenue, over the length of several blocks, was one of St. Paul's most vibrant streets, and was home to a number of festive restaurants and shops. The Wild Onion, a restaurant-bar that offered burgers, beer, and other like fare, was one of them.

"Why don't we say four-thirty," Camron proposed.

"Sure."

Camron suggested she give him a number at which he could

reach her in case their plans got kinked. She gave him her cell number.

"Thanks for calling, Paris. I'm looking forward to dinner."

"Me too," she said.

"If I don't see you this weekend out and about, I'll see you next Tuesday."

"All right. You have a good afternoon."

"You too," Camron said. "Bye."

"Bye."

That was a pleasant surprise, he thought as he hung up the phone. There was a slight smile on his face. *Looks like I'll get a chance to see what Ms. Paris is about after all.*

Camron stretched and yawned, fighting off a laziness that always seemed to accompany the early hours of a workday afternoon. He went next door to the small room that served as his laboratory to check out the simple setup Bob had constructed for him—a tabletop pump, mixing tank, and filter, all connected by flexible tubing. He poured a few gallons of water into the tank, and, to check for leaks, turned the pump on to recirculate the liquid through the system. Finding no drips, he turned the pump off, made a quick trip to the men's restroom, then returned to his desk to author some e-mails. In the middle of typing his first one, the phone rang again.

"FPC, Camron Dickerson."

"Camron!"

The excited voice at the other end was his co-worker/friend, Renee Johnson. She was calling, no doubt, about their dinner engagement slated for later that day.

"What's up, Ms. Johnson?" Camron said.

"Nothing. What's up with you?"

"Hey, Camron," said another voice over the phone.

"Hi, JaLisa," Camron said.

Renee apparently had arranged a three-way call to include her best friend, JaLisa Maxwell. JaLisa worked for Bidell as well, and for about the last two years, the three of them had got together monthly for lunch or dinner. It had become a ritual: a way for them to relax, let their hair down, and get country after being cramped in their corporate environs.

"So how's the day going for you ladies?" Camron asked.

"Mine is going great because I'm on vacation," JaLisa said.

"She's on vacation today, tomorrow, and Friday," Renee informed him.

"Must be nice," Camron said.

"It is," JaLisa assured them. "And while I'm out, you guys keep making that money. Keep my benefits rolling in."

"Somebody got to make the money," said Camron.

"We're meeting at Bob's, right?" Renee asked.

Bob's, or more correctly, Bob's Big House Bar-b-que, was the appointed location for this month's affair.

"Yeah. Five-thirty," Camron replied.

"Hey, Renee. Can you swing by and pick me up?" JaLisa asked.

"Now, Camron, can you believe this?" Renee queried. "She at home sittin' on her butt all day, but yet and still want me to pick her up and chauffeur her around."

"Hey. Supervisors got it like that," Camron said.

"I guess so," Renee replied.

"Yeah right," JaLisa said. "All Bidell give this supervisor is a hard way to go. That's why I had to get up outta there the rest of this week. Clear my head."

"I know that's right," Renee said.

As of late, things hadn't been going well for JaLisa at work. Jealous and backbiting co-workers, and a boss she felt was guilty of favoritism, were beginning to work her nerves.

"And I got to talk about some things at dinner," Renee said.

"What?" Camron asked.

"She needs some feedback," JaLisa said. "A male perspective on some issues."

"Some issues involving a man I'm sure," Camron said.

"Of course," JaLisa said, confirming his suspicion.

This should be interesting, he thought. Things generally were when it came to Renee and her men.

"All right, ladies. I'll see you at five-thirty," Camron said, then added, "Oh, Renee. It's your turn to pay, so bring a lot of money. I'm gonna throw down on me some ribs."

Renee quickly corrected him. "No it's not my turn to pay. I paid last time. And JaLisa paid before that, so actually it's *your* turn to pay."

Camron knew it was his turn to cover their meal, but he just wanted to get a rise out of Renee. Put some tease into her afternoon. He laughed, then allayed her fiscal fears. "I know, I know. Calm down."

"We'll see you there at five-thirty. Not five-forty-five or six, but five-thirty," Renee reminded him in no unsubtle terms.

"I'll be there," Camron chuckled. "Bye."

"Bye," Renee and JaLisa replied in unison.

Camron hung up the phone and left them to continue conversing.

8

JaLisa & Renee

BY THE TIME CAMRON CLICKED himself out the front entrance of his building with his magnetic ID card at 5:13 P.M., it was already dark outside. By virtue of its proximity to the top of the world, Minnesota's winter days were short. For the same reason, when, in summer, the tilt of the earth's axis brought the sun closest, Minnesota days were long. The longest Camron had ever experienced. So long that, on some days in June, remnants of sunlight scattered across the northwestern sky till nearly ten at night.

But it wasn't June. It was December, and summer seemed so far away that there was no use thinking about it, or even trying to imagine it. Winter's glacial grip was in full command, and now had Camron firmly in its grasp.

It was three degrees Fahrenheit outside. So cold Camron wondered how the air itself could stand it. To keep himself warm while traversing down the sidewalk and the fifty yards across a near-deserted parking lot to his car, his upper body was covered in three layers—a blue denim shirt, light gray sweater, and a three-quarter length, charcoal-gray wool coat. He was also wearing thin leather gloves, a black fedora, a black wool scarf wrapped twice around his neck, blue jeans, and thick-soled, steel-toed work shoes. Even so, by the time he reached his car, the frigid air had thoroughly chilled him, and the interior of his vehicle provided only a modicum of relief. As he fumbled to get his key into the ignition, he let out an audible "Woo!" in response to the teeth-chattering temperatures. Turning the key, his car came to life, and he set it in motion without waiting for it to warm.

Camron maneuvered to the service road that ovaled and bisected the myriad of buildings that made up Bidell's corporate campus, and was soon traveling east on Interstate 94. He exited onto Radio Drive, then veered south. Two miles later he reached Valley Creek Road, turned left at two successive stop lights, and wound his way into the parking lot of the giant log cabin structure that served as Bob's Big House Bar-b-que Restaurant. He found a place to park and walked inside.

Thirty minutes later, JaLisa, a tall sistah in her early forties with cinnamon brown skin and short-cropped, natural hair, was admonishing Camron. "I don't know how you can eat all that nasty pork," she said.

"How? Watch this," Camron responded, then took a big bite from one of the meaty bones of his half-slab of ribs.

"Uh huh, it's funny now," JaLisa said, "but wait till that first heart attack sneaks up on you."

"I'll deal with that when it comes," Camron said, dismissing her concern. "So, Renee, what particular man problems are you having now?"

"She's having problems with Steve again," JaLisa said.

Renee posed a question. "Camron, what's wrong with the brothas today?" Renee had a hazel complexion, medium-length, beauty-shop-relaxed hair, and a voluptuous body that attracted men for the wrong reasons. At twenty-eight years old, she was the youngest of the trio. "You a man. Explain it to me."

Camron could sense Renee was about to go on a mental warpath against the latest man that had done her wrong, and the defense of the American Black male—nay, all men—would soon rest on his broad shoulders. But before beginning his joust for mankind, he wanted one more bite of the tender, succulent, barbecued pork ribs he was enjoying.

"I'll tell you what the problem is," JaLisa offered. "Men want to have their cake and eat it too."

"Wait a minute," Camron interjected as he dabbed his mouth with a stiff paper towel, the only style of napkin the restaurant offered. "Let me break it down for y'all. Can I do that?"

"Okay, break it down," Renee said, her voice almost an octave higher than when she previously spoke.

They were now moving flush into a Black male-female relationship conversation, a favorite topic of their monthly get-togethers.

"We're in a new millennium, right?" Camron asked rhetorically.

"Well, yeah, we will be in 2001, which is a couple of weeks

away still," JaLisa said.

"Whatever," Camron said. "My point is this. Women have spent much of the past century fighting for equal rights. They got the vote, access to good jobs, and are operating closer to their full potential."

"And what does that have to do with the way Steve is treating me?" Renee asked.

"Hold it, Renee. So what are you trying to say, Mr. Dickerson?" JaLisa asked with a grin and a twinkle of anticipation in her gray-brown eyes.

"I'm saying, things are more equal now. Women are independent. Because what did Destiny's Child say in their li'l song? *'Shoes on my feet, I bought it.'*" Camron sang the melody like a tone-deaf rapper, then carried on with his sermon. "So we hear that and we say, 'Okay. You're completely independent now. Don't need us men. All right. Cool. Give us a li'l bit every now and then, then you can put on your independent shoes, get in your independent car, and drive back to your independent apartment or house. That way you got your independence, and we got ours.'"

"Camron, you're being silly now," Renee insisted. "Let me tell you what happened." Renee had to get whatever it was on her ample chest off it.

"Okay, listen to this and tell me what you think is going on," JaLisa said to Camron. She obviously had already heard what Renee was about to tell him.

"I went over to Steve's house on Saturday," Renee began. "We had a pretty lazy afternoon, just lying around by his fireplace watching TV, which was nice 'cause it was cold outside all day anyway. But early that evening we were getting cabin fever, so we decided to go to a movie. Saw, ah ... what was it, JaLisa?"

"Tom Hanks, *Cast Away*," JaLisa reminded her.

"Yeah, *Cast Away*," Renee said.

"How was that?" Camron asked, taking Renee off-subject.

"It was good. I liked it." But Renee quickly steered back to the matter at hand. "So we saw the movie, went back to his place, and I spent the night there. We really had a nice, full day together, which I really appreciated because we hadn't done that in a while."

"Tell him 'bout the glass," JaLisa said, apparently losing patience with Renee's pace of delivery.

Renee continued. "Anyway, that Sunday morning I went downstairs to get something to drink. There were already a few dirty glasses in the sink, so I decided to take one of those and wash it instead of dirtyin' up another glass. So, took one of 'em out the sink, and noticed all this lipstick on it. That threw me for a loop, but I was cool about it. Didn't say nothin'. But I was thinking about it, and the more I thought, the more it bothered me."

"All right, hold it right there," Camron interrupted. "Now see that's the first problem. You let your emotions take control and drive your thoughts, all under the assumption that the lipstick belonged to some woman he was kickin' it wit'. As far as we know, those lipstick prints could have come from the person who delivers his mail. The mailwoman could have gotten to his mailbox, realized she was tired and thirsty, and decided to ask for a glass of—"

"Listen!" Renee insisted. "Later, Steve was in the shower and I was still thinking about this, and getting mad. So I scrolled through his caller ID, and there was this female on there—actually a couple of females—but there was this one named Veronica, which for some reason—I don't know why—rang a bell."

JaLisa spoke. "Now I didn't necessarily agree with her there, rambling through the boy's caller ID. Camron, would you be upset if a woman scrolled through your caller ID?"

"Yes I would," Camron said with mock matter-of-factness. "How upset would depend on how long we've been dating."

"Well Steve and I, we've been dating for almost five months," Renee said.

"That's not long enough for me," Camron insisted. "If we've been dating for eight months *and* have decided to date each other exclusively, then she can scroll. Matter of fact, if *that's* the situation, she can answer my phone."

"So eight months is the amount of time necessary before scrolling," JaLisa said, a grin on her face.

"Exactly," Camron answered along with a single nod of his head. He was smiling too, and both he and JaLisa were on the verge of having fun at Renee's expense.

"Well I did it and there's nothing I can do about it now," Renee conceded. "But he gets out of the shower and I decide I'm gonna ask him about this. So I walked in the bathroom while he was drying off and said, 'So when was Veronica over for a drink?' "

"What did he say?" Camron asked.

"Nothing really, other than what y'all usually say: 'What you talkin' about?' So I showed him the glass with the lipstick, then he was like, 'Can we talk about this later?' I didn't tell him about the caller ID though."

"Since you said the girl's name, he probably already done figured out you was all up in his caller ID," Camron said.

"Is this girl a detective or what?" JaLisa said with a bit of pride in her voice.

"Mm-hmm. She a detective all right," Camron said. "Done detected onto something she didn't want to find out about."

"It doesn't matter now because that relationship is over," Renee said.

"Y'all didn't talk about it later?" Camron asked.

"He didn't want to talk about it," Renee said. "If he wanted to talk about it, he would have. Instead, this sorry-ass man calls me when he knows I'm not gonna be home and leaves a message saying he needs some space."

"I reckon he does," JaLisa stated with sass.

Exasperated, Renee said, "Anyway ... I just don't get it." She shook her head. Her voice sounded weary.

"Don't wor' 'bout it, girlfriend," JaLisa said. "There are more fish in the sea."

"Guess so," Renee said.

JaLisa looked at Camron as if he was the one who had done Renee wrong. "You mens is just so ... so difficult."

"And women aren't?" Camron retorted.

JaLisa answered. "We have our shortcomings. But men, I don't know. Sometimes y'all are so—"

"Slutty," Renee said, finishing her friend's sentence.

"Oh, okay, I'm a slut now," Camron said with feigned indignation. He turned to an imaginary waiter and raised his hand. "Garçon. Check please."

"Men are just dogs," JaLisa said.

"And why is that?" Camron asked her.

"Oh, I don't know," she said, then put on a pretense of searching her mind for an answer. "Ahm ... born that way maybe?"

"I'll admit, we are inclined to stray," Camron said. "But some women, not all, but some—well quite a few, actually—need to improve their skills."

"Skills? What skills?" Renee asked.

"Relationship skills," Camron said. "See here's the problem. Too many sistahs lack the skills necessary to keep a man around. Or if they do have 'em, they seem reluctant to put 'em on display."

"But what skills are you talking about?" Renee asked.

"All right, say when you first meet a woman," Camron said, but then decided to go in another direction to make his point. "Okay, let me give you a real-life example. I was at The Quest a couple a' weeks ago. Asked this sistah to dance." Camron crinkled his mouth into a sneer, then snarled, " 'Naw!' I had hardly gotten the question outta my mouth, and that's her response. 'Naw!' Like I had slapped her momma or somethin'. Made me wanna go dance wit' a White girl."

"Well maybe she didn't feel like dancin'," Renee said.

"And that's fine," Camron said in a high-pitched voice. "My point is, it wouldn't have taken no more energy for her to say, 'No, thank you. Not right now,' than it took to growl 'Naw' at me. Matter of fact, it would have taken less. So that's one skill I'm talkin' about: basic common courtesy." Camron took a sip of his water, then added, "And I'll tell you this. After a brotha gets that kind of attitude about a thousand times, there's more resentment there than you might think, or even he might realize.

"Now let's say you get past that kind of attitude or whatever initial front she's putting up. Then you got to deal with that I'm-just-as-tough-as-you-are façade. Hey, I'm not interested in an arm wrestlin' contest to see who's strongest. I mean if I'm out with a female, I don't think it's too much to expect some femininity. That's no different than a woman, when she's out with a man, expecting him to exude masculinity. Wouldn't you agree?" The question was to both JaLisa and Renee.

"But that's you, Camron, and the kind of women you deal with," Renee said. " 'Cause you're out at these clubs all the time, so you're more likely to meet the women that lack these 'skills,' as you put it."

"And where'd you meet Steve? At a club, right?" Camron asked.

Renee gave up a weak smile, hesitated, then exclaimed, "That's different!"

"I believe you said you met him at the Riverview, if I'm not mistaken," Camron reminded her. When Renee did go clubbing, the Riverview was one of her favorite locales.

Satisfied he had successfully put Renee in her place, he continued. "Now let's say you're in a relationship that's matured a bit. Y'all been dating for a few months. In that situation you need maintenance skills. 'Cause see, too many sistahs get settled, get lazy. 'I *got 'em girl. Shit, I'm 'a relax now.'* Get lazy in the bedroom, gain a bunch a weight, disrespect you quicker. Which is the wrong thing to do 'cause we always on the prowl. And if you fall short on the maintenance skills, we'll do more than prowl. We'll stray."

Renee busted back up into the conversation. "Y'all gonna stray regardless of what we do. We can treat y'all like kings. Cook ya' dinner, wash ya' crusty feet, do all kinds of tricks in bed. Y'all still gonna stray."

Camron chuckled at Renee's comeback, then looked heavenward, shaking his head. "Well, Lord, I tried. Tried to edu-ma-cate 'em here a li'l bit today. I did my best. That's all I can do."

"No, some of your points are valid," JaLisa conceded. "But all that stuff, the issues revolving around how we relate to each other, can be traced back to slavery."

"Uh oh, here we go," Renee said as she rolled her eyes.

"It's true," JaLisa declared.

Over the course of their last few monthly parleys, JaLisa had spoken on—as numerous Black scholars had for years—the adverse effects slavery had heaped upon Black male-female relations. That slavery had, as JaLisa put it, "flipped the scrip" on the roles Black men and women had to play. White slave owners, she related, were fearful of the big Black buck males, and demanded meekness from them. In the absence of strong male leadership, female slaves then had to become stronger. "They had no choice *but* to become more masculine," JaLisa had said at their October dinner two months earlier. Subsequently, she argued, girl slaves were taught to be strong, while slave boys were taught to be submissive. She further contended that this abnormal role reversal continued many score years after slavery, especially in the Jim Crow South, where, well into the 1950s, a Black man could be strung from a tree without fear of reprisal and for no greater crime than looking at a White person the wrong way. At any rate, Renee couldn't see what goings-on from years ago had to do with her current personal tribulations.

"Well, I've never been a slave, and neither has Steve," Renee stated, "so I'm not gonna give him that as an excuse for his behavior."

"But it's not an excuse, just an explanation," JaLisa told her. "Not only for Black male behavior, but Black female's too."

"I kinda feel ya' on that," Camron said to JaLisa. He'd gradually been warming to her thesis. "Because I can see where—like you were sayin' last time—if a Black woman back then didn't know on any given day if her man was gonna be beaten, or sold, or lynched, she would *have* to become stronger. Stronger even than the man."

"Right," JaLisa said.

"But now today, when some of the brothas are stepping up to the plate and sayin', 'I'm ready to take my rightful place in the relationship,' a lot of women don't know how to ease up; let go of the reins a little bit."

"Yeah. Let go of the reins and get driven over a cliff," Renee chirped.

Camron shook his head and laughed. "You a mess, girl." He looked at his watch, then asked, "Are we 'bout ready to get outta here?"

"I'm ready," JaLisa said. "Renee, you getting any dessert?"

"Nah."

"Okay, cool," Camron said. "It's my turn to pay, so if you ladies wanna take off, I'll square things with our waiter."

"All right, Mr. Dickerson," JaLisa said as she and Renee rose to their feet. "It was fun and real as always."

"Yes it was."

"Bye, Camron," Renee said. Camron thought she seemed a bit despondent still.

"Bye," he replied. "And, Renee. Trust me. Tomorrow will be a new and brighter day."

"I hope so," she said, smiling weakly.

9

First Date

I KNEW I DIDN'T LOVE KIMMA, but, over the three months we'd been together, I had grown very fond of her, so the thought of us breaking up made me sad. However, after my first date with Mara, I was having to confront just that possibility.

Such thoughts first entered my mind while I was driving home from that inaugural date. The scent of Mara's perfume remained fresh in my nostrils. I could still taste the cherry flavor of her lip-gloss, feel her soft lips pressed against mine. And all I could do as I made my way home was smile, and occasionally shake my head in near disbelief at just how beautiful a woman she was. Physically beautiful, yes. That I knew from the wedding reception. But—without the distractions and background noise of a postnuptial celebration—the beauty of her personality, her smile, her laugh, and her eloquence amazed me, and nearly took my breath away.

So at that moment I was afraid about the future for Kimma and me. And afraid as well at the strong impression this new woman had put on me. I searched my mind. *Had I ever had a first date like that before?*

We had rendezvoused at Sidney's, a restaurant near the Uptown section of Minneapolis. I got there before her, so I sat down at a bar that was just inside the front entrance and secured an MGD. Five minutes later, through the windows of the restaurant, I spotted her walking across the parking lot—actually prancing was more like it, prancing with a sly twist—through the vestibule, then the front door. She was smooth too. So smooth in her effortless stride it seemed as if she were being swept along by a breeze.

She saw me and suddenly, again, there was that dazzling smile. I smiled back, mine fueled by the energy from hers.

"Hi, Camron. Sorry I'm late," she said.

"You're not late," I lied as I stepped down from a high wooden bar chair and gave her a hug. "I just got here no more than five minutes ago myself."

She smelled nice. Like lilacs and rose petals rolled into one sweet fragrance. And I told her so.

"You smell good."

"You too," she said.

I had sprayed on cologne from a black bottle just before leaving home. I had no idea what it was. Something I'd picked up weeks earlier on my way out of a Kohl's department store.

"Let's find a place to sit," I suggested.

We walked up to the hostess, who led us to a table near one of the two large fireplaces found at either end of the restaurant. There was no fire, though, because the mild September weather made it unnecessary. And that was fine because the warmth of Mara's smile was plenty heat for me.

She took off her black, wool, near-knee-length swing coat and hung it around one of the four chairs at our table. Underneath it she was wearing a short red dress that displayed her curvaceous figure quite effectively. As I was removing my own full-length coat, also black, I wondered if I should help her with her chair. But by the time I had thrown my coat across the chair next to mine, she was already seated.

"You look nice tonight," she told me as I sat down across from her.

I was wearing a long-sleeve silk shirt the color of tarnished gold, and loose, black wool pants with shiny, black, thick-soled shoes.

"So do you," I said, returning the compliment. "You didn't have any trouble finding the restaurant did you?"

"No, not at all. I've passed this place before, so I kinda knew where it was. But this is my first time coming here. It's nice."

Sidney's—with its mud brown ceramic-tile floor, wood-frame windows, and vaulted and flat sections of ceiling supported by thick wood logs and two-by-fours—was both rustic and bright. Latino and Anglo cooks in plain view behind the bar counter, their white chef hats drooping limply down the back of their heads, added to the restaurant's festive feel as they prepared meals on hot grills and open, wood-fired, brick stoves.

"Yeah," I agreed. "They have some good chicken dishes."

Our waitress dropped off waters, and asked if we wanted something else to drink. I was content with my beer. Mara ordered a glass of white Zinfandel.

"How was your work week?" I asked.

"Not bad. Just daily trips to Washington," she replied.

"D.C.?"

"Yeah."

An image of Mara serving a meal to Kimma in midflight popped into my head. That, thank goodness, couldn't have happened because Kimma hadn't flown to Washington on NorWest Airlines, but Delta.

"The days are long, but I like the daily trips because I get to sleep in my own bed," she said.

"I can understand that." I sipped my water, then admitted to her, "You know, I was kind of anxious about our getting together tonight."

"Why is that?"

"I don't know. Maybe I'll figure it out over dinner."

"Okay," Mara said with a smile. "Let me know when you do."

It wasn't so hard to figure, really. Here before me was a beautiful brown-skinned lady who was articulate and had an engaging personality. Someone who had a sense of style and sophistication, yet seemed down-to-earth. And was, as far as I could see, available.

"I was somewhat anxious too," she confessed.

"And what had you anxious?"

"Well, Camron, you strike me as a very nice brotha. Professional. Handsome. Someone who has his act together, you know? And while that's not a rare thing, it's not something you run into everyday either."

"Thank you."

"Oh, and Patrice said you were nice too."

"When did she say that? I know she didn't call you from Hawaii."

"No," she chuckled. "We talked some more at the reception after you left."

"How long have you known Patrice?"

"I met Patrice just a few days after I moved here. At The Riverview." She was referring to a Black-owned nightclub in North Minneapolis. "I was sitting at the bar, and she came up beside me and ordered a drink," Mara recounted with a broad smile. "Anyway, the bartender shortchanged her, and Patrice got mad, so she was fussin' at him and complaining to me, talkin' 'bout, 'He must think I'm dumb thinking I thought I gave him a *ten* when I know it was a *twenty*. He just wanted to see if I would say anything, 'cause if I didn't he was gonna put that extra ten in his pocket.' And I was like, 'Yeah you right, girl.' "

"I can easily picture that scene," I said with a laugh as I imagined Patrice and the bartender butting heads.

Mara continued. "So after she got her correct change, we just kept talking and really hit it off. And we've been good friends ever since."

Our waitress returned with Mara's drink and to take our order, but we hadn't even looked at our menus. I asked her for two more minutes.

"So what do you recommend?" Mara asked me.

"I really like their fettuccine and hot sausage dish."

"Where's that?"

I reached across the table to point it out to her on her menu.

"Mmm, that looks good," she said in that sultry voice of hers.

"It is. I had it the last time I was here, so I think I'll try something different. But you should try it."

Our waitress returned shortly, and Mara went with my suggestion. I ordered one of the chicken entrées—a quarter chicken, rotisserie baked and spiced with herbs, lemon, and garlic, served with mash potatoes and a vegetable mix of carrots, zucchini, and squash.

As we continued our conversation, which darted from the lack of local cultural outlets to our ages (she was nine months younger than me) to dogs versus cats to how much screwing Patrice and Donnell were doing on their honeymoon, I couldn't help but notice how comfortable and natural it felt to be around her. I decided not to analyze it, as my engineering mentality sometimes led me to do, but to just enjoy the moment.

As we were taking the first bites of our dinner, Mara took our conversation in yet another direction. "So what has your experience been with the dating scene here in the Twin Cities?"

"Ah-mm ... varied," I answered.

"I take that to mean you've dated a lot of White women."

Where in the hell did that comment come from? I thought to myself. "No not really," I laughed.

"Now there you go with that 'no not really' stuff again."

"I've dated a couple," I admitted. "Which is different from *a lot*."

"Well that's not exactly a news flash. What brotha who's lived here more than six months hasn't? 'Cause they're all over you Black men up here. And you know what? Y'all love it."

"Oh we do, huh?"

"Yes y'all do."

"What about you? What's been your experience dating the brothas here?" I asked. "No, let me rephrase that. What's been your experience dating men here, because I don't want to assume you've just dated Black men."

"I'll be honest," Mara said. "I went out with a White guy here two or three times. He was a nice man too. I just felt weird being out with him though."

"Why was that?"

"Maybe it's because I was raised in the South, you know? 'Cause down there you'd get a lot of stares, which would make you feel self-conscious. Here, of course, you don't get that, but maybe I was expecting it."

"So just *expecting* stares made you feel uncomfortable?" I asked.

"Yeah. And we did get some. But not like we would if we would have been walking down a street in Podunk, Mississippi," Mara said. "But even beyond that, culturally we just didn't mesh."

"Yeah, I know what you mean," I told her. "Okay, now what about the brothas?"

"Well," she began with a smile, "you brothas here are interesting."

I chuckled. "How so?"

"First of all, you've got Black men here that date White women exclusively. And once I see that's the case, I don't deal with 'em at all because there's some kinda self-hate thang goin' on there."

"Wait a minute," I said. "Didn't you just tell me that you went out with a White man a few times?"

"Yes, but I don't take the position that I'm gonna date *only* White men or Black men or Hispanic men."

"Which is different?"

"Yes. I think so," she said. "Then you got brothas that are always on the lookout for the BBD."

"BBD? What's that?" I asked.

"Bigger Better Deal. This White girl, Cindy, that I work with—

she's a mess—she taught me that term," Mara said snickering. "She and her boyfriend are always breaking up and getting back together, and she'll complain that he's constantly looking for the BBD—someone with a better body, better face, better job. You know?"

I took advantage of an opportunity to flatter. "Well, I couldn't imagine a bigger better deal than yourself."

"Aaah. You're so sweet. But you say that now because we just met."

"Yeah. And I'm sure I'd say it six months from now too," I assured her.

"Hmm. Six months. That's a long time."

"Not as long as you might think. Especially if you're having fun."

"That's true," she agreed.

"So what you're saying is, there are two types of brothas here: those that are completely into White women, and those that are constantly in search of the BBD."

"Well those are the two types I always seem to run into. Like the last guy I dated, who was actually a bit of both."

I smiled at her. "And which type am I?"

She smiled back. "Oh, time will tell."

Our conversation proceeded with an ease that was almost unsettling to me. In between the words, laughter, and teasing glances, we were able to finish much of our food. During a second round of drinks, I asked her, "So what else did Patrice say about me?"

"Hmm," Mara said as she took on a look of thoughtfulness. "She said she was surprised you weren't married by now."

I had to laugh at that comment. "That's interesting."

"So? What would your response to that be? Or do you prefer to plead the fifth?" Mara had a mischievous grin on her face.

I considered her offer to cop a plea. But for some reason, I wanted to give her an explanation. "I guess, up until the age of thirty, marriage never crossed my mind because I was having too much fun being single. Then thirty came and went, and I thought, 'Okay, maybe it's time to get into that mindset.' "

"Mindset?"

"Yeah. There's a certain mindset a man has to get into to prepare for marriage. An openness, at least to the concept, of a lifetime commitment."

"And you weren't able to get into that?"

"I think I was open to the notion of marriage," I said, "but the right person never showed up."

"So you're no longer looking?" Mara wanted to know.

"No. I just don't look as deliberately as I used to."

"Does that make it easier? Not being so deliberate in your search for love."

"Yes. Much," I said as I raised my near-empty beer bottle for one last swig.

A few minutes later I was walking Mara to her car. In my left hand, I was carrying her leftovers. The waitress had placed them in a small, white, paper carton, the kind used for takeout Chinese food, and on the top of it had scribbled the date in blue marker ink. In my right hand, I was holding Mara's left.

"How'd you like the restaurant?" I asked.

"Oh that hot sausage pasta was good. I can eat the rest of that for lunch tomorrow."

"Or breakfast."

She gave me a dubious look. "I don't know about that now."

"Sure. You can scramble the hot sausage and pasta in with a couple of eggs, make you some toast, add a little jelly, and just like that, a delicious breakfast."

She laughed at my weak humor, which I thought was nice of her. "Okay, I'll do that. And if it's not good, I'll bring it over for you to eat."

"Mmm. I can't wait."

As we strolled down the sidewalk beneath tall trees that would soon bloom with the colors of fall, I felt as light on my feet as one of the Nicholas Brothers. I didn't want the evening to end. There was something present between us that I think we both were feeling. It was that all-elusive mishmash of emotional-physical attractions that many describe simply as "chemistry"; at that moment we had it, and I was almost afraid to let it go. But our evening together was nearly over. The best I could do at that point was plan for another.

"Speaking of cooking, you should let me cook dinner for you sometime," I offered.

"Oh. So you cook?"

"Li'l bit. When I put my mind to it," I said. "I make a mean spaghetti sauce."

"Sounds delicious. When were you thinking?"

"This weekend. Saturday."

"Hmm. That should work," Mara said. "I don't fly again until Sunday."

"Good. I'll call you Saturday morning and give you directions to my house."

"All right," she said as we approached a red '92 Geo Metro. "Here's my car."

"This is cute," I commented.

"It gets me there and back. And that's the important thing."

"Exactly," I agreed as we reached the driver's door. "Listen. I had a nice time."

"Me too."

I'd wanted to kiss her ever since she'd come into the restaurant, and we'd finally arrived at the perfect time for me to make that move. I decided to take a gentlemanly approach.

"Can I kiss you?" I asked.

"Sure," she replied. "If you don't mind me kissing you back."

I smiled, then moved closer and hunched down to her level. Our lips met. Just lips at first. Then she returned an invitation from my tongue to hers. Her hands went from around my neck to the broadest span of my shoulders. From the sidewalk, I heard the steps of another couple passing, but hardly noticed them otherwise. I held her tighter, fell deeper, and was soon oblivious to everything but the moment we were in. A few seconds passed, maybe more, before I caught myself and pulled back. I didn't want to offend her. But I had a feeling she was nowhere near so.

"Mmm," I murmured as I erected myself. "That was nice."

"Yes," Mara said. Then she smiled. "You got my lipstick all over you. You might want to wipe that off before you walk back to your car." She brushed around the corners of my mouth with her finely manicured index finger. I licked my lips to aid her effort. "You know how Uptown is." She was making reference to the perception of a higher-than-average gay population in that part of Minneapolis.

I laughed lightly. "I'll be okay. But what about you? Those two Zinfandels don't have your head spinning too much, do they?"

"No, I'm fine."

"All right. Drive carefully."

"I will. You too," Mara said.

"I'll call you Saturday," I promised.

"Okay. Talk to you then."

"All right."

I stood on the sidewalk and waited until she drove off.

As I was walking, on air it seemed, back to my car, I suddenly remembered that I needed to call Kimma to confirm a date we had scheduled for the next day. But as I drove down Hennepin Avenue towards I-94, I could hardly think of anything or anyone but Mara.

10

P

IT WAS 7:21 P.M., THURSDAY, four days before Christmas 2000, and Camron was primping in his bathroom mirror with nothing on save a pair of gray athletic briefs, preparing for his eight o'clock date with Paris. Their original plan to get together two days earlier hit a snag when Paris had to work late, so they rescheduled. Upon doing so, Camron suggested, instead of meeting at a restaurant, that he pick her up at her apartment.

As he was raking a damp brush through his hair, searching for waves, the phone rang. Camron placed the brush on the sink, made a counterclockwise turn, walked into his bedroom, around his bed and past the corner TV that was blaring a *Saturday Night Live* rerun, then up to the sunken oak headboard, where the cordless phone was cradled. He picked up the phone and saw on the caller-ID panel that the area code of the number was 2-1-5. He didn't need to look at the name to know it was his best friend, Peter Smith, calling from Philadelphia. Concerned a long conversation would make him late, Camron nearly let the call carry over to his voice mail. But he hadn't talked with his friend in more than two weeks, so he pressed the "ON" button.

"What up, P?" Camron blurted into the receiver as he fell across the black- and white-striped comforter covering his bed. Ever since they had met as freshmen at North Carolina A&T State University in '82, Camron had always called him "P." He just couldn't bring himself to call him Peter, which he thought was too dorky a name for a brotha.

P asked essentially the same question, but louder. "What's up, Negro? Just checking to see if you still alive out there in that cold-ass place."

"Yeah, I'm still kicking. How are things in Philly?"

"Aside from this bullshit job of mine, everything's fine," he said in his rich baritone voice.

P was a sales rep for a trucking company. He was good at his job, but was growing increasingly frustrated at what seemed to be ever-changing, ever-escalating sales quotas.

"What's the temperature out there?" P asked. He was fascinated at how cold the winters could be in Minnesota

Camron grabbed the TV remote and lowered the volume on the television. "It's about ten right now, but I think it's suppose to be dropping to around zero later tonight."

"Now, boy, you know that ain't no place for a Black man. You need to just come on back home."

"It's good for ya'," Camron said in regard to, and in weak defense of, the icy temperatures. "Wakes ya' up."

"You got that right. Wake you up just long enough to freeze yo' ass to death."

"So how things rolling?" Camron asked.

"Everthang's cool," P said. "Last night was interesting."

"Oh yeah? How so?"

"You remember that girl I was telling you about a few weeks ago? Diane?"

"The light-skinned Amazon?"

"Yeah," P said. "Finally got up in that last night."

"How was it? Babe got skills?"

"I couldn't tell. I was too distracted by her *lack* of hygiene skills."

Camron chuckled. "What you talkin' 'bout, man?"

"Man, I don't know if the babe forgot to take a bath or what, but she had the smelliest coochie I've ever encountered."

Camron howled with laughter. "Maybe she had a rough sweaty day at work."

"Something. I don't know what the problem was."

"P, it couldn't have been that bad," Camron said, traces of laughter still in his voice.

"Camron, I kid you not. It didn't hit me until I got up in there. But once it did, I just wanted to get it over with."

"Whoo," Camron said laughing and sounding like an owl. "Dayum. I hope you were wearing a condom on that one."

"Yes, sir, I was, and happy I did. And I thought about that shit afterwards while I was laying there and that funk was wafting up my nose. 'Cause with that kind of smell, no telling what might be crawling up in there."

"Did you tell her?" Camron asked.

"No. She wanted to get busy again, but I told her I had to get up early. So I put on my clothes and took her ass home."

"So what you gonna do? Y'all gonna hook up again?"

"Man, if that's what I got to look forward to, hell naw!" P declared. "I can't operate under those conditions."

"Well you need to tell the girl," Camron said, still unable to stop laughing as he spoke. "Write her a letter or somethin'."

"For what?" P asked. "She know her pussy stink."

"Hey. Maybe she don't."

"Shit. I don't know how she wouldn't. Funked up the whole bedroom."

"I apologize, man," Camron said with mock sincerity. "Sorry you had to go through that."

"Man, fuck it," P said as Camron laughed some more. "So what's up at your end?"

"Hookin' up with this new female for dinner tonight."

"What she look like?"

"She's cute. Her name is Paris."

"I like that name. Hope she's more hygienically inclined than my babe last night."

"Well since this is our first date, I don't think I'd get far enough tonight to find out about that. But listen, I gotta get outta here 'cause I have to pick her up in a few."

"Aw'ight, man. Enjoy yourself," P said.

"I will. And hey!"

"What?" P asked.

"Go take a bath," Camron teased.

"Man, shit, I already have. But I might just go take another one."

"Negro, you crazy," Camron said giggling. "Okay, P, take it light."

"You too. Peace."

"Peace."

Camron hung up the phone and let out another hearty laugh. "Damn, that's fucked up," he said out loud as he rolled off the bed and stepped toward the bathroom.

He completed his grooming and pulled on black dress pants, black socks, and a brown pullover knit sweater with one button at the top. After turning off the TV and bathroom lights, he went downstairs and chose from three pairs of shoes, all black, that were lined up against the wall near his front door. He sat on the next-to-bottom step of the stairs, slipped into the pair of his choice, and tied them snugly. He moved toward the side door that led to his garage, stopping at the closet adjacent to it to grab his tan trench coat. He buttoned the coat its full length, then walked into the kitchen to retrieve his black leather gloves and thin, foldable cell phone. Both were on the kitchen counter, next to days of unopened mail. He slipped the gloves on his hands, shoved the phone in his coat pocket, and dimmed the living room chandelier, now the only light in the house, to a hazy brown. Camron retraced his steps back to the side door leading to the garage, opened it, and was smacked in the face by the cold dry air. The temperature was nine degrees Fahrenheit, and falling.

It was a kind of cold difficult to imagine in his home state of North Carolina. Down South, evening temperatures in the teens would be sufficient to keep virtually everyone indoors. But there, frigid temperatures of that sort were short-lived. In Minnesota—in the winter—days, even weeks, could pass without the air rising to twenty degrees, day or night. And so with no other choice, Minnesotans embraced their winters. Indeed, between snowmobiling; skiing; ice hockey and ice fishing on frozen ponds and lakes; carnivals; parades; and other winter activities, they reveled in them. And while Camron found certain aspects of Minnesota winters oddly appealing, he much preferred the warmth of indoors.

He reached into the dark of his garage, feeling for the wall button that controlled the garage door. Finding it, he pushed, and the cold, calm silence was abruptly shattered by the sounds of the large door being pulled up and in. Lights attached to the opener itself illuminated what had been a nearly pitch-black space.

Camron looked down onto the cement floor to be sure a mouse wasn't scurrying about. Two or three usually found their way into that part of his home during the first truly cold days of the season. However, they soon met their demise via disposable traps baited with peanut butter, or from tiny, dark brown boxes filled with pellets of poison. Nevertheless, Camron always checked before taking the two steps down onto the garage's floor because he was as squeamish about rodents as some women.

Confident the coast was clear, he stepped down, locked the

house door behind him, and took three tight paces along the length of his car. He opened the driver's door, climbed behind the wheel and into an interior that was only slightly less cold than the outdoors, and started the engine.

As he backed out of his driveway, with previously shoveled snow piled three feet high on either side of it, Camron wondered what he and this lady named after the City of Lights might do tonight. Their original plan had been to go to the Wild Onion in St. Paul, but since they were closer to the weekend, Camron was in the mood for something more entertaining than just a meal. Jazzmine's, a stylish bistro in Minneapolis that featured live jazz and good food, struck him as an attractive option.

Driving westbound on I-94 toward St. Paul, a myriad of thoughts were running through his mind: his vulgar conversation with P; how Paris might look in more than just the dull lighting of a nightclub; and backup plans in case she stood him up.

He also thought—just for a moment—about Mara. Where was she right now, this second? Was she happy, sad, lonely? But, with hundreds of miles and a divorce now separating them, what business was it of his?

Camron was jarred from his mental gyrations when the driver of a rusting jalopy traveling eighty miles per hour cut across Camron's lane, and did so with no more than ten feet between his rear and Camron's front bumper.

The nutty driver was quickly many yards in front of Camron before he had a chance to curse him. "Mothafucka!" Camron shouted at him through furrowed brows, his Southern accent aroused. "Der he is, ladies and gen'a'men: Mr. Dunce."

That was a game Camron sometimes would play, identifying the "Dunce Driver of the Day." It was a harmless tension release, and alternative, he reasoned, to more flagrant forms of road rage.

Regaining his cool, Camron flipped on his interior light, scanned numbers scrawled across a white Post-It note that was on the passenger seat, then punched the digits into his cellular phone.

After the second ring, a gentle voice at the other end answered: "Hello."

"Paris?" Camron asked.

"Yes."

"Hey, it's Camron. I'm almost there."

"Okay. I can meet you on the west side of the building. By the steps."

"I'm in a black Dodge Intrepid. I'll be there in about two minutes."

"Okay. See you then," she said, then hung up.

As he whizzed through the traffic and ever closer to Paris, Camron curiously found himself unexcited about the date. Perhaps it was because, as far as he was concerned, one of the more invigorating aspects of the dating game, *the chase*, was over.

The whole point of the chase was to get beyond the incidental conversations at nightspots, and get together one-on-one. In other words, the chase was all about *getting* a date. Consequently, a first date to Camron signaled the end of the chase and the beginning of *the dance*, that process of flirting and wooing, which, if attractions held, culminated in *the conquest*.

But Camron, recently and for reasons he couldn't quite understand, hadn't been much interested in anything beyond the chase. The allure of pursuit itself—and the adrenaline rush that accompanied it—had lately proven to be satisfaction enough of his urge to court a woman.

But with Paris, the chase was over, and now it was time for the dance, which raised the stakes a bit. Camron wondered if he would be interested in continuing to play the dating game with her after tonight.

He steered into his left lane and exited off the interstate onto Sixth Street, which led directly into the Lowertown section of St. Paul. That was where Paris lived, in a double-towered amalgamation of tan- and brown-bricked, purple-glass tinged, high-rise apartments and condominiums known as Galtier Plaza. The north side of Galtier Plaza was adjacent to Sixth Street. At Jackson Street Camron made a left, which put him on the west side of the building, and there he found Paris, standing just inside double-glass doors. She was wearing a long, sky blue wool coat, and all of her head, except the top, was wrapped in a blue and white silk scarf.

Recognizing his car as he came to a stop, she stepped out from the warmth of the building's ground floor and into the frosty night air. Camron waved to confirm he was whom she was looking for. He followed her with his eyes as she walked—with her arms crossed and the shoulders of her tall frame arched against the chilling temperatures—down a short flight of cement steps that led to the sidewalk. She passed in front of his headlights and across to the passenger side.

Camron clicked the doors unlock, and Paris swung the front passenger side door open.

11

Paris

"HI," CAMRON SAID WITH A SMILE.

"Hi," Paris said as she fell into the passenger seat. "Ooo!" she exclaimed, then sucked in air between clinched teeth. "Cold out there."

"Hey. Minnesota in December. What can you do?"

"Turn the heat up!" she said in answer to his rhetorical question.

Camron chuckled at her vibrancy as he turned the car's fan to near full blast. "How's that?" he asked as the warm air came streaming from below the dashboard and onto their legs.

"Better," she said. "So how are you tonight?" she asked smiling and displaying a perfectly straight, pearly white set of teeth. Her smile maximized her beauty, blending well with her deep-set, light brown eyes, narrow congenial nose, and moderate lips.

"Fine. And yourself?"

"Pretty good. Nice to be off for a few days."

"You off the rest of the year?" Camron asked.

"I wish. I'm off till Tuesday. What about you?"

"Monday and Tuesday are holidays at Bidell," he said. "And so is the following Monday, New Year's Day. So I decided to make it a long break by taking vacation tomorrow, next Wednesday, Thursday, and Friday, as well as the following Tuesday. Which means I won't have to join the ranks of the common worker again until January third."

"Lucky you," she said.

"Ain't I though?"

They both laughed.

"I'm not nearly as fortunate," she said. "I'm off through Christmas, which I'm happy about, but I work the weekend before New Year's, including New Year's Eve."

"That's terrible. I think you should go on strike."

"Well if you put together a picket line, I'll be right there to support it," she said.

"So, you said you don't like being a nurse anymore, huh?"

"No, I don't. Do you know that one of my patients cursed at me today?"

"You're kidding."

"No. This grumpy old White man. Told me to kiss his ass."

Camron smiled and shook his head.

Paris said, "I've been a nurse for over nine years, but I can't see myself doing this from now to retirement."

"What else are you considering?"

"I've been thinking about accounting or teaching."

"Those are good fields. Probably wouldn't have to worry about getting cursed at."

"You know?" she said with a rising voice. "Although, bad as kids are these days, it probably could still happen if I were a teacher."

"That's true."

"But I'd like to start taking courses in one of those disciplines next fall. I don't know where I'm going to find the time though."

"Just start with one course at a time," he suggested. "At least until you get back into the swing of school."

Camron confessed he wasn't overly enamored with his occupation situation either. Told her it felt like, after almost ten years with his current employer, he was fast approaching a dead end.

"But, short of finding a new job and having to start all over with respect to benefits, what can you do?" he said with a tad of resignation in his voice. "I'm taking a weekend Java class this spring though."

"Java? What's that?" Paris asked.

"A computer programming language. My company is paying for it, so I decided I may as well see what it's about. If I like it, maybe it'll be the start of another career path."

"You never know," Paris said.

As they continued floating toward Minneapolis, he asked her about other ordinary things. She was born in Baton Rouge, Louisiana, but had moved to Chicago as a toddler with her parents. And that was where she remained—through high school, a community college and Loyola University, and her first nursing job—before relocating to St. Paul in the fall of 1998. Every few months she returned to Chicago by car or plane to see her parents and her older brother, Nathan. Her oldest sibling, Deanna—who was visiting Paris at the time Camron saw her at South Beach—lived in Kansas City with her husband, Jake, and their three-year-old daughter, Cicely.

"What prompted the move here?" Camron asked.

Paris paused in response to his question, stared straight through the windshield, and seemed to be focused on some distant object. On her face Camron thought he detected minute elements of a frown. But then her mouth formed a fragile smile. "It was time for a change," she said.

Camron turned left off Hennepin Avenue onto 3rd Street. They were now back near the point of their last encounter, in Minneapolis's Warehouse District, so named because many of the buildings had once been warehouses. The streets were crowded, filled with the first revelers of a long holiday weekend.

Jazzmine's was situated in a first-floor corner of an eight-story brick office building. Camron pulled to the left curb near the building's entrance between signs that read "Valet Parking Only."

"Here we are," he said to Paris, then stepped out of the car and up onto the sidewalk, leaving the engine running and the driver's door open.

Paris joined him as a parking attendant, a young White dude wearing a thick black parka, appeared. Camron reached between the buttons of his coat, fished out his wallet, found a five- and a one-dollar bill, and surrendered them to the attendant. The attendant gave Camron a claim ticket, then sped away in Camron's vehicle to some unseen parking spot. The warmth of the car had made it easy to forget the night air was now a frigid seven degrees, but they were immediately reminded of that fact as the relentless cold reintroduced itself to them.

"Have you ever been here?" Camron asked as he extended his gloved hand out to Paris.

"No, but I've heard nice things about it," she said as she accepted his hand into hers. "They've been open ... a year maybe?"

"Something like that. It's nice. Kinda small but cozy."

They climbed seven steps to the elevated ground floor, their frozen breaths preceding them. They walked through the glass doors of the office building, then turned left into the club. A smiling maître d', with brown short-cut hair and wearing a white button shirt and red vest, was on guard just inside the entrance. He reminded Camron of Pee Wee Herman, the once popular children's TV host. The resemblance caused Camron to stare more than was warranted as he gave him a ten-dollar bill, five dollars cover for each of them. The maître d' handed them off to a young hostess with long blonde hair, who led the couple past the bar and its grain wood floor, and to a booth by windows that faced the street they were just on. At the far end of the club, a quartet of musicians was already performing on a small stage, providing soft, cool jazz sounds for the thirty-plus customers present.

They removed their coats and hung them on pegs next to their table. Paris was dressed mostly in black: black polyester pants that outlined thighs and hips more shapely than Camron had remembered them to be at South Beach, and a knit top with horizontal black and white stripes.

"This is a nice club," Paris said as she demurely squeezed into the booth and looked around. "It *is* small."

Jazzmine's was much longer than it was wide: fifty feet by thirty-five, much of which was occupied by the bar and the stage. Besides seven booths abutting the windows facing the street, there were several small tables that could each accommodate up to four people. Twelve or so people could also sit comfortably at the bar, which was close to a banister that separated it and its adjacent aisle from the carpeted dining space. With the club being so small, a hundred patrons could make for a standing-room-only crowd.

"Yeah," Camron agreed. "The ambiance is cool though."

The high ceiling, which was rough and black with twinkling lights embedded in it, opened up the room some. The ceiling space was also decorated with eight unconventional wicker ceiling fans, each shaped like a huge flattened teardrop, swaying in tandem like slow-moving pendulums.

A waitress, with long straight black hair and lipstick that seemed way too red for her fair skin, came to their table, gave them menus, and took their drink orders.

After she went away, Paris asked, "When were you last here?"

"Three weeks ago. I was hanging out with some alumni from my school that were here for a basketball tournament."

"What school?"

"North Carolina A&T State University."

She asked, "That's a Black school, right?"

"Yeah. For now anyway. Who knows what it'll be in ten years."

"Why do you say that?"

"Well, the powers that be have been pushing for a higher percentage of White students."

"What's wrong with that?" Paris asked.

Her question made Camron hope she wasn't too unconscious.

"Maybe nothing. I hope nothing," he asserted. "But we're hardly thirty or forty years removed from the time when we couldn't even get into a White school in the South. So there are reasons the Black schools are there. And some of the reasons they were built in the first place are still valid." Camron added, "Of course, that's just my humble opinion."

"I suppose that's true," Paris concurred.

By the time the waitress returned with a beer for Camron, and a glass of Merlot for his date, Paris had learned he had four siblings— an older brother, and two older and one younger sister. After sitting down their drinks, the waitress took their order, then disappeared again.

"So are you ready for Christmas and Kwanzaa?" Paris asked.

"Let's see," Camron said, feigning contemplation. "Kwanzaa is the one where you don't have to spend any money, right? I'm definitely ready for that."

"Oh, you've broke the bank for Christmas already?"

"No. Not really."

Besides a hundred- and a twenty-dollar bill he had sent to his father and a favorite niece, and a few things he had bought as presents to himself, Camron hadn't spent anything on Christmas. He didn't have to because, for the first Christmas in years, he found himself with no girlfriend, fiancée, or wife upon whom to shower gifts of the season. And as far as his siblings were concerned, phone calls would suffice. *At least I can save some money,* he had thought just earlier that day.

"How about you? You done a lot of Christmas shopping?" Camron asked.

"Lord yes. Too much."

Paris told Camron about the gifts she'd bought: a dress for her mother, gloves and a hat for her father, fragrances for her sister, a coat for her brother, and a brown doll for her niece.

"Does your family always get that kind of treatment at Christmas?" Camron asked.

"No. But I've been blessed, so I just wanted to share that with my family this year."

"You going to Chicago over the weekend?"

Paris shook her head. "Mm-mm. I was home for Thanksgiving, but since I have to work the day after Christmas, I'll stay here," she said. "Deanna and Jake and my niece are driving up from Kansas City to spend Christmas with me though."

"That should be nice," Camron said.

"Yeah, I think it will be. What about you? What are your plans for Christmas?"

"Nothing really. I'll make some calls to my family, slow cook something for dinner, and check out whatever bowl game will be on that day."

"That sounds lonely," Paris said.

"Depends on your perspective. I tend to think of it as 'blissful solitude': nice, peaceful, and quiet." Camron said this with a smile to hide his own doubt. How *would* he feel spending Christmas alone? Sad and blue? Or relaxed and content. As he had discovered since his separation and divorce, there was sometimes a thin line between those two worlds.

"Do you miss not having your family closer to you?" Paris asked.

"Sometimes. My mother died in '95—"

"Oh, I'm sorry to hear that."

"No need for sorries. She had a good life. But since she passed, the urge to go back home hasn't been as strong or as frequent as it was when she was alive."

"How old was she?" Paris asked.

"She had just turned seventy."

"How'd she die?"

"Well, it wasn't a sudden thing. A buildup of things, I guess. First her kidneys failed, and she had to go on dialysis three times a week. That not only sapped her of her energy, but of a lot of her independence as well. And that was devastating to her because she had been a strong, do-for-self kind of woman all her life. Anyway, she went through that for a couple of years, then fluid began to build on her heart, which led to medication and some hospital stays. That depressed her even more. Ultimately she just got tired of fighting and let go. And everybody in my family I think understood that. But the doctors, as far as I'm concerned, hastened her death."

"What makes you say that?" Paris asked.

"Months before she died, during one of the times she was in the hospital, an intern had run a tube down her throat. He didn't do it right or something because she couldn't breathe. They ended up slitting her throat to create an air passage. She seemed to go downhill faster after that. I told her she should sue them. But she was such a sweet soul. She'd just say, 'They're doing the best they can.' "

A few minutes later the waitress brought their food. Camron requested another beer, and Paris another glass of wine. On the stage, a female vocalist, a White girl with permed, medium-length, brunette hair, had joined the quartet of musicians. The band's sensibilities had shifted to the pop end of the jazz spectrum, as they were now delivering an effective interpretation of Sade's "Sweetest Taboo."

"So what finally made you decide to call me?" Camron asked before taking a bite of his veal scaloppini.

Paris, who had shrimp scampi on her plate, smiled a little. "When I saw you the last time and you gave me your card again, I felt guilty about not having called the first time. But I didn't want to call out of guilt either. You know what I mean?"

Camron nodded.

"So I said, 'If I call, what would be the motivation?' And I decided that the fact that you were a gentleman about the whole situation the second time we saw each other at the club was reason enough."

"Well I'm glad you called," Camron said smiling. Thus far he thought *the dance* with Paris was going well.

As they finished their meal, they played "Try To Remember The Seven Days of Kwanzaa," at which they both failed miserably. By the time their waitress had removed their plates, the number of people in the club had nearly doubled, and the bar was full, with many standing and waiting for an opportunity to squeeze up to the counter and order their drink of choice.

When they were ready to leave, Camron left $60 cash on the table, enough to cover the tab and a tip of near twenty percent. They collected their coats, walked out of the restaurant-club, and into the building's vestibule.

"Wait here while I get the car," Camron told her.

"No problem," Paris said as she, in anticipation of the cold, buttoned every button on her coat.

Camron returned two minutes later. "The car should be around in a few."

"Okay. Hope you told them to turn the heat on," Paris said with a smile.

When the car was delivered, Camron tipped the valet two bucks, then he and Paris got into the waiting vehicle. Paris was delighted to find the heat on full blast.

"Mmm," she purred with enough sexual content that it raised the hair on Camron's arms.

As he drove over the dry, salt-ashened streets of downtown Minneapolis, Camron reflected on the date. The tranquillity and calm of Paris's personality he had noticed during their previous encounters was complemented by the more vibrant side of her essence. An impulse to extend this first dance with her took hold of him. He glimpsed at the glowing blue clock on his radio-CD player. 9:57.

"Are you turning in early tonight?" Camron asked.

"Not likely. I'm so excited about not having to work tomorrow I probably won't be able to sleep."

Camron chuckled at her exaggeration, then followed through on his impulse with a suggestion. "Well it's not *too* late. Would you like to stop somewhere on Grand for a nightcap?"

"Sure," Paris answered.

Ten minutes later, they were in St. Paul at the intersection of Grand and Victoria. On one corner was Ciatti's, an Italian eatery, and Cafe Latté, a cafeteria-style establishment infamous for its wide selection of tasty desserts. On the other corner, across Grand, was Billy's, a pub with an inviting fireplace and a slightly raucous air.

Camron searched for a parking space, and had the good fortune of locating one three-quarters of a block later. They got out of the car, with Paris stepping onto the sidewalk, Camron into the street. Camron clicked the doors locked with his key chain remote, and jammed his hands and keys into his coat pockets as he walked around the rear of the car and toward his waiting date. Without any coaxing, Paris passed her right arm through his left, clasped her hands, and they moved together through the hyperborean night air.

"So where are we going?" Paris asked.

"How about Ciatti's?" Camron offered.

"Okay. But let's run," she suggested. Camron quickened his step to a lazy jog. Paris giggled as she struggled to keep up with him, but he quickly slowed to his original pace.

"We'll be fine. It's not that cold," he said.

"Yeah right. And what do you consider cold?" Paris asked.

"What would I call cold? Negative thirty. That was how cold it was a few years ago when me and my friend-at-the-time went to a Frankie Beverly and Maze concert at Northup Auditorium."

Northup Auditorium was on the University of Minnesota campus, in Minneapolis, on the east side of the Mississippi River. The "friend-at-the-time" was his ex-wife during the early days of their love affair.

"We couldn't find parking near the auditorium," Camron related, "so us and a whole lot of other Black folk ending up walking—running really—two or three blocks in that cold. And the wind was blowing a li'l bit too, so that negative thirty felt more like negative sixty."

"Damn. Was it worth it?" Paris asked.

"The concert? Yeah. Frankie and the boys were in rare form that night. It was cold outside, but it was definitely a hot show."

By the time they reached the entrance to the building in which Ciatti's was located, the vessels in their faces had contracted, and much of the blood in them had retreated, leaving that naked portion of their skin to battle the cold as best it could. As they walked through the insulating warmth of the vestibule, to their right they could see a long line of people in Cafe Latté, waiting their turn to select their favorite sweet.

Ciatti's was to their left. Just inside its entrance was a counter, behind which stood a hostess. Camron barely broke stride as he mouthed and said to her, "We're going to the bar," and pointed toward the back portion of the restaurant.

The bar region was dimly lit by sunken ceiling lights, and its mostly burgundy coloring gave it an even darker, romantic blush. They found an empty stool at the bar. Paris sat on it, and Camron stood beside her as they again shed their coats and gloves. Camron threw his coat across his arm; Paris put hers across her lap. The bartender was quickly in their faces.

"What can I get for you?" she asked, dropping two napkins on the counter.

Camron ordered his usual beer, and Paris a Bailey's, Kahlua, and coffee with whip cream on top. Two minutes later, their beverages were in front of them. Steam wafted upward from the top of Paris's hot drink.

Paris asked, "So how long were you married?"

"Two years," Camron answered. "Wait a minute. How'd you know I was married?"

Paris pointed at the ring finger of his left hand. Camron looked down and saw the faint but obvious indentions from where his wedding band had once been. He smiled in compliment of her keen observation.

"And of course I'm assuming you still aren't," Paris said.

"Your assumption is correct. I've been separated for a year, divorced for nearly three months. And yes, I was married for two years," Camron reiterated. He was a little embarrassed that she had unearthed a piece of his history without his permission.

"That wasn't long."

"No."

"What happened?" she asked then flicked her tongue into the whip cream floating on top of her drink. "If you don't mind my asking."

"No, I don't mind," Camron assured her. "We were both stubborn. Too stubborn." He took a small gulp from his beer bottle. "Two stubborn people."

"That's the whole story?"

"Pretty much. It seemed all our problems stemmed from that. You know? We'd have a spat or disagreement about this or that, then we'd sulk for hours—days even—both of us too stubborn to say 'I'm sorry' or 'Let's talk about this.' After a while, it just got tiring going to bed mad at each other so often."

Camron noticed a couple, sitting in a corner on a low gray love seat, rise to their feet and leave.

"Let's sit over there," he suggested as he moved to claim the abandoned sofa. It was almost too small to even be considered a love seat, but that was fine by Camron because it would allow him and Paris to get close, literally.

After situating themselves, Camron asked, "What about you?" He looked at her ring finger, searched it for any perfect scars, but saw nothing other than unblemished skin. "Have you ever been married?"

"No. I was engaged for a year though, when I was living in Chicago. We were together for two years total."

"So what happened there?"

"After we got engaged, he changed. He became more controlling, jealous." Her voice trailed off slightly. "And abusive."

"Physically?"

"Mm-hmm. Which really scared me. So I had to step away from that situation."

"I can understand that."

Paris took a nip of her hot liquor. "He ended up getting thrown in jail."

"Things got that crazy?" Camron asked.

"Yeah. We were living together in my apartment, but after the relationship fell apart and he moved out, he'd showed up at all times of the night buzzing me. Finally I had to get a restraining order. But he still came back, and some cameras at my complex caught him on tape."

"How long was he in jail?"

"Oh, he was out on bail in a few days. He ended up with probation and a fine. He didn't come back though. Or, I should say, he didn't get caught coming back."

"Wonder what made him go off like that?" Camron asked.

"I don't know. We'd have our spats every now and then, but nothing as bad as the last few months of our relationship. Anyway, soon after that episode, I moved here. I had been considering moving anyway, but that just kind of sealed the deal for me."

"So where is he now?"

"I have no clue. I would imagine he's still back in Chicago." Paris took another sip of her drink. A bigger one this time. "What about your ex? Where is she?"

"North Carolina. She moved back there last summer."

"You guys talk much?"

"No. Not much."

Camron noticed Paris staring at his face, as if she was searching for something. Some trace, perhaps, of a connection that might still exist between him and his former wife.

"The good thing about that situation, if there was a good thing, was that we didn't have any kids," Camron said. "So the break was fairly clean. I gave her $20,000 and a car, and that was it."

"How'd you decide on that?"

"I just didn't want to argue over things, you know? The house, alimony, my 401(k). So I made that offer, and she accepted it. No lawyers. Nice and clean."

Paris said, "I think the institution of marriage can be a beautiful thing, but when marriages turn sour these days, things can get ugly real fast."

"That's true. And after what I've gone through, I'm not even so sure about the institution itself anymore."

"So you don't think you'll ever get married again?" Paris asked.

"I'll put it this way," he replied with a smile. "The money that I pay every month to cover that $20,000 settlement is a monthly reminder that marriage is not a move I want to consider right now."

Camron swigged his beer, let out a jocular, "Humph," then said, "JaLisa—a friend of mine at work—I think she has a good approach to marriage."

"What's that?"

"She thinks a marriage license should be like a driver's license: renewable every four or five years."

Paris laughed. Camron chuckled.

"And both parties have to agree to renew," he added. "And pay a hundred dollar renewal fee just to show they mean it."

Paris laughed again. Her laugh was pleasant, a lilt that rose easily from her bosom.

They spoke of other relationships in which they had been involved. Recent relationships with less depth, less drama, that neither seemed very interested in elaborating on to any great degree. Paris mentioned a guy named Leon, whom she only described as "a jerk," and Camron talked about a girl, Michele, who, after a month of dating, decided to go back to her old boyfriend. They then traded thoughts and personal philosophies on what it took to make a relationship successful: honesty, communication, money, good sex. Camron took issue with the honesty part.

"I mean, what if your wife or significant other asks you if she looks fat in a certain dress? And she *does* look fat. What do you do? Be honest and say, 'Honey, you *do* look kind of piggish in that dress.'?"

"Nooo," Paris said smiling. "If you lied about that, that would be a white lie. We like those kind of lies. Sometimes. I'm talking about something bigger than that. Like if the man comes in at ten o'clock at night and his wife asks him where he's been. Some honesty would be appreciated in that instance."

"Of course," Camron agreed.

Thirty minutes after their claim on the love seat, they put on their coats and gloves, and headed back out into the winter air.

As they continued to discuss the major elements necessary for a successful relationship, Camron drove east on Grand, turned left on Dale Street, and made a right on Summit Avenue. That section of Summit was where many of St. Paul's old-money residents resided in weary mansions from another era. Near the end of Summit, on a hill that overlooked downtown, sat the majestic St. Paul Cathedral. On a grassy knoll in front of the cathedral, a manger scene with plastic, incandescent moldings of the Three Wise Men, surrounding like representations of Joseph, Mary, and the baby Jesus, served as a reminder of the true meaning of the Christmas season. Just past the cathedral, Camron took another right that took them down the hill and back into the downtown district. Four minutes later they were at Galtier Plaza, where he had picked Paris up three hours earlier.

"I'm glad we finally got a chance to get together," Camron said as he pulled to a stop. This time she had directed him to the north end of her building, the proper entrance for the side of the complex on which she lived.

"Me too. I had a nice time," Paris said.

"Likewise. Thank you for the company and conversation. We should do it again real soon."

"Definitely," Paris said as she nodded her head.

"Maybe next week. After Christmas."

"Okay. Give me a call."

"I will."

Camron took her gloved right hand, and began pulling at the fingers.

"What are you doing?" Paris asked with a smile.

"Getting ready to kiss you good night."

He removed the glove and kissed her on her hand.

Her smile became broader. "Silly man," she said as she leaned in and gave Camron a peck on the lips. "Call me."

With that, Paris got out of the car and walked into her building. She turned a corner, looked back, smiled and waved, and with her lips gave a silent "Goodbye." Camron returned the smile and wave, and pulled away.

Hmm. That was better than I expected it would be, he said to himself.

He checked his radio clock. 11:17. Given that he didn't have to work the following day, Camron considered swinging by another nightspot. But his time with Paris had temporarily loosened the lust knot—that primal, sexual tension that made him, and most every other male, want to be close to a female. So instead of heading west on I-94 and back in the direction of Minneapolis, he drove east, toward the safety and security of the lily-white suburbs and his suburban abode.

Camron was soon home under the warm covers of his bed, TV remote in hand, racing through channels. More of the beer he had drank wanted out, so he made his way to the commode. As he relieved himself, he noticed that he was partially erect. He hadn't been with a woman in nearly five weeks. Not since Michele, the lady he had mentioned to Paris. And now it seemed his penis was looking back at him, the slit serving as its eye, evidently disgusted at its own recent lack of activity beyond just passing water. The slit suddenly transformed itself into a mouth. *"Man, you need to get on the stick,"* his Johnson said in a munchkin voice. *"Shit."*

The phone rang, bringing Camron out of his goofy hallucination.

He shook his manhood gently, stuffed it back into his underwear, and walked into the bedroom and toward the ring of the phone. Picking up the receiver, he looked at the caller-ID screen. It showed "EDWARDS, PARIS."

"Hello," he said as if he had no inkling whom it was.

"Camron?"

"Yes."

"This is Paris."

"Hey. What's up?"

Did she forget something in my car?

"I should have asked you this before I got out, but you told me you didn't have any plans for Christmas Day, right?"

"Right. Nothing in particular."

"Well, would you like to join me and my sister's family for dinner?"

"Sure," Camron said. "That would be cool."

"Good. Why don't you plan on arriving around three o'clock."

"Okay."

"Great," Paris said. "I'll see you then."

"See you then."

So, it seemed, his dance with Paris would resume sooner than he had expected.

12

Love

MARA AND I MADE LOVE for the first time on a Friday night, five weeks, six days, and five hours after we first met. I had made dinner, and I think we both knew early on that evening that we would end up in bed together. It probably would have happened sooner if I had pushed things. But a part of me wanted to savor the innocence of our fresh, newly found adoration.

We were cuddling on my living room sofa—this sofa—full from a meal of baked pork chops, rice, and green peas, and barely paying attention to whatever movie was playing on HBO. Instead we were kissing; necking like high schoolers.

"Let's go upstairs," I whispered.

"Okay."

I stood and pulled her to her feet. I kissed her again, my tongue flirting with hers, before re-aiming our bodies and walking slowly towards the steps, forcing her to walk backwards in the process. Our awkward movements caused Mara to stumble.

"Camron, you're gonna make me fall."

"No, sweetie," I said as I grabbed her waist tighter. "I would never let you fall."

We climbed the stairs, she ahead of me. Her beautifully round behind looked enticing in the tight denim jeans she was wearing. As we reached the top of the steps, I put my hands on her shoulders and massaged them. She rubbed her hands over mine.

"Mmm, that feels good," she moaned.

"Why don't you go on up and relax. Let me turn off this TV," I said, and returned downstairs.

I loaded both discs from a Luther Vandross greatest hits collection into my CD player, programmed some of the slow jams, and pressed the "PLAY" and "REPEAT" buttons. I turned off the television, darkened the living room, then went upstairs to join the Mara.

Mara had strewn herself diagonally across my waterbed and was lying on her stomach, her magnificent form made visible by the dimmed headboard lights. I laid beside her, and watched her backside go up and down as the water beneath the mattress conformed to accept the both of us. She turned her head to face me, and I kissed her softly on her lips.

"Camron," she said, looking at me through lovely slanted eyes.

"Yes?"

"What do I mean to you?"

"What do you mean to me?" I repeated, buying time.

"Yeah. What am I to you? A friend? A girlfriend?"

I measured my words and spoke slowly. "Well, of course I would consider us friends. But, even though we haven't known each other long, I think of us as more than friends. I would say we're friends that are enamored with each other. I certainly know I'm enamored with you."

Mara smiled.

I added, "Enamored friends ... quickly heading towards something more."

I kissed her; a deep kiss. "I wanna make love to you."

"You do, huh?" Mara said, a sly smile etching across her face. "And what's gonna happen after that?"

"Bigger and better things."

I gently rolled her onto her back, and massaged her neck with my tongue. Her chest rose as she took in a deep breath.

"Take this off," I said as if it were an idea that had just popped into my head. I was alluding to the white, V-neck, long-sleeve sweater she was wearing.

She raised up, threw her hands over her shoulders, and began pulling the sweater over her head. Leaning on one elbow, I assisted her, then licked my lips at the sight of her smooth, brown back, a portion of which was covered by the strappings of a shear, tangerine-colored bra.

I pulled her down beside me. She nuzzled her nose into my neck and kissed me gently there. I began unbuttoning the red button-down shirt I was wearing. Mara ran her hand across my chest and began helping me, her fingers interwoven with mine as we moved further and further down, from one button to the next.

I was about to begin working on my belt, but Mara's fingers

were on the buckle before mine, deftly pulling at the metal. She had it undone before I had a chance to help, which left me impressed. And the member between my legs burgeoning.

I pushed her onto her back once more, and kissed the middle of her chest, just below where the cups of her bra were joined. From there I slid downward, my tongue leading the way. I made a circle on her stomach, then puckered my lips over her innie bellybutton. I unfastened the lone button on her jeans and unzipped them. Underneath were panties that matched her bra. I planted wet kisses on both sides of her waist, right on her hip bones, and ran my hands across the soft, blue denim that covered her thighs so snugly, it made me wonder how she got them on.

"I don't think I can get these things off," I said in jest. "They're too tight."

"Guess they'll have to stay on then," Mara replied.

"Wait a minute," I insisted, not quite sure if she meant what she had just said.

Four seconds later I was standing at the foot of the bed, tugging first at the left leg of her tight-fitting pants, then the right. Mara lifted her bottom, and, with her hands, slid the jeans below her waist and over her ample rump. I pulled and they came off easily. Wearing nothing but a bra and panties, Mara struck a cute-sexy pose by bending her legs slightly at the knees and turning her hips sideways. I dropped her pants to the floor, then my own beside them. Her eyes followed me as I moved around the side of the bed, pulled off my shirt, and let it fall to the carpet as well. I crawled back onto the bed beside her. Her skin was velvety soft. I gathered her into my arms, and we moaned in unison as our tongues met again and toyed with one another.

One of my hands, wandering about her shoulder blades, found the clasps of her bra. With an adroit, one-handed finger move that had proven useful to me as far back as high school, I flicked the tiny metal hooks loose, and her brassier dropped limply about her shoulders. She pulled her arms through the straps, and I tossed the bra over the end of the bed.

I brushed my hand across one of her soft, brown breasts, and made small circles around her nipple with my index finger. I took the nipple of the other in my mouth, massaged it with my tongue, held it gently between my teeth, and gave it a little tug before letting it drop from my snare.

"Ouch," Mara said. "Ooh. Do that again."

I smiled at her. "I'll be right back."

"Okay."

I went into the adjoining bathroom, flipped on the switch that controlled the numerous vanity bulbs above the large mirror, and partially closed the door behind me. I opened the left-hand drawer that was just below the sink counter and peered into the back of it. Three condoms were there. I grabbed one, and, looking at the package, realized it was a novelty condom: one that glowed in the dark. I smiled, threw it back in the drawer, and reached for one of the other two, both Trojan brands, ultra ribbed. Then I thought, *Why not have some fun?* I retrieved the glow-in-the-dark condom, looked at the package more closely, and tossed it on the sink. I returned to the bedroom, closed the bathroom door, but left the light on to allow the glow condom to energize.

Mara was lying on her stomach, displaying her luscious, lovely bottom. At five-feet-four-inches tall, she was a small woman. But somebody forgot to tell her ass that, 'cause it was more than a handful. Some basic instinct made me wanna slap it; get some jiggling going. But I resisted the temptation.

"Where you get all this from?" I asked as I slid next to her, and instead massaged my hand over her gorgeous mounds of backside flesh.

"My mama," Mara said. She turned onto her side to face me. "And where'd you get all this?"

I was lying on my side as well, and Mara's eyes had lowered to my crotch. Her hand eased down along my belly until it reached the bulge in my bright white athletic briefs. Once there, she gave it a gentle squeeze.

"My daddy," I said.

We both chuckled.

She pulled her body closer to mine, kissed my chest, and teased my nipples with her tongue. She tugged and pulled at my underwear until they were nothing more than another garment on the floor, then took me to higher levels of arousal with the warmth of her mouth and tongue.

After a bit, I inhaled and exhaled deeply, then said, "Let me grab some protection."

" 'Kay," she said with a breathy whisper.

I returned to the bathroom and grabbed the glow-in-the-dark

condom off the sink. After getting it out of the pack, I rolled it onto my anxious appendage. I shut off the bathroom light to see if the condom worked as I anticipated. It had a hazy, hot-white glow. I smiled in amusement as I flexed my groin muscles and watched it bob up and down.

Going back into the bedroom, I walked to the opposite side of the headboard to turn out the headboard lights. I wanted to enhance the effect of my gleaming masculinity, which Mara had yet to notice.

Mara's eyes were closed as I peeled off her tangerine panties, raised her legs, and planted wet kisses on the back of her thighs. My tongue traced along her inner thigh before finding her sweet spot. Mara began to rotate her hips, and her vaginal muscles flexed and twitched. Moans, originating somewhere deep within her body, became more intense, more frequent, and excited me further.

Moments later I raised up, and positioned my glowing sheath between her legs.

Finally noticing, Mara said, with surprise and a giggle, "What is that?" She arched her back and raised her butt a bit to help me get to where I was trying to go.

"My own personal light saber," I said as I made a slow, gentle thrust.

"Camron, you ain't got no ... ooh ... sen-se."

Mara raised her legs higher as I entered her completely. I watched as my member disappeared inside of her, then reappeared, then disappeared again, looking like a fluorescent lamp—with a slight bend—moving in and out of her feminine fleshpot.

"Ooh, baby, you feel so good," Mara purred. "Don't stop. Don't stop. Take it, baby."

I dropped down on top of her, and grabbed both cheeks of her soft behind in my hands. Mara wrapped her arms around my back and held me tight, her movements in perfect sync with my own. With each stroke, the passion between us escalated, and soon fully possessed us. Her knees were near her head as she jostled her hips in time to my rhythm. Primitive grunts and groans filled the room. Our hearts and breaths raced. As Mara approached her climax, she crashed her pelvis repeatedly into mine with sweet abandon. In my own loins, that familiar knurl of pleasure began to build, like a rolling snowball, until I could no longer contain it. Waves of ecstasy swept over us, engulfed us, demanded the attention of every fiber in our bodies. Our muscles tightened, brought us deep inside each other, and—for a single, perfect, rapturous moment—we were one.

The swell of carnality quickly subsided, and left us weak with pleasure. A few minutes later Mara, searching for her breath, said, "That was wonderful, Dickerson." It was the first time she had called me by my last name, the start of a habit that would continue from that point on.

After that first night of lovemaking, my quandary with Kimma thickened. She had sensed that I was drifting away. So when, the following week, I gave her the proverbial line about needing more space, I don't think it was totally unexpected to her. Nevertheless, in the darkness of my bedroom, she cried in my arms, her shoulders heaving heavily. She cried so hard it momentarily frightened me, and made me realize just how deeply she'd fallen into the relationship. After a few minutes of tears, she bolted from the bed, and began to hastily dress.

"Take me home," she insisted as she fumbled in the dark for her clothes.

"Kimma, please," I said with as much sympathy as I could muster.

"Take me home!" she repeated.

I let out a sigh of resignation, then rolled and twisted until I was sitting on the edge of the bed, my elbows on my knees. As she continued, on the opposite side, to pull garments over that lovely, chocolate frame of hers, my fingers slowly scratched the top of my nappy head. God, I never wanted to hurt her like that.

As I drove her home, the new day—a Sunday—was not quite two hours old. With the exception of an occasional sniffle and a Con-Funk-Shun CD playing in the background, we rode in silence.

I found myself wishing she had never met me.

"I'll call you," I said as we came to a stop in front of her apartment building.

"Don't bother," she replied. She got out of the car and slammed the door behind her.

As fall turned to winter, Mara and I spent more and more time together. We shared Thanksgiving dinner at the home of our newlywed friends, Patrice and Donnell, where we ate and drank and laughed and laughed until late into the night. We woke up together on

Christmas Day. We rang in the New Year kissing on a dance floor amidst a sea of lip-locked strangers. And on Valentine's Day of 1997, my thirty-third birthday, I told her—over a dinner of veal and au gratin potatoes at a dark, sleepy piano bar in Minneapolis called Sophia—that I loved her.

"I didn't expect this," Mara said, not so much in response to my confession of deep affection, but more so as to how quickly our relationship had blossomed. "I really didn't. But I love you too, Camron."

I wanted to kiss her, but she was on the other side of the table, too far away for me to reach. So I rose to my feet, took one giant step in her direction, and leaned and gave her a short but amorous kiss. I noticed a few couples staring at us as I returned to my chair, but I didn't care.

My kiss left a soft smile on Mara's face. She looked radiantly beautiful in the soft lighting of the restaurant. "Love is a scary thing, Dickerson. You know?"

"It doesn't have to be," I said, trying to assure both her and myself.

She twirled her fork in her potatoes. "What's the name of that song? 'Now-that-we've-found-love-what-are-we-gonna-do-with-it'? You know the one I'm talking about?"

"Yes."

"So what are we gonna do with it?"

I pondered her question for a moment. "Embrace it."

In my twenties, I had been in what I thought was love a couple of times. During one such instance—in the fall of my junior year in college—a cute AKA soror named Sheila with skin the color of honey had blew my mind. We had met at a party in the basement of a raggedy dorm. She liked my smile; I liked her ass. We dated, and later got creative in finding places to make love (outside, hidden by the night, in the recessed corner of some campus building; in my dorm room while my goofy roommate was away at the library; et cetera, et cetera). When Christmas break started, we intentionally stayed behind for a few days, spending nearly the whole time in my room, screwing till it hurt. I thought, Surely this must be love. But by the end of the following spring semester, the infatuation had run its course, and we both had drifted on to other things.

Then there was Lauren, whom I had met in April of '94, three years and one month after my arrival in the Twin Cities. Lauren was very light-skinned, a trait attributable to the union of her Black father and White mother. Her body was thick, but not fat, and she had one of the most beautiful faces I had ever seen. But she was so weird. For instance, she never felt she was clean enough, so as soon as we'd get to my house, she'd jump in the Jacuzzi, and would stay in it until she had used up all the hot water. Also, she was often quiet and distant, and in the bedroom she was essentially frigid. I never could quite figure out what was wrong with her. And actually, now that I think about it, I don't think I ever really loved her. I wanted to, though, because she looked so damn good. But in the end, she proved to be too much of a conundrum to me, and, after nine months, I decided to let the relationship go.

So as I sat there with Mara on that Valentine's Day having revealed my soul to her, I knew she was right about love. It *was* a scary thing. And although I was trying to play it cool, it was a tad frightening to think about what might lie ahead for us: Commitment and marriage? Or disaster and heartbreak.

13

Christmas Morning

CHRISTMAS MORNING, 2000. Camron, still in bed, scrolled through numbers stored in the memory of his phone until he reached that of his oldest sister, Lena. He pressed the "ON" button and heard the faint tones of the numbers being automatically dialed. The phone at the other end rang twice.

"Hello." The female voice that answered was dispassionate, flat.

"Merry Christmas and Happy Kwanzaa," Camron said.

Silence was followed quickly by recognition.

"Hey, baby! How you doing?" Lena said, her voice instantly animated.

"Fine. And how are you, sis?"

Camron loved all three of his sisters, but Lena was his favorite. She was the first person to take him to see a movie and to eat pizza, both great adventures for a five-year-old, his age at the time. And as far back as he could remember, she always made him feel special and loved.

"We are doing wonderful, jus' wonderful," Lena assured him. "We're about to get outta here and head down ta da house."

"Da house" was the home in which they had all been raised, and was where their father still lived. It was located in a sleepy North Carolina hamlet called Spivey's Corner.

"Y'all gonna have dinner der?" Camron asked. His Southern dialect asserted itself almost anytime he talked with anyone back home. But he liked *talkin' Southern*. Liked the lazy efficiency of it.

"Yeah. We're gonna *fix* dinner der ac'chally."

"That's good. So er'body jus' gonna meet der den?"

By "er'body" he meant Wonetta and Tammy, his other sisters; Dwight, his brother; and their respective families.

"Mm-hmm," Lena said. "That way Daddy du'n' have to get up

out da house."

"Well I jus' wanted to wish you a Merry Christmas," Camron said. " 'Specially since I didn't send anythang. But dollars tight deez days."

"Baby, you got that right. I'm jus' happy the Good Lord has brought us all around to see another Christmas. We certainly miss Momma, but we can all be thankful that we got our health and are managing to hold it together. And that's enough of a present for me," Lena said. "So what are you doing today, baby? You should be down here wit' us."

"Yeah, you right. I'll make it down next time. But I'm having dinner wit' a friend of mine and sum' a her fam'ly."

"A new girlfriend?"

"No," Camron said with a chuckle. "I haven't known her too long. She seems nice though."

"Well that's good. I was thinkin' about cha' last week. I said, 'Now my baby brother up there in that cold place all by hisself.' And this is the first Christmas you and Mara are spending apart too. So I was jus' worrin' about cha' a li'l bit, that's all."

"No need to worry. I'm fine. I'm gonna get up from here in a li'l while and get ready to go to dis dinner. But since er'body gonna be der at da house, I'll call down der before I leave to say hello."

"Yeah you do that. They'll all be glad to hear from ya'."

"How's Phil and the girls?" Camron asked.

Phil was Lena's husband, a driver for a package delivery company. "The girls" were their two daughters, Cecilia, twenty, and Missy, eighteen. Missy wasn't the real name of the eighteen-year-old, but everyone had called her that for so long, Camron didn't have the foggiest idea what her birth name was.

"They're fine. The girls are gonna meet us down der. And Phil is sittin' in the living room in front of the TV waitin' on me. So I better go before he gets too involved in whatever it is he's watchin'."

"All right," Camron said.

"Okay, baby. I'll talk to ya' later today when you call, okay?"

"Okay."

"All right den. Love you," Lena said.

"Love you too."

"Bye-bye."

"Bye."

It wasn't quite 10 o'clock, and, through the slits in his blinds,

Camron could see the sky was gray. Excellent conditions for a nap, he felt. He pulled the covers up, turned down the volume on the TV, and was soon asleep again.

The phone rang and jolted Camron back to consciousness.

He grabbed the receiver. "Hello," he said. His voice was groggy.

"Merry Christmas." It was Paris.

"Merry Christmas to you."

"So where are you?" she asked.

"At the number you just called, home."

"Now, Camron, I know you aren't still in the bed."

What time was it? he thought. He knew he couldn't have slept the afternoon away.

"We've got dinner on the table," Paris said. "We're just waitin' on you."

"What time is it?" Camron asked hurriedly. He looked at the cable-box clock on top of his TV. It said 11:23.

"Now, Paris, you oughta quit playin'," Camron admonished. "It's not even eleven-thirty."

"You were knocked out, weren't you?" she said.

"I was just takin' a li'l nap."

"A little nap or a big nap?"

"Well, maybe a medium nap," Camron conceded.

"But you *are* gonna get up eventually, right?"

"Yes I am."

"And hopefully in time to get here by three."

"Yes."

It was clear Paris was amused by Camron's laziness. To get her off his case, he asked, "How long have you been up?"

"I've been up cookin' since seven o'clock."

"By three you'll have put in a full day's work. You'll need a nap by then yourself."

"I'm fine. My sister's been helping."

"When did they get in?"

"Yesterday afternoon. She's anxious to meet you."

"She is, huh? Is that good or bad?"

"I don't know. You can ask her when you get here," Paris teased.

"You want me to bring something?" Camron asked. He had purchased two bottles of wine a couple of days earlier to take with him. But if she requested something beyond that, he didn't know what he'd do since most stores were closed.

"No. Just yourself," Paris said.

"All right. I'll see you at three."

"Okay."

Camron turned off the TV, went downstairs, and programmed songs from CDs by The Sounds of Blackness, Take 6, and Michael Franks. Going back upstairs, he went into the bathroom. He was about to turn on the shower, but instead decided to take a bath in his Jacuzzi tub. *I've got plenty of time*, he thought, and began filling the tub with a mix of hot and cold water.

Prior to moving into his house, Camron had always taken showers. In fact, he had lived in his house for nearly a year before he tried out the Jacuzzi. But once he did and discovered what a relaxing experience it was, he found himself in that big tub three times a week or more.

Once, around a few of the guys at work, he had made the mistake of mentioning something about taking a bubble bath after work. Bob, his technician, was amongst the group, and seized upon the opportunity to rib him. "Take a bubble bath? What are you gonna do after that? Shave your legs?" Camron's co-workers guffawed. Camron couldn't help but laugh too, even as he retorted, "A *Jacuzzi* bubble bath, man. There's a difference!"

After placing his cordless phone on the ceramic tile that surrounded the tub, he climbed into the warm water and reclined, bringing his head to rest on a white inflatable pillow that was covered with fabric on one side. He added some freesia-scented liquid bubble bath, and pushed a button in the corner of the Jacuzzi, causing the six water jets to whir to life. Within two minutes, the tub was filled with tiny white bubbles that covered Camron like a blanket of whip cream. He closed his eyes, and let the warm water soften and relax his muscles.

A few minutes passed before he opened his eyes and looked at the phone. His lids had been lifted by the thought of calling Mara to wish her Happy Holidays. She would most likely be at her mother's by now. He could remember the first few digits of the number, but wasn't sure about the rest. The number was in his electronic organizer, but that was downstairs on the kitchen counter. Well enough, he thought, because he wasn't sure he wanted to bring Mara further to the fore of his mind by calling her on Christmas Day.

He picked up the phone, and instead dialed a number he did know: home.

"Yello." It was Camron's father.

"Merry Christmas, man," Camron said.

"Hey now!" his father half-shouted. "Merry Christmas."

"How's it going, Pop?"

"Fine. Get'n' ready to sit down and eat here in a minute."

"Er'body get there?"

"Yeah, dey all here. 'Cept for your baby sister."

Camron's father was talking about the youngest member of their family, Tammy, twenty-seven years old and a newlywed of four months.

"Where's she and Marcellus?" Camron asked. Marcellus was her husband.

"Dey on dey honeymoon."

"Oh yeah. That delayed honeymoon of ders. Where'd dey go?"

"Way down yonder."

"Florida?"

"Naw, man. Down there. You know." Camron's father seemed frustrated that Camron couldn't read his mind. "Where *did* dey go?" his father asked himself aloud. Suddenly remembering, he said, "The Mahamas."

"Mahamas?" Camron refrained. "You mean the Bahamas?"

"Yeah, that's where dey went."

"How long dey down der?"

"I think dey gonna be down there till ah ... the day after New Year's," his father told him. The volume of his voice dropped as he tossed a query away from the phone's mouthpiece. "Lena, when Tammy and Marcellus coming back?"

Camron heard Lena from a distance say, "January third."

Having resolved that issue, Camron spoke some more with his father, then with other members of his family that were there, wishing them all—their Southern accents in full effect—a Merry Christmas and Happy Kwanzaa.

14

Christmas Dinner

CAMRON FOUND A PARKING SPOT, guarded by a gray parking meter, a half-a-block from Paris's apartment building. He got out of the car, the loops of a plastic bag in one hand, black leather gloves in the other. He was about to pull the gloves onto his hands, but instead put them in his coat pocket, reasoning that the short walk and jostling he would have to do with the bag didn't make it worth the effort of squeezing into them. He clicked his car doors locked, and closed his tan trench coat loosely with its belt.

The day was calm, gray, hazy, and cold. However, it seemed a bit warmer than the previous few days had been. Camron guessed it was about fifteen degrees.

The streets were quiet on this midafternoon Christmas Day. So quiet Camron could hear the gritty crunch of his footsteps echoing off the surrounding buildings. A few cars passed, but most of the vehicles he saw were stationary and parked along the streets.

He reached the vestibule of Paris's complex. A black phone was there, and beside it a list of resident names. Camron ran his index finger down the list until he found "Edwards, P." He picked up the receiver and entered the code that was beside the name.

The phone rang only once before a genial female voice came on the line. "Merry Christmas."

"Hey, it's Camron. I'm downstairs."

"Who?"

"Camron," he said. "Paris, are you still being silly?"

"Would you like to speak to Paris? This is her sister, Deanna."

"Oh, I'm sorry, Deanna. You sound just like Paris."

"No no. She sounds just like *me*. Which was probably why she wanted me to answer the phone. Just to confuse you. Anyway, hold on for a sec, Camron, and I'll buzz you in."

In the background, Camron heard Deanna ask Paris how to buzz the door open. "Press the pound key," came the faint response. The lobby door made a humming sound and Camron pulled it open, hung up the phone, and walked through the lobby to the double elevators. He rode one of them to the 24th floor, found his way to Paris's apartment, and knocked on the door. A few seconds passed before it swung open. Behind it stood an attractive sistah with a cheery smile.

"Hi," she said. "I'm Deanna."

She extended her hand and Camron gave it a weak shake. "And I'm Camron."

"Nice to meet you, Camron."

"You too."

Deanna was a tad darker than Paris's rosy brown complexion, and not as tall. Her face was just as attractive and favored her younger sister's, but was fuller. Her straight black hair was pulled back into a neat bun. Camron could tell that she was shapely, despite the loose-fitting, full-length teal dress she was wearing. He thought a woman who covered her body in that fashion, but was obviously fine, always added an air of mysterious sensuality to that part of her being.

"Forgive me for giving you such a hard time on the phone, but you can blame Paris for that," Deanna said.

"She's to blame, huh?" Camron said.

"Don't believe a word she's saying, Camron," Paris countered. Paris was in the kitchen, the first doorway to Camron's left as he walked in, tending a pan of frying chicken. "She did that all on her own, without any encouragement from me. Five minutes before you came she said, 'I'm 'a let Camron think I'm you.' "

Paris had a casual but sexy look in some snug fitting, dark blue jeans and an aqua, short-sleeve, pullover top.

"I brought two bottles of wine," Camron said, raising the thin, translucent, plastic bag he was carrying. "A Merlot and a Chardonnay."

"I told you you didn't have to bring anything," Paris scolded.

"I didn't want to come totally empty-handed."

"Mmm, let's get one of these open," Deanna said, then took the bag from him, and turned and walked down the entryway and toward the dining room.

"Deanna, don't open those yet," Paris hollered at her sister. Paris shook her head and looked at Camron. "Don't mind her."

"How are you?" Camron asked.

"Fine," Paris said. "You look well rested."

Camron chuckled. "I am. Thank you."

"You can hang your coat in the closet behind you," she told him. "Then go on in and meet Jake and Cicely."

"Okay," he said.

After Camron hung up his coat and kicked off his shoes, he walked further into the apartment: through the dining room, and to the edge of the living room. Deanna was placing a covered dish on a dining room table with a smoky glass surface.

"Camron, that's my husband Jake," she said nodding her head in the direction of the living room.

Jake, who was watching a televised football game from what appeared to be a comfortable perch on the living room's green leather sofa, pulled his 6'3" frame up, and reached to give Camron a soul handshake.

"Hey, how ya' doing?" Jake said with a lot of bass in his voice.

"Fine, how 'bout yourself?"

"Just kicking back and enjoying these few days of vacation."

"I heard that," Camron said, trying to get as cool as Jake.

With deep-set eyes and a narrow nose that gave him a Roman-esque look, Jake was a handsome man. His mustache thinned as it traveled down his mouth, then curved upward until the narrow lines of hair widened and met his sideburns. It was a look Camron imag-ined Jake spent a considerable amount of time maintaining. There were speckles of gray in both his facial and short-cut cranium hair, and just a touch of potbelly was pushing against the light blue, silk button shirt he was wearing. He was about the same color as Cam-ron, but the dullness of his complexion made him appear darker.

"And that's our daughter Cicely," Deanna said, gesturing toward a cute little girl with big eyes and two tightly braided pigtails stick-ing out the sides of her head. "She's three and a quarter."

Cicely, who had a skin shade between that of her father and mother, was sitting on a matching love seat adjacent to her father. She was dressed in black Capri pants and a pink turtleneck top, and was holding a Black Barbie doll.

Deanna encouraged her daughter to speak. "Say 'Hi, Camron.' Can you say that?"

Cicely looked at her mother, then at Camron, then back at her mother.

"Hi, Cicely," Camron said, which caused her to look at him again. "How you doing, sweetie?"

Cicely's only response to Camron was a doe-eyed stare.

"She's so shy," Deanna said. "I'll be glad when she grows out of that."

Seeing he wasn't going to coax a response either, Camron posed a question to Jake. "Who's playin'?"

"Boston College and Arizona State. The Aloha Bowl," Jake said. "They're playing in Honolulu."

"Camron, we've got some beer in the fridge," Deanna said. "Would you like one?"

"Sure," Camron said. "Whatcha got?"

"Let's see," Deanna said and walked into the kitchen and opened the refrigerator door. "We've got Heineken, Miller Genuine Draft—"

"I'll take an MGD," Camron said.

Paris walked into the dining area with a large platter of the chicken she had been frying, and placed it on the dining room table. Half of a baked ham, green bean casserole, rice, greens, and potato salad were already there.

Deanna handed Camron a can of beer. "Thank you," he said.

"You're welcome," Deanna responded as she walked past him and sat down beside her daughter, then began running her fingers through the hair of Cicely's doll.

"This looks good," Camron said to Paris as he moved toward the dining room table and admired the spread of food. He popped the top of his beer. "How much of this did you do?"

"Deanna did the potato salad and green bean casserole," Paris said. "I did the rest."

"I hear somebody talkin' about me?" Deanna's voice chimed in from the living room.

"I was just telling Camron you made the potato salad and green bean casserole."

"Yes, and they're both quite delicious, so be sure and get two helpings," Deanna recommended.

"I'm impressed," Camron said loud enough so Deanna could hear him as well.

"You might want to reserve judgment until after you've tasted it first," Paris said.

"If it tastes anything like it looks, I'm sure it'll be delicious," Camron offered.

From behind him, Camron heard a whirring noise, then Deanna's voice once more, this time chastising her daughter. "Cicely, don't start that truck up again."

Off to one side of the living room, Cicely was sitting in a bright pink, motorized, toy four-wheel drive truck, and had set it in motion.

"That was one of her presents, and she's been in it all day. You'd think the batteries would be dead by now," Deanna said. "Get out of that thing. We're gonna eat in a minute."

Cicely quietly heeded her mother's command.

"Hey, you guys. Come on so we can bless the food," Paris shouted in the direction of the living room. "Camron, you want to bless the food?"

Camron froze. The only blessing he knew was that semirhyming one he'd learned as a kid: *God is great, God is good, and we thank him for our food....* He could try freestyling, but then he would really make a fool of himself, he thought. Why did Paris have to put this kind of pressure on him? He looked at her. She was looking at him with an anticipatory gaze. Then he noticed just a crack of a smile at the corner of her mouth, which let him know she wasn't totally serious.

"Naw, you can go ahead," Camron said weakly.

"You sure?" she asked, smiling even more.

"Positive," Camron assured her.

Jake, Deanna, and Cicely arrived at the table.

"Let's all join hands," Paris directed.

They formed a semicircle around the food, and Paris delivered a short, sincere blessing, at the end of which the adults said "Amen" in unison. The silence that punctuated the prayer was immediately replaced with the sounds of a small group about to feast.

"Camron, you want to open the wine you brought?" Paris suggested.

"Sure," Camron responded.

"There's a corkscrew in the drawer beside the refrigerator," Paris said. "Deanna, can you put those plates on the table?" She was speaking of eight blue ceramic plates that were on the kitchen counter. "I think it will be easier to just pick up your plate closer to the food. Leave the silverware on the counter though. Everybody fix your own plate. That way you can get as much of whatever you want.

"After y'all get your food, just take a seat in the living room.

Trays for your plates are on top of the microwave. Cicely, come here, baby, and show me what you want so I can get you squared away."

"That ham really came out nice," Deanna said as she sat the plates at one corner of the table, then took one for herself.

"Yeah it did, didn't it?" Paris said as she placed some ladling utensils in the casserole, rice, greens, and potato salad, and a fork on top of the chicken. "Camron, can you slice up the ham?"

"Yes," Camron said quickly. Slicing up a ham was a cinch compared to delivering an original blessing.

Everyone was soon seated in the living room, their blue plates heaped with food. Jake and Deanna were sitting on the sofa, Paris and Camron on the love seat. Cicely was on the floor with the brown Barbie, her plate on a tray in front of her, gingerly picking at a table-spoonful of potato salad with her fork.

"Quite good, ladies," Jake said between bites of chicken.

"Yes it is," Camron concurred. "Who's winning?" he asked Jake of the football game.

"They're tied. It's just about halftime."

"Jake, is something else better on?" Deanna asked.

Jake lied with authority. "Nah, this is all that's on right now."

"Lord, why'd I even ask," Deanna said.

"Girl, you put the hurt on this green bean casserole," Paris said to her sister, turning Deanna's attention away from her momentary discontent with her husband.

Deanna returned Paris's compliment with one of her own. "And this chicken is so good. You got to show me how you spiced it."

Later, the desserts (apple and sweet potato pies; a yellow cake with chocolate frosting) proved to be just as scrumptious. Camron especially enjoyed Paris's sweet potato pie.

"This sweet potato pie is delicious," Camron said.

"Thank you," Paris replied.

"Reminds me of my mom's. Hers had this glazed coating over the top as well," he said.

"Your family's all in North Carolina, right?" Deanna asked.

"Yeah," Camron said. "I talked with everyone earlier today."

"Your mom's probably serving up some of her own sweet potato pie right now," Deanna suggested. Paris momentarily stopped chewing her food.

"Well, my mother's dead," Camron said to Deanna. Saying it

still felt awkward to him. "She passed in '95."

"Oh, I'm sorry," Deanna said.

"No, nothing to be sorry about. She had a good life," Camron told her.

"How old was she?"

"Seventy."

"That's not much older than our parents right now. Let's see. Mom is sixty-seven, right, Paris?"

"Mm-hmm," Paris confirmed. "And Daddy will be sixty-nine in July. So they're getting on up there too."

"It's hard to imagine them not being around," Deanna admitted. "I know we all gotta go someday. But still—"

"Now you know our parents aren't going anywhere anytime soon," Paris said. "They're having too much fun being retired."

"And too much fun gettin' their freak on," Jake added.

A suspicious grin came over Paris's face. "Jake, what are you talking about?"

Deanna answered for him. "Nothin'."

"Deanna didn't tell ya'?" Jake asked. "We heard 'em in their bedroom screwin' one night when we were there for Thanksgiving."

"Jake!" Deanna slapped her husband on the leg and pointed at Cicely to remind him his daughter was within earshot. "They wasn't doing nothing like that."

"Now come on, Dee. You know what they were doing and I do too. I know 'crewin' when I hear it," Jake said, this time mangling the word for purposes of disguise.

"No they wasn't, was they?" Paris said in disbelief. "How did I miss this?"

"You were downstairs in the corner bedroom, so you probably couldn't hear it," Deanna said. "A little bit of noise was coming from their bedroom, but I don't know if that's what they were doing or not."

"You saw how chipper they were the next morning," Jake said.

Camron was amused. "Hey. Ain't nothing wrong with that."

"That is so cute," Paris said. "Their for'd selves. It's a good thing I didn't hear them 'cause I would have just asked them straight up: 'Clarence and Sarah Mae Edwards. Were you two doing the wild thang last night?' "

The sisters laughed heartily at the prospect of an amorous episode between their parents, while the men went into the kitchen—

Jake to get another piece of pie, Camron for another beer.

"That's funny," Camron said to Jake.

"At first I didn't know *what* they were doing," Jake recounted. "But after a while, you know, the rhythm of the springs let me know that's all that could have been going on. Deanna was half-asleep, but I woke her up and told her, 'Your parents are getting' their freak on.' I almost busted out laughin'."

Camron could recall only once, as a preadolescent boy, where late-night sounds emanating from his parent's bedroom may have been sex noise. The sensation from the imagery of that thought was—then and presently—interestingly weird to Camron because, like most children, he didn't think of his parents as sexual beings. But obviously they were. He and his siblings were proof enough of that.

As the afternoon hour approached 5:30, the cold gray day transformed into an even colder night. However, the scene in Paris's living room remained lively and warm. The sisters were enjoying the wine Camron had brought and reliving childhood memories.

"Deanna was so mean to me when we were little," Paris said to Camron and Jake.

"*Au contraire,* my sister. When I baby-sat you, I let you stay up way past your bedtime. I let you talk on the phone. I let you do whatever you wanted to do as long as you didn't get me in no trouble."

"What about that Easter Sunday you sprayed me with the garden hose and got my new outfit soaking wet?" Paris asked.

"Now that's a shame," Jake said. With the outcome of the football game a forgone conclusion, his interest in the contest had waned.

"She was asking for that," Deanna explained. "She had been picking on me all day about Daryl Rodgers, this skinny boy I used to like. Besides, church was over and you were about to change clothes anyway."

"And what about that time you put all that bubblegum in my hair?" Paris asked.

"That was an experiment," Deanna said with seriousness, then laughed. "From back when I thought I wanted to be a hairdresser."

Everybody laughed except Paris, who had a contrived sneer on her face. "It took me a week to get all that gum out my hair."

A few minutes later, Paris suggested a game of cards. "Who's up for Spades? Me and Camron against you and Jake," she said to

Deanna.

Jake objected. "Spades? That boring game? If we gonna play something, let's play Bid Whist."

"Don't nobody know how to play Bid Whist but you, Jake," Deanna said.

"Camron, you know how to play Whist?" Jake asked.

"Yeah," Camron said.

"There you go," Jake said triumphantly.

"That still just makes two that know how to play Bid Whist," Deanna countered. "But all of us know how to play Spades. You know how to play Spades don't cha', Camron?"

"Yeah," Camron said again. He didn't want to get in the middle of Jake and Deanna's little disagreement, so he decided to remain succinct.

"So we'll play Spades," Deanna said.

With the matter settled, Deanna and Paris cleared away the remaining food, and, for the next two hours, cards—accompanied by boasts of all sorts—were slid, flipped, and smacked onto the dining room table. The commotion drew little Cicely to the table's edge, her doll gathered in one arm, where she stood wide-eyed and silent, wondering how such small rectangular pieces of stiff paper could have so profound an effect on grown men and women. By the end of the competition, Camron and Paris had won three out of four games.

Jake was less than thrilled with his wife's play. "Baby, you were underbidding too much in that last game."

In her own defense Deanna cried, "Well that's better than getting set."

"It's just a game," Paris assured them. "Y'all got whooped, that's all. So just deal wit' it."

"Whatever," Deanna responded. "You and Camron got lucky is what it was."

The intimacy bred by the card game made Camron feel comfortable participating in the braggadocio. "Nope. No luck involved. Just skill. Pure skill," he said as he walked back into the living room and plopped down on the couch.

"Baby, you 'bout ready to get outta here?" Jake asked his wife.

"Yes, honey," Deanna replied. "Paris, I'm gonna fix me a li'l plate for the road."

"Okay," Paris said before joining Camron in the living room.

Jake walked into Paris's bedroom.

"Jake, can you grab my coat too?" Deanna shouted from the kitchen.

"They're leaving tonight?" Camron asked Paris with a lowered voice as she sat down beside him.

"No. They got a hotel room. I told 'em they could have my room, and Cicely and I could sleep out here. But they insisted on getting a room. Cicely's been staying with me though, so that should tell you right there what's on their minds. You see how all of a sudden they're getting all sweet with each other."

Camron smiled and knowingly nodded his head.

Paris continued. "They're leaving tomorrow morning around ten. I'm working second shift this week, so I don't have to be at work until three tomorrow afternoon." She raised her voice and directed it at Cicely, who was back on the living room floor with her doll, staring at the television. "So Miss Cicely is gonna stay with her Auntie one more night, right, baby?"

Cicely looked in the direction of the couch and nodded her head.

"Well I'm sure you ladies will have fun," Camron said. "Anyway, I better get ready to get outta here too."

"No, sit with me for a while," Paris cajoled.

Camron paused just long enough to not seem too eager before answering. "Okay."

"Let me get these guys out the door. You want another beer?" Paris asked.

"Yeah, that would be nice," Camron said.

Paris walked into the kitchen. He could hear her hashing out details with her sister for their pickup of Cicely when Jake came into the living room. He had on a light brown, full-length wool coat, and was carrying a dark gray wool coat over one arm.

"Nice meeting you, man," he said as he walked over toward Camron and extended his hand.

"You too," Camron replied before slapping his hand into Jake's and giving him a another soul handshake, curling and momentarily locking their fingers on the pullback. "So y'all heading back to Kansas City tomorrow?"

"Yeah. We'll be back by here tomorrow morning to pick up Cicely. You gonna be around?" Jake asked, a sly grin on his face.

"Naw, man," Camron said smiling. "I'm 'a get up outta here in a few."

Deanna's head poked from around the corner of the kitchen. "It was nice meeting you, Camron. Hope to see you again soon." She was waving with one hand and had a stiff, white, paper plate of food covered with aluminum foil in the other.

"You too," Camron replied automatically.

A minute later they were gone, anxious, no doubt, to reach the seclusion of their hotel room.

"They seem like a nice couple," Camron said to Paris as she rejoined him on the couch and handed him an ice-cold can of beer. In her other hand she had a wineglass that was half-full of deep, purple wine.

"Yeah. They're pretty happy most of the time."

"How long have they been married?" he asked.

"Six years. So if they can make it through the seven-year itch, then maybe they'll have it made."

"I don't know if I'd say that. Because after the seven-year itch comes the eight-year itch, which is immediately followed by the nine-year itch. And of course you can't forget the ten-year itch."

Paris laughed. "So you're saying every year is a challenge."

"Every year of my marriage was a challenge. And I was only married for two."

Paris laughed again while Camron forced a chuckle.

"Marriage isn't something I'm that anxious to try," Paris confessed. "Some of my girlfriends think I'm crazy. But it's just not a big priority. At least not at this point in my life."

"I don't think there's anything wrong with that. Marriage is definitely not something you want to force. As a matter of fact, love itself is sometimes a foolish move."

"Camron. I can't believe you said that. How can falling in love be foolish?"

"*Sometimes* foolish. If you fall in love with the wrong person. Someone you're not compatible with."

"Well if you're not compatible, you shouldn't let it get as far as love," Paris declared.

"Ideally yes. But what if you don't find that out until after it's too late? You're already in love and married, then all of a sudden one day, for whatever reason, the relationship just doesn't work anymore."

"Is that what happened in your marriage?" Paris asked.

Camron thought for a moment. "I guess it did."

"But, Camron, seriously though. Two years? Seems like you

guys could have hung in there longer than that."

"We probably could have. But I think the results would have been the same whether we stuck it out one year or ten. So I figured it was best to let it go while we both were still young."

Paris took a drink of her wine, then placed the glass on the coffee table. "Did you talk with your ex today?"

"No. Why would I have talked with her today?"

"It's Christmas."

"Yeah, but she has her life and I have mine."

A half-smile appeared on Paris's face. "It's funny how, one day, two people can be living inseparable lives, and the next, it's the total opposite: separate lives with lots of distance in between them."

Camron absorbed her words, then said, "Just another peculiar aspect of relationships."

Paris nodded her head, then glanced across the room and noticed that Cicely was lying flat on her stomach, her small head resting on the bend of her arm.

"That girl is falling asleep," Paris observed. "Cicely, go get your pajamas out of your suitcase."

Cicely raised her head and Paris repeated her request. "Go get your pajamas, boo, so you don't fall asleep in your clothes."

Cicely slowly rose to her feet and dragged herself into Paris's bedroom to retrieve her pajamas. She returned a minute later with a blue, one-piece pull-on with booted feet that featured Winnie the Pooh and friends. Paris undressed Cicely down to her panties and helped her slide into her sleepwear.

"You want to lay down on my bed?" Paris asked her niece.

Cicely shook her head.

"I think she's afraid to be in my room by herself," Paris said to Camron. "Come over here, baby, and lie down on the love seat. You can watch TV from there."

Cicely climbed onto the small couch. "I'm gonna go get something to put over her," Paris said.

Paris went into her bedroom and returned with a crocheted afghan covered in concentric hexagons of brown, yellow, and white. She placed it over Cicely, whose eyes were again focused on the television.

Paris sat down on the couch beside Camron and tucked her legs underneath her. They talked for another half-hour and few minutes, mostly about their families. From their discourse, Camron learned

Paris was especially close to her mother.

"I think part of the reason my mom and I are so close," she explained, "is because I was her last child. So I didn't have to share her that much with Deanna and Nathan."

"That's the way it was with me too. Until my youngest sister came along," Camron related.

"Now were you mad at her for stealing the spotlight from you?" Paris asked.

"No, not really. I was almost ten, so I was beginning to kinda pull away from my mom some anyway. And then, during my teenage years, I went into something of a rebellious stage. But my father was always around to keep that in check."

"You don't see much of that today."

"What?" Camron asked.

"Fathers being around to keep their sons in check."

"That's true. But even when I was rebelling—you know, staying out late or wanting to talk on the phone for as long as I liked—my mom and I were close. And once I left home and became a man, so to speak, we became even closer."

"My mom and I never had any real rifts," Paris related. "Other than when I was dating Charles." Charles was her ex-fiancé. "She didn't care too much for him, and of course in the end he proved her right. But I love my mom to death. I don't know what I'd do if she wasn't around."

"Yeah. Mothers are special. Mine was certainly the most important influence in my life. I can still hear her voice guiding me."

Camron looked at his wristwatch. It said 8:53, but it was, as always, ten minutes fast. He wasn't totally sure why he set it that way. His thinking was that it provided a psychological jolt helpful in getting him moving to wherever his next appointment in life happened to be, and, in transit, some comfort that he wasn't yet late. But in reality his watch mostly made him have to do arithmetic, simple though it was, every time he looked at it.

"You know what? I better get going," Camron said.

"I *have* had you over here a while, haven't I? I'm sure you're getting bored by now."

"No, not in the least," Camron insisted. In fact, he *was* getting a tad bored. Some other things—physical things—they could do that would maintain his interest sauntered through his head, but it was too early, he concluded, for them to take the relationship there. "I've had a very nice time. I'm glad you invited me."

"And I'm glad you came."

They both stood and began moving toward the front door.

"Everything was delicious," Camron said. "I'll have to return the favor sometime soon."

"You're gonna fix dinner for me, my sister, Jake, and Cicely?"

Camron smiled at her humor. "I could, but I'd prefer to start with dinner for two."

"That sounds nice. When would you like to do that?"

"I'm off the rest of the week, so I'm free anytime."

"You just have to rub it in, don't cha'," Paris said, reminded by Camron's comment that she had to work for much of the coming week.

"No, I'm just saying we can get together anytime. It just depends on your schedule."

"My next day off is Saturday," Paris said.

"All right, well, let's make it Saturday."

"Okay. Let's talk later this week and we can plan from there."

"Sounds good."

Upon reaching the door, Paris said, "Let me get your coat."

"Thanks."

Camron slipped into his shoes while she fetched his coat from the hall closet. Paris helped him into it by holding it up and open as he slid his arms into the sleeves. Having a woman help him into his coat momentarily left him feeling awkward.

"Thank you," Camron said as he put his arm through the last sleeve and spun around to face Paris.

"You're quite welcome," Paris said with a smile.

Camron gave her a hug, and she wrapped her arms around his shoulders. Pulling back, he kissed her once, then again lightly on the lips, which were soft, responsive, encouraging. The second kiss transformed into a deeper one as their lips gave way to tongues. Paris moaned ever so slightly. Camron pulled her closer, eliminating what little space remained between them.

Suddenly, the sound of a child's voice was in the air. "Auntie, I got to go to the baf-room."

They both looked down, instantly terminating their kiss and the mood created by it. It was Cicely, standing no more than two feet away. Her tiny voice had caught them both off-guard. Especially Camron, as he had not heard the child speak a word until that moment.

"Honey. What are you doing up?" Paris said as she, in one continuous motion, moved away from Camron and to Cicely, bending at the knees until she was nearly at eye level with her niece. Cicely, who, in her left hand, was dangling her Black Barbie by one arm, looked confused and a little scared.

"You gotta pee?" Paris asked her.

Cicely nodded while rubbing one eye with the back of her other hand.

Paris looked up at Camron. "Can you wait one minute? Let me get her started."

Camron released a throaty close-mouthed chuckle and nodded his head. Paris picked Cicely up into her arms, scurried down the hall, then made a right around a corner.

Returning a few seconds later, Paris was shaking her head and had a look of exasperated bemusement. "Can you believe that girl? Done snuck and woke up."

Camron grinned. "Guess she didn't want us to get too far gone."

"Apparently."

"Did she finish her business?" he asked.

"No. She's sitting. Her doll baby is keeping her company."

"Well, let me go. Cicely will probably need your assistance again any moment now."

"Yeah," Paris acknowledged. "Okay then. Thanks for coming."

"Thanks for inviting me. It was fun."

"So I'll talk to you later this week?"

"Yes," Camron said.

"All right."

"Okay, sweetie. Good night."

"Good night."

Camron gave Paris one last peck on the lips, opened her door, and stepped into the hallway. The apartment door shut behind him, followed by the metallic click-clack of Paris engaging her dead bolt lock.

Camron gained his bearings, moved toward the elevators, rode the twenty-three floors down to the ground level, and was soon outside on the sidewalk, his senses alerted and his gait quickened by the single-digit temperatures. Walking east, he crossed Sibley Street, which placed him no further than twenty-five yards from his car. To his right was a small enclave of leafless trees and crisscrossing walkways called Mears Park. Twinkling miniature white lights were strung back and forth through the naked limbs of the trees. He thought of his family and imagined that their celebration of Christmas had ended as well, especially given the fact that the time there was one hour later than the street on which he was walking.

Twelve minutes later Camron arrived home. Once inside, he took off his shoes, then his coat. The only light in the house was from the tiny, off-white bulbs—much like the lights he had just seen snaked through the trees of Mears Park—on his four-foot tall imitation Christmas tree.

He walked into the kitchen and poured himself a glass of cranberry juice. As he drank it, he noticed two neatly wrapped boxes under his tiny tree. Those were presents he had bought for himself five days earlier. In one box, the larger of the two, were two pairs of dress pants—one black, one tan—and three pullover sweaters. In the other was a three-quarter length black leather jacket.

As he looked at them now, it struck him as a silly thing to do, wrapping presents for one's self. But for some reason, at the time, the idea of seeing wrapped presents under the tree appealed to him. He wondered if he should unwrap them before Christmas slipped away. Rip the multicolored paper off and tear open the boxes, the way he used to as a child.

But he wasn't a child anymore. He was a thirty-six-year-old divorcé standing in the dark kitchen of his suburban residence. An abode that often felt more like a house than a home.

He climbed the stairs and went to bed instead.

15

Engagement

BY JUNE OF '97, MARA AND I were essentially living together. She spent nearly all of her off days from her flight attendant job at my house, and had almost as many of her clothes in my walk-in closet as I had of my own. She cooked, cleaned, placed scented candles in the bathroom, added fabric softener to the wash, and, in general, brought the touch and feel of a woman into my environment. And I liked it. I liked it a lot.

It was also in June that the thought of marriage first entered my mind. That first mental encounter—images of me walking down the aisle and exchanging vows—left me baffled and dumbfounded. Could it be that I, Camron Dickerson, a confirmed bachelor, was thinking of hanging it up and turning in my bachelor's license? I spent much of the next few weeks talking to myself, mirror images of my psyche sparring for and against matrimony.

I sought P's advice via e-mail.

June 3, 1997

What up P? How are things in Philly these days? Did you ever hook up with that babe with the Hottentot ass?

Man I been having some weird thoughts lately concerning Mara. I've been thinking about asking her to marry me. Am I being delusional?

P, who had met Mara in April when I had accompanied her on one of her flights to D.C., responded to me the next day.

Yeah you are being delusional! Give it a few days and it'll pass.

No man seriously, Mara is a fine lady. Very sweet and down to earth. And you two were obviously smitten with each other when I met you guys down in D.C. So I'm not surprised you feel the way you do. And in the end you got to go with how you feel.

Oh and the babe with the phat ass? (or the hottentot ass as you call it). Yes I did get with that. And it was quite nice sir.

Later.

P

To help further straighten my thoughts, I put a list of pros and cons associated with marriage on paper. The pros boiled down to having a friend, companion, and lover for life, and—although children were not at the front of my mind—having someone with whom to raise a child or two.

The cons included having to wake up beside the same woman day after day after day, and no longer being able to play the field. But I was getting a little tired of playing the field anyway, so I made it one of my pros as well, with a slight change in wording: I no longer *had* to play the field.

By late June, I had yet to make up my mind, and Mara began to notice that I was mulling something.

"What's wrong?" she asked me early one evening as she was washing and I was drying dinner dishes.

"Nothing. What makes you ask that?"

"You're kinda quiet tonight, Dickerson. As a matter of fact, you've been quiet a lot lately. Something bothering you, honey?" she asked me with a sympathetic look in her eyes. "Am I over here too much? Invading your space?"

"No, sweetheart. I love your company. And you too. You know that."

"And I love you. So what's wrong?"

"Nothing. Just thinking about some things."

"About what?" she persisted.

"Just some problems at work with my boss," I lied. "We're not seeing eye to eye on a few things."

"Such as?"

"Some technical stuff. How much time and effort should be spent on this project versus that one."

"Have y'all talked about it?"

"Yeah, we've had a few conversations."

I had to figure a way out of the loop of questions I unexpectedly found myself in. "I have a meeting scheduled with him and our department manager next week, so we should be able to straighten things out then."

"That's good," she said, and left it at that.

A week or so later, on the evening of the Fourth of July, I finally made up my mind that I would ask Mara for her hand in marriage. I came to that decision when we were in St. Paul, sitting on a blanket that was spread upon the grass near the cathedral, watching, along with hundreds of others, a fireworks display. Mara was sitting between my legs, delighting in the bursts, booms, and bright sparkles that were painting the sky. A feeling of warmth and comfort spread through my chest, generated by just having her there beside me at the close of a lazy summer holiday. I recalled P's advice about going with the way I felt, and, at that moment, I felt I wanted Mara to be in my life forever.

The ride home for me that night was relaxed. Having made my decision, my mind was content and at ease. We talked about the fireworks show and her upcoming work schedule before we both grew quiet. Suddenly Mara asked, "Did you resolve the issues you had with your boss?"

I smiled a little inside before answering. "Yes. I did."

The following week I visited a jewelry store and chose an engagement ring. My selection was a simple solitaire design: a single carat, marquise diamond in a six-prong platinum band, size 6.

A few days later, on an evening when Mara was working, flying high in the sky somewhere between D.C. and Minneapolis, I called P to let him know I had bought a ring and was about to pop the question.

"How you gonna play it?" P asked.

"I was thinking we could go out to dinner, and I'd just ask her then."

"You gonna get down on one knee?"

"Hell naw," I told him. "I'd feel too self-conscious and silly doing that."

"Man, you better go on and do it. You know the women love it when you do that."

"You do it when *you* get engaged, Negro," I suggested.

"Don't hold your breath waiting for that to happen."

"I won't."

"You pretty certain she gonna say 'yes,' right?"

"Of course she'll say 'yes,'" I scowled. "Shit. She better."

"Where y'all gonna have the wedding?"

"Probably back home. At my church or hers."

"Damn, man. This some heavy shit," P said.

"Yeah, marriage ain't no joke. But, after debating about it back and forth for the past few weeks, I feel good about it. Better than I expected to feel. Kinda like when you fight against something all your adult life, then when you give in to it and it feels good, you wonder why you ever fought against it in the first place."

P went even further down the philosophical path. "Right. Like if you were drowning, struggling and kicking, but then you realize you're gonna drown anyway, so you just say 'fuck it' and give in to the water. And just before you pass out and die you think, 'Hey. Drowning isn't as bad as I thought it would be. At least not as bad as being burnt up or something.' "

"I wouldn't quite put it that way, but if that's the best analogy you can come up with, I guess so."

"I'm just fuckin' with you, man," P said. "I'm happy for ya'. And I'm sure you guys will have a fine life together."

"That's the plan, my brotha. That's the plan."

That was indeed the plan, and the next step was to get the question out of my mouth. An opportunity to do that arose soon after I had gotten the ring. It was a Friday and our intention that evening was to have dinner at the Caribbean Splash, a Black-owned restaurant in downtown Minneapolis with great food but poor service. From there we were going to meet Patrice and Donnell, who were ten months into their own marriage, at the Riverview.

I hadn't determined precisely how and where I wanted to ask Mara to jump the broom, and as we were driving to the restaurant— with the ring resting beneath my seat—I was debating whether I should ask her there or at the club. The thought of proposing in the club didn't appeal to me because I didn't want to do it in front of Patrice and Donnell. So it seemed the Caribbean Splash would be the special place.

But as we were getting out of the car, I realized I couldn't reach under the seat and get the ring—which was still in its case—and put it in my pocket without being conspicuous. So I left it there, thinking I could come up with an excuse to return and retrieve it later.

Fortunately, we had found a parking space on the street less than a block from the restaurant. That would make going back to my car that much easier. However, as soon as we walked into the Caribbean Splash and I saw the many faces, some familiar, I immediately felt I didn't want to do it there either. The extremely personal nature of a proposal left me reticent about baring myself when anyone else with whom I was even vaguely acquainted was around.

So how was I to do it? As we scanned the menu, I decided not to concern myself with it for the time being.

The décor of the Caribbean Splash was mostly dark—black tables, black chairs, black bar counter, dark green interior walls. However, pane walls that faced the streets, and the relative small size of the restaurant, gave it an open yet intimate feel.

Mara ordered the oxtail dinner, a favorite of hers. I ordered the blackened fish with rice and, as an appetizer, a pair of their spicy meat pies. The service, as usual, was slow, and nearly fifty minutes had passed before we got our entrees. While waiting, Mara, in between stealing pieces of my meat pies, expressed her excitement about seeing Patrice later that evening.

"I haven't seen her in nearly two weeks," she said. "I wonder how her project is coming along."

"What project?" I asked.

"She's trying to get pregnant."

"Already?"

"She says she wants three kids, so she's anxious to get started."

"Whatever makes her happy."

"What about you, Dickerson? You want children?"

"One day. Not right now though. Maybe at the start of the new millennium."

"I'll pencil that in." Mara touched the tip of her index finger to her temple and took on a look of concentration, appearing as if she were trying to stencil something on her brain. "Make baby in 2000."

Mara was eager to get to the Riverview, so we didn't linger at the restaurant much beyond the time it took for us to eat. The walk back to the car, however, returned me to the dilemma at hand. I opened Mara's door, let her in, and, as I was walking to the driver's side, contemplated canceling my planned proposition. I could make my request for her undying love on another day, and just leave the ring where it lay until we came to a time and place that felt right. But as I was about to start the car, something stopped me.

"Mara, I ah ... I need to talk to you for a minute ... about something," I stammered.

A look of concern spread over Mara's face. "What's wrong, sweetheart?"

Words over which I seemed to have no control spewed forth.

"I've never thought much about a long term commitment, and all that that entails. There's been no need to really. And I'm not sure I even know what that means—'long term commitment.' But I do know this. With you I feel like I've found my soul mate. And that's something I never want to lose." I paused. Fortified myself. "I love you. You know that, right?" She nodded her head and looked at me intently. Her eyes and face had an almost-sad look. "And I want us to be together forever. So with that in mind, I'll ask this question. Mara, will you marry me?"

Did I just say that? It didn't even sound like my voice.

At first she said nothing. Then her face transformed from the almost-sad look into an expression of joy.

"Yes, Dickerson, I will."

I guess I did say it.

I leaned in towards her; kissed her. She kissed me harder. A passionate kiss that mutated into a hug. A hug in which Mara held my neck so tight, I thought she would asphyxiate me. I finally managed to pull away.

"Let's make this official," I said.

I reached under the seat. My hand landed directly on the gray velvet case in which the ring was enclosed. As I brought it up and into view, Mara's eyes trained on it. I opened it, pulled out the ring, dropped the case to the floor, and slipped the ring onto her finger. It fit perfectly, and the diamond seemed bigger and brighter than any of the previous ten times I had stared at it.

"Oh my goodness," she blurted, then looked at me and kissed me softly. "Oh my goodness," she said again. "This ring is beautiful, honey. I love white gold."

"Actually it's platinum."

Mara didn't acknowledge my correction, but instead continued to admire the ring that was sitting nicely on her finger. Her lips were shaped into a nervous smile, a pained smile that placed her somewhere between joy and tears.

"Dickerson, you have just totally shocked me," she said. "I must admit. This is a total shock. I don't know what to say."

"You said 'yes,' which was the important thing."

"Why would I have said anything else?" Mara stated. "I love you. But this is just so overwhelming."

"To me too. If someone had told me a year ago that I'd be getting engaged, I would have asked them what narcotic were they on. But I guess this was inevitable."

"Inevitable?" Mara quizzed.

"Yeah. Our fate was sealed after you caught that bouquet at Patrice's wedding."

"That *was* funny, wasn't it? I caught the bouquet, totally by luck, and now here we are."

"Here we are," I said, then puckered my lips and kissed Mara once more.

I mentally searched myself for traces of regret or fear. But there were none to be found. Nothing but a warm, fuzzy feeling as it was then clear to me that this beautiful woman would one day, someday soon, be my wife.

Having removed the burden of the proposal from my conscious, it occurred to me that there was more on the evening's agenda.

"Are you ready to head out to the 'View?" I asked.

"The 'View?" Mara said as if she'd never heard of the place she and Patrice had first met.

"Yeah. We're meeting Patrice and Donnell there. Remember?"

"Oh. Okay. You still want to do that?"

"That's what we'd planned. And I thought you wanted to see Patrice?"

"I do. But I wasn't expecting this, Dickerson. Now you got me all flustered."

"We don't have to go," I said.

"No, we can go. If you want to."

"Fine with me, sweetie."

I started the car, and we headed in the direction of the Riverview. During nearly the entire four-minute drive, Mara was staring at the ring, her fingers spread.

"Did Patrice know you were gonna do this?" Mara asked. "Tell the truth."

"No. No one knew. Other than P."

"Oh, honey, I love you," Mara gushed, then kissed me on my cheek.

"I love you too."

The Riverview was located on a grassy bank at a calm, lazy section of the Mississippi River. There was no charge to get into the club at the early evening hour we arrived. Consequently, we simply passed through the unmanned metal detector that was just beyond the club's front door, and into the club itself. As we entered, we could hear the live band—which was to our left and more and more behind us as we walked further into the venue—performing on a small dance floor that served as their stage. We veered left and walked behind the main bar past tall sets of pane, which afforded a spectacular view of downtown Minneapolis. All the while, I was holding Mara's left hand, the one with the newly engaged finger. As we came around the backside of the bar, we spotted Patrice waving at us from a raised section of six booths adjacent to the far end of the bar. Donnell was sitting quietly next to her, smiling, with a drink in his hand, which he raised towards us in salute. Mara ran in front of me and around a banister that separated the booths from the rest of the nightclub. Patrice left the booth at which she and Donnell were sitting and met Mara halfway. They hugged and smiled and laughed as if it had been months or years, as opposed to days, since they had last seen each other.

"Guess who's engaged?" I heard Mara say to Patrice.

"Oh my God, girl, no," Patrice responded.

"Yes," Mara said.

They screamed in unison and jumped up and down without letting their feet leave the ground. Folks sitting in the booths, and some on the main floor, turned and looked at them, perhaps wondering if one or both had lost their mind. Not wanting to get struck by a flailing limb in the wake of their excitement, I sidestepped the two ladies and walked to the booth at which Donnell was sitting.

"What are they so excited about?" Donnell asked me.

"Mara and I just got engaged," I told him.

"What!?" His smile broadened. "When did this happen?"

"About fifteen minutes ago."

"Aw, man, congratulations."

"Thanks," I said.

Donnell stood and slapped his hand into mine. We gave each other a shoulder bump and a stiff hug, then sat down—me on one side of the booth, he on the other.

Mara and Patrice arrived right after, their four hands clasped into a ball.

"Donnell, they're engaged!" Patrice announced.

"Camron just told me," he said.

"And all this started back at our wedding," Patrice said. "Can you believe that!? I just told Donnell the other day, I said, 'Donnell, they are going to get married one day. You mark my words.' Didn't I say that to you?"

"Yeah she did," Donnell concurred.

"I just didn't expect it to be this soon. Girl, let me see that ring." Patrice grabbed the fingers of Mara's left hand and rocked them from side to side, admiring the diamond. "Mmm-mm. That is so beautiful. Camron, you got good taste, man. How you feelin', girl?"

"Patrice, I did not know what to say," Mara admitted, her face all smiles. "And I still don't. He shocked me good."

"We got to celebrate this," Patrice proclaimed, then looked at her husband. "Honey, let's get a bottle of champagne and some chicken wings."

"You got some champagne money?" Donnell asked her.

Mara interjected. "No, Patrice, don't do that."

"Donnell, they just got engaged," Patrice said. "Get us some champagne. Please, baby?"

"And we definitely don't need no chicken wings," Mara told her. "We just ate."

"We'll get the chicken wings for me and Donnell then 'cause we haven't had a thing to eat," Patrice said.

Patrice waved down a waitress, and ordered chicken wings and a bottle of champagne. Moments later I offered Donnell a twenty-dollar bill to help cover the cost of our minicelebration, but he declined.

"That's all right, man. We got it," he said cheerfully. "I'll get Patrice's part when we get home."

In the midst of the champagne and 20 Questions from Patrice, there was a break in the live music. Patrice suddenly became frantic.

"Listen, listen," she implored and directed our attention towards the band. They vaguely reminded me of Sexual Chocolate, the band one of the Eddie Murphy characters, Randy Watson, had fronted in *Coming to America*.

"How ya' feelin' this e'nin'?" the band's leader—a fortyish-looking, dark brown-skinned brotha with relaxed hair—asked the crowd. They responded with a few smattered whoops of approval and moderate applause.

"We want to send out a congratulations to a lovely couple that's here ta-night," he said, then looked down and squinted at a small piece of paper he was holding in his hand. "Cam-a-ron and Myra. They just got engaged. Give 'em a hand, ladies and gen'a'men."

The crowd applauded, and many of the women looked around, trying somehow to pick us out, despite the fact there was no such-named couple in the club.

"This next song's for you," he announced.

The group then launched into a fairly credible rendition of Al Green's "Let's Stay Together." At the chorus, Patrice and Mara, their champagne glasses raised high in the air, sang along with gusto.

Two hours later, Mara and I were home in bed, making love with a passion that reached deep, and turned our souls inside out. Afterwards, Mara was cuddled in my arms, her head on my shoulder. A few moments passed before I felt the soft saline moisture of falling tears. Then I heard a sniffle.

"Mara, what's wrong, sweetie? Why're you crying?"

"I don't know," she said between her tears. "Just happy I guess."

I smiled, pleased, on some level, at her unabashed display of emotion.

"I'm happy too," I said. "Happy that you'll be my wife. And that we'll be together forever."

I pulled her towards me and kissed her. One of her tears landed on my cheek, and ran down my face.

16

Marriage

IN AUGUST OF 1997, I TRADED my emerald green '94 Mazda 626 for a new black Dodge Intrepid.

Another significant happening that month was Mara moving into my home, despite the fact that the lease on her South Minneapolis apartment didn't expire until the end of October. Consequently she just paid the rent as it was due, and kept the keys to her empty place.

"Long as I'm paying the rent, I may as well keep the keys," she reasoned.

But her landlord offered to return $300 of her October rent if she relinquished her keys early, which she did by the end of September. And with that, we were officially "shacked up," an outdated, derogatory term for two unmarried people living together that I used to hear as a boy in North Carolina.

As far as a wedding was concerned, we discussed it a time or two, and August of the next year was mentioned, I think by me, as a possible date. But I wasn't anxious to get into the nuts and bolts of nuptial planning, and, interestingly, neither was Mara.

During a visit we made to North Carolina in October, the inevitable question of exactly *when* we were getting married came up more than once from members of both our families. The tentative August date served well enough as a convenient answer. However, Mara's youngest sister, Kera, took more than a passing interest, and was soon discussing wedding planning issues in earnest with Mara.

Patrice also began offering more and more advice, and would sometimes come over to our house and discuss this and that detail for hours. Once, she arrived at the start of a Minnesota Vikings football game and so disturbed my focus on the contest, I had to make a suggestion.

"Ladies, listen," I said. "Can y'all go upstairs and discuss that stuff? I'm trying to check out the game."

"All right, Mr. Dickerson. Don't get your underwear all in a bunch," Patrice said before she and Mara retreated to the upper level of the house.

By late November, the only thing I had done that had anything to do with a wedding was ask P to be my best man. He seemed genuinely flattered.

"I'd be honored," P said to me over the phone. "Just let me know the exact time and place, and I'll be there."

"I will do that, sir," I said.

"Y'all decided where you want to do it?"

"Her sister is looking at a church in Raleigh."

"Raleigh? Seems like it would be easier to do it there in the Twin Cities. You got any idea how much it's all gonna cost?"

"I don't know. But however much it costs, I'm sure I'll be paying for ninety-five percent of it."

"Weddings are expensive, man," P said soberly. "I've seen couples drop thousands and thousands of dollars on a wedding, then spend the next five years struggling to save up enough money for a down payment on a house."

"Exactly. Especially for us Black folk because we get so caught up in this Eurocentric idea of what a wedding ought to be. Problem is, we ain't got that Eurocentric kind of money."

"You got that right. Like this White couple across the street. They got married three years ago. His daddy paid for the wedding; her daddy gave 'em the down payment on the house."

"How you know all that?"

"Rick, the husband, told me when I was over there for a party they had a couple a' months ago. He'd had a few drinks and was talking away. They're cool people though."

"I'm sure they are. And it's no fault of theirs that their parents got money, or even that their parents' parents probably had money. But that doesn't change my reality. Shit. To cover a big-ass church wedding, I'd have to spend every penny I got in savings *and* borrow from my 401(k)."

"You'll just have to scale back, man," P said. "Like at the reception have people bring their own sandwich and stuff."

I laughed. "Negro, you crazy."

"Well whatever you do, don't let the costs spiral too much outta control."

"Oh, don't worry. I won't," I promised him. "I can't."

As the weeks passed, the thought of a wedding, and the aggravation and expense of executing it, became a burden on my mind. I didn't share my concerns with Mara. However, I knew I would have to discuss it with her eventually. My personality was such that I could keep things inside for long periods of time, if for no other reason than to maintain the peace. But eventually the need for a resolution would overwhelm my desire for tranquillity.

Finally, one midweek day in January, while driving home from work in a relentless downpour of snow, a solution to the wedding predicament came to me. The following Saturday morning, I shared it with Mara.

"You know what," I said to her as we both lounged in bed, her back against my chest, watching nothing of much interest on TV. "Let's not have a big wedding. Let's just get married."

"What?" Mara said with surprise.

"Let's just get married," I repeated.

"When?"

"Today."

"Today? Where can we get married today?"

"Las Vegas."

"Las Vegas?" Mara turned to face me and surveyed my expression for any signs of illness. "Camron, have you lost your mind?"

"No. Listen. We can be on a plane by this afternoon, and be in Vegas almost at the same time we leave here. Walk into one of those infamous Vegas chapels as an engaged couple; walk out as man and wife."

"Are you being serious?"

"Yes. I'm very serious."

"But, honey. That doesn't sound very romantic. You know?"

"We can have a romantic church wedding in North Carolina if that's what we really want to have. But look at all the headaches we're gonna have to go through to get there. I mean, your sister is already calling up here every other day to talk about the wedding. And Patrice is over here all the time."

"Patrice hasn't been here in almost a week," Mara reminded me.

"Well it seems like it's all the time. And it's only gonna get worse. And be honest, Mara. You're not too into all of this wedding-planning stuff yourself."

"I will admit that much," she said. "Some people are fascinated by weddings. But it's not something that really turns me on. Certainly not as much as some women I know."

"Like Patrice."

"Yeah, like Patrice."

"Plus we can get outta this cold for a while. You don't have to be back at work till Wednesday, right? I can take a couple of days off, and we can get married, gamble, eat, and screw till our hearts content."

"Dickerson, you are crazy," Mara said, smiling.

Four hours later we were on a plane to Las Vegas. And thanks to the fact that Mara was one of the airline's employees, we got a steep discount on the flight.

Las Vegas was surrounded by sunny skies and wrapped in fifty-five-degree air. Cool, chilly even, but a far cry from the subfreezing temperatures we had left behind in Minnesota.

"I can't believe we've eloped to Las Vegas," Mara said right after we got off the plane.

"Well believe it, because we're here. The slot machines tell you that much," I said in reference to the colorful, money-gobbling, stationary robots that were all over the terminal.

"Where are we staying again?"

"Ah ... we'll figure that out shortly."

"Dickerson," Mara exclaimed as she slapped me lightly across my shoulder. "I thought you said you'd made reservations before we left."

"I thought I had too, but the lady at the MGM got confused. Told me she had some rooms, then said she didn't."

"Are you sure she was the one confused?"

"Don't worry. Vegas has plenty of rooms," I said confidently. "Especially in January."

"You did get a car, I hope."

"Yes, I got a car," I said. "I'm not *completely* inept when it comes to planning a wedding."

Mara gave me a grin that didn't totally convince me she was amused. "It's already four o'clock you know."

"I know. So what are you trying to say?"

"I'm saying by the time we find a room and get settled in, it may be too late for a wedding."

"There's always tomorrow."

"Are these wedding places open on Sundays?"

"I'm sure they are. If not, then we'll do it on Monday."

"No. We're not getting married on no Monday."

"We'll find a place tomorrow then. Maybe we can find one where Elvis is the presiding pastor."

"And I don't want to get married by no Elvis either."

"Okay. No Elvis. How about Little Richard?"

"Camron, you're so silly," Mara said with a laugh as we stepped on an escalator that took us down to baggage claim.

After some driving around, we found a room on the Strip at a hotel shaped like an Egyptian pyramid. We checked in, then approached the concierge's desk.

"My fiancée and I are getting married tomorrow," I said to a clean-cut, tall, young gentleman at the desk.

"Congratulations," he said.

"Thank you. I was wondering if you knew of some good places for a wedding."

"Oh, there are lots of good places for a wedding here in Las Vegas. As a matter of fact, we have a chapel right here in our hotel."

"Really? That's convenient," Mara said.

"How big of a wedding is it going to be?" he asked.

"Just us," I told him.

"You might want to consider one of the smaller chapels then. Let's see … there's Victor's. They're on Sahara Avenue. I've also heard good things about Cupid's Li'l Wedding Chapel, which is at the south end of the Strip."

"Can we get a wedding dress and tux at these places?" I asked him.

"Some of them, yes. There are also places you can go that just specialize in rentals for weddings. They can get you fitted and ready to go in a half-hour."

"Great," I said. I wasn't sure if he was being sincere about the half-hour service promise, though.

"What about a marriage license?" Mara asked.

"You'll need to go by the courthouse for that," he said. "They're pretty much open all the time, so that shouldn't be a problem."

He wrote his chapel suggestions down on a slip of paper and gave it to me. I gave him a five-dollar tip, and Mara and I moved towards the elevators, pulling our wheeled suitcases behind us.

"So it looks like we'll need to get the license, tux and wedding gown, then go to whichever chapel we're going to do it at," I said as we rode the elevator to our floor.

"I'm going to have to try and get in a rental car wearing a wedding gown?"

"No. We can rent a limo for two or three hours, have them pick us up here, take us to the courthouse, then to a tux and bridal gown place, to the chapel, then back here."

"And we're going to be able to arrange all of this by tomorrow?"

"Sure. Vegas handles this kind of stuff all the time."

"What about rings?" Mara asked.

"Oh, that's right. I guess you'll have to give me the one you got on back. Then we just have to find one for me. They probably have some at the tux and gown places."

"Dickerson, this is going to start getting expensive."

"Not nearly as expensive as a church wedding in North Carolina would have been," I reminded her.

Once in our room, we unpacked the two black denim suitcases we had brought with us: one large (Mara's) and one small (mine). I got in the shower, and Mara began calling the chapels recommended by the concierge, as well as some others she found in the yellow pages. As I was toweling myself dry in front of the bathroom mirror, she shared with me what she had discovered.

"They all have different packages," she shouted from the bedroom. "And the packages include bouquet and boutonniere, pictures, champagne, and stuff like that. I kind of like Cupid's because after the ceremony she said we can take pictures in the chapel and in their courtyard. They also videotape the ceremony."

"Okay, let's go with that," I said.

"You want to ride by there and see what it looks like?"

"We can. I'm sure it's fine though. They're on the Strip. Plus the concierge recommended them. Call 'em back and book it for tomorrow at three or four o'clock, somewhere in there. Then we'll ride by there. If it doesn't look cool, we'll cancel and go somewhere else."

Mara called Cupid's and reserved their "Always & Forever" package for four o'clock. She then took her turn in the shower while I arranged for a limo to pick us up the next day at noon. I also set a one-thirty appointment at a tuxedo and bridal gown rental store, which I felt would give us enough time in between to go by the courthouse to secure a marriage license.

With the both of us clean, refreshed, and relaxed in the thought that all necessary plans had been laid for our nuptial, we returned to the main level of the hotel and feasted on a buffet dinner. Afterwards, we went into the hotel's casino section, where Mara watched me lose sixty dollars at a blackjack table, and I watched her lose forty at some slot machines.

The next morning we had breakfast in bed—scrambled eggs, bacon, sausage, toast, Danishes, and orange and cranberry juice.

"So today will be our first day as man and wife," I said as I salted my eggs.

Mara smiled. "Mm-hmm. The first day of the rest of our lives together. Are you nervous yet, Dickerson?"

"No. Are you?"

"No I'm not, actually."

"Did you think you would be?" I asked.

"A wedding would have made me nervous. You know? Walking down an aisle full of people with all eyes on me would have made me extremely nervous. That's the way I was at my first wedding anyway. But now it'll just be you and me." Mara took a bite of her bacon, then took on a thoughtful expression. "It almost seems like a game. Like we're about to play dress-up and pretend we're getting married."

"Nope, it's not a game. A dream maybe."

"So we might wake up and find ourselves back in bed in Minnesota, surrounded by snow?"

"That could happen."

Mara sighed. "We're not being too crazy getting married this way are we, Dickerson?"

"No. We're going to be man and wife a year from now regardless. We may as well do it now, and save ourselves a lot of time and money and headaches."

"Patrice is gonna shit when she finds out," Mara said. "Maybe I should call her."

"No, let's make this an official elope-tion."

"I don't think that's a word."

"You know what I mean. Let's keep it a secret until we're married."

"Fine. But I *have* to call Momma," Mara insisted. "She might lose her mind too."

"All right. Go ahead and ruin the surprise."

We finished breakfast and Mara called her mother, whose initial response (Mara told me later) was, "Lord, gurl, hush yo' mouf!" The conversation was periodically interrupted by loud bursts of laughter from Mara. Within three or four minutes, Mara's mom insisted on speaking with me.

"Hey, Ms. Riggs," I said.

"Camron, what you doin' draggin' my daughter way out there to Las Vegas?" she asked.

"Well, Ms. Riggs, we're getting married anyway, so we decided to go ahead and just do it. You know, like the Nike commercial."

"Like the what?"

"Nothing."

"Well, I just wish y'all good luck. It's not my place to say whether this is the best way to do it. Course I never heard of such foolishness, but y'all grown so I reck'n you can do what you wanna do."

"Yes, ma'am."

"So congratulations. Y'all enjoy yourself and we look forward to seein' the both of you soon."

"Thank you, ma'am. We look forward to seeing you all soon too."

"And, Camron."

"Yes, ma'am?"

"You take care of my baby girl now."

"Yes, ma'am. I will."

"All right. God bless you both."

With the blessing of Mara's mother in hand, thirty-five minutes later we made our way downstairs, reaching the lobby a few minutes before noon. We were both dressed casually, Mara in a flowing dress with small floral print, me in loose-fitting black jeans, and a roomy, brown and black button-up shirt.

"Are you ready to do this, Ms. Brown?" I asked as we walked briskly and in lockstep past the registration desk.

"Yes I am, Mr. Dickerson," Mara said. A big toothy grin covered nearly her whole face.

I gave her a quick kiss without breaking our stride. Two sets of double doors, ten feet apart, opened automatically to let us out of the hotel and into the guest arrival area. To our left, fifteen yards away, we noticed a long, sparkling white, Lincoln limousine.

"That must be us," I said.

"Oh my goodness. That is a nice limo," Mara declared.

"For $75 an hour, it should be," I said.

As we approached the stretch vehicle, we could see the driver standing near the front of the car holding a sign with "Dickerson" scribbled across it.

"I think you're the one we're looking for," I said to him.

"Yes, sir," he responded, then walked quickly around the vehicle, past us, and to the long back door. He opened it, inviting us in.

Mara and I climbed into the roomy back seat of the exaggerated car. The interior was also, for the most part, white: white leather seats across the back and along the length of one side of the passenger area. On the other side was a minibar. A portion of the bar was sunken and filled with small cubes of ice, in the middle of which sat a large, green, unopened bottle of champagne. At the end of the bar, eight champagne glasses were hanging in a rack.

"Did you request a white limo?" Mara asked.

"They gave me a choice of white or black. Black limos make me think of funerals, so I told them to send a white one."

The driver climbed behind the wheel, looked over his shoulder, and said in a thick Brooklyn accent, "So there's going to be a wedding today I hear."

"Looks like it," Mara said smiling.

"Congratulations. My name is Antonio, and, as you may have guessed by now, I'm your chauffeur for today. If there's anything else I can do to make your day as enjoyable as possible, please don't hesitate to let me know."

"Thank you, Antonio," Mara and I both said in unison.

"I believe the first stop is the courthouse," Antonio said.

"Right," I confirmed.

"Is that ours?" Mara said to me, pointing towards the champagne bottle.

"Yes," I said. "It came with the rental. You want some?"

"I do, but maybe we should save it until after the wedding."

"We don't have to. Another bottle comes with the wedding package."

"That's right," Mara said. "I forgot. Open it up then."

I removed two of the champagne glasses and handed them to Mara. I then positioned the bottle of champagne between my feet on the floor of the limo, grabbed a corkscrew that was on the minibar, and twisted and pulled at the cork.

"Careful, honey," Mara told me.

The cork came out with a loud pop, and behind it a spewing of bubbly liquid. I jerked my foot away to avoid the flow of champagne, which subsided as quickly as it had begun.

"Hon-eey," Mara moaned.

"It's cool," I assured her. "Let me have your glass."

I filled one glass, gave it back to her in exchange for the other, then filled it too.

"We made a little mess back here, Antonio," I said with a raised voice.

"No worries, Mr. Dickerson. I'll get that cleaned up after we get to the courthouse."

"Thanks," I said as I placed the bottle back into the ice. "And, Antonio, feel free to take the long route to the courthouse. It'll give us a chance to work on this champagne."

"Sure thing, Mr. Dickerson."

"So what should we toast?" Mara asked.

"Hmm. Let's see," I said, thinking out loud. "Okay, how about this?"

I raised my glass. Mara did the same with hers and brought it close to mine. "To love and marriage in Vegas," I pronounced.

Mara smiled her approval. "To love and marriage in Vegas."

We clinked our glasses and took a big sip of the effervescent wine.

"Mmm. That's good," Mara said.

"Yes it is," I said, then moved my lips closer to hers.

We kissed a kiss punctuated by moans as our tongues frolicked with one another.

I pulled back a bit, brushed my cheek against hers, and whispered in her ear. "Love you, baby."

"Love you too."

I took Mara's glass, and returned it and mine to the rack. With our hands unencumbered, we resumed our kiss as Antonio took us ever closer to our date with matrimony.

Two days later, Mara and I were hovering above the Twin Cities, returning home as man and wife. I was seated at a window, and Mara, sitting next to me, was sound asleep.

I stared at the gradually expanding earth below. From the air, the snow-covered landscape of Minnesota looked like a desert blanketed in white sand. The sky was shades of gray, and, as we continued our descent and approach into Minneapolis-St. Paul, one of the pilots announced it was twenty-two degrees outside.

I looked at the gold wedding band on my finger. We had purchased it for one hundred and seventy-six dollars at the tux and bridal gown shop. For a last minute selection, it didn't look too bad. The only problem I had with it was the fact that it was a half-size too big. But getting it properly fitted was a fairly simple matter. Mara had suggested that, later, we choose something better. But I decided right then and there to keep it. The simplicity of its design appealed to me, and it was, after all, the ring we had used in the ceremony.

As we wove through the sky, I tried to discern if it felt any different being a married man. Mara and I had been in a comfortable groove for months, so I wasn't sure if it *felt* any different or not. Intellectually, though, I knew that things were not the same, and never would be. The fact that there was someone there in my corner, unconditionally, gave me a feeling of comfort. But I was fearful too because I knew there would be days when our happy home would seem as cold as the twenty-two degrees on the other side of my window.

As we neared the ground, I woke Mara to keep her from being startled by the landing. "Wake up, sweetheart. We're about to land."

She blinked herself into consciousness, stretched, and yawned.

"Woo," she uttered through her yawn. "We're here already? That was a quick flight."

"Yeah it was. You know what? I think I like this ring."

Mara looked down at my finger. "It's not too bad."

"Think I'll keep it."

"Well, if you like it, I think you should."

When we arrived home, there were sixteen messages on our voice mail. Five were from Patrice, the last of which had a scolding tone.

"Mara, why haven't you returned my calls? Where are you? I guess you must be working. Anyway, Camron, give me a call to let me know if that's the case so I won't have to worry. Call me, girl. I got something I need to show you. Bye."

"Let me call this girl," Mara said, a mischievous grin on her face.

"Put her on speaker phone. I want to hear this."

Mara dialed Patrice at work. Patrice answered on the second ring. "TMB, Patrice Sanders."

"Hey, girlfriend," Mara said.

"Where have you been, Ms. Thang?" Patrice demanded.

"Girl, let me tell ya'," Mara said.

"You got me on speaker phone?"

"Yeah. Camron's here."

"Hey, Camron."

"Hi, Patrice," I said.

"So where have you been? And why you just now returning my calls? I was getting ready to ride over there to see if the house had burned down or something."

"No. We're fine," Mara said. "But we got something to tell you."

"What?"

"You're not gonna believe it," Mara insisted

"What is it?" Patrice asked. "What are you two up to?"

"Listen," Mara said. "We just got back from Las Vegas. We were there this weekend."

"Vegas? For what? Gambling? Don't tell me you won some big jackpot."

"Yeah, we were gambling, but we didn't win any money though."

"Well what made y'all up and go to Vegas?"

"You're not gonna believe me when I tell you."

"Tell me what?"

My patience evaporated. "Mara, tell the girl!"

"Camron, what is it?" Patrice asked.

"We got married," I said.

"No!" Patrice cried.

Mara laughed. "Yes. Can you believe it?"

"No, I can't," Patrice said. "Are y'all playin' with me?"

"Nope," I said.

"We got married in Vegas on Sunday," Mara said. "And we got a marriage license, wedding pictures, and a video to prove it."

"What made y'all decide to do that?" Patrice asked.

"Camron, my crazy husband, woke up Saturday morning—oh my goodness, Patrice, it sounds so funny me saying 'husband.' But that's what he is now, right?" Mara turned her gaze towards me. "My husband," she said again, then leaned over and gave me a smack on the lips. "Mm-whaa.

"Anyway," Mara continued. "Camron woke up Saturday morning, and from out of the blue said, 'Let's get married. Let's go to Vegas and get married right now.' And before the sun was down we were in Vegas."

"My Lord. You two are nuts!" Patrice said. "If you're not pulling my leg, I guess all I can do is say congratulations. But, Mara, I'm mad at you. You done messed up our wedding plans. Y'all just gonna have to do it again in August."

I couldn't help but roll my eyes at that comment.

"But I got to come over there and see those pictures and video," Patrice insisted.

And she did just that, arriving at our house, with Donnell in tow, around seven-thirty that evening. She complimented Mara on her choice of wedding dress—a full-length strapless, pearl-colored, knockoff Wang with a smooth satin bodice—and me for the classic black, double-breasted tux I was sporting.

By the time they left, it was after ten. Afterwards, Mara and I fell into bed, and, unlike the previous three nights, we were too tired to make love. So instead we cuddled and settled for dreams of our wonderful adventure in Vegas.

17

The Quest

THE NEW YEAR OF 2001 was ninety minutes away, and Camron Dickerson was leaning on one end of a long black bar in a downtown Minneapolis nightclub called The Quest. "MGD," he said to the bartender, and dropped his charge card on the counter.

Like South Beach, The Quest was located in the Warehouse District of the city. Unlike South Beach, The Quest was large. The vastness of the club's interior seemed apropos to its location: the wide openness of the space easily brought to mind a warehouse.

The Quest was a dark, box-shaped club with two levels. The lower level had two bars, parallel and on opposite walls. Beneath each bar, blue light glowed through letter-shaped cutouts in wrought iron sheets that angled up from the floor. In keeping with the occasion, the front edges of the bars were adorned with parabolic waves of green tinsel. The tinsel itself was dotted with tiny white lights. Scattered along the top of each bar were party favors—black and silver top hats, feathered eye masks, colorful beads, and noisemakers. Streamers of assorted colors were suspended over the bars as well.

A wide aisle, that would later be crammed with moving and stationary bodies, was adjacent to one of the bars. Adjacent to the other, the one at which Camron was located, was an even wider aisle, sparsely littered with round high tables and chairs, all occupied by groups of women and a few couples. Maroon clothes were spread over the tables, on top of which were many of the same party favors found at the bars. Hovering over the center of each table—and held in place by silver, jellybean-filled bags on small round mirrors—were shiny, helium-inflated balloons.

In between the bars and their aisles was the dance floor, a wooden surface nearly forty-five feet long and twenty feet wide. A stage, twenty-five feet deep, was at one end of the dance floor. At the other end was a DJ booth, as wide as the dance floor and a quarter its length, surrounded by floating balloons. On the side of the DJ booth opposite the dance floor was more aisle space (which seamlessly connected the bar aisles). Adjoined to this aisle, and festively decorated in a fashion similar to the rest of the club, was a raised section with additional seating.

Tall columns around the dance floor and at the bars supported the twenty-two-foot ceiling and upper-level floor. Numerous televisions hung from the ceiling, which operated not only as regular TVs, but also as screens to relay video images of the stage action during live performances.

Camron grabbed the beer the bartender had just placed in front of him, took a swig, then strode down the aisle toward the stage. The bulk of the bass driving the party came from stacks of speakers that were on either side of the stage. Walking past them, one had to be careful not to get too close, lest their eardrums would be in jeopardy. And such was the case now as Camron approached the speakers because the rappers of Outkast were blaring from them, declaring to Ms. Jackson that they were sorry. But walking in front of the speakers and across the dance floor was a relatively quick and inconspicuous way to get to the steps that led to the upper level. And that, for no specific reason, was where Camron wanted to go.

He observed the stage as he passed it, and memories of Prince, Morris Day and The Time, Chaka Khan, George Clinton, Miles Davis, and others he'd seen perform on it over the years flashed through his mind.

He looked down at his shoes as he stepped off the dance floor and back onto the dull, gray, outdoor carpeting that covered nearly everything but the dance floor and restrooms. He was checking to make sure the shine was adequate. Maintaining shined shoes was one of only two pieces of advice his father had ever directly given him. The other was never drive a clean car with dirty tires, which somehow seemed related to the advice about shoes.

The stairway, with the flat purple-blue paint that covered the stone and plasterboard walls, was the most ragged looking part of the club. It was also an interesting location for people watching because, from a lighting standpoint, it was the brightest portion of the club. The extra illumination allowed a woman to see precisely what a man (who was trying to talk to her) looked like, and vice versa. Also, if an appreciator of the feminine form, while going upstairs, were fortunate enough to get behind a female with a plump and shapely derrière, the incline of the steps provided for a fantastic view.

The upstairs region of the nightclub contained a bar and reserved booths, as well as open tables, and encircled the dance floor below. Nearly all of the wall space was covered with brilliant fluorescent paintings of the cosmos, which, when brought to life under black light—as it was at that moment—had the illusion of three dimensions.

Camron reached the upper level and strolled into the men's restroom, relieved himself at one of the two urinals, then walked up to the mirror and checked his look. The long-sleeve, red, silk shirt that flowed over the top of his crisply pleated, black dress pants was, as far as he was concerned, working well enough. He patted the top of his slicked-back hair, walked out of the restroom, and to the rectangular balustrade that separated the second level from the twenty-two-foot drop to the dance floor below. He peered over one of the rails. Despite the fact his view was obstructed by three huge plastic bags—each filled with dozens of colorful balloons and suspended with string above the dance floor—Camron could see, and hear, that the club was filling quickly with merry revelers anxious to bring in the New Year.

He took a seat at one of the few remaining empty tables surrounding the railing and looked at the party favors scattered across it. He considered donning one of the masks, a black one that mostly covered the eyes, but decided it would make him look more funny than cool.

From where he was seated, he could easily see the top of the stairway and the increasing number of people filtering through it to the second floor. He noticed four extremely attractive sistahs in a range of brown skin tones come up the stairs and strut to the bar, laughing and talking with each other every step of the way. Camron recognized one of them. She had dull brown skin, and was the least attractive of the bunch, mainly due to an ever-present, close-mouthed snarl she kept at the ready to scare off any unwanted advances. Camron knew her to be a "pro-ho," a name he'd heard attached to a woman who was always on the lookout for a stray professional athlete.

Years ago, Camron had made the mistake of asking her to dance. She consented quickly. Much too quickly, as he found out moments later, when, upon reaching the dance area, he turned around to find her not behind him, but still standing at the spot where he had first approached her, laughing. Camron marched determinedly back to where she was standing, all the while struggling to maintain his composure.

"What the fuck is your problem!?" he demanded as the space between them narrowed to inches.

"Nothin'. What the fuck is yours?!" she barked back, then added dismissively, "I'm here with my boyfriend." The snarl on her face became even more twisted. Suddenly, to Camron, she looked like a witch.

"You should have said that in the first place," he volleyed angrily at her lie.

Fearing he would lose total control, Camron gave her one last glare, then walked past her, and to the men's restroom to attempt to restore his wounded pride.

Despite the brevity of that run-in, it affected him permanently in one respect: since then when walking to the dance floor with a partner, he made sure she was within arm's length.

Camron saw this female at different nightspots many times after that, in the company of, or chasing after, someone six-feet-four or more. And every time he saw her, he was reminded of how much he hated her for what she did. In fact, the sight of her now was nearly sickening to him. For the sake of putting some distance between them, he rose to his feet and walked back downstairs.

With the nightclub approaching capacity, the energy level had increased substantially during the short time Camron had been upstairs. The DJ was letting some rapper named Ludacris thump the room: "*I wanna … lick, lick, lick, lick you from your head to ya' toes….*"

Well over a hundred people were on the dance floor, and many more were milling about, talking, laughing, shouting, and drinking or ordering a drink. Most everyone was dressed regally—a brotha in a white tuxedo and tails; a sistah styling a turquoise miniskirt with a matching sparkling halter and fringed, velvet jacket; two White girls, one in blue, one in cream, dressed like flappers from the 1920s; and an alluring beauty in a full-length, glittery, bronze-colored gown who, from twenty feet, could have passed as Halle Berry. Her attractiveness captured Camron's eye for a few seconds before she turned to accept a drink from a tall, almond-colored brotha in a handsomely cut black suit.

Camron retraced his steps, walking directly across the dance floor near the stage. This time, though, he had to measure his movements so as not to bump into the dancers. One of them, near the very middle of the floor, reminded him of Paris, and he thought, for an instant, it was her. But Paris was working, often the lot of nurses on such occasions, whose duties and responsibilities did not break for holidays.

Returning close to the section of the bar he had occupied earlier, he hoped for quick service from the bartender that had first waited upon him. However, it was clear that was not going to happen, as there was now a crush of people there, each waiting their turn to order. He got as close as he could to the bar's counter, then turned slightly and refocused his attention on the dance floor. He peered toward the area where he had seen the dancer that had brought Paris to mind, but she had disappeared into the crowd.

From Camron's vantage, things were going well between him and Paris. And were it not for the fact that she was at her job, they undoubtedly would have been ringing in the New Year together. Still, he faltered mentally, hesitated, when thoughts of elevating their relationship entered his mind. He enjoyed her company but wasn't certain he wanted to go deeper. Didn't know if he wanted to deal with the additional expectations that accompanied a blooming relationship. Also, he had adjusted to, and was beginning to relish, the freedom of being single again; unfettered and available to court (or attempt to court) anyone who struck his fancy.

The funny thing about that—courting anyone who struck his fancy—was that he knew if, through some idiosyncrasy in time, space, and memory, he were able to see Paris—the real one—for the first time that night, he would approach her again. During the first two instances when their paths had crossed, there was something about her quiet disposition in the midst of celebratory chaos that had drawn him to her. But now that she had responded to his overtures, did that somehow make her less desirable? Was her attraction to him the panacea for his attraction to her?

"Are you waiting to order?" someone asked, breaking his thoughts.

The words came from his left, the source an enticing sistah with a golden brown complexion.

"Yes," Camron answered with a smile.

Her straight, black hair was short and comfortably layered about her head. She had a round face, full lips, and a nose that started narrow at the bridge and widened slightly as it went down her face. Her inquisitive dark eyes had a seductive glint. She appeared to be in her late twenties, thirty at most.

"When you get to the bar, can you order something for me? I'll give you the money," she said.

"No problem," Camron responded. "What are you having?"

"A Singapore Sling."

She was wearing a black, long-sleeved, one-piece pants suit, which complemented her athletic figure quite well. The legs were flared and slit along the side to just above her knees. Around her waist was a silver, chain belt with large links. Her black, velvet, high-heel shoes were sprinkled with small, shiny, counterfeit diamonds. Camron supposed that, if a half-length cape had been added to her outfit, she could easily have passed for a superhero of some sort.

"Things are getting tight, but I should be able to get to the bar in a minute," he said.

"Great. I'm Vonda, by the way." She extended her hand, revealing elegant slender fingers with well-manicured nails swirled in an assortment of shiny pastels.

Camron gently grasped it for a moment. "Hi, Vonda. I'm Camron. Happy New Year."

"Happy New Year to you," she replied.

A fat dark-skinned brotha in front of Camron, the last person between him and the bar counter, picked up three drinks with both hands—two iced teas and a sex on the beach—then turned and walked carefully through the tight mesh of people.

" 'Xcuse me ... 'xcuse me," he said repeatedly as he made his way past Camron and others. Camron quickly squeezed into the position vacated by the man before someone else could. Vonda moved a step closer.

"So how is your New Year's Eve going so far, Vonda?"

"So far so good. And yours?"

"Fine. Just glad to have made it through another year."

"Aren't we all," she said.

"You have a long list of resolutions?" Camron asked.

"Don't have any. I don't believe in New Year's resolutions."

"Why is that?"

"They're a setup for failure."

"Hmmm," Camron hummed, not quite sure what she was talking about. The bartender appeared in front of him. "Singapore Sling and an MGD," Camron shouted at him.

"New Year's resolutions are more wishes than anything else," Vonda continued. "There usually isn't much conviction behind them at all. For example, what's the most common New Year's resolution?"

"Ahmm ... lose weight," Camron guessed.

"Yes. But if you don't have a plan to lose weight—and most people who say that at the beginning of the year don't—then it's just a wish."

"I see your point."

Vonda gave Camron a five-dollar bill, which he stuffed into his pocket. He doubted that would cover a Singapore Sling, but he wasn't about to squabble over the dollar or whatever difference. He was going to charge it to his tab anyway, which always created the illusion he was spending less money than he really was.

"Who are you celebrating with tonight?" Camron inquired.

"I'm here with a girlfriend of mine and her boyfriend."

"So you left your friend at home?"

"Friend as in boyfriend? I don't have one of those right now."

"A lady as lovely as yourself with no boyfriend? That's surprising."

"I had a friend up until a month ago," she said. "But we were beginning to bore each other."

"In what way?"

"In more ways than you could imagine," she said.

"How long were you together?" Camron asked.

"Eight months. Which was about six months longer than we should have been," she declared. "What about you? Do you have a lady friend? Or guy friend?"

"I don't have a lady friend right now. And as far as a guy friend goes?" Camron smiled broadly at her insinuation and shook his head. "The only thing I can say to that is 'Hell naw.' I don't swing like that, darling."

"No harm in asking, right? Because you never know these days."

The bartender returned with their drinks. "Put it on my tab," Camron said to him. "Dickerson."

When Camron turned back to her, she was looking in her purse for something. He quickly saw what she was searching for when she pulled out a pack of Salem Light cigarettes.

Cigarettes were always an attraction killer for Camron. Smoking was something he had abhorred ever since one of his sisters, as a source of entertainment for her and her boyfriend, had made him take a drag from a cigarette. Being only seven years old at the time, Camron did as he was told, and, given that smoking was a grown-up thing to do, even expected some kind of tasty pleasure from it. But instead it made him cough, and left his mouth stinking and feeling dirty. He had avoided those tiny sticks of tobacco and their residue ever since.

As soon as Vonda had placed the cigarette between her lips, a skinny dark-skinned brotha, wearing a blue derby and a blue zoot suit with white pinstripes, leaned in with a gold-colored lighter to offer her a light. The tip of the cigarette came to life as she inhaled deeply. He then placed the small flame in front of his own mouth, from which a cigarette was also dangling.

"Thanks," Vonda said to him.

As Camron handed Vonda her drink, she redirected her lips nearly ninety degrees, and blew the smoke from her first drag in someone else's face, a bit of courtesy that he very much appreciated.

"Thank you," she said with a smile as she took the Singapore Sling from Camron.

In a way, he was relieved that she was a smoker because it instantly halted any interest he had in her, thereby averting potential complications between he and Paris. Not that having an interest in someone else was out-of-bounds, because Paris, in Camron's mind, wasn't his girlfriend, nor he her boyfriend.

However, he could sense, despite the brevity of their acquaintance, that they were approaching a crossroad, and decisions would have to be made as to the direction their relationship would take. He knew from experience he was not very adept at platonic friendships, so he saw only two options for them: proceed to intimacy, or retreat back to occasional encounters at various night venues.

"Well listen, Vonda, I'm gonna make my way to the li'l boys' room," Camron said.

"Okay. Maybe we can get a dance later."

"That would be nice. I'll find you," he said, knowing he most likely wouldn't put a lot of effort into doing so.

"All right," Vonda said cheerfully.

The main-level restrooms were near the other bar. Camron moved in that direction, following the aisle connecting one side of the club to the other. En route, he passed a scantily clad blonde girl standing on a platform selling bottled beer and other such drinks from a tin tub filled with ice. While admiring her figure, Camron nearly bumped into a tall, slim, fudge brown sistah who was shouting into the mouthpiece of a cell phone, with the receiver end away from her ear, as if it were a walkie-talkie.

With midnight just twenty-eight minutes away, the club was now full, and perhaps a smidgen beyond its legal capacity of 1600 bodies. The crowd, as was the case with most of the downtown nightclubs that featured hip-hop and R & B music, was primarily Black: a mix of professionals, working-class people, and the ghetto fabulous.

Aware more ladies were about, Camron put a little extra smooth into his walk. His walk, or pimp as it was called back in the day, was a gliding, even gait with hunched shoulders. It was an amble he had perfected as a preteen by emulating his older brother.

As he pushed the swing door of the men's restroom inward, he found that space filled as well, which in this instance meant there were twelve men waiting to use three urinals and a commode.

Camron took a position behind a brotha, about the same height as he, sporting a jheri curl that appeared to have been heisted directly off one of the members of '80s R & B group Ready For The World. It was difficult for Camron to imagine someone styling a jheri curl on the eve of 2001, but there it was before him, in all its glistening glory. In front of the jheri-curled man, at one of the urinals, was a blonde fellow dressed in a shiny silver suit. Behind Camron were two other brothas, looking in the opposite direction at themselves in the restroom mirror.

"Man, Traci gettin' on my nerves," said one to the other. "Gettin' mad 'cause I'm lookin' at asses."

"Hey. A brotha gonna look. I'll tell you that right now," his compadre replied with a chuckle. "And with all deez hos up in here tonight, I might have ta do more than look. Might have ta slip somebody my phone number fo' it's all over wit'. Shit. You know me, dog."

"I heard that," his friend concurred.

The entrance to the ladies' restroom was right beside that of the men's, and two minutes later, as Camron was exiting the men's room, he caught a glimpse of a familiar face and form going into the ladies' room. Wanting to confirm if it was whom he thought, he positioned himself at a column just outside the lavatories, and leaned back, intent upon waiting there until she came out.

That column was a location he knew well, as he had stood there many times before. It was one the best locations for a comprehensive examination of the women in the club because, at some point, nearly all of them passed that spot on their way to the restroom.

Nine minutes later, the lady he was surveilling came out of the women's room with a girlfriend, and they both walked past Camron without noticing him. He watched them as they stepped into the mass of people and toward the dance floor. Not wanting to lose her, Camron followed. The two ladies came to a stop near the middle and edge of the dance floor, where they joined two other females, one wearing a feathered mask and the other a silver top hat that was tilted slightly to one side of her head.

A groove from the recent past, "Still Not A Player," by Big Pun, the deceased Latino rapper, and Joe, was booming loudly, and as Camron moved closer to the four ladies, he could tell from their smiling conversation that they were in a cheerful mood.

He walked up behind the one he had been watching, and spoke close to her ear. "Excuse me. Would you like to dance?" Two of her girlfriends looked at him as if he were crazy.

She jerked around, slightly alarmed at his audacity, but recognized him right away. "Heeey," she sang and gave him a hug. It was Kimma, his Liberian girlfriend at the time he had met Mara. "What's up, stranger?"

"Not a thing. What's up with you, sweetie?" Camron replied over the beat of the music.

"Nothing much," Kimma said. "Haven't seen you in a while."

"It has been a while, hasn't it? What? Three years?"

"At least."

Four years, two months, and five days to be precise. Not since that early Sunday morn when she, heartbroken by the demise of their relationship, had slammed Camron's car door shut.

"So how've you been?" Kimma asked, her face fully consumed by her ultracute smile.

"Fine. And you?"

"Great."

"But you didn't answer my question," Camron insisted.

"What?"

"Would you like to dance?"

"Sure," she beamed. "Come on."

As they searched for a place on the crowded dance floor, Camron couldn't help but notice how pretty Kimma looked. Prettier than he had remembered. She still had the same cute stubby nose, drowsy eyes, and silky skin. However, those attributes were now joined and made more attractive by an air of carefree confidence.

She would now be twenty-eight years old, but if she had entered a room filled with a hundred people and announced to them she was twenty, none would have doubted her. She had always looked young like that. But the four years since he'd last seen her had added a sexy maturity to her look and demeanor.

Her skin was a shade darker than Camron's own rich, toffee complexion, and the white she was wearing—loose-fitting white pants; white, open-toed, strapped heels; and a gleaming white tube top—accentuated that difference even more: beautiful, unblemished black skin, directly from the earth of the motherland, that did not require the aid of makeup.

She moved her body in the same seductive way she did the first time they had danced together years ago. They danced to a second song, stealing glances, exchanging smiles, at times so close Camron would wrap one hand around her naked waist and place his leg between the both of hers.

The music, the rhythm, the bass carried them into another song, this one by Ja Rule. *"Where would I be without you-oo ..."* he sang as best he could.

Feeling the groove, Kimma's mouth was pursed, and the skin between her eyebrows was crinkled like a collapsed accordion. It was the same sensuous look of desperate sexual frustration that used to be on her face when they made love.

She reached out, touched Camron's hard stomach, and grabbed a handful of his shirt. She turned her back to him, relinquishing her grip on the cloth only when the spin of her body forced her to. She thrust her behind into his crotch, where a hard-on was being nursed, then spun around to face him once more, gripping his shirt again.

The heat was still there, and couldn't have been any hotter at that moment than it was the time they had—in the company of soft shadows created by slow burning candles—got physical on the countertop of his bathroom sink. Or when they had once made love in the front seat of his car. That particular time Camron had just pulled into his garage, but their lust—powered by alcohol and an unusually long absence between them—had already taken flight. "Let's do it right here," Camron had whispered. Kimma mustered just enough breath to sigh "Okay." And so they didn't bother to take the few steps necessary to reach the bedroom, or living room floor for that matter, but instead quenched their desires in his automobile, which was soon bouncing and made hot, humid, and foggy by the thrashing of their bodies.

He wondered what could have made him leave her, surrender all that passion. Camron, of course, knew the answer. In a word, Mara, who not only matched and often surpassed Kimma's physical ardor, but also brought a sophisticated maturity that seemed capable of sustaining a long-term relationship. He just didn't count on Mara's stubbornness to be as intensely unyielding as his own, which, in the end, served as a major driving force in the disintegration of their union.

Near the end of the third song, the music stopped, and the DJ began barking into the mike. "Peo-ple! Are you ready to have some fun in two thousand and one?"

A loud chorus of voices in a variety of pitches arose from the crowd. "Yea-ahh-wooo!"

"I can't hear you!" the DJ shouted in a singsong fashion. "Are you ready to have some fun in two thousand and one?"

The crowd responded even louder.

"Thirty seconds! Thirty more seconds and the New Year is here!" the DJ hollered.

"Come on," Kimma said to Camron, then took his hand in her own, and led him off what was now a dance floor full of people standing in place, clapping and screaming. They returned to where her friends had been situated, and Kimma let Camron's hand drop from hers.

Two of her three girlfriends were in the same spot, screaming with the rest of the crowd and holding clear, plastic, two-piece cups shaped like champagne glasses in each of their hands. The shallow cups were filled with champagne.

Kimma took a cup from one her friends, then reached out to take another from the other friend, who seemed reluctant to relinquish it. Kimma gave her a frown, said something to her, and was then able to wrest it away without too much additional effort. Kimma gave the cup to Camron, who felt a bit guilty about her commandeering champagne on his behalf. He didn't linger on it, though, because, besides being provided gratis by the club, the amount of champagne in the cup was, at most, four ounces.

As soon as the DJ said "Ten!", everyone joined in the countdown.

"Nine ... eight ... seven ... six ... five ... four ... three ... two ... ONE!" the people screamed in unison, then whooped, hollered, and blew and spun noisemakers as if the New Year had just erased every problem they may have had in their lives a minute earlier.

As balloons fell from the nightclub's sky, people tapped their cups to anyone else's that was near, then gulped down their champagne. Many couples in the crowd were kissing. Depending upon the relationship, the kisses ranged from short lip smacks to visible tongue wrestling. Camron noticed a couple of lip-locked women as well.

He tapped his plastic glass to Kimma's and they each drank their mouthful of champagne. She threw her arms open, inviting him into her space. He reached for her waist, and as they came closer, in slow motion it seemed, Camron decided he would go for no more than a kiss on the lips. If she wanted to take things farther, he wouldn't hesitate to accommodate. But he'd start with just an innocent kiss.

Kimma's face was just inches from his, moving closer and closer. Camron puckered his lips ever so slightly, and expected Kimma to do the same. But she had a big grin on her face, her teeth on full display. *She needs to get ready to kiss me,* Camron thought, *or my lips are only gonna hit teeth.*

Suddenly, unexpectedly, Kimma turned her head, and instead of kissing, they were hugging.

"Happy New Year, Camron," she said into his ear.

Camron was surprised, because he just knew he was getting a kiss; especially after their fiery dancing.

"Happy New Year to you too," he managed to respond.

Chords of an instrumental, rock-guitar-driven version of "Auld Lang Syne" came over the speakers, and the crowd began to sing along. But White people didn't even know that song, much less Black folk. So after the first line—"Should auld acquaintance be forgot"—the crowd's singing became a muddle of nonsense words, and everyone was soon impatient for more dance music. Moments later, the DJ obliged the people by putting on some Jay-Z, which quickly packed the floor.

"You want some more champagne?" Camron asked Kimma.

"Yeah. This was nothing," she said looking at her empty cup.

"Walk with me to the bar," he said.

"Okay."

Camron reached out and grabbed Kimma's hand, and turned toward the bar. But as he was beginning to negotiate the maze of people, Kimma pulled her hand back. Not abruptly, but it was a clear enough signal to Camron that she didn't want him to hold her hand. Instead, she patted him on the shoulder to let him know she was behind him. That was as curious to Camron as the hug-instead-of-a-kiss had been.

They planted themselves at an open spot at the bar, and waited for the bartender to work his way toward them.

"So how's married life?" Kimma asked.

Through sporadic exchanges of e-mail that began soon after their breakup, Kimma knew Camron had got engaged. However, after he shared that bit of news with her, they soon lost touch with one another all together.

"I wouldn't know," Camron said.

"What do you mean?"

"We divorced this past fall."

"Oh, Camron. I'm so sorry to hear that."

"Don't be. Marriages end all the time."

"Don't tell me that," Kimma said warily.

"Why? Are you married now?" Camron asked with a throaty chuckle.

"No. But I'm engaged."

"Oh," Camron said as he raised his head high, then began nodding slowly. "Congratulations."

"Thanks."

"When's the big date?"

"August. August 18th. My birthday month."

"That's great, sweetie. I'm happy for you."

"Thank you," Kimma said and smiled broadly. She looked back toward the dance floor, where the DJ was raising a ruckus.

"Do my ladies run this mothafucka?" he asked loudly and in time to the beat of the music.

"Hell yeah!" came the high-pitched response from the females.

"Or do the fellas run this mothafucka?"

"Hell yeah!" the men responded gruffly, with many of the ladies simultaneously sprinkling in "Hell no!"

Kimma waved at one of her girlfriends who was dancing. "That's my fiancé's sister. She's crazy."

Camron looked at Kimma and smiled at the joy that was on her face as she waved to her future sister-in-law. He *was* happy for her. He truly was. Happy she had found the man of her dreams. He couldn't help, though, but feel some jealousy as well.

So he was both happy and jealous.

Mostly jealous.

18

Money Blues

THE FIRST YEAR OF MY LIFE as a husband to Mara was fairly blissful: dinners by the fireplace, bubble baths by candlelight, snowball fights, and lovemaking in every room of the house several times over.

However, that first year, blissful though it may have been, was far from perfect. We had our share of disagreements, which sometimes escalated into arguments. Arguments that commonly ended with me sulking on the living room couch, stretched out in front of the TV with remote in hand, and Mara upstairs in the bedroom, reading some trite romance novel.

Passage of time—thirty, forty minutes, maybe an hour—and, if it were evening, sleepiness, would eventually dull my anger, often to the point that I'd forget exactly what we had argued about in the first place. I'd climb the stairs and find Mara asleep, the book she was reading abandoned and lying across her chest. The quaint beauty of my lovely, caramel brown wife slumbering would wash away any residual bitterness, and I'd soon be in bed beside her. Stirred by my presence, she'd snuggle into me, and, without opening her eyes, whisper, "I'm sorry."

"I'm sorry too," I'd say.

And all was forgiven.

One day—the next day after one of these arguments—Mara shared with me some advice she had once gotten from her mother. "Never go to bed angry," she recounted. "Whatever it is, talk it out. Don't go to sleep mad at each other."

And, early on, we adhered to that doctrine.

Most of those first-year arguments involved, in some form or fashion, money. One of the earliest that I remember occurred during the spring following our elopement. It wasn't an argument really, but a few moments of contention over a phone bill. A three hundred-sixty-five-dollar-and-forty-eight-cent phone bill.

"Mara!" I hollered upstairs from the living room couch. I was sitting in front of the television with that month's bills, all of which were strewn across the living room's glass coffee table. However, for the moment I was fixated on the $365 and forty-eight cents.

Mara came to the balcony and peeped down at me. "Yes?"

"Do you know how much this phone bill is?" I asked.

"How much?"

"Three hundred sixty-five dollars."

"How'd it get so high?" she asked innocently.

"You tell me. Most of the calls are to Raleigh, Newark, and Orlando," I said as I leafed through the pages detailing the charges. Mara had family/friends in each of those places.

"Let me see that," she said with concern in her voice as she made her way down the steps.

She took the papers detailing the phone bill from me, sat down on the love seat, and looked at some of the calls, one of which especially caught her eye.

"Seventy minutes!" she cried. "There's no way I could have been talking that long. No way."

"Well if you want to call the phone company and dispute it, be my guest," I said. "In the meantime, I suspect they'll be wantin' their money."

There was a long pause as Mara continued to stare at the bill.

Finally she said, "I'll give you some extra money for my calls. Just tell me how much they are."

Tired from a long day at work, and irritated by the other obligations that were spread out before me, I said, "You got the bill in your hand right there. Just ca'culate it out."

She gave me a look of exasperation and sighed loudly.

"What is it?" I asked in response to her reaction.

"Nothing," she said curtly, which of course meant *something.*

"Mara, you see I'm going through the rest of these bills. It won't hurt you to figure out how much those calls come to. 'Specially since most of 'em are yours."

She rose, turned, and walked quickly up the steps, the pages of the phone bill fluttering in her hand.

I shook my head, then returned my focus to the other invoices.

Ten minutes later, I walked upstairs, accompanied by a somber mood. Mara was sitting on the bed, her focus oscillating from the list of calls to a calculator into which she was punching numbers.

"Mara, I'm sorry," I began, but she hushed me with an open palm in my direction, and the look on her face became even more concentrated as she struggled to keep from losing her place amongst the jumble of numbers.

I walked into the bathroom, closed the door behind me, took a long pee, washed my hands, and came back into the bedroom.

"My calls total two hundred seventy-eight dollars and twenty-two cents," she announced. "I'll give you that in addition to the usual."

The "usual" was six hundred dollars. That was her monthly contribution in our crusade to keep a roof over our head, maintain two cars, provide for household essentials, keep food in the fridge, and entertain ourselves via the occasional dinner and movie-or-live show.

I apologized for a second time. "I'm sorry, sweetie."

"Sorry for what, Camron?"

"For snapping at you."

"That's okay," she said tersely. She extended her hand towards me, at the end of which was the freshly analyzed phone bill. "That's just your style. Snap now, ask questions later."

I reached out and took the papers from her, ignored her last comment, and instead tried to put the situation in perspective. "Listen. You're trying to save money, and I'm trying to save money, which is hard to do if ... you know ... if we aren't careful in controlling some of these bills. Our trip to North Carolina last month and, after that, your car blowin' up, have made things tight enough as it is."

"I know," she responded. "I'll just be a little more careful with the long distance calls. That's all I can say, you know?"

Mara flipped on the television.

"All right. As long as we're both aware," I said. "So you're not mad, right?"

"No."

"You sure?"

"Camron," she said as she looked at me. There was annoyance in her voice. "I'm not mad."

As I walked back downstairs to rejoin the other bills, it was clear to me that—if she wasn't mad—she certainly was far from happy.

Mara eventually gave me a portion of the money she promised for the phone bill: one hundred and fifty dollars. That was indicative of her casual approach to our financial commitments, which irritated me to no end. Especially when it came to her base obligation of six hundred dollars per month, because often she would give me those monies at her leisure: at the beginning of the month; two weeks into the month; half at the beginning of the month, half in the middle; or whatever other payment combination one could imagine. And sometimes, by the end of the month, when all was said and done, she'd be short by a hundred or more bucks.

"Mara, you got the rest of your bill money?" I asked her early one mid-August evening. She had given me four hundred dollars at the beginning of that month, and had promised to give me the balance the next week.

I hated asking her about money she owed. There was something distasteful about it, and, to a degree, I resented that she put me in a position to have to do so.

"Can I give it to you at the beginning of next month?" she said to me.

We were both in the kitchen helping ourselves to slices of a just-delivered pizza.

I smirked and shook my head. "You know what? This is getting tiring."

"What?" Mara asked, knowing full well what I was talking about.

"Me having to beg you for your share of the bill money every month."

"What difference does it make if I give it to you now or two weeks from now?" Mara asked.

"Good question. I'll pose it to the mortgage company and see what they have to say.

"But I'll tell you what the problem with that is," I said. "The problem with that is, come September, you'll give me four or five hundred dollars—maybe—and delay the rest until later that month, which will turn into October. And by then you'll have extra expenses and won't have it. Isn't your sister getting married in October?"

"Yeah," Mara answered.

Kera, her sister in Raleigh who was so into the early planning of *our* wedding, was getting married herself.

"And you're in the wedding," I reminded her. "So that's gonna cost. The dress; getting down there."

"I'll give you the money, Camron. Dang."

"Am I asking for too much? Is six hundred a month too much?"

"No," she said.

"Then what's the problem?"

"It's expensive in some of these cities, you know?"

"What are you talking about? The airline covers your expenses."

"Yeah, we get a per diem. But that doesn't nearly cover the real cost of meals in a place like D.C. or Miami," Mara insisted.

"Nor, I imagine, does it cover the new outfits and shoes you seem to bring home with you from every trip."

Mara stopped abruptly, narrowed her eyes, then hurled a double negative at me. "I don't bring no new outfits home with me that often."

"Mara, look in the closet. I've moved most of my stuff to the other bedroom closet, and there's still hardly any room left."

Mara shook her head and strolled into the living room with her two slices. "Camron, I'll give you the money."

I followed her. "Listen. I've been thinking of a better way we can do this. We can set up a joint account, have our checks deposited into that, then draft from the joint account into our own separate accounts everything except money for the bills. That way we don't have to go through this every month."

"Whatever you want to do is fine with me."

The following week we set up our accounts as I suggested, and with that most of our money issues were laid to rest. But we'd find other things over which to disagree in Year Two.

19

Patience

"SO WHAT'D YOU THINK OF THE MOVIE?" Camron asked Paris as they walked out of the old, elegant, single-screen theater and onto a sidewalk being dusted with new snow. They had just seen *Crouching Tiger, Hidden Dragon.*

"It was all right," Paris said. "I don't care much for subtitles though. That's too much work, trying to watch the screen and read at the same time."

"I didn't know it was gonna be subtitled till it started. I thought it was gonna be dubbed like the old-school karate films."

"Some of the fight scenes were a bit absurd," said Paris. "You know, where they were flyin' and runnin' across rooftops."

"Yeah, that was a little off-the-wall. It was choreographed pretty tight though. Not quite as tight, of course, as my favorite karate movie of all time."

"Which is?" she asked.

"*Enter the Dragon.* With my boy Bruce Lee," Camron said proudly, as if he and Bruce were kin.

"I've seen bits and pieces of that on video," Paris said. "That wasn't dubbed, was it?"

"No. It was in English. Which Bruce couldn't talk worth a damn. But English wasn't something me and my boys paid much attention to in a Bruce Lee movie anyway because we were too busy watching Bruce kick ass."

They moved briskly through the chatty Uptown crowd, their shoulders stiff, braced against the cold. The fat flakes of snow were falling at a moderate pace.

"As a matter of fact, Bruce Lee was my inspiration to take karate as a child," Camron admitted.

"You studied karate? For how long?"

"About two days," he answered. "That was how long it took for this kid to kick me in the nuts, and me to decide immediately thereafter that being a Kung Fu master was not the move for me."

Paris laughed. "You should have kept trying. If at first you don't succeed, try try again, right?"

"Wrong," Camron corrected her. "That cliché doesn't apply after one gets kicked in the balls."

Paris laughed again, this one heartier than the first.

A minute later they had reached the relative warmth of Camron's car.

"Winter in Minnesota. Don't you love it?" Camron said as he turned the key and ignited the engine, which roared, then settled quickly to a high idle.

"Oh yes," Paris replied unconvincingly as she rubbed her black-gloved hands together. She exhaled and her own breath appeared in front of her. "The fresh snow does make things prettier," she conceded.

Looking in her direction and noticing a few flakes of snow that had yet to melt on the shoulder of her light gray wool coat, he said, "Yes, it does."

Camron leaned toward her. Taking notice, Paris did likewise, and they kissed softly, but with a fervor that quickly warmed their cold lips.

"What was that for?" Paris asked as Camron pulled away just a little.

He was silent for a moment, then said, "My way of saying thanks for a lovely evening."

"And thank you. Dinner was nice. The movie was pretty good too, despite all the reading."

"Yeah," Camron agreed.

He turned on his wipers, which responded by pushing away the inch of fluffy snow blanketing the windshield. He pushed the radio on and set it to a low volume, then backed out of the parking spot and guided his vehicle toward the busy streets. "It's still early so ... what do you want to do now?" he asked as he pulled into traffic.

Paris looked at the car's CD-radio and saw that it was 9:45. "I don't know. What do you suggest?"

"I suggest ... we go to my house ... start a fire ... and open a bottle of wine."

"Sounds cozy. But what about this weather? I might get stuck at your place."

"I think they're only predicting four inches, and it looks like half of that has fallen already." Camron smiled before saying, "And what would be so terrible about getting stuck at my place?"

Paris twisted her mouth to one side, then formed a smile of her own. "Hmm. That could be dangerous."

"Think so? What could make it so dangerous?"

"Lots of things."

"Such as?" Camron asked.

"A warm fireplace and wine for starters."

"You don't trust yourself under those conditions?"

"Yes, I trust me. But you know what almost happened the last time I was at your house." Paris was alluding to the previous Sunday evening. That night had ended on Camron's bed, and, although they remained clothed, their passions nearly convinced them otherwise. "Something that I'm not sure I'm quite ready for."

"You told me that," Camron reminded her. "And what did I say? When you're ready, just let me know."

"You did say that," she said. "And I appreciated it."

Paris thought for a moment, then said, "Are *you* ready?"

"I'm comfortable with where we are," he said. "But I want you to be comfortable too. And when you are, we'll take that next step."

Paris smiled. "Thank you for your patience."

As for Camron, he was disguising the fact that, in actuality, his patience was wearing somewhat thin. It was now the last Saturday in January, so they had been dating steady for over five weeks, and Camron wanted to get closer to her. But Paris's presence was a comfortable one, and it was for that reason that Camron didn't feel an urgent need for sexuality.

The rest of the drive to Camron's house was consumed by conversations about work, much of it concerning recent drama between Paris and a co-worker.

"Let me tell you what this heifer did," Paris said. She was talking about a nurse named Cathy. "Brings all these charts into my office and says, 'These are some extra patients you're going to have to handle.' I say to her, 'Says who?' And she's like, 'Ms. Reynolds.'"

"That's your supervisor, right?" Camron asked.

"Ms. Reynolds is. But not Cathy, although sometimes she seems to think she is.

"So I said, 'Well why didn't Ms. Reynolds tell me that?' And she says, 'Ms. Reynolds had somewhere to go and she won't be back for a couple of hours, so she asked me to tell you.' I was so mad at that girl. Always got her nose up Ms. Reynolds's behind, and then, every chance she gets, tries to act like she's my boss. I'm telling you, that girl just gets on my last nerve.

"She wants to be a supervisor so bad. And you know what? She will be one day because she and Ms. Reynolds are just so chummy. That's another reason I've got to get out of there because there's no way I could work for Cathy."

As Paris continued to seethe, Camron pulled into his driveway, which was completely covered by the still falling snow. He reached up toward the visor and touched a button on his garage remote. The garage door raised and he pulled inside. It was during these times of the year, when snow and cold blanketed everything, that he most appreciated his attached garage.

Paris followed Camron into the house, and he took off his leather jacket, underneath which he was wearing black, baggy, corduroy pants and a roomy, blue-green pullover sweater.

Turning to Paris, Camron said, "Let me have your coat."

Paris spun until her back was to him, then let her coat drop from her tall frame and into Camron's hands. He peaked at her round bottom, which was framed well by the tightness of the tan jeans she was wearing. The clingy, long-sleeve, off-white nylon top she was sporting fit high and snug around her neck, and displayed the outline of her buxom (he'd been debating for weeks as to whether she was a B or C) quite nicely.

He wondered what it would be like when they finally made love. How would her skin feel next to his? What would she taste like? How would she respond once he was deep inside her? What would her femininity feel like to him and how would his masculinity feel to her? But Camron forced such thoughts of physical rapture from his mind by reminding himself again about patience: that it was a virtue.

He kicked off his shoes onto the long thin floor mat that covered much of the foyer, then raised the temperature setting on the wall thermostat by six degrees.

"Let me light this fire," he said.

He walked across the living room's bone colored carpet to the fireplace, and placed a prepackaged imitation log in it.

"You want me to get the wine?" Paris asked as she tugged at the calf-hugging black boots she was wearing.

"Yeah. There's a bottle of white Zin' in the fridge. The wine-glasses are in the cabinet to the left of the stove."

As Paris walked into the kitchen, her feet covered by sheer brown stockings, Camron was thankful he had cleaned the house some before their date. Especially the kitchen, which had been a complete mesh hours earlier.

He lit the log with a long wand lighter, then stretched out across the living room floor in front of his compact disc player.

"Where's your corkscrew?" Paris shouted from the kitchen.

"In the second drawer below the microwave," Camron hollered back, then began programming songs from CDs by R & B singers Joe and Case.

Paris walked into the living room with a full wineglass in each hand just as Joe was beginning to proclaim to some woman that he would do all the things her man wouldn't. She handed one of the glasses to Camron, and sat down on the carpet beside him.

"Let me get something for us to sit on," Camron said. He stretched to reach the thick glass top of the coffee table and placed his glass of wine on it. He got up and went quickly upstairs. After walking into his bedroom, then the bathroom, and finally his guest bedroom, he returned with a king-sized comforter, purple on one side, burgundy on the other.

"Hop up," he said to Paris.

She stood and moved to a corner of the living room by one of the two nine-foot tall windows that were on either side of the fireplace. Camron threw the comforter up and out, and let it float like a para-chute down onto the floor.

"There," he said.

They both sat down close to the fireplace on the purple side of the soft comforter, Camron cross-legged, and Paris facing him, her back to the fire, legs together and bent at the knees.

"You look tired," Camron remarked as he retrieved his glass of wine.

"You know what? I am a little bit. It's been a long day."

Earlier that day Paris had worked from seven to three.

"Are you going to church tomorrow?" he asked.

"Yeah. If there isn't too much snow on the ground. I need to go regardless because I haven't been in two Sundays." Paris took a sip of her wine. "Speaking of church, you've been promising to come with me."

"I will. Next Sunday."

"I work next Sunday."

"The Sunday after that."

"You don't have to wait on me you know," Paris told him. "You can go by yourself and tell me what you think."

"I'd rather go with you."

Paris clamped her lips shut and shook her head, then said, "Any excuse is better than none."

Camron chuckled. "My mother used to say that to me all the time."

"Really?"

"Yes. I was so young the first few times she said it, I didn't know what she was talking about."

"You miss your mom a lot?"

"I do," Camron said. "But she's with me every day in spirit. I'll catch myself saying something or doing something that she used to say or do, or I'll see something that reminds me of her, and suddenly I feel her presence. And that always makes me feel good. You know?"

Paris smiled. "I talked with Momma yesterday."

"How's she doing?"

"Fine. Complaining about something my father was suppose to get fixed on the car."

Camron looked down into his glass of wine and the reflection of the flames dancing in it. He smiled inside, happy for Paris that she was yet able to share moments with her mother.

"How's Deanna and Jake?" he asked of Paris's sister and her husband.

"I talked with her earlier this week. They're doing fine. She told me to tell you hello. And Cicely is growing like a weed."

"Good. I was afraid we'd stunted her growth or caused some kind of permanent psychological damage after she caught us necking at your front door on Christmas."

"Cicely didn't pay us no mind," Paris said laughing. "She just wanted to go to the bathroom."

Paris looked over her left shoulder and out the tall window she had stood by earlier. "Is it still snowing out there?" she asked herself aloud, a touch of concern in her voice. She sat her wineglass on the coffee table, stood, and walked to the window. "You said they were only calling for four inches? Looks like more than that." She crossed her arms as she looked out at the falling snow. "The weathermen here are so bad at predicting things."

"They are," Camron agreed as he drank more of his wine, rose to his feet, and joined her by the window. "Back home, old people sitting on the porch could tell you what was going to happen better than these guys here."

A smile came over Paris's face. "When I was growing up in Chicago, there was this old lady next door to us. What was her name? Miss King. Anyway, she'd say, 'Tell your mama her flowers should get some rain tomorrow.' I'd say, 'How you know that, Miss King?' And she'd say, 'My knees been actin' up all day.' Sure o' 'nough, that night or the next day it would rain."

"Old people have a knack for that," Camron said. "She's probably still giving your parents regular weather updates."

"No. Miss King died years ago. Poor thing. I always felt sorry for her because she seemed so lonely. Momma told me she had been married at one time, but her husband had died many years earlier."

The smile that was on Paris's face a few moments before was gone, replaced by a look that was faintly sad as she remembered her old neighbor. Camron looked at her as she stared into the cold snowy night.

He touched her chin with his finger, diverting her attention from Minnesota in winter, and turned her head toward him. He kissed her affectionately as the crackle of the fire and Case played in the background.

Couldn't we be-ee happily ever after....

He relinquished her lips, gently brushed her cheek with the back of his hand, and whispered, "I think you should stay with me tonight."

"Is it too bad for you to drive me home?" Paris said softly.

"No," Camron said before kissing her cheek. "I just think it would be nice if you stayed."

"If I stay, we're just sleeping. You know that, right?"

"Yes, I know," Camron agreed as he pulled back enough to look into her eyes to see if she was serious about what she had just said. "All I want to do is cuddle anyway. Tonight's a perfect night for cuddling, don't you think?"

"I can't disagree with that," Paris acknowledged. "What time are you going to take me home?"

"Uhmm ... how about nine-thirty? Will that give you enough time to get ready for church?"

"Yes."

Paris gazed at Camron for an instant. "You planned this all along, didn't you?"

"Me?" Camron said. "No."

They talked by the fire for another twenty minutes, then made their way upstairs. Before leaving the living room, Camron put the music that was trickling from the stereo in repeat mode, and lowered the living room chandelier to a dusky brown.

"You got a T-shirt I can sleep in?" Paris asked as they walked into Camron's dark bedroom. The only lights in that room were from the headboard, which Camron had turned on and positioned to a dim setting when he had went upstairs to get the comforter.

"Yes," Camron said and moved in the direction of his walk-in closet. He walked in and came out with two T-shirts: one black, one red; one for him, the other for her. He gave Paris the red shirt, and she went into the bathroom, flicked on the light, and slammed the door behind her.

"Sorry," he heard her say from the other side of the door, apologizing for the slam.

Camron sprawled across his bed. *Wonder if she gonna gi' me some tonight,* he said to himself. He thought about her declaration that they were only going to sleep. And his admission that he was interested in nothing more than cuddling. *Yeah right.* But since he'd indicated that cuddling was the thing foremost on his mind, he'd attempt no more than that. That is, of course, unless she wanted more.

Camron rolled off the bed and quickly undressed down to his white athletic briefs. He pulled the black T-shirt over his head, turned the ceiling fan that hung over his bed to a slow, counterclockwise spin, and got under the covers. Snug in bed, he could now avoid having to clumsily undress in front of Paris. He reached over his head and snagged the remote from the headboard, turned on the television, and adjusted the volume just high enough so that he could hear it over the music from downstairs.

After a few minutes, Paris walked out of the bathroom, her off-white top replaced by the red T-shirt.

"Anything good on?" she asked as she strolled to the side of the bed and began undoing her pants.

"No. Just flipping through channels," Camron answered.

"You men and your remotes. I don't know what you'd do without them."

"I don't know either. I'd probably hire a midget to sit by the TV and change the channel," Camron said as he pulled back the covers on her side of the bed, inviting her in.

Paris laughed. "You're terrible."

Still standing, she shimmied from side to side until the tight jeans she was wearing made it past her hips, then slid them over her thighs. She reached down and pulled one leg of the pants, then the other, past her feet. Camron wanted to look, sneak a gander at her body in a state of undress. But he played it cool, nonchalantly staring in the direction of the television.

She threw her limp pants on the wicker trunk in which Camron stored his clean towels, then sat on the edge of the bed and slipped her knee-high pantyhose off. Now with nothing on but a T-shirt and a thong, Paris climbed into bed, pulled the covers over her, and scooted sideward till she was next to Camron. He placed his arm under and around her shoulders. Paris's silky-smooth, cool, naked legs intertwined with Camron's warm hairy ones.

"Ooo, you're warm," she purred.

As her legs caroused with his, he said, "This feels nice." Despite the T-shirts that were between them, he could also feel her soft breasts against his chest. "The perfect way to get through a snowy night."

"Mm-hmm," Paris moaned as she snuggled closer, gave him a brief but lustful kiss that had him hoping for more, then closed her eyes.

Camron turned off the television, and the only sounds left were the sweet strains of Case and Joe.

Someone was cajoling, urging him on.

"Take it, baby. Take it."

The voice was Mara's, and Camron was on top of her, pumping furiously. Mara was returning every thrust she received with one of her own, and with one hand was grabbing and smacking at Camron's muscular behind as if she were driving a racehorse home to the finish. Every nerve in his body was alert and on edge, every muscle tightened in response to some animalistic calling. Sweat formed running wet lines down his face and dripped onto Mara's chest, which was also glistening with moisture. Camron moaned audibly as he approached climax.

Suddenly, Mara disappeared. Camron blinked his eyes once, then twice. No Mara. Only the barely visible, foggy images of the blades of a ceiling fan twirling slowly overhead. As the fan came into focus, Camron realized he was in his bedroom. And that he'd just been dreaming about making love to his ex-wife.

However, he could feel that he was erect, and that was no dream. Indeed, he was more than erect. He was bone hard, his shaft spontaneously pulsing. It was the most satisfying erection he could ever remember experiencing. Becoming self-conscious, he looked to his left. *Paris is here, isn't she?* he thought. But he didn't see anyone. Did he take her home? Had she witnessed him in this state of inexplicable pleasure? And what about this pulsating zone of delight present below his waist that seemed to be intensifying? Was he dreaming still?

He looked down and saw a big bump in the covers. A bump that was moving up and down, and had the roundness of a person's head. A moist suctioning was prodding him to even higher heights of passion. Fully conscious now, he realized it wasn't a dream, but a reality that his manhood was wrapped in the warm splendor of Paris's mouth!

Camron pulled back the covers and there she was, bobbing and slurping all over his hardened prong, the elastic band of the front of his underwear underneath her chin.

Guess she changed her mind about cuddling.

He began to gently pump his hips in time to her motion, and ran his fingers through her short, soft, curly hair. Realizing he was conscious and there with her, she increased the ferocity of her juicy movements.

Camron soaked in all of her rapturous affection, but at the same time was somewhat taken aback by it. It seemed incongruent with her otherwise laid-back disposition. But he wasn't complaining, nor about to ask any questions.

Camron pulled Paris by her shoulders up toward him. Reluctantly, she let his manhood flop from her mouth and smack against his flat belly, then followed in the direction of his tug. As Paris's face came closer, Camron could see, despite the scant lighting, her sleepy eyes. The sluggish look was not from drowsiness, but was the result of a salacious drunkenness that had taken over her body and soul.

She locked her mouth onto his and tried, it seemed, to drag Camron's tongue out of his head. But he countered the move and soon possessed *her* tongue.

With one hand he worked off his briefs, and they began clawing at each other's T-shirts.

"Hold up your arms," Camron whispered.

Paris did so, and he lifted the T-shirt over her head so fast that her naked breasts, with their silver-dollar-sized nipples, were bouncing even after he had sent the shirt drifting to the floor.

Definitely C's, he thought as he visually consumed her vivacious mammaries.

Camron raised up; Paris jerked his shirt over his head and arms, and tossed it over her shoulder. He pulled her close and rolled her onto the bed, then pulled the nipple of her left breast into his mouth.

"Oh ... ah," Paris gasped as she threw back her head.

Camron rubbed his hands over her flat stomach. He looked down, and saw her beautiful long legs apart and bent at the knees, her feet flat on the bed. A major portion of the thong, which was white and shear, was covering her crotch.

He gripped the thin waistband of the thong on one side between his right thumb and forefinger and tugged at it. Realizing that getting the spaghetti-stringed panties off would be easier if he used both hands, he got on his knees and curled his fingers around the sides of the thong, slid it from her waist, and over her smooth thighs. Once the thong was below her knees, Paris slowly bicycled her legs, and Camron removed it completely, leaving nothing between their bodies.

He took in the full view of her honey-colored physique. She was even finer, thicker with no clothes on.

He was about to part her legs, provide oral pleasure to other parts of her body, but Paris pulled herself up from the bed. Her head moved in the direction of Camron's swollen manhood, and, without using her hands, she again attached her puss to it, feverishly pulling him inside of her, then withdrawing, over and over again. A couple of minutes of this passed before Paris's body contracted and she began to moan. The vibrations of her mouth caused tremors up and down Camron's organ. She was orgasming, full mouth and all.

Seconds later, her body relaxed, and Paris stopped for a moment, like a suckling babe on the verge of sleep at its mother's breast.

Camron, for the first time since awakening from his dream, heard the faint sounds of the music he had left playing downstairs.

Paris's mouth went into motion again, slowly at first, then with increasing alacrity. Soon she was climaxing once more in much the same way she had minutes earlier.

All the while, Camron, still on his knees, but leaning back to the point that his bum was resting on the heels of his feet, was enjoying her handiwork, at times with his eyes closed (to better relish the pleasures she was bestowing upon him), at other times with them open (to take in the sensuous sights of her romping mouth and fine body). As Paris climaxed that second time, Camron thought no guy in the Twin Cities was luckier than he this night.

He felt a familiar welling in his loins that let him know he too was approaching his peak. Not wanting things to end just yet, Camron hesitantly pulled away. At first Paris resisted his retreat, but finally, again, let his appendage pop from her mouth.

"Turn around," he whispered.

Needing no further inducement, Paris turned her backside to Camron, got on her knees, and tilted her behind heavenward. It was one of the most glorious sights he'd seen in a while.

"Don't move. I'll be right back," Camron said before crawling off the bed.

"Hurry," Paris said in a voice that sounded pained and desperate.

He went into the bathroom, and, without turning on the light, rambled through a drawer and found a condom. He opened the pack and rolled its contents onto his erection, then walked back into the bedroom, his masculinity bouncing up and down with each step.

Paris was waiting as he had left her—on her knees, butt high in the air, back slightly arched, and resting on her elbows. Camron grabbed her buttocks with both hands and gently directed her closer to the end of the bed, where he was standing on the floor. He wove one finger through her soft, curly, pubic hairs. She was, as he suspected, drenched with juices from her own body. She was ready and so was he.

He looked toward the head of the bed. The orange-red glowing numerals on his clock-radio, which, like his wristwatch, was ten minutes fast, said 3:19.

As he guided himself into her, Paris let out a guttural murmur. Camron's masculinity jerked and flexed with satisfaction at her reaction. As he moved in and out of her warm, moist den of pleasure, filling her space then retreating again and again, Paris's amorous clamors grew louder. She raised her behind higher, curved her back more, and Camron's thrusts became more intense, more forceful, more rapid.

Paris's moans and groans evolved into screams of passion. "Oh! Mmm—ah—oh. Damn, damn, damn, damn it!"

As sweat beads began to form on his forehead and air rushed between his curled upper lip and clenched teeth, Camron was relieved the neighbor closest to his exterior bedroom walls was sixty yards away.

Paris's body began to tremor and quake as she, for a third time, found her sexual nirvana. Camron, no longer able to hold back the tide of his own fast-rising desire, fell over the edge of sexual delirium and into ecstasy with her.

He pushed himself deep inside her, held it there as waves of prurient satisfaction coursed through his midsection, then spread to other parts of his body. Camron's shoulders slumped as, with each pulse of his heart, his lust ebbed. Paris, in her own world of fulfillment, was moaning, but, with the exception of her labored breathing, was motionless.

Exhausted and spent, Camron slowly extracted himself from Paris, who was wetter now than she had been when he first entered her.

"That was good, baby," he managed to say.

"Mm-hmm," Paris moaned.

"I'm gonna get a cloth."

He dragged himself to the bathroom, peeled off the condom, and dropped the partially filled latex balloon into the commode. He noticed he too was quite wet, covered in Paris's love flow.

Damn. Never would have thunk she was that wild, Camron said to himself. He was delighted, though, with her wanton sexual nature. It ensured they wouldn't get bored with each other anytime soon in the bedroom.

He flushed the toilet, then wet a washcloth with cold water that soon ran hot, wrung it, and carried it with him into the bedroom. Paris had rolled onto her side and curled into a loose fetal position. Camron slid behind her and gently touched the cloth between her legs, which she opened to give him easier access.

As he kneaded the warm cloth into her femininity, Paris moaned with pleasure from the heat.

He folded the cloth, wiped himself, then threw it in the direction of the bathroom. It landed on the carpeted floor just outside the bathroom door with a sloppy plop.

He pulled the covers over them. Paris turned to face Camron, and they brought their bodies close.

Camron spoke. "So ... that was all a dream, right?"

"Yes. It was all a dream," Paris said without an inkling of facetiousness. "Something that happened in our minds."

He could, however, hear the smile in her voice.

"Thanks for a wonderful dream," she said.

"No. Thank you," he insisted, then kissed Paris passionately. Satiated, Camron closed his eyes. "Good night, sweetie."

"Good night," Paris said.

For a few moments, everything was still, and—except for the music from downstairs—quiet. Then Paris rubbed her hand over Camron's chest, across his stomach, and down to his limp manhood.

Did she want more? Camron wasn't sure he had the energy.

Her tongue darted onto his nipple, then went under the covers with her as she snaked a path down to his stomach. He felt a tingle, an electric pulse below his waist. Perhaps he *could* find the energy for another round.

Paris threw back the covers. Her wet mouth was now past his navel.

"Time for seconds," she said as she continued her descent.

20

Brunch

CAMRON LEANED OVER PARIS'S SHOULDER and peered down at her.

"So what was that about?" he asked.

Paris smiled. "What?"

It was Sunday morning and they were in bed naked, Camron behind Paris, watching a jazz program.

"Last night," he said. "Thought you just wanted to sleep."

Paris stared at the television screen. "That was your fault," she said with an impish grin.

"My fault? How was it my fault?"

"You got all hard and stuff," she said as if it was a complaint.

"I was dreaming."

"About what?" Paris asked.

"I don't remember," Camron lied.

"Whatever it was, you definitely got hard. Real hard. So I figured, why let all that go to waste?"

Camron chuckled. "Interesting. I'll have to have that dream more often."

Paris, still grinning, said with an air of nonconcern, "Suit yourself."

Camron licked the smile that was on his lips. "Never would have guessed you to be such a lioness in bed."

Paris turned her attention away from the television screen and looked directly up at him. "Now what does that mean?"

"Just that … you surprised me. In a good way. A very good way."

"A lioness in bed?"

"Yeah. That's a compliment."

She twisted her mouth, thought for moment, and gave a sigh. "I do like sex," she confessed. "Wait. That sounds too unaffectionate. I do like making love. As much as the next woman. And I probably liked it more last night because I hadn't done it in a while. So maybe I was slightly more energetic than usual, if that's what you mean."

"That's sort of what I mean. But it wasn't a wasted energy either. There was a lot of skill and dedication behind it."

"Sounds like you're giving me an evaluation."

Camron was afraid he wasn't making his point as well as he would like. "Listen, let me just say this: I really enjoyed last night. And I'll leave it at that."

"And so did I."

Camron pursed his lips; Paris, responding to his cue, did the same, and they smacked them together.

He looked at the clock that sat within the headboard of his bed, and estimated that it was several minutes past 10:30. "You're gonna miss church."

"I know. Don't remind me. I'm feeling guilty enough already," Paris said. "I'll just go to the seven o'clock service tonight."

"Good enough. Anyway, I don't know about you, but I'm getting hungry. Let's go get some breakfast."

"Okay."

"I gotta go out here and shovel this snow first so we can get outta the driveway. Why don't you take a bubble bath while I do that."

"That sounds good. Can I light the candles around your tub?"

"Sure. Just don't burn the house down," Camron said.

Paris gave him a you-silly-boy look.

"I'll shower when I get back in," he added. "Then we'll go."

"All rightie."

After donning the underwear he had discarded earlier that morning; some black sweatpants; a blue sweat shirt; clunky orange-brown work boots over white athletic socks; a blue and black checkered scarf; an old, gray, wool coat; a wide brown band that went around his head and covered his ears; and thick insulated black gloves, Camron went into his garage and raised the door.

The sun was shining brightly. Indeed, the sun's reflection from the snow was nearly blinding. So much so that Camron immediately went back into the house to retrieve sunglasses with gold rims shaped like those made famous by Malcolm X, a final touch to his mismatched ensemble. Fashion displays, however, were a minor concern when it came to shoveling snow. Especially when it was only eighteen degrees outside, which it was on this day, despite the beautiful, bright sun.

Returning to the garage, Camron reached for the shovel—with its long, tan, wood handle and wide, black, hard plastic face—and began the arduous task of clearing the millions of snowflakes that covered his driveway. The scraping of the shovel against the driveway's black asphalt and packed snow from previous snowfalls cut through the silence of the late morning.

Starting at the driveway's center and working his way down its length, Camron pushed the shovel with long, angled strokes, forcing the snow to one side. Upon nearing the end, he came back to where he started, and repeated the process on the other side of the drive. He then trimmed the drive's edges by lofting the snow in short strokes into his yard, where it would remain until it melted completely in early spring. He shoveled his walkway and front stoop, then removed the snow at the end of his drive, which had been left dense and packed by plow trucks.

Every winter Camron would swear he was going to buy a snowblower. But he would procrastinate between snowfalls until late March. By then the first signs of spring would appear, and his intended purchase would be forgot.

In reality, Camron didn't terribly mind digging snow from the fifty-foot length of his driveway. Especially when it was fluffy and light, as it was now. He found it to be good exercise. And on nights and days when the temperature would drop into the low single digits, or even below zero—and the wind would howl—manual snow removal became his most intimate contact with the more treacherous face of Minnesota winter: a test of his fortitude against raw brutal cold, all within a few feet of the seventy-plus degree warmth of his house.

Completing the shoveling job twenty-five minutes after he started, Camron knocked the snow from his boots at the garage step and untied them. Walking inside, he kicked them off onto a dark blue door mat. He took off his gloves, headband, and scarf, and threw them on the top shelf of the entryway closet. He peeled off his coat, then slung it over the post at the end of the banister. As he went upstairs, he could hear sounds of cascading water, which let him know Paris was still in the tub, refreshing her bath with hot water.

"Finished," he announced. "Hope you haven't used up all the hot water."

"No. I don't think I have. Guess you'll find out for sure when you get in the shower," Paris said as Camron peered through the door separating the bedroom from the bathroom.

The only lighting in the bathroom, beyond what was filtering from the bedroom, were soft, orange-yellow glows emanating from six apple-shaped candles clustered at one end of the Jacuzzi.

Paris was reclined in the tub, smothered in bubbles. The only visible parts of her body were her head—which was resting on the inflatable pillow—shoulders, and bent knees poking out of the foam.

"You look comfortable," Camron remarked as he stopped near the edge of the tub and smiled down at her.

"I am. Very," Paris confirmed. "Instead of taking a shower, you should just join me."

It was a nice offer, but Camron had some doubts. "I don't know if the both of us could squeeze in there," he said. "I'll just take a shower."

"Suit yourself."

By the time Camron had got out of the shower and dried his body, Paris was in the bedroom lubricating hers. Noticing she was still naked, he couldn't keep himself from walking into the bedroom for a better view.

He wrapped a towel around his waist and moved in her direction. Even though they had made ferocious love just hours ago, he would have been self-conscious without the towel around him. Not because of any concerns about his body. On the contrary: his physique was sculpted quite nicely for a man soon to be thirty-seven. Pushups, sit-ups, and some free weights he kept in his basement had aided him in staying trim and muscled. But there was a part of him that was a little self-effacing, one of a number of traits he acquired from his mother.

Paris, on the other hand, seemed oblivious to her own nakedness. Why shouldn't she? Camron thought. Her body was spectacular: beautiful long legs, an athletic but feminine derrière, and breasts that accentuated her womanhood without overpowering it. She was thirty-three years young, but her body seemed younger: the toned figure of a woman who had yet to birth a child.

Camron noticed, too, an interesting grooming touch. She had trimmed and shaved her pubic hairs to the point that all that remained was a tiny rectangle, which looked like a portion of a Hitlerean mustache positioned vertically.

As he moved closer and invaded her space, Paris—busy massaging baby oil into her arms and shoulders—looked away from the TV and at him.

"What?" she asked smiling.

"Nothing," Camron said as he put his arms around her waist. "Just admiring this fine body of yours."

"And when did you come to the conclusion I was fine?"

"Just now."

"Oh, you didn't notice last night?" she asked.

"Yeah I did. Actually, I came to the conclusion that you were fine last night. But seeing you standing here in the light of day with no clothes on, I realized you're *super* fine."

"Super fine? Hadn't heard that term in a while. Well I'm glad you like."

"Mm-hmm. Make a brotha wanted holla," Camron said before burying his head into Paris's neck and teasing it with his tongue and teeth.

Paris put her hands on Camron's shoulders and pushed away weakly. "Okay, come on now, we got to get ready for breakfast. Or brunch I should say 'cause the morning's about over."

"We can have brunch right here in the bedroom," Camron said. "Just let me go downstairs and get some syrup."

"Hey. Don't start nothing you don't want to be responsible for finishing." Paris pushed with a tad more resistance. "Camron. Stop! Come on, honey. Let's get ready to go. I'm hungry."

Camron relented and let Paris put some elbowroom between them. "Okay. Let's get outta here," he said.

He didn't press things any further because he was hungry too. A hunger now accompanied by pangs strong enough to trump his carnal urges.

He smacked Paris's tight butt with the palm of his hand and walked into the closet to find something to wear.

"So as far as food goes, what do you feel like? Breakfast? Lunch?" Camron asked as he steered onto a main artery out of his neighborhood. Since last night's snowfall, the snowplows had already made one or two passes on the roads, so the streets—although wet—were quite navigable.

"Breakfast sounds good," Paris said. "A ham-and-cheese omelet would be delicious right about now."

Camron thought of a place on the south side of St. Paul that, in addition to the ordinary array of omelets, featured mouthwatering Belgian waffles as well. It was also a place he and his ex-wife had once had a brief but memorable spat. But it was beyond Paris's downtown apartment by a few miles, which is where he would be taking her after their meal, and he wasn't interested in driving the additional distance. So he opted for an en route Denny's restaurant instead.

Camron parked in a section of the parking lot that was behind the Denny's and adjacent to a lake. The lake, like all lakes in Minnesota in January, was frozen, covered with ice at least a foot thick. A quarter mile in breadth at its widest point and three-quarters of a mile long, it was littered with people sitting or standing outside tiny shacks. Two four-wheel drive vehicles were also parked on the lake. The people were ice fishing, a popular Minnesota pastime. Having dug holes in the ice with the aid of manual or gasoline-powered augers, they would spend days and sometimes nights collecting as many perch, pike, and walleye as they could. The colorful shacks, which were about the size of outhouses, provided some relief from the cold.

"We should do that sometime," Camron said, jerking his head in the direction of the lake.

Paris looked across the perfectly flat expanse of frozen water. "The only way I'll be out there on that ice with you is in spirit," she said, which made Camron laugh.

They made their way across the snow and ice that covered the parking lot, and toward the front door of the restaurant. Once inside, they requested a booth in the nonsmoking section, and were soon being led to their seats by a tall, brown-skinned sistah with a modest Afro who appeared to be in her early twenties. Something about her aura suggested to Camron that she was African.

"Your waiter will be right with you," she said with a jaunty West African accent, confirming his suspicion. Nigerian perhaps, he thought.

No sooner than they had taken off their coats, and seated themselves on opposite sides of the booth's table, their waiter appeared, a bespectacled young White guy, short and stocky in stature.

"Good morning," he said cheerfully and with a smile. "Would you like something to drink? Coffee? Orange juice?"

"Coffee for me," Paris said. "Extra cream."

"Sure. And for you, sir?"

"Diet Coke," Camron said.

When it came time to order, Paris requested the ham-and-cheese omelet she was craving, and Camron selected a hash consisting of scrambled eggs over diced ham, pieces of bacon and sausage, and fried potato bits, all topped with grated, melted cheese.

Twelve minutes later, as their waiter placed their food on the blue-speckled, pressed-wood top of their booth table, Camron asked Paris, "What time did you say you were going to church tonight?"

"The evening service starts at seven," Paris said before closing her eyes and silently mouthing a prayer to bless her omelet and the side of hash browns that came with it. Camron thought about doing the same thing, but, since they were sitting at the same table, felt sufficiently certain he was covered by Paris's prayer.

"You want some company?" he asked.

An astonished look came over Paris's face. "Sure."

"Okay. I'll pick you up at six-thirty," Camron offered. "Do I need to dress up?"

"No. Not necessarily. A step up from what you have on now maybe," Paris said of his attire: blue jeans and a purple sweatshirt with "VIKINGS" in gold letters emblazoned across the chest.

"I know that," he said. "I was just wondering though, because Black people here dress a lot more casually for church than they do down South. Especially for an evening service."

"People dress up more in Chicago too," Paris said as she picked up a plastic bottle of ketchup, and turned it upside down over her hash browns. When she gave it a first squeeze, the bottle made a gurgling sound and dispensed nothing but air and a spray of ketchup droplets.

"Sound like you last night," Camron said as he spread strawberry jam over his wheat toast.

Paris tilted her eyes up at him and hid her embarrassment behind an amused frown. "You so nasty."

He smiled, then returned to what they had been talking about before the splutter of the ketchup bottle. "I remember the first few times I went to church here, I was amazed by how casually people dressed. 'Cause in North Carolina people always dressed up for church. Whereas brothas here, especially the young people, might show up in a pullover sweater and jeans."

"Yeah, that's true," Paris agreed, then smiled. "Last year I spent Easter weekend back home. Now you talking about some people dressing."

"And I'm sure you were right in the thick of things."

"I was holding my own," Paris said. "No, I was doing more than holding my own. I was looking good that day. I was wearing this porcelain-colored dress with a layer of chiffon, matching shoes, and a pillbox hat."

Camron smiled as he tried to imagine what she might have looked like that day.

"I was styling. I'll show you a picture," she promised.

As Camron digested a mouthful of his food, Paris's comments triggered thoughts from his own, even more distant past that made him chortle.

"What?" Paris asked.

"I was just thinking about some of my Easter outfits. As an adult I've been, for the most part, pretty conservative. But back in the 70s? Now that's another story."

"Let me guess. Platform shoes."

"Oh, most definitely. *Color-coordinated* platform shoes. Me and some of my childhood buddies, we were really into the new Easter outfit thang for a while. Every year we'd try and outdo one another. I remember one Easter—I was eleven or twelve—I broke up in church with a lime-green leisure suit with bell-bottom pants, the big wide tie, the shirt with the giant butterfly collar, *and* the lime-green platforms."

"No you didn't," Paris said.

"Yes I did. And there was no way you could convince me I wasn't the shit. And my Afro was so blown out—you know that blow-out cream they used to have—I could have passed as one of The Jackson Five."

"I'd love to see a picture of that," Paris said, giggling.

"I don't have one. But I'm sure somebody back in my neighborhood does," Camron said.

A few minutes later, they had finished their meal, and Camron was lamenting the quick end of the weekend, when he noticed a couple—a man and a woman—walking toward them, then turn a corner. They were trailing the African hostess as she led them to a seat.

Recognizing the female, Camron's heart skipped a beat, and his body temperature dropped a degree or two as he looked back at Paris. He hoped there were no external hints of his sudden anxiety for her to notice.

"What's wrong?" Paris asked as that hope vanished into the aroma of the food the wait staff was feverishly shuffling to hungry customers.

"Nothing. Just noticed someone I know."

"Who?"

"An old friend," he said with a weak smile.

The African hostess seated the couple along the same windowed wall at which Camron and Paris were sitting, with just one other booth separating them. The woman had a complexion the color of the yellow scrambled eggs Camron had just eaten, a color down South that would have been described as "high yella." She sat opposite her companion, a brown brotha an inch or two taller than Camron. She was facing Camron, making the distance between them nearly three booths in length.

"A woman?" Paris asked.

"Yeah."

"Oh. Someone you used to date?"

"For a minute."

"That short, huh?"

"Almost."

The persona that had jarred Camron was Michele, the woman he had dated just prior to the start of his courtship of Paris. They had dated for a month, and had got sexual three times before an abrupt change of heart caused her to return to her previous boyfriend.

"You should say hello," Paris suggested.

Just moments after those words had come out of Paris's mouth, Michele's wandering eyes landed on Camron. At first her gaze was nothing more than that glance of solidarity Black folk sometimes gave each other when they were surrounded by White people, which—in this now-frozen Midwestern metropolis of 2.4 million inhabitants—was nearly all the time. A look that most often resulted in nothing beyond a friendly, knowing smile and nod: a fleeting acknowledgment of a cultural kinship. But this time it became more than that as Michele recognized Camron almost immediately, grinned broadly, then sent a brisk wave in his direction. Camron responded likewise, although with noticeably less enthusiasm.

"There. Good," Paris said with a bit of curtness. "How long did you two date?"

Camron saw Michele say something in a hurried fashion to her companion as she slid out of her seat, stood, and walked toward him and Paris.

"Not very long," he said as he braced himself.

"Hi, Camron. Long time no see," Michele said as she approached their booth.

Paris, who couldn't see Michele coming, looked left and up in the direction of Michele's high-pitched voice.

"Hey, Michele," Camron replied as he etched a cheesy smile across his face. "Yes, it has been."

"How you doing?"

"Fine. And yourself?"

"Very well, thank you."

Michele looked down at Paris, who was wearing a demure smile.

"Michele, this is my friend Paris," Camron said.

"Hi, Paris. I'm Michele."

"Hi. Nice to meet you," Paris said as if she really meant it.

"You too," Michele said extending her hand. Paris reached out and lightly clasped it. A funny feeling came over Camron as the last two women with whom he had been intimate were now before him, hand-in-hand.

As the ladies released their grasp, Michele returned her attention to Camron. "I was about to go to the restroom when I saw you, and I told Terrence I wanted to say hello." Michelle looked back in the direction of her companion. "Terrence, this is an old friend of mine, Camron."

Camron thought it interesting that Michelle considered him to be an "old friend" as well, even though they had met at The Quest only four months earlier.

Terrence looked over his shoulder, and threw a wave and a smile in their direction.

"And his friend Paris," Michele added.

Paris looked over her shoulder too and exchanged "Hi's" with Terrence before he returned to studying his menu.

"Terrence and I just got engaged a month ago," Michele announced.

"Congratulations," Paris and Camron said at nearly the same time.

"When's the big date?" Paris asked.

"We haven't decided yet," Michele said. "We were thinking maybe sometime this summer, but I don't know if we could pull together a wedding that quickly. So it may not happen until next spring because I couldn't imagine trying to get married here in the winter."

"Right," Paris said.

Fixing her eyes on Camron once again, Michele said, "Well, Mr. Dickerson, you certainly look nice. Keeping yourself in shape I see."

"Thank you," Camron said with a grin. "You're lookin' pretty good yourself."

"I try," Michele said breathily, as if the mere *thought* of the effort necessary to keep her waist trim and butt tight was exhausting. "I was going to ask you guys to join us, but it looks like you're nearly finished."

"Yeah," Camron confirmed. "We're about to get out of here."

"A nice thought though," Paris added.

"Oh well," Michelle said. "Maybe next time."

"Yes, maybe so," Paris said.

Michelle looked back in the direction of her fiancé. The same waiter that had served Paris and Camron was at their table.

"Could you bring me an orange juice?" Michele said to the waiter. He nodded and scampered away. "It was nice seeing you again, Camron. Is your address the same?"

"Yes. Yes it is."

"I'll have to send you an invitation once we get a date. And it was nice meeting you too, ahm—"

Paris helped Michele refresh her short-term memory. "Paris," she said firmly.

"That's right. Paris. I'm sorry," Michele squeaked. "That's such a pretty name."

"Thank you," Paris said.

"Anyway, you guys take care."

"You too," Camron said. "And congratulations again."

"Thank you," Michele said graciously. "See you guys later."

"Bye," Camron said.

Michele turned, walked quickly down one of the aisles of the restaurant, and in the direction of the restrooms. Camron took in a hasty glimpse of her butt as it moved away, swishing from side to side. A picture of her naked in front of his bathroom mirror, with her back toward him while he watched from the softness of his waterbed, inadvertently danced into his head.

Camron blinked the image from his mind. "You ready?" he

asked Paris.

"Yes, if you are," she said.

Camron dropped a twenty-dollar bill on the table, they put on their coats and gloves, and walked back out into the sunny winter day.

21

Stubborn Daze

As THE SECOND YEAR OF MY LIFE as a husband to Mara unfolded, things became increasingly cantankerous. We argued a lot over various things that were usually of little significance.

Looking back on it now, it doesn't seem as if it could have been as bad as it actually was. But time tends to dull one's remembrance of unpleasant things in life. Instead, people seem to remember the good in a greater proportion than which it truly existed. My theory on this method we humans have of filtering, and in some cases altogether eliminating, bad memories from our conscious is that it is our way of protecting our souls from being too burdened, and eventually overcome, by things we'd rather forget. A survival mechanism of sorts.

So while, in retrospect, I can't recollect all of the acrimonious moments between Mara and me, I do know we were at odds quite often. But even to this day—nearly a year after our separation, and nine weeks and three days after our divorce—I don't precisely know why we argued as much as we did.

I do know, however, that we were both stubborn, which enhanced greatly our tendency to disagree, and gave us the ability to pout for days over the most trivial of matters.

For instance, I recall a midspring morning in 1999 when I was about to leave for work. It was raining and Mara had to work later that morning herself. My car was parked in the garage and Mara's was in the driveway. Now, the garage was big enough to hold both vehicles, but it was so cluttered that only one of our cars could be in there at any given time. So who got the space generally depended on who got home first. And, since Mara's job as a flight attendant sometimes kept her out of town one or two nights a week, it was often mine by default.

Anyway, that particular morning my car was in the garage, Mara's was in the driveway, and I was in front of the bathroom mirror putting some finishing touches on my hair. Mara, in bed watching a morning news program, made a suggestion.

"Camron, why don't you drive my car today and I'll drive yours," she said casually.

"Why?" I asked.

"Because I don't want to get my hair wet. You know I just got it fixed yesterday."

"Mara," I said as I patted a few stray hairs on my own head into place, "it's only thirty feet from the front door to your car."

"Do you know how wet my hair can get by the time I get to the car?"

"Well that's what umbrellas are for," I said.

Mara went silent. *Mad that quick*, I thought. But, as I had learned during the first year of our marriage, that was her way. Once she got upset, she'd get quiet, which often meant the discussion was over, leaving me trapped in a talk-to-the-hand scenario.

What was the big deal about walking the few steps to her car? Once she reached her employees parking lot, she'd have to get out into the rain anyway, at which point, of course, she'd hoist her umbrella to protect that just-fixed hair of hers. Besides, she knew I didn't like driving her blue '96 Hyundai Excel. That was a girl's car. I much preferred the brooding, masculine look of my black '98 Dodge Intrepid.

My image in the mirror smirked at me and shook its head. Suddenly, I *wanted* to be at work. I went downstairs and slipped into my steel-toed safety shoes, and pulled my arms into a thin, light brown jacket.

As I was about to start towards the door that led to the garage, a desire to ease that early-morning rift topped my intransigence. I hollered back upstairs. "Mara! I'll drive your car. Where're your keys?"

Her voice came down at me from the bedroom. "That's okay, Camron."

"Mara, gimme the keys," I said, exasperation in my tone.

"Naw just forget it," she insisted.

I kicked off my shoes, walked back upstairs, and into the bedroom. I leaned across the bed until my face hovered over hers, which was intently focused on the news show, then kissed her on the cheek.

"Have a good day," I said.

"You too," she replied dryly.

Had she not been working that day, I probably would have bypassed the kiss, and instead just bid her goodbye from downstairs. But I didn't like us parting on a sour note, however petty, when she had to fly. God forbid that something happen, but, if it did, the memory that our last exchange had been tainted with anger would have been a difficult one for me to live with.

As I made the five-mile drive to work, I wondered why was Mara so stubborn. I wasn't certain. And why was I? To that I did have an answer.

I inherited my stubborn nature from my mother, who, ironically, was also the first victim of it. I say she was the first victim because, in my earliest display of obstinate behavior, I ended up biting her. On the butt. In church on a Sunday. In front of everybody.

I was about five years old at the time. That Sunday after preaching, Sacrament was held, which I liked because I relished drinking the thimbleful of Welch's grape juice and eating the miniature crackers.

As was the custom at our Methodist church, the first people to go to the altar were the elderly, then the middle-aged, followed by the mature adults, young adults, and so on, down to the children big enough to kneel at the altar and still reach the juice and crackers. The juice and crackers, of course, represented the blood and bones of Jesus Christ, but to us kids, they were just that—juice and crackers, an early afternoon snack on church time.

As the moment approached for my mother to go to the altar with her group, the mature adults, I became increasingly anxious. It was an anxiety not much different from that of a starving airline passenger watching the peanut-and-pop cart, rows away, slowly make its way down the aisle towards them. But such anxiety in the body of a boy was bewildering and significantly more difficult to temper. So I was becoming more and more fidgety with each passing minute, and increasingly eager to fill my mouth with as much of the juice and crackers as I could get my little hands on. However, I was painfully shy and didn't want to go up to the altar with the other children, but in the easing presence of my mother.

"Momma, I wanna go wit' you," I told her as the middle-aged people ambled to the altar.

"No, baby, you wait here while I go up. Then you can go up wit' the chi'ren," she said gently.

"Nooo," I moaned. "Momma, pleeease."

I was petrified by the thought of having to go to the altar with my peers. Even so, I wanted my fair share of the juice and crackers.

When it came time for my mother to go up, she offered me a bribe to keep me in my seat and in line for the few minutes she would be gone: "Wait here and I'll give you a peppa'mint when I get back."

But as she started to the front of the church, my stubbornness took over, and I followed her. She was nearly at the altar before she realized I was behind her. Turning and giving me a look that let me know she was more than just a little irritated with me, she put her hands under my shoulders, lifted me and my tiny blue suit from the floor, and sat me at one end of a front pew.

"Listen. Don't chu cut the monkey up in here with me ta-day," my mother whispered sternly. "Now you sit yo' behind down right here and wait till I get back."

A female usher policing the adjacent aisle and wearing a white dress, white shoes, white stockings, and white gloves, moved closer to me and gently touched my shoulder, alerting me to her presence. So, as my mother leaned at the altar, I sat there, becoming more and more upset.

My displeasure quickly turned to a burning anger, and tears began to well in my eyes. With her back to me, all I could see of my mother was her big butt poking out from the altar. And since that was what I could see of her, that became the focus of my rage. In the blink of an eye, I had convinced myself it wasn't my mother, but her butt that had denied me the opportunity to imbibe (free from the abashed fear I would experience if I were to go up with my peers) in the Welch's grape juice and miniature crackers.

My tears obscured my vision, causing the butt to go in and out of focus. I could see it well enough, though, up there enjoying delicious refreshments in which I felt I should have been partaking. Incensed, I could no longer take it.

I jumped from the pew, open-mouthed and wailing, and charged the butt like a child gone mad. As I ran towards it, the butt got closer and closer until it consumed my entire field of vision. Before I knew it, I had come to an instant stop, my momentum halted by the butt itself. I buried my face into its expansive softness, bit down as hard as I could, and locked my jaws in place. The clinch, however, was short-lived as the usher, who supposedly had been guarding me, rushed to my mother's aid and pulled me away.

I was hysterical—screaming, kicking, and hollering, with tears covering my distorted, ugly face, and slobber stringing from my mouth to the floor. My mother, embarrassed, rose to her feet and escorted me back to our seat. I don't know if she got to taste the juice and crackers, but I did know, as I began to calm down and come to my senses, that I was in trouble.

Later, as we walked out of church and people queried my mother as to what was the matter with me, she handled herself with her usual aplomb, preserving her own public persona as a kind and easy spirit. Which she was, but of course I had crossed the line big time by biting her behind. So I knew I was in for a whipping. But as we drove home, my mother chastised me only a little, then seemed to forget the entire incident. That is, until we got to the house.

No sooner than we had walked through the front door, she gave me an order: "Go get me a switch. And don't come back here with no li'l one either, 'cause you don't want me to have to go get it."

I had just begun to relax, so her directive shocked me. But I had no choice other than to obey and walk into the sparse woods behind our house, where I found a thin limb from a sapling that I thought would be suitable. I carried it back to my mother, stripping the leaves as I returned. Dissatisfied with my selection, my mother took it from me and whacked me with it one time across my back.

"I said don't come back here with no li'l switch. Now go get another one!" she barked.

I returned to the woods, and, as I walked back to the house after harvesting a thicker limb, I felt like a death row inmate marching to the electric chair who had been ordered to pull the switch himself. Which may have been preferable to the beating I got, one that easily went into my personal Top Three Whippings of All Time.

My stubborn side revealed itself to me in dramatic fashion that day, and has been with me ever since. Often it has served me well, not allowing me to give up at different points in my life when giving up was an attractive option. But, since *both* Mara and I were stubborn (she perhaps more than me!), in our marriage, stubbornness was a liability.

Lying here now on this couch, I'm remembering so many silly little things over which we butted heads. Whether it involved shopping at the mall (me wanting to leave, Mara wanting to shop some

more); music in the car or at home (my tastes leaned towards a peculiar mix of hip-hop and public radio, Mara's more in the direction of
jazz fusion); church ("Are you coming with me to church?" Mara
would ask on a glorious Sunday morning. My frequent reply at such
times: "Naw. The Vikings play at noon."); control of the TV remote;
housework (neither of us were premier housekeepers, so the house
was often a mess, and whose turn it was to do dishes, launder, vac-
uum, et cetera, were constant points of contention); or money, it
seems we always found something over which to disagree.

One Sunday afternoon, one on which Mara and I *had* attended
church together, she told me of plans she'd made for us to visit
Patrice and Donnell (and their year-old baby boy).

"I talked to Patrice yesterday," she said, "and she asked me if
we'd like to have dinner with them today. I told her 'Sure.' "

We were upstairs, changing out of our church clothes and into
something more comfortable.

"Well thanks for telling me," I said sarcastically as I slipped out
of my pants.

"You got plans?"

"Sort of. I was gonna go down to Arnellia's and watch the
Lakers game, then come home and relax."

Arnellia's—people pronounced it as if there was no "i"—was a
Black-owned St. Paul bar-slash-nightclub with a '70s decorum (other
than the 52" color television in one corner) and atmosphere.

"You can watch the game with Donnell at their house," Mara
suggested as she pulled the straps of the mauve dress she was wearing from her shoulders. She let it fall to her waist, then stepped out of
it, leaving her with nothing on but control top, sheer, black pantyhose and a black bra. Seeing the strain her voluptuous thighs and
booty were putting on the hosiery suddenly put a hanker in me for
some after-church sex. But it appeared I would have to defend my
afternoon intentions instead.

"Mara, listen, I don't feel like being sociable today. And don't
you think it would have been a little more considerate if you had
asked me before making plans on my behalf?"

"Camron, I didn't see where it would be that big of a deal. We
would just be over there for a couple of hours."

"Yeah right. You mean four or five hours. We ain't never been
over to Patrice and Donnell's for less than that."

"She's gonna be cooking. Aren't you hungry?"

"I was gonna get some chicken wings at Arnellia's. Patrice can't cook no way."

"Patrice can cook fine," Mara said, then abruptly changed the spin on her objection. "So you were just going to go to Arnellia's and leave me here?"

"You're welcome to come. But you know ain't nobody there on a Sunday afternoon but mostly men."

"Oh, so you don't want me to come with you then."

"Mara, what I just say? You can come if you want to," I said with a chuckle, a subconscious reaction meant to ease the rising discord.

"I see what this is all about," Mara declared. "Patrice and Donnell don't have anything to do with it. You just don't want to spend time with me this afternoon. Is that it, Camron?"

All I could do was shake my head at the incredible talent Mara had for turning my words against me. Although in this instance, maybe she was right. Maybe I *didn't* want to spend the afternoon with her. But what was wrong with having a little space sometimes?

"Well go watch yo' game and get yo' chicken wings then," Mara said. "But I'm going over to Patrice's 'cause I told her I was coming."

"Fine," I said with a shrug of my shoulders.

"And what do you want me to tell Donnell?" she asked. "That his company wasn't good enough for you this afternoon as well?"

"Just tell him I already had plans to meet some co-workers to watch the game."

"So it's not okay for me to make plans on your behalf, but it is okay for me to lie on your behalf," Mara said.

I didn't say anything to that. Didn't know what to say to settle the frivolous conflict we were having. Not that anything I could have said at that point would have helped anyhow because it seemed the matter was settled. She was going to Patrice's and I was going to Arnellia's. Case closed.

As I dressed, I watched Mara sashay and twist in a near-naked state from the bedroom to the bathroom to the closet to the bedroom again, and was beginning to find myself more and more in the mood for sex play. We had made love right after church before, and I had found there to be something erotically sinful about sitting prim and proper in a pew one minute, then screwing with abandon a fraction of an hour later. But at that moment I had the feeling Mara wouldn't be open to any sexual advances on my part. Maybe that night after we both got back home I could get a little taste, I thought. I felt my Johnson jerk inside my drawers in protest of my decision to defer any overtures. I ignored his complaint, finished dressing, and left ahead of Mara for Arnellia's.

Once there I watched the game, laughed at the witty banter and high jinks between some of the brothas, and ate my fill of chicken wings and beer.

I arrived home early that evening, before Mara. I anticipated, when she got back, that she would still be upset at me for not going with her, so—in an effort to abate any residual anger—I parked in the driveway, leaving the garage spot available to her if she wanted it. I also took advantage of the solitude and put on one of her Joe Sample CDs. Thirty minutes later, she walked in through the garage door.

"How was dinner?" I asked from my outstretched position here on the couch.

"Fine," she said as she hung her coat in the foyer closet. "You missed a good meal."

"What'd you do besides dinner?"

"Just talked. Had a bottle of wine. They wanted to play Spades," Mara said, then added as a not-so-subtle reminder of my absence, "but, of course, you can't play Spades with three people."

Mara walked upstairs without asking me how my afternoon went, further indication that she was still peeved. The sound of heavy running water rushed from the bathroom; she was filling the Jacuzzi. A few minutes later, the bathroom and bedroom doors slammed shut. She had retreated to her corner of the house, and I was comfortable in mine. Things would be better between us, I thought, after some make-up sex later that night. With two different remotes, I turned off the CD player and turned on the television, but soon fell asleep.

I was awakened by Mara's voice. "Camron, you want some tea?"

"Huh?" I said as I returned to consciousness. My eyes darted about the room as I regained my bearings. *How long have I been dozing?* I wondered.

Mara repeated her query. "You want some tea?"

I was still on the couch, lying on my stomach with my head facing the television, which was on but not being watched. I tilted my eyes upward in the direction of my forehead, and Mara came into view. She was standing, sideways it seemed, at the entrance to the kitchen.

"No, no, thanks," I said groggily. "What time is it?"

"Nine-ten."

I had been asleep for over an hour.

I heard the beeps of the microwave as Mara set the timer to warm a cup of water for her tea, then the hum of its bowels after she pressed the start button.

At least she had been courteous enough to ask me if I wanted some tea too, and in a tone that was fairly more cordial than it had been since right after church. Maybe she was through sulking for the evening. I decided I would take advantage of the thaw and try to converse, maybe squeeze in an apology of some kind. But what was that she was wearing? I hoped it wasn't what I thought it was.

When she walked out of the kitchen and towards the stairs, hot tea in hand, I saw that she was wearing precisely what I didn't want to see: that ugly, pink, cotton pajama set of hers. It was a sweatsuit really. The outfit she would wear to bed when she wanted to send a clear signal that sex was out of the picture for that night: her ain't-gonna-gi'-you-none pajamas.

Despite the mental body blow the sight of those things delivered, I went with my initial impulse and initiated an exchange.

"Mara, can I talk to you?" I asked just as her foot touched the first step of the stairway. Perhaps I could eventually talk her out of that scraggily outfit. What was the lyric from that old-school funk song, "Snap Shot," by Slave? *The upper persuasion for the lower invasion.*

She shuffled towards the couch in her big bunny slippers, but sat on the love seat some six feet away from me.

"Are you still mad about this afternoon?" I asked as I spun slowly from a reclined to a sitting position.

"No, Camron, I'm not mad. I just thought it would have been nice to have gone over to Patrice and Donnell's together. You know? And just have a relaxing, fun, Sunday afternoon with friends."

"So you don't think I should have gone to Arnellia's?"

"That's what you wanted to do, so you did it. No biggie. But I think you would have had just as much fun over there. Donnell had the game on most of the time anyway."

"Well, the next time you want to go, I'll go. But do me one favor. Let me know a day or two ahead of time so I won't have my mind set on doing something else. Okay?"

"I will do that," Mara said.

"Good."

I paused, half-expecting her to say something more. But she didn't, which made way for an awkward silence to creep in between us.

Another moment or two passed before I said, "What are you doing upstairs?" It was just a filler question because I knew what she was doing.

"Reading," she said, which was as I suspected.

The phone rang, piercing the stale air that had engulfed the room.

"That's probably Cindy," Mara said in reference to her co-worker and friend.

Mara returned to the kitchen, moving gingerly so as not to spill her tea. She lifted the light tan phone—one of three that was in the house, this one cordless—from its wall base.

"Hello," she said. "Hey, Cindy! How you do-in', girl?"

She turned, walked up the steps, and back into the bedroom, chatting happily as she went. It was interesting to watch her go from sulky to cheerful in the blink of an eye. Observing her transition left me musing as to why I was getting that kind of positive energy from her less and less.

Mara was on the phone with Cindy for almost thirty minutes, then called Patrice and talked twenty more, laughing and giggling to the point that she didn't even seem like the same person in whose presence I had been for much of that day.

When I turned off the television and finally went upstairs around 10:30, Mara was on the bed reading by the faint light from the headboard. Three fluffy pillows were behind her back.

I went into the bathroom to relieve my bladder, closing the door to the bedroom only halfway. "How's Cindy?" I asked as water left my body and fell noisily into the commode.

"She's fine," Mara said with a yawn. "She's got an early morning flight to Seattle tomorrow."

"You don't work tomorrow, do you?"

"No. I have an overnighter to Miami on Tuesday, then nothing till the weekend."

I was curious as to whether or not her weekend work included overnight duty as well. If so, that might be a nice opportunity to hit a club. Since we'd been married, I could count on one hand the number of times I had been to a nightclub without Mara. But there was a restlessness stirring deep within me: a slow, swirling, miniature windstorm in the pit of my stomach. It was something that, at the time, I couldn't explain. But almost instinctively, I knew a flirtatious conversation and a dance or two with a pretty lady would calm me, put me in a more natural biorhythm.

I moved a few steps from the toilet and turned on the shower. I stripped off my clothes, and tossed them over the front edge of the Jacuzzi tub, which I noticed Mara hadn't yet bothered to clean. After bathing and meditating under the warm spray of water for a while, I felt fresh, relaxed, and ready for some sex.

I dried myself, then strolled into the bedroom with nothing but a towel wrapped around my waist and a bottle of baby oil in one hand. Once I got to my side of the bed, I contemplated turning on the TV. But Mara was still intently reading, and I didn't want to risk intruding upon her concentration. So instead I dispensed some of the baby oil into my hand and began spreading it over my arms, chest, and legs. My movements loosened the towel, and it fell from my waist to the carpet. I didn't bother reaching for it, though, but continued smoothing the oil over the rest of my naked body. Afterwards, I walked into the closet, and found and donned a clean pair of black athletic briefs. Returning to my side of the bed, I pulled back the sheet and comforter, and climbed in under them.

"You can turn the light out," Mara said as I pulled the covers up to my neck.

Good, I thought. Now maybe we could get physical, something I had been wanting to do since we'd gotten back from church. But even before I had turned the light switch—a tiny gold knob deep inside the headboard on my side of the bed—and enveloped the room in darkness, Mara had rolled onto her side, leaving her back to me. Undaunted, I slid close to her and put my hand on her waist. Blood rushed to my manhood and it began to swell in anticipation. I moved even closer until the front of my pelvis was snug against her bottom. I put my hand under her pajama top and touched the hot, naked skin of her stomach.

"I 'on't feel like it tonight, Camron," Mara said abruptly, bluntly.

I held my breath for a second to counter my disappointment. I wasn't totally surprised by her rebuff, especially given what she was wearing. But we hadn't made love all weekend, plus a couple of days preceding, so I was kind of hoping for some physical intimacy before the new week began.

Unaware of the rejection, my Johnson continued to grow, forcing my briefs to make more room to accommodate him. Poor ignorant fellow. He didn't have the brains to know there would be no haps that night.

My disappointment transformed into a soft anger; I moved away from my wife and rolled onto my stomach. And as laid there, with a hard dick but nothing to do with it, the thought of going out the coming weekend seemed even more attractive.

22

Corporate Blues

THE FRIDAY LUNCH CROWD AT ROSETTA'S, a downtown St. Paul cafeteria that specialized in Italian food, was near capacity.

"So it's official, huh?" Camron asked JaLisa as he, she, and Renee sat down at their table.

"Yes it is," JaLisa proclaimed. "As of the end of the day on February 28, 2001, I will no longer be an employee of the Bidell Corporation."

"Hallelujah!" Renee cried. "I wish I could join you."

Many times during their monthly gatherings, JaLisa had expressed dissatisfaction with how her career was progressing. And now, after a twenty-year stint with Bidell, she was resigning. That she had finally decided to leave her job, and the benefits that came with it, stunned Camron more so than Renee.

"That's great. That really is great," Camron said with an admiring smile on his face. "But what are you gonna do now?"

"Relax awhile, then become self-employed," JaLisa said.

"Doing what?" he asked.

"Same thing I'm doing now. IT systems analyst. I'll just add 'consultant' to that title. Or something fancier if I can think of it."

"How about IT Consultant Specialist?" Renee offered. She set her garden salad to one side and prepared to attack her linguini.

"Sounds a little redundant to me," Camron said.

"Or IT Consultant Extraordinaire," JaLisa suggested.

"Well, information technology is a hot field right now, so whatever you put on your card, you should be cool," said Camron.

"I think so," JaLisa agreed.

"I'll be taking a Java class soon myself," Camron said.

"That's right. I remember you mentioning that," JaLisa recalled. "When do you take that?"

"It starts in April. The class will meet all day on Saturdays for six weeks."

"Six Saturdays in a row?" Renee huffed. "Humph. I don't know if I could do that. Give up six of my Saturdays? No way."

Camron, paying no attention to Renee's comment, asked JaLisa, "So how did your boss react when you gave him your resignation?"

"He was scared," Renee interjected.

"Scared? Why was he scared?" Camron asked.

"Scared JaLisa was going to sue Bidell for racial discrimination."

"What is Renee talking about?" Camron queried.

JaLisa explained. "Okay. This is how it went down. I called my boss this past Tuesday morning and told him I needed to talk with him as soon as possible. I think he kind of sensed it was something heavy, so he suggested we meet in his office after lunch. And of course I already had my resignation letter typed out and everything.

"So I get to his office and I say, 'Bill, I've enjoyed my tenure here at Bidell, but I would be lying if I said I haven't had some disappointments, the most recent of which you're well aware of.' "

"Now you're talking about the promotion the White girl got, right?" Camron asked.

"Yes. Marjorie," JaLisa reminded him.

"You mean Margarine," Renee said. "I call her Margarine 'cause her teeth are so yellow."

Camron laughed. "Renee, you silly."

"Well they are," Renee insisted.

JaLisa continued. "And he says, 'If you're referring to Marjorie's promotion, that was a committee decision,' and I say, 'That may well be, but I've been here longer than Marjorie, I've worked on a much wider variety of projects than Marjorie—' "

"And what did he say to that?" Camron asked.

JaLisa lowered the tone of her voice to emulate a man's. " 'Well ahm … JaLisa, that position was about more than experience and projects. A very strong set of soft skills was necessary as well. And Marjorie was very well regarded in those areas.'

"So I told him, 'Bill, we don't really need to go back over all that because I've voiced my displeasure with that whole incident. The real reason I wanted to meet with you was to tender my resignation.' And when I said that, his mouth just about dropped to the floor."

As they continued to eat their food, JaLisa related the rest of the story.

———————

"JaLisa, don't you think you're overreacting a bit?" Bill asked.

"Bill, it's not just Marjorie's promotion I'm reacting to. In the last three years, two other people have come into this department and were soon promoted to higher positions. And frankly, I felt I was more qualified than either of them. And these were women as well, so the only real difference I could see between us was skin pigmentation."

Bill seemed puzzled. "Skin pigmentation?"

JaLisa made it plain. "They were both White, Bill. Just like Marjorie."

"So you think there's some sort of racial thing at play here?"

"That would be one way to put it."

"If you honestly feel that way, JaLisa, you can always request assistance from Human Resources."

"Bill, I already been there and done that. I had a back-and-forth with HR when one of the other promotions occurred—before you came to this department—and it ended up being a lot of headaches and drama for nothing because nothing ever came of it. So if I were ever to initiate something like that again, it would be external of Bidell."

Bill was quiet, then said, "I see."

He then picked up JaLisa's letter of resignation, and there was an even longer period of silence as he read parts of it again. Afterward, Bill looked up at JaLisa. "So you're sure this is what you want to do?"

"I've given it a lot of thought, and I think this is what would be best for me right now," JaLisa said.

"This is a two-week notice. That might put us in a bit of a bind. Would you be open to working through the end of February?"

"What would be the benefit to me of working two more weeks than I need to?" JaLisa asked. "Other than, of course, two more weeks of pay."

"I'm sure we could come up with something that could make it worth your consideration," Bill said.

"Okay. Let me know what you come up with."

JaLisa stood and was about to walk out of Bill's office, but was stopped by his voice. "Oh, JaLisa."

"Yes?"

"Have you discussed this with anybody else in the group?" he asked.

"No."

"Good, because I think it would be better if we keep things confidential until we come up with some arrangement that would allow you to stay with us through February."

"That's not a problem," JaLisa told him.

"And if there's anything I can do to help with your transition, don't hesitate to let me know."

"I won't. Thank you."

"Now can you believe that?" Renee asked. "JaLisa turns in her resignation, then all of a sudden they need her more than ever."

"So what did he offer you to stay till the end of February?" Camron asked JaLisa.

"Pay through the end of March."

"What! Shit. I ought to turn in *my* resignation," Camron declared. "So you think that subtle threat of legal action scared him?"

"You mean where I told him that if I were to make another complaint it would be external of Bidell?"

"Of course it did," Renee said.

"Probably not," JaLisa countered. " 'Cause Bidell isn't going to be afraid of anything until it's right up in their face. But if it did scare *Bill*, that's good because that'll be helpful when I talk with him next week."

"About what?" Camron asked.

"She's going to talk with him about a contract for her company," Renee said.

"I'm going to ask him what do I need to do to get a contract from Bidell for the company I plan on forming. If he helps me and it results in a business account, I'll let bygones be bygones. Otherwise, I just *might* consider a discrimination lawsuit."

"You're vicious," Camron said.

"That ain't vicious," JaLisa refuted. "What's vicious is bringing these people in with a helluva lot less experience than me, and a helluva lot less know-how than me, grooming them, and sending them on their merry way right up the corporate ladder."

Renee offered an opinion. "You know, it's almost as if there's some kind of secret development and promotional program that some of these White women have been plugged into."

"It's not almost, it is, whether they want to admit it or not," JaLisa assured her. "I mean, think about it. Let's suppose it's 1950 and you a big White man with a company. It's all hunky-dory then 'cause you ain't got to deal with us Negroes, other than to direct us to what office to clean. Then comes 1964 and the Civil Rights Act saying you can't discriminate. You get a *little* nervous, but that specific piece of legislation at that time is just words with no teeth. So you and your good ol' boys are able to continue to hold on to the lion's share of the wealth. Now never mind that some of your best customers are us good ol' loyal Negroes.

"But at the end of the '60s, the government realizes the '64 Civil Rights Act is a joke, and they demand affirmative action, *affirmative* action as far as job hiring goes. So finally we're able to get some decent jobs. Some decent starter jobs anyway. Now in come the '80s and you got Blacks and Asians and Latinos and women all up in the corporate mix. Then you, the boss, figure I got to promote somebody other than the people that look like me, or this is going to start to look funny."

Renee broke in. "And Coca-Cola, Microsoft, and some of those other companies that have recently lost some *huge* racial discrimination lawsuits know just how funny things were looking."

"Right," JaLisa concurred. "But you as the HCIC—"

"HCIC?" Camron said.

"Head Cracker In Charge," JaLisa explained. "You figure, 'I got to promote somebody.' Then it hits you: 'I'll promote my wife. Or my best friend's wife. Or his friend's daughter. Because they're a part of this big group of people that fell under the umbrella of the '64 Civil Rights Act as well. That way we can keep it all in the family.' "

"Girl, you a mess," Camron said, marveling at her analysis.

"But am I right or wrong?" JaLisa asked.

"You right," Camron agreed.

"And that's why Bill was scared," Renee said. "Because he nor nobody else in the upper ranks of Bidell want it to be the next company to face—and most likely lose—some kind of class-action discrimination lawsuit."

"Well, like I said. If they give me a decent contract, they don't have to worry about me starting a lawsuit," JaLisa said.

"So when are you going to start this new company of yours?" Camron asked.

"I don't know. A month or two after I leave Bidell maybe. If I don't get a contract from Bidell right away, I might just go into semiretirement and not do anything for six months. Hell, Jamal is encouraging me to take a *year* off and spend more time with the kids."

JaLisa was referring to her husband of eighteen years and their two children, Imani, eight, and Malika, thirteen.

"Mmm, mm, mm. Girl, what I wouldn't do to have a man like yours," Renee stated. "Now, Camron, that's a real man," she said to him, then turned her eyes back on JaLisa. "If you ever decide to divorce him, please let me know."

"You'll be the first one I call, baby girl," JaLisa promised her. "Anyway, enough about the exciting new life path I'm about to embark upon. What about you, Mr. Dickerson? Heard you got a new love in your life."

"Where'd you hear that from?" Camron asked as he looked at Renee.

"Don't worry about that," JaLisa said. "Now what was her name again?"

"Paris," Renee said.

"That's it," JaLisa said.

"What is the deal with you and her, Camron?" Renee asked. "Last time we got together, y'all had just met. But the way you were talking about her over the phone the other day, sound like it's a love thang already."

"Who said anything about love?" Camron asked.

"You said everything but 'we're in love,' " Renee said. "Talking about how fine she is, how much time y'all have been spending together, and that you might take a trip to the islands."

"Listen," Camron said. "Just because two people spend time with one another, appreciate each other's company, and even consider a li'l winter getaway doesn't mean they're in love."

"True," JaLisa agreed. "But once things like that start happening, you're well on your way to love land."

"If you ask me, I think you need to get back with your wife," Renee said.

Camron was about to take another bite of his lasagna, but felt the need to respond immediately to Renee's suggestion. "Number one, I don't have a wife. That's one of the residual effects of a divorce, in case you didn't know. It leaves you *wifeless*. And number two, nobody did ask you. Okay? Ms. Advice Lady."

"I'm just saying," Renee said. "I think y'all should have stayed together and worked it out. Mara was a sweet girl."

"And she still is a sweet girl, as far as I know, " Camron said. "But sometimes things don't work out."

"True that," JaLisa said. "Marriage can be a challenge even under the best of circumstances."

"You and Jamal have fared pretty well," Renee said. "What's y'all's secret?"

"I don't know if we have a secret. Giving each other space maybe. Knowing when to push, knowing when to pull. Knowing when to do nothing. We've had our issues though."

"But you're still together, even after eighteen years," Renee asserted.

"And we've separated twice during those eighteen years," JaLisa said.

Renee froze. "I didn't know that."

"Because I didn't tell you."

"How long were you separated?" Camron asked.

"Two weeks the first time, two months the second." JaLisa wiped the corners of her mouth with her napkin. "Sustaining a marriage is a job. It takes effort. It truly does. And if it's not working, I wouldn't advise anybody to try and force it. My parents were married for over thirty-five years before divorcing in their sixties."

"Your parents divorced in their sixties?" Camron asked.

"Yes. Now isn't that crazy? Thirty-five years together, then divorcing. But you know what? They probably should have gotten divorced twenty-five years earlier because, after ten years, the marriage was too broke to fix anyway. It seems like such a waste of life. Because my mother could have remarried. My father too. They both could have had another chance at happiness. Instead, they spent twenty-five years making each other miserable."

"But your parents were probably like mine," Camron said. "Had that old-school approach to marriage. That once you got married, that was it; you're together forever, through thick and thin."

"They did," JaLisa confirmed. "But it just got to be too much, even for their old-school mentalities."

"Being together through thick and thin is the way it should be, I think," Renee said. "Once you're married, it *should* be a lifetime commitment."

Camron looked at Renee. "I'll be glad when you get married so I can witness firsthand these extraordinary marriage skills you must have."

"You might get to see 'em sooner than you think. She and Steve got back together," JaLisa said.

"Oh really?" Camron remarked.

Renee smiled. "We have reconciled and are quite happy, thank you."

"It'll be interesting to see how long it lasts this time," Camron said.

"Maybe forever," Renee said, still smiling.

"Good," Camron said, then offered her some advice. "Just keep your heart closer to your chest this time. At least for a while."

"He's right about that, Renee," JaLisa said.

Camron posed a rhetorical question to the ladies. "You know what marriage is?"

"What?" Renee asked.

"I was thinking about this the other day," Camron said. "What marriage is. Or what it is far too often."

"What?" Renee asked again.

"An irrational response to insecurities," Camron said.

"What are you talking about?" Renee asked.

"Just what I said. Marriage is, much too often, an irrational response to insecurities."

"An irrational response ... to insecurities," JaLisa said slowly, regurgitating his words in an effort to better understand what he was trying to say. "In what way?"

Camron explained. "People get insecure about this and that—about getting old, or less attractive, or being alone. Then, all of a sudden, they see marriage as a way to calm these growing self-concerns. And that's not a good basis for a marriage."

"Is that why you and Mara didn't make it?" JaLisa asked. "Because the marriage was based on insecurities?"

"The marriage itself wasn't," Camron said, "but the breakup was."

23

Guilt

"CAMRON, WHAT THE FUCK IS THIS?"

I was reaching into the refrigerator for a jug of cranberry juice when Mara appeared in the doorway of the kitchen and wolfed that question in my direction. Until the moment I heard her voice, I thought she was in the basement sorting clothes for laundering, so her sudden appearance, as well as her demanding timbre, startled me.

In her left hand she was holding up a small, white, square napkin, the kind you find on bar counters in restaurants and nightclubs. Something was scribbled across it in blue ink.

"What?" I asked, injecting some ignorance into my tone as a shield against whatever charges might be forthcoming.

"This note I found in your pants pocket."

"I don't know. Let me see it."

"No, I'll read it to you. 'Evelyn, 7-7-7-93-24.' "

"You found that in *my* pants pocket?"

"Yes I did."

"If that's where it was, I don't know how it would have gotten there."

"Maybe we should call Evelyn and see if she can shed some light on how her number got in your pants."

"Which pants?"

"Those grayish blue pants of yours that were laying across the bed in the guest bedroom."

"Why were you in my pants pockets?" I asked.

"Because I'm doing laundry."

"Those pants are dry clean only."

"I know that," Mara said. "That's why I was about to put 'em in the dry-clean bag. But even the dry cleaner appreciates empty pockets."

I couldn't argue with that.

Mara asked, "Weren't those the pants you were wearing when you were hanging out the other night?"

"Yeah. I believe so."

"So you're collecting numbers when you go out now?"

"Mara, don't be silly. If you found a napkin with a number on it in my pocket—"

"Not *if*, Camron. I *did* find a napkin with a woman's name *and* number on it in your pocket."

"What I was about to say was, it could have gotten there any number of ways."

"Such as?" Mara wanted to know.

"I might pick up a napkin to wipe my face or whatever, and maybe somebody already done wrote something on it. You know?"

That explanation sounded weak *to me* even before I had gotten all the words out of my mouth, so I knew Mara wasn't buying it.

She looked at me with fiery eyes. "Is the word stupid written across my forehead this morning, Camron?"

She then turned in a huff and walked back downstairs to the basement.

I had been busted, and as I stood there getting chilled by the cool air from the open refrigerator, I contemplated what to do next.

Damn. I should have flushed that number down the toilet before I left the club. It wasn't like I was going to use it anyway, even if it was genuine, because to me those digits were nothing more than a token prize: an ego-pleasing reward in the coy game men and women play when circumstances ignite an attraction.

I had met the supposed owner of that number about thirty-four hours earlier at a nightclub on the west side of the Cities called Sharks. She was walking towards the ladies' room, and I had just walked out of the men's. A recent inattentiveness by Mara, when it came to all things intimate, had put me in the mood to flirt, and Evelyn's radiant, dark brown skin and shapely figure were the ideal catalysts for my inclinations.

I stopped in my tracks and smiled directly at her. She smiled back.

"Hi," I said.

"Hi." Her tone was lively.

"Can I do something for you?" I inquired.

"Can you do something for me?" Evelyn said, mildly bemused. "I don't know. Can you?"

"I could hold the bathroom door open, or buy you a drink, or take you out on the dance floor and twirl you around."

A big grin spread over her face. "A drink or a twirl are possibilities. I think I can handle the bathroom door myself though."

"Okay. Let's talk about it after you come out."

"Let's do," she said.

She disappeared into the ladies' room and I stood nearby, vibing off the music and the buzz of the crowd. I started to step to the closest bar—which was within eyesight of the entrance to the short hall that led to the ladies' restroom—get another MGD, and wait for her there. However, I decided to stay put. That way I wouldn't run the risk of losing her attention to some other knucklehead that might attack between the restroom entrance and the bar.

A few minutes later she came out of the ladies' room. As she walked towards me in the tight, shiny, red pants and black, midriff-baring top she was wearing, I was glad I had waited because she was definitely fine.

"So what should we start with?" I asked her. "A drink or a dance?"

"A drink."

I took her hand in mine and we fought our way through the shifting crowd to the bar counter, where I ordered a beer for me, a Tanqueray and Seven for her. She had an easy, inviting smile, and was as much in the mood for flirting as I was, both perfect salves for my ailing machismo. We danced to four songs, flirted some more, and shared another drink. I suggested she give me her phone number. It was more out of habit than anything else: the Pavlovian reaction of a sexually frustrated male to a lovely, receptive female. Evelyn quickly wrote her digits on the napkin that would eventually find its way into my wife's possession. Soon after, I wished her a good evening, kissed her on the cheek, and left.

On the way to my car, I reached in my pocket, found my wedding band, and slipped it back on my finger. I knew that, other than by chance, Evelyn and I would never talk again. But our brief flirtation had been a pleasant diversion. A diversion that helped relieve some tension I didn't even know was so strongly present within me. So as I drove home I was relaxed. As relaxed as if I'd just had sex.

I heard footsteps, softened by the carpeted stairs, coming back up from the basement. I was sitting at the kitchen table by the bay windows, the cranberry juice in a glass before me, but I had yet to take a drink.

Mara again appeared in the kitchen doorway. "You want to talk about this?"

I mustered enough resolve to say, "Yeah."

"So who's Evelyn?" she asked.

No more evading. It was time to come straight.

"Someone I met at a bar."

"What bar?"

"Sharks."

Mara's voice increased a notch in volume and scale. "That ho house! You must be kidding me." She shook her head, looked down at the floor, then back at me with an intense glare. "Is this what you do when I'm out of town, Camron?"

"Mara, I was just being flirtatious."

"Collecting numbers is more than flirtatious, don't you think?"

"No. Because a man taking a woman's number doesn't mean a thing unless he uses it."

"And when were you planning on doing that?"

"Never. Shit, I'd forgot I even had it."

"It slipped your mind that quick? It happened when? Friday? And you forgot all about this skank's phone number already? Yeah right."

There was a pregnant pause as Mara stared at me, and I stared at my glass of juice. Heat was welling in my chest, and I could feel my pulse through a vein in my neck.

"Don't any of these tricks ask you about your wedding band?" Mara asked. "Oh, let me guess. You leave that in the car, right?"

"No," I said. But she was close enough with her guess that I remember at that moment thinking she might want to consider a career as a psychic. The humor of my thought, however, was lost in the midst of the emotional turmoil.

"Well you know what, Camron? You're gonna have to give your behavior some thought."

Mara again fixed her eyes on me. There was still anger in them, but some sadness as well. She turned and went upstairs.

Fifteen minutes later, I was outside washing my car, not because it was in dire need of cleaning, but more so to escape the poignant ire that had swamped the house.

Soon the garage door raised and Mara's car slowly backed out of the enclosure. She brought her car to a stop when it was directly beside mine. She lowered her window, and I walked around the front end of her vehicle from the passenger to the driver's side. However, before I got a chance to reach Mara's door, she said, "I'll be back in a while." Without further elaboration, she rolled out of the drive and sped away.

I eventually left the house too, driving about aimlessly before deciding upon the Mall of America, the largest mall in the country, as a destination. My motive wasn't to shop, but to think. For some reason, I always mulled best in the company of disinterested, disconnected strangers.

I found myself in one of the food courts, which reminded me I was getting hungry. I bought a *stromboli* and sat overlooking the huge, silly little theme park that engulfed the entire center of the shopping complex.

What should I have said to Mara? That I was sorry? That would have been a good start. But should I also have told her how frustrated I was becoming that our marriage wasn't what it used to be? That I longed for the sweet, vibrant woman I had wed? That our sex life, once full of vigor and passion, had become tepid and limp? That we were no longer nurturing the relationship or ourselves?

When I got home, Mara was still gone. I walked inside the empty house, and was amazed by how exhilarating I found the quiet and solitude to be. For the first time since we had met, an image of my home without Mara flashed through my head. My brazenness in entertaining such a thought made me feel guilty. More guilty even than when Mara had found the napkin with Evelyn's phone number on it in my pocket.

24

Valentine's

CAMRON LOOKED OUT OF THE LIVING ROOM window of Paris's apartment, down twenty-four stories onto the streets of St. Paul. Miniature cars, buses, and people were moving in straight lines through the gray, wintry, February Friday morning to predetermined destinations they'd most likely rather not be.

Paris's voice wafted from the kitchen. "Honey, you want toast or muffin?"

"Toast," Camron answered.

Paris did not have to report to her nurse's job until midafternoon, and Camron had started his weekend early with a day of vacation, so the pace of the morning was slow and comfortable. Last night he had taken her to dinner at the Rock Brewery Cafe, a restaurant in Minneapolis's little theater district that featured American cuisine and beers made on-site. He had taken her there partly as a way of saying thanks for the unforgettable evening she had given to him the previous week on Valentine's Day.

Valentine's Day was also his birthday. Typically on that day he would have a Sweetheart Dinner, complete with flowers and candy, with whomever his lover happened to be that year, and occasionally would receive a gift as well. But Paris had told him that she wanted to treat him to a special celebration. "Forget that it's Valentine's Day," she had reiterated to him over the phone the day before Valentine's. "Let's just focus on the fact that it's your birthday." Explaining, she said, "You've always had to share your birthday with a holiday."

"Valentine's Day isn't a holiday," Camron had told her.

"No, but it is a big day. And you have to share your birthday with it. It's sort of like having your birthday on Christmas."

"Maybe. But Christmas is a much bigger deal than Valentine's."

"True. But still. Doesn't it kind of make you feel secondary to the day itself?"

"Sometimes," he admitted.

"Now with my birthday, I don't have that problem. Wait. Do you remember when it is?"

"Your birthday? Of course," Camron said.

"When?"

"Listen. I know when your birthday is."

"Well tell me," Paris insisted.

"Is this a test?"

"Yes."

"It's in September, right?"

"No," Paris said.

"Wait, wait. October."

"No, Camron."

"July."

"Keep guessing," she encouraged. "Only nine more to go."

"June 27th."

"Right," Paris said, pleased he had remembered.

"I knew that. I was just playin' with you."

"But see, I don't have to share my birthday with any other occasion because there's nothing special about June 27th."

"Isn't June Black Music Month?"

"That's a whole month," Paris said. "That doesn't have anything to do with a single day. You silly pumpkin head."

"Pumpkin head? Are you trying to say my head is big?"

"Well you *were* having trouble pulling that T-shirt over your head the other morning."

"That's cold."

Paris laughed before saying, "No, honey, your head is the perfect size. Especially when it's between my legs."

"Girl, you are too bad."

"And you love it when I'm bad too, don't cha'?" she said. "But back to your birthday celebration. All you have to do is be here at my place at six-thirty. Okay?"

"Got it," Camron said.

"Now don't get colored on me and get here at six-forty-five. Six-thirty and not a minute later. As a matter of fact, let's make it six-fifteen."

"Okay, okay. I'll be there at six-fifteen," he promised.

"And be sure to take the day off."

"My birthday?"

"No. The day after," Paris said. "You won't have the strength to work anyway."

"Is that right?"

"That's right, sir."

"Sounds good to me," Camron said. "I'll see you tomorrow then."

"Okay."

"Hey. How should I dress?" he asked.

"Nicely."

When Camron arrived at Paris's apartment the next evening at 6:23, she opened the door wearing a red dress with spaghetti straps, shear black hose, and black, shiny, high-heeled pumps. She ran her right arm up the side of the door, let her fingers curl over the top of it, and struck a dainty pose.

"Hi, birthday boy," she purred.

Paris's tall frame and sexy legs made him want to ravage her right there.

"Mmm. You look delicious," Camron said as he came closer for a kiss while keeping one hand behind his back. He wanted her lips, but, to avoid spoiling her auburn lipstick, Paris turned her head and gave him her cheek instead.

"So do you," she told him. Underneath his soft, flowing, black trench he was dressed in an athletic-cut, dark blue suit; light brown shirt; and a silk tie with a repeating watercolor pattern of blues and purples, and winding slivers of white. And the black wide-toed dress shoes he was sporting had a shine that would make his daddy proud.

"What you got behind your back?" Paris asked.

Camron brought his right arm around to reveal a dozen red roses and a big heart-shaped box of chocolates. "Sweets for my sweetie."

"Camron. I told you today is not Valentine's Day, it's your birthday." Paris took the flowers and candy into her hands. "Thank you though." With the fear of damage to her lipstick melted by the gifts, Paris gave him a light lip-smack on his mouth.

Camron smiled at her appreciation, which suddenly changed.

"And you're late too," Paris said as she walked to the dining room table, where she laid the candy and flowers.

"I'm not late," Camron said, then looked at his wristwatch, which, even after subtraction, confirmed that he was. "Ten minutes late. What's ten minutes?"

"One minute more than nine," Paris said. "I'm glad I told you to be here by six-fifteen, 'cause if I had said six-thirty you would have gotten here at six-forty-five, and that's the exact time we have to be in the lobby."

Paris opened a cabinet under the kitchen sink, pulled out a glass vase, and began filling it with water.

"In the lobby?" Camron said as he walked to the dining room table and sat down. "What's happening in the lobby?"

"You'll see," Paris said.

"Are we riding with someone else?"

"You can say that."

Paris put the flowers in the vase and distributed them evenly. She slid the vase of roses to the center of the table, placed the large cellophane-wrapped box of candy beside it, and briefly admired her arrangement skills.

Pleased, she said, "There. Let me get my coat and we'll be ready to go."

Paris went into the bedroom and donned a jacket that matched the color of her dress. She then went to the closet by her front door, reached in, and pulled out a black, full-length wool coat. Camron joined her there and helped her into it. They then proceeded to the elevator and down to the lobby.

"So where are we going?" Camron asked as they stepped out of the elevator.

"The Dakota Bar and Grill."

The Dakota Bar and Grill was a restaurant in St. Paul that offered dinner and live jazz. Camron wasn't surprised by her selection because she had commented more than once how much she had enjoyed Jazzmine's, the site of their first date.

"That sounds nice. And who are we riding with?"

"You'll see," she told him again.

As they walked hurriedly to the west entrance of the complex, their shoes clopped noisily across the blue, tan, and white miniature tiles of the lobby floor.

"What time is it?" Paris asked.

"Six-forty," Camron said as he quickened his pace to keep up with her. "We're not late, sweetie, slow down." He reached into his coat pocket, pulled out his black leather gloves, and pulled them onto his hands.

Paris was nervously looking out the windows to the street as she and Camron moved. Then her face relaxed into a smile. "Our ride is here already," she said.

Camron followed her gaze as they walked through the vestibule. At the bottom of the steps was a black limousine.

"Paris, no. This limo?" Camron said.

Paris was beaming. "Yes, this is our ride."

"Sweetie. We could have just as easily driven to the restaurant."

"Now what would have been special about that?" Paris said.

The driver, a middle-aged White male with graying hair peaking from beneath the black cap he was wearing, was behind the wheel reading a newspaper. Upon seeing them approach, he quickly got out and opened the back door. "Good evening, sir, ma'am," he said, touching his thumb and index finger to the brim of his cap.

"Good evening," Paris and Camron said together.

They barely had a chance to notice the six-degree air temperature before they were comfortably situated in the back seat of the warm limousine.

Camron didn't know how to react, other than to smile and shake his head.

Paris was smiling too, which turned into a grin when she realized he could find no words.

"Happy birthday, honey," she said, then wrapped her arms around his neck and gave him a kiss. This time it was a lipstick-be-damned kiss as their lips and tongues melded.

"Dakota Bar and Grill?" the driver asked.

Paris pulled her mouth from Camron's just long enough to say "Yes," and, as they continued their amorous embrace, the driver whisked them away to the north side of town.

Staring out Paris's window and reminiscing of that evening as she prepared breakfast, the same smile Camron had when they first climbed into the limousine was planted on his face.

The limo ride, his first since he and Mara had eloped to Las Vegas three years earlier, wasn't the end of the surprises Paris had up her sleeve that evening. After dinner, the driver dropped them off at a nearby hotel, where she had reserved a room for the night, replete with wine, chocolates, and strawberry-scented candles. They made love to the point of exhaustion before falling asleep in each other's arms. When they awoke the next morning, their grogginess was soon replaced with more friskiness, and their bodies became as one again. Finally leaving the hotel a few minutes after eleven that morning, a cab returned them to Paris's apartment.

Valentine's had been nine days earlier. Now, outside Paris's window, little flakes of snow were beginning to swirl, floating down slowly onto the cars, buses, people, and earth below. The flurry of white particles reminded Camron that spring was still far away. However, a respite from winter's grip was forthcoming, as he and Paris, on their next adventure, would—in a week—be basking in a five-day weekend in Montego Bay.

Leaving the thought of island breezes and the memory of his most wonderful birthday ever by the window, Camron walked into the kitchen.

"Need some help?" he asked Paris, who was busy scrambling eggs.

"No, I got it."

As he watched her dish the eggs from the frying pan onto two plates, he wondered if he'd found love again.

25

Crossroads

WHAT IS THE ANATOMY OF A BREAKUP? If we knew its shape, its form, could we then—upon recognition—avoid it? Remove ourselves from its path the way we might flee a hissing snake, a rabid dog, or the giant, fast-moving funnel of a tornado?

Whatever its form, Mara and I didn't see it coming, and had started down the slippery slope of separation well before either of us had realized it.

Our arguments became more frequent, more extended. And the emotional remnants of yesterday's or last week's or last month's quarrel would linger and, like a sore, fester until they were pricked by fresh altercations.

And none of the arguments was ever really forgotten. They were all stored somewhere in our individual memories, remembered as we wished to remember them, and built upon to the point that, under the pressure of their own weights, they became slow-burning, inextinguishable resentments.

One Saturday, early in the summer of 1999, I was sitting in a restaurant on the south side of St. Paul, waiting on Mara to join me. I was looking forward to the meal because the old family-owned eatery I had chosen offered delectable Belgian waffles. However, I was mad at Mara because she was thirty-five minutes late and counting.

She had left the house early that morning for some training associated with her job.

"When do you finish?" I had asked her as she was preparing to depart. She was standing on her side of the bed making some final adjustments to the tan pants suit she was wearing, and I was on my side, ensconced beneath the covers.

"Eleven," she said.

"You want to meet for lunch?"

"Sure. Where?" she asked as she scampered to the bathroom mirror.

"Ah ... let's see," I said, trying to think of a place. "How about the Copper Dome on Randolph?"

"Okay."

"Eleven-thirty?"

"That should be fine," she told me.

Some four-and-a-half hours later, at seven minutes past noon, an elderly waitress was placing a refill of diet pop on the booth table at which I was seated, and Mara still hadn't arrived. I glanced at my cell phone, which was on the table as well. Its face showed no indication of a call.

Ten minutes earlier, I had called Mara on her cell, but it was, according to the recorded message, turned off. That wasn't unexpected because she normally had it off. A $400-plus cell phone bill she had gotten one month the year before had forced that habit upon her.

As the time approached 12:20, my anger leveled to a simmering boil. I felt disrespected, not only by her lateness, but also by the fact that she hadn't even bothered to call to tell me she *would* be late. Disgusted, I placed my order.

My anger softened when the thought occurred to me that she could have been in a car accident. But it returned with a vengeance when she finally did come prancing to the table at 12:32. At that point, my mood couldn't have been anymore sour than if I had just feasted on a bowl of lemons.

"Sorry I'm late," she said with a sheepish grin as she slipped into the booth, opposite and facing me.

"No you're not," I challenged.

"Why am I not sorry?" she said, with an even wider grin and trying to sound perplexed.

"Because if you were sorry, you would have called me long ago to say so."

"Camron. Are you mad?"

"No, Mara," I said, raising the volume of my voice a bit. "I'm happy. I'm happy as a hot pile a' shit on a snowy day."

"You know what? The sarcasm isn't necessary," Mara said, still grinning, but only a little.

"What's not necessary is you disrespecting me by being this damn late without even calling."

What was left of her grin dissipated into something less than a smile. "If you're gonna be this ugly, maybe I should leave."

"Well if you leave, the atmosphere at this booth won't be any different than it was two minutes ago, or for the last hour for that matter."

"You sure are being stupid," she said, this time with no trace of amusement on her face.

"Stupid? I'm not too stupid to know what time it is."

The insides of her eyebrows curled down. "Fuck you, Camron."

"No, fuck you," I said loud enough that it garnered attention and stares from several nearby tables.

Mara got up and stormed away, her head high and arms straight, just as the old-woman waitress came to the table with my food. The waitress turned her head to witness the last wisps of Mara's presence. She then placed my food on the table.

"Will she be joining you?" she asked.

"No," I said. "She decided she wasn't hungry."

A few of the patrons, all White and mostly middle-aged or older, stopped chewing their food and gave me that uh-oh-there's-a-crazy-nigga-in-the-house look. But their sanctimonious peers didn't bother me. Even if they did, I wasn't going anywhere because my waffle had arrived.

And I definitely wasn't going to go running behind Mara. If anything, she should have been coming back to the table and apologizing to me like she meant it, then sit and bathe quietly in the fumes of my anger because, shit, I wasn't the one who was over an hour late, she was.

When I arrived home forty-five minutes later, Mara was in the living room, talking on the phone with someone (probably Patrice). I went upstairs to the bathroom, made some water, and came back downstairs. Mara was stretched out on the love seat, gabbing away. I spread my body on the couch, pulled myself up to grab the TV remote from the coffee table, then reclined again. I began flipping through channels, to which Mara immediately objected.

"Camron, I'm watching that," she said, interrupting her own conversation.

"How? You're on the phone," I said, intent upon escaping from the Lifetime Channel the television had been tuned to before I had turned it.

I continued channel surfing, searching for nothing. Mara glared at me for a second or two, rolled her eyes, then resumed talking. By the time she hung up the phone ten minutes later, I had yet to find anything interesting to watch.

"Was that really necessary?" Mara asked before she had even placed the phone on the coffee table.

"What?" I asked.

"That little scene in the restaurant."

Oh, that. I thought she was preparing to harp some more about me turning the TV from Lifetime.

I pulled at the lower end of my mustache and, for a few seconds, mulled my response. "Was it necessary? You tell me. If you're asking was it necessary for me to express to you that I was upset that you were over an hour late without calling, then yeah I think that was necessary. I'm sure if the tables were turned, you would have found it completely necessary to do the same."

"I told you I was sorry," she reminded me.

"And I appreciated the apology. But couldn't you have called me and let me know you were gonna be late?"

"The training went longer than I expected, and afterwards me and some of the girls I work with got to talking—"

"And you couldn't stop talking long enough to call and say, 'Camron, I'm talking with my girls so I'm gonna be late,' or 'Camron, I'd much rather be here gabbing with my co-workers than having lunch with you, so go ahead and eat, kiss my ass, and I'll see you later'?"

"Camron, I *wanted* to have lunch with you."

"Well that was an interesting way to show it."

"And that was an interesting way you showed your behind in public by cursing at me."

"If I recall correctly, I think you cussed at me first."

"Whatever, Camron. Let's just forget it."

"See that's the problem right there, Mara. You always want to forget stuff. That's why this relationship is in the shape it's in now."

"And what's wrong with this relationship?"

"Mara, are you serious?"

"I'm very serious. What's wrong with this relationship?"

"Given that you're one half of this marriage, I would think you'd know. But since you're pretending you don't, where should I start?"

"Wherever you like."

"Okay. We can start with the lesson you delivered today at the restaurant: disrespect. I found your lateness to be highly disrespect-ful. Especially when you consider that everybody you ran into to-day—your employer, your co-workers—*got* respect from you. Everybody, that is, except for me."

"Camron, I said I was sorry. What else do you want me to do? Get on the floor and grovel and beg?" Mara asked. "But you know what? Respect goes both ways. I mean, I'm not the one coming home with phone numbers in my pocket."

"Oh Lord, there you go."

"Oh Lord nothing. Is that respectful? A married man collecting phone numbers at a club?

"Well you know what, Mara? If you were handling your wom-anly business around here—"

" 'Womanly business'?"

"That's right. Handling your business in the bedroom. In case you haven't noticed, sex has gotten to be an endangered activity around this house. So if you were doing that, maybe I wouldn't be inclined to put myself in the kind of situation where I'm asking—or a woman is offering—her phone number to me in the first place."

"You're being full a' shit now, Camron, because nobody's forced you to be in a club flirting. You went there of your own accord, and behaved exactly as you wanted to."

Camron shook his head, and, for a moment, couldn't remember precisely what they were arguing about: her disrespecting him or he disrespecting her.

"So disrespect and sex. What else is wrong with our marriage, Camron?"

"Never mind."

"Oh, so now *you* want to drop things. Thought you wanted to talk."

"It doesn't do any good because you're just looking to accuse and attack," I submitted.

"Isn't that what you're doing to me? Accusing and attacking me?"

"I'm not attacking you. I'm just telling you how I feel."

"How *you* feel? I hope my feelings count for something in this relationship too," Mara said.

"Your feelings count just as much as mine."

"That's nice to know."

"And really, to be frank about it, I think I'm very considerate of your feelings," I insisted.

"Maybe. Sometimes. But you can be very selfish too, Camron. You know that?"

I didn't say anything. The conversation had disintegrated into an exchange of charges and countercharges, and had become tiresome to me. So, other than a shake of my head, I said nothing more. Just stared at the TV.

"Do you know that?" Mara repeated.

A few more seconds ticked by. Seeing that I was through with our little tête-à-tête, Mara sighed heavily. "Fine, whatever," she said, then popped up from the small couch and went upstairs to the bedroom. With us both tucked in our familiar corners, leaden air rolled in, and consumed our home like a fog.

There was one other odd thing about that day that stands out in my memory. Despite the discord, that night Mara and I made love. Actually we had sex. Sex stripped of its affectionate content and reduced to nothing more than a physical means to a climax. I think she was guilt-prodded by my comment about her handling her "womanly business." But she was hardly there during its execution. And neither, till near the very end, was I.

The next day I wrote Mara a note.

Dearest Mara,

Just wanted to apologize for anything that happened in the restaurant—or anything that was said in our conversation afterwards—that might have upset you. It's just that I'm a little frustrated right now by how things are going for us. I'm sure it's nothing that we can't get beyond. Just part of the growing pains of marriage I guess.

Love You Always,
Camron

For a couple or so weeks after the restaurant incident, things were better between us. The reason may have been that we were both ready for a break from our intransigent standoffs (and their peripheral effects). Especially me because I truly despised arguments. In fact, I recently came to the conclusion that I am a pacifist when it comes to emotional discord, and now, as a single man once again, I avoid such conflicts as much as possible. However, Mara, at least on the surface, tolerated them better than me. Indeed, sometimes she even seemed to revel in our heated parleys! But, of course, Mara and I, despite that brief respite from our angry discourses, were still the same people, with our same foibled personalities. Consequently, the dynamics of our everyday interactions eventually made way, almost naturally, for a return to the same obstinate behavior patterns.

Seeking diversion from what was quickly becoming a stale marriage, I would still, on occasion, hang out at nightclubs. One such night, later that same summer, I returned home around 2 A.M. to find Mara's car in the garage. She had flown out early the previous morning, and I wasn't expecting her to return until much later that day, so her presence startled me. I lowered the garage door, moved my car over on the driveway, and walked towards the house. As I unlocked the front door, the eight beers I had drank that evening were whirling through my system.

"Hey, hey!" I sing-shouted, announcing my presence as I walked through the door. It was the same empty salutation my father used to use when he'd return home late and inebriated.

The only light in the house was a dim one from the upstairs bedroom. I climbed the steps, and, as I ascended, could see Mara sitting at the foot of the bed, slipping her feet out of the black pumps she was wearing, looking in the direction of the running television. Apparently she hadn't been home too long herself.

"What's up?" I said as I walked into the bathroom. "Didn't think you'd be back till da'mar." My Southern accent was intensified by my drunkenness.

At first Mara said nothing, but after a few heartbeats, and over the sounds of the TV, and me peeing, she said, "I deadheaded on a late flight out of Miami."

Deadheading was commercial aviation jargon for an airline employee who rode a flight as a passenger for positioning purposes, or simply to return home.

"So did you have a good time hanging out?" Mara asked. There was more contempt than sincerity in her voice.

I came out of the bathroom and walked past her. The perfume she was wearing pierced through the haze that enveloped my head. "It was aw'ight," I said.

Mara stood, moved a step or two in the direction of the closet, and pulled the smart jacket of her flight attendant's uniform off her shoulders and down her arms. I reached my side of the bed near the headboard, which put me opposite and diagonal from the bed corner that she was most near.

"How many numbers did you collect?" she asked. That question sounded almost polite in relation to her previous one.

The alcohol was keeping my mood light, so I said, "I 'on't know. I'll count 'em da'mar."

Suddenly something soft but fast-moving struck my head. The whooshing sound of flailing cloth filled my ears, and fabric swaddled about my noggin. A small, hard object slapped against my cheek, causing me to jerk involuntarily. The room went black as whatever had struck my head continued to wrap about it and covered my eyes. I reached up, snatched the material from my head, and flung it on the bed. I looked at it and saw that it was the brass-buttoned jacket Mara had just taken off. Overtaken by rage, she had flung it at me at light speed.

"What the hell wrong wit' chu?" I demanded.

"What the hell is wrong with you, Camron?" Mara spat back. "Hanging out at clubs all the time."

I looked directly at her with as much anger as I could summon from my drugged body. She returned my enraged peer with one of her own that was even more fearsome. The insides of her eyebrows were furrowed deep into the lids of her eyes, while the outsides were raised. It reminded me of the intimidating scowl of the rapper Ice Cube, that—during his musical heyday—I had seen frozen in marketing photos.

It was a look that a nephew of mine had demonstrated mastery of as well many years earlier. He was around five or six when he fell into the habit of serving up that stare if he were more than a little upset about something. And he was so small that an adult—or teenager, as I was at the time—hovering over him could only see the whites of his eyes as he displayed his anger. A couple of times my mother had quickly rid him of the expression with a slap across his face. But he hardly would hesitate to use it again during his next episode of displeasure.

Ironically, it was also a look I had seen my mother give to my father once and, to the best of my recollection, only once. My father had said something with which my mother took issue, and she gave him that look: that silent, angry glare, her mouth protruding and locked shut. At the time, it struck me as too severe a punishment for whatever my father's infraction may have been. It wasn't until much later that I realized that look was not only for his transgression of the moment, but for years of transgressions. For many nights over many years of coming home late, alcohol-tainted blood running through his veins, the smell of perfume in his shirt. It was a look that communicated the heartbreak of living for decades with the knowledge that her husband was the father of two other children that she had no role in bringing into the world. A look that reflected years of disappointment. It was a look of hate. And when I saw it that one time, I thought, *I never want a woman to have to look at me that way.* But there before me was my wife of nearly eighteen months, glaring at me in nearly that same exact fashion.

"Shit, girl, you could have put my eye out," I said, pulling part of the jacket up from the bed by one of its buttons. I then picked up the whole thing and tossed it back in her direction. The jacket landed at her feet.

"Camron, what exactly are you trying to accomplish with all this clubbing? What are you looking for? An affair?"

Funny she should ask because, since our love life had become so drab and listless, I *had* recently been entertaining thoughts of having an affair. And while I had no candidate in mind, I had considered the logistics of it, what lies would have to be told, and the mechanics of concealing them.

"Will you quit being so paranoid. Damn," I said, then complained, "E'r since you found that li'l phone number in my pocket, you been trippin'. Yeah I hang out a li'l bit. But it's better than just sittin' here at the house on a weekend night."

Mara picked her coat up from the floor and tossed it over the wicker trunk. She then walked into the bathroom and slammed the door behind her.

I stripped down to my underwear, spread my clothes neatly on the floor, got in bed, and, sedated by the beers, fell asleep, the image of Mara's scowl still clearly visible to the eyes of my mind.

Nearly two weeks later, I was at work, sitting behind my computer playing a virtual card game. It was 6:40 P.M., over an hour past the regular time I left work. But the workplace at that early evening hour was peaceful and stress-free, which was not the case often enough at home for my tastes. So my overstay on the job had more to do with mental relaxation than some kind of dedication to work or love of occupation. In retrospect, staying late at work simply to avoid, or delay, conflict at home was one of my earliest pacifistic tendencies when it came to domestic discord.

As I was trying to decide how I was going to get the Queen of Clubs beneath the King of Diamonds, the phone rang.

"FPC, Camron Dickerson," I spoke into the receiver. I was expecting to hear Mara at the other end. She was the only one I could imagine calling me at such an hour at work.

"What up, Negro?"

The voice wasn't Mara's.

"What up, P?" I said, smiling at the sound of my best friend's voice. "How'd you know I was here?"

"I called your house, but Mara said you were probably still at work. What the hell you still doing at work? It's time to go home."

"I'm leaving in a few. Just tying up a few loose ends."

"Yeah, I bet you are. Tying up a few loose ends with some secretary."

"Don't I wish. So what's up, man?"

"Nothing. Same old, same old."

"How's your girl?" I asked. "What's her name?"

"Audrey."

"Yeah, Audrey." I was about to call her Big Butt Audrey, which was what P had called her the first few months they had dated. But given that it was August, that would make it six months for them as a couple, so some measure of respect was in order. "Y'all still dating, right?"

"Yeah, we still hanging," P said.

"Damn. That's a rare occurrence for you, P. Dating one female for half-a-year? What's going on, boy? Sounds like it's gettin' serious."

"Well I doubt if we'll make it to three-quarters."

"Why you say that?"

"You know what attracted me to her in the first place, right?" he asked.

"Of course. The same thing that attracts you to every woman you date: that phat ass of hers."

"Right. That's my weakness, what can I say?"

"It's one of mine too," I said. "But you're on a different level than me because with you, the bigger the ass the better."

"Anyway, the fascination I've had with that ass has worn off, and, now that I'm getting to know more about her, I'm discovering we don't have that much in common. As a matter of fact, her ass has more personality than she does."

I laughed. "Well hey, my brotha, hopefully one day you'll find that perfect combination of both personality and ass."

"And if I don't, I'll sure as hell have fun trying," P said, at which we both laughed. "So how are things with you and Mara?" he asked. "Y'all still arguing?"

"Three or four times a week over something," I said. "Last night when she got home from work, she was mad because I hadn't cooked anything to eat. But I'd had two grilled ham-and-cheese sandwiches earlier, so I wasn't hungry. Yet and still, it seemed as if she was expecting me to have a four-course meal hot and ready to go when she walked in the door at eight-thirty last night. I started to tell her, 'You better get on in the kitchen and fix yourself a bowl of cereal.'"

"I know that's right," P said.

"I don't know, man. I been thinking a lot lately about this marriage," I said. "Can I tell you something?"

"You can tell me anything, man."

"Straight up?"

"Straight up," P said.

I took in a deep breath, then heaved it out, leaving my lungs empty. "I don't think I want to be married anymore."

26

Loss

FROM THE VESTIBULE OF PARIS'S COMPLEX, Camron lifted the black phone from its cradle and dialed the three-digit number to her apartment.

"Hello," Paris said with a sniffle. She sounded congested, as if she had a cold.

"It's me," Camron said. His voice was somber and tight.

The door buzzed, he hung up the phone, jerked the door open, and walked inside. He moved quickly to the elevators and pressed the white button with the black "up" arrow stenciled on it. Neither of the two elevator doors opened. Camron moved back a step, threw back the sides of the three-quarter length, black leather jacket he was wearing, and stuffed his hands in the pockets of his blue jeans. He began to tap the heel of his right foot against the burgundy and white floral-patterned carpet, anxiously waiting for one of the elevators to arrive. Five seconds passed, then ten.

Damn it, come on.

He tapped his heel faster, trying in vain to dissipate his impatience. He clenched his jaw, forcing his top and bottom molars to come together tightly. His cheeks flexed in response, reinforcing the look of sternness on his face.

Fifteen seconds. He looked to his left at a glowing red exit sign, and briefly considered taking the stairs. However, with twenty-three floors between him and Paris, that thought was summarily dismissed.

Finally, the doors of one of the elevators parted. Camron took a step toward it, but two people, a man and a woman, walked out. He let them pass, got aboard, and pushed the button labeled with his destination. The doors closed and the big rectangular box of metal sped skyward. Hoping he wouldn't be stopped by someone else seeking to go up—or a playful child—Camron watched the light over the elevator door as it jumped from floor to floor. It didn't stop until it reached "24," a small blessing for which he was grateful.

He scurried through the hallway maze until he arrived at Paris's door, then knocked thrice. The door opened almost immediately.

"Baby, you okay?" Camron asked.

Paris, her eyes reddened and moist with tears, didn't answer, but instead brought her body and soul into his open arms.

"I can't believe this. I can't believe it," she sobbed.

Forty-seven minutes earlier, Paris had called Camron at work, unusual for her.

He'd answered the phone in his customary way: "FPC, Camron Dickerson."

"Camron?" she had said. Her voice contained an urgency and tenor he'd never heard, so for an instant he didn't recognize it.

"Paris?"

"Camron?"

"Yeah it's me, sweetheart. What's wrong?"

"Something terrible has happened," she said.

"What is it?"

"My daddy's dead."

"What! How?"

"This morning. They found him this morning."

"Where?"

"Outside the house. In the snow."

"Oh my God," Camron said. He exhaled hard through his mouth. So hard his cheeks puffed out. "Sweetheart, I'm sorry. Are you okay?"

"I'll be okay. I just ... just need to get home."

"You're at work?"

"Yeah. I'm going to be leaving in a few minutes though."

"Listen. I'll come pick you up," he said.

"No. You don't have to do that. I need to get my car back to my apartment anyway."

"I'll meet you at your place then."

"Honey, I'm okay," Paris insisted.

"No. I'll meet you there," Camron said firmly. "When do you think you'll leave work?"

"I don't know. Sometime in the next ten or fifteen minutes."

"All right. I'll be there at—" Camron looked at a clock on a nearby wall, "Twelve-forty-five."

"Okay," she consented.

Standing now in her apartment, Camron held Paris tight, trying somehow to transfer her pain into his body.

"I'm sorry, baby. I'm so sorry," he said as she cried on his shoulder. Then he was quiet because he didn't know what else to say, and the only sounds were Paris's soft sobs. Time sputtered to a stop as she grieved for her father and Camron grieved for her.

Finally he said, "Let's sit down," and time struggled to start again as they moved from the foyer to the living room couch.

Paris wiped at her cheeks with a balled-up paper towel moistened by tears, and began to take the first few steps toward understanding death by confronting it head-on.

"He was ah ... ," she began haltingly. "He was shoveling snow this morning, and Momma was in the house, when this lady knocked on the door, and told her a man was in the yard lying face down in the snow. It was Daddy. They called an ambulance, and a man who was with the lady turned Daddy over, and they wrapped him in blankets while they waited. They took him to the hospital." Paris stared at the air in her living room. "But he was dead before they got there."

Camron said nothing. Just shook his head as he held Paris's hand tight in his.

The silence was abruptly shattered by the simultaneous ringing of phones, one from the kitchen, another, muffled, from the bedroom.

"You want me to get that?" Camron asked.

"No, that's probably Deanna," she said referring to her sister in Kansas City. "She was the one who called me at work and told me."

Paris walked into the kitchen, her gait labored by the weight of this new, unexpected burden.

Camron heard her say "Hello," then "Hi, Peggy." The name was unfamiliar to him, and as the conversation from Paris's end became stiff and monosyllabic—"Yes," "What time?", "Thank you"—Camron drifted into contemplation of some of the concerns at hand. How would she get to Chicago? It was a six-plus-hour drive or a one-and-a-half-hour plane flight. If she opted to go by car, he would most definitely do the driving. And if he did end up driving her there, how long should he stay? A day? Two days? Should he plan on attending the funeral? The funeral, and everything before and after it, would keep her in Chicago for close to a week or more. Would her absence from work for that long cause any on-the-job problems, rankle any feathers?

Other concerns, also practical but selfish too, entered his head. Their trip to Montego Bay, scheduled to begin in three days, would have to be postponed. And during her absence, he would miss not only her company, but her passionate touch as well.

Camron heard Paris reading off some numbers—"4892 ... 6378.... Okay.... All right.... Call me right back and let me know. I'll be here.... Thank you so much, Peggy. I really appreciate it.... Bye."

When Paris returned to the living room, her disposition seemed no more somber, but certainly no less, than before she had walked into the kitchen. The black cordless phone on which she had just been speaking was in her right hand.

"That was Peggy, a girl who works with me," she said as she sat back down on the couch beside Camron. "She's such a sweetheart. She's calling the airlines to reserve a ticket for me. She's trying to get some special price the airlines give when there's a death in the family. I gave her my credit card number so she could get it."

"That's nice of her," Camron said.

Paris placed the phone on her coffee table, but no sooner than she had done so, it came to life again.

"Hello," she said blankly into the mouthpiece.

This time it *was* Deanna.

"Paris, it's me," Deanna said.

"Hey, sis," Paris said. "You doing all right?"

"Yeah. Just doing what we need to do. What about you? You hanging okay?"

"I'm fine. You talk with Momma?"

"Just got off the phone with her."

"Was Nathan there?" Paris asked.

"Yeah he's there," Deanna said of their brother. "Uncle Jesse and Aunt Liz are too. And so is Aunt Sara."

"Good," Paris said. "What time are y'all getting to Chicago?" By "y'all" she meant Deanna; her husband, Jake; and their daughter, Cicely.

"We're leaving here a little after five and should be in Chicago by six-thirty. What about you?"

"Hopefully I'll get there around that time or earlier. A friend of mine at work is checking on a ticket for me."

"Did you talk to Camron?"

"Yeah. He's here right now."

"Oh good," Deanna said, the relief in her voice apparent. "We'll be here for a while still, so call me back when you find out your itinerary."

"I will."

"And don't worry yourself. Let's just focus on getting home."

"Okay," Paris said.

"Love you, sis."

"Love you too."

Paris again set the phone on the coffee table.

"They'll be getting to Chicago at six-thirty," she said.

"Peggy shouldn't have any problem finding a flight for you," Camron said. "NorWest has quite a few going into Chicago every-day."

"Yeah."

"Is there something I can do?" he asked.

"No," she said, then reconsidered. "Drive me to the airport, I guess."

"Of course. I mean anything besides that."

"No. Thanks for being here though."

There were more calls made and received by Paris. She called home and spoke with her mother, who was now, without warning, a widow. Paris was pleased to hear that additional family and friends were there, weaving a web of sympathetic, loving support. Peggy called to let Paris know she had reserved a seat for her on a 3:40 P.M. flight to Chicago. Afterward, Paris called home yet again, this time speaking with her brother. She let him know the time of her arrival, and he promised to arrange for someone to pick her up at Chicago's Midway Airport. Then she called Deanna and shared the same information with her.

Having been on the phone for as long as she cared to be, she said to Camron, "I better pack a few things." Just before disappearing into her bedroom she said, "Oh, I thought of something else you can do for me."

"What?"

"Water my plants."

"I can handle that," Camron said with a little smile.

Paris returned his smile with one of her own, although more faint than his. But it was a smile nonetheless, which he found heartening.

It was just after two-thirty when they left Paris's apartment. Sixteen minutes later, they arrived at the Minneapolis-St. Paul International Airport. Camron parked in the short-term parking garage, and he and Paris walked to the ticket area, each pulling luggage-on-wheels behind them. Given that it was a Monday afternoon, traffic was sparse and they were soon at the counter. Paris received her ticket, checked her luggage, and they proceeded to the gate. Upon reaching her departure gate, they sat in two of the small, gray, vinyl-covered seats that populated much of the terminal space.

"Who's picking you up in Chicago?" Camron asked as he slid Paris's apartment key onto his key ring.

"My brother said it would be either him or my Uncle Jesse."

"You got everything you need?"

"I think so," Paris said.

"If not, let me know. I can go by your apartment, pick it up, and have it shipped to you next-day air."

A female voice came over the PA system. *"Ladies and gentlemen, welcome to NorWest Flight 394 nonstop to Chicago. We would like to begin preboarding with first class passengers...."*

"If I'm missing something, I'm sure it won't be that critical," Paris said. "I won't be gone more than a few days anyway. Probably come home Sunday or Monday."

Sunday was six days away, Monday even longer, Camron thought.

"I'm worrying about Momma though," Paris said. "She and Daddy have been together so long."

Trying to assuage her concern, Camron said, "I'm sure she'll find the strength to carry on."

"I know she will. It'll be hard for a while. But I know God won't put on us no more than we can handle," Paris said.

"I'm sure He won't."

"Ladies and gentlemen, I would like to call all passengers sitting in Row 20 and higher...."

"That's me," Paris said.

They both stood and faced each other. They hugged and Camron kissed Paris on her cheek.

"All right, sweetie. Be strong," Camron said. "And call me the moment you get there."

"I will," Paris promised.

He kissed her lightly on her lips. "Have a safe trip."

"I will," she said again.

"I'll talk to you this evening."

Paris nodded her head, mouthed an inaudible "Bye," then moved into a line that led through a door, out of the terminal, and to the plane. Camron stood near a steel beam column and watched her slowly advance. She reached a female attendant, who took her ticket, ripped away part of it, and gave the rest back to her. Paris looked back at Camron just before she walked through the door. They gave each other smiles, then she was gone.

Camron turned and began walking the way they had come. Suddenly, as his concern for Paris's well-being was replaced by a sadness and sense of loneliness all his own, he became lightheaded and could barely feel his feet touch the floor. He wondered, if he were by her side on the flight to Chicago, would such feelings go away as quickly as they had come.

On the drive home, imagining what Paris would have to endure the next few days, he recalled his own mother's funeral in '95: the late night phone call from an aunt letting him know his mother's condition was worsening, and that he should get to North Carolina as soon as possible; arriving home five hours after his mother had taken her last breath; he, his father, and his sister, Lena, discussing details of the grim ceremony with the director of the funeral parlor; the shock of seeing his mother's dead body for the first time, bloated and discolored by embalming fluid; the kind and touching words of remembrance from dozens of friends and relatives; the mass of people at the funeral; his family debating and arguing over the design of his mother's tombstone and wording of its epitaph; and, finally, the dark, empty void after everything was all over and he was back in Minnesota, twelve hundred miles from his mother's fresh grave. He knew many or more of those things Paris would now experience in some form or another.

Camron had been home for just over two hours before Paris called. "Hi. I'm here," she said. Her voice was more resonant than earlier that day.

"How was the flight?" Camron asked.

"It was good. Not too long."

"Your brother pick you up?"

"No. My uncle. He was waiting at the terminal when I got

there."

"How are things there?"

"A lot of people are here, but things are quiet. Kind of weird. The mood is heavy, somber. But that's to be expected, I guess."

"Your mom doing all right?"

"Yes she is. I thought I would have to provide support for *her*, but, to be honest, it's been the other way around."

"Really?"

"Yeah. I think she's done more to lift my spirits than I've done to lift hers."

"Mothers are like that."

"Mm-hmm," Paris hummed in agreement.

Camron looked at the bedroom clock. "Deanna and Jake should be getting there soon."

"Yeah, they should. They're renting a car at the airport and driving from there."

"So you're doing better too then?" Camron said, wanting to be sure.

"Hanging in here. Dealing with things minute-by-minute."

"That's all you can do, sweetie. That's all you can do."

"Well," Paris sighed, "Let me get back downstairs and see what else needs to be done. The kitchen's beginning to fill up with food."

"All right. Stay strong and call me when you can."

"I will. Probably tomorrow."

"Okay," Camron said. He knew they were about to hang up. But something else was on his mind. "Paris."

"Yes, honey?"

"I love you," he told her for the first time.

The phone line went silent for a moment, and Camron's heart-beat spiked.

"I love you too," Paris said.

27

Dissolution

ONCE THE THOUGHT OF SEPARATION entered my head, I couldn't escape it. It was with me at work, at home, in the car, or wherever I happened to be, haunting me like the ghost of a long-lost relative.

The omnipresence of such ruminations strengthened my resolve, and one day, on a sunny, cloudless, fall afternoon in 1999—not much more than three years to the day since Mara and I first met—I awkwardly initiated the dissolution of our marriage.

We were in my car, returning home from the grocery store.

"Mara, I've been thinking about some things. About this marriage really. That maybe we made a mistake."

I braced myself for her response. I was expecting something severe, but instead she calmly said, "Maybe we did."

There was a terse silence for the rest of the short drive home, which, when juxtaposed with the glorious day, seemed especially odd and unnatural. More silence followed when we arrived home.

As we were putting away the groceries, Mara shattered the muteness. "How long have you felt this way?"

"For a while now," I said. "A couple of months I suppose."

She made an audible "Humph" sound. "So what do we do?" she asked. "Get a divorce?"

I almost laughed at her question. "I think we'd have to start with a separation first."

"If that's what you want, Camron, that's fine with me," she said as she put some perishables into the refrigerator. "Because obviously you're not happy. You know?"

After shoving two big boxes of cereal into the cabinet over the stove, I replied, "And neither are you." I turned to face her. "The thing about happiness is, it can't be manufactured. And it can't be made to exist through pretense. It's either there or it isn't."

"I don't believe that," she retorted. "I think people can make a situation happy or sad. To a large extent it's up to them."

"To an extent, yes. But I think two people have to at least be close to being on the same page. With us, I don't know. Our personalities are similar in some ways. A lot of ways actually, but our approach to dealing with conflict is totally different. And right now, I just don't see that there'll be any changes in that aspect of this relationship."

"So we just throw in the towel?"

"This marriage isn't working, Mara. And it's nobody's fault. It's not your fault. It's not my fault."

Mara sat down at the kitchen table. "Is being married something you ever wanted to be in the first place, Camron?"

"Yes. I think so. But marriage shouldn't be this hard. If it were supposed to be this hard, why would it ever be desirable over just staying single?"

Mara looked out the bay windows of the kitchen into the beautiful day, then back at me. "Am I that difficult?"

"Mara, it's not you. Maybe it's me. Maybe marriage requires too much of too many things that I'm not good at. Like patience, understanding, humility, compromise. All I know is, the last few months have been trying, and I couldn't imagine living like this for the next forty years."

"I'm not sure anybody looks that far into the future," Mara said.

"Well I couldn't see living like this for the next five."

I opened the cabinet above the microwave. In it were several bottles of liquor.

"I'm gonna fix a drink," I said. "You want one?"

"No," Mara said, but quickly changed her mind. "Yeah, I'll take one. Whatever you're having."

I didn't have much skill when it came to mixing drinks, so I kept it simple. I pulled down a bottle of rum and, from another cabinet, two short glasses. I filled one glass a quarter full with rum, the other a bit more than that. I snatched a two-liter bottle of Coke from the refrigerator and added some of the cola to the glasses of rum. From the freezer I grabbed some cubes of ice and plopped two or three in each glass. I gave Mara the drink with the least amount of liquor, and sat down with her at the opposite end of the kitchen table.

"This doesn't surprise me," she said looking into her drink. "I knew it was coming."

"How's that?" I asked.

"I just knew. I felt it. It was just a matter of when."

I looked at Mara. Her eyes were soft and sad, very much unlike when they had accented the scowl she had given me that was so reminiscent of the one with which my mother had seared my father.

28

Homeward

PARIS'S NAKED BODY WAS THRASHING on top of Camron's, her grunts and moans shattering the quiet of the otherwise peaceful Saturday morning. Camron matched his thrusts with hers as she alternately sat atop him ramrod straight, palming and kneading her own breasts, then with bent back, her torso huddled over his, their tongues flailing. Paris's moans escalated, which Camron knew was a sign of the imminence of her climax. He wrapped his arms around her shoulders, brought her chest close to his, and pistoned himself deep inside her over and over. Her sensual grumblings morphed into cries of passion, and her entire body tremored and quaked as the waves of her orgasm washed over her from head to toe.

As the intensity of Paris's sexual release subsided, her skin's nerve endings—clenched like a million tiny fists—began to unwind and relax into a tranquillity. Camron and Paris's bodies, in constant motion just moments earlier, slowed to erratic throbs, then to no movement at all. He, however, was not finished. *She got hers,* Camron thought, *Now it's time for mine.*

He allowed her several more breaths before, in one seamless rolling maneuver, and without pulling himself out of her, he spun her body onto the bed. Using the momentum to spin himself, he quickly reversed their positions. Now on top, Camron began to move again. Paris, although still blissfully reposed in her own personal ecstasy, answered the pulses of his pelvis with pumps of her hips. Content in the knowledge that she was satisfied, Camron focused on his own pleasure. Soon, like a slow-climbing roller coaster, he could feel the insistent rising of his libido until, unable to go any higher, it fell over the edge and plunged into an ethereal abyss of satisfaction. A few more moans, then silence.

"Mmm," Camron sighed as his racing heartbeat slowed. "Did I tell you how much I missed you?"

Paris smiled without opening her eyes. "I think you just showed me. But I don't mind if you tell me again."

"I missed you," he said. He looked at her mouth. "And you," he said, and kissed Paris on the lips. "And you," he said to her neck, then kissed it as well. "And you," he repeated to her left nipple before kissing it also. To the right nipple: "And you too." *Smack.*

Paris's close-eyed smile blossomed into a wide grin as Camron persisted in teasing her breasts. But then she protested. "No no no, baby. I can't take anymore this morning."

After nine days in Chicago, Paris had returned from burying her father, and last night till now was the first chance she and Camron had found to spend any real time together since her arrival back in St. Paul.

"I'll fix us some breakfast," Camron offered. He rolled out of his bed naked, walked downstairs, and into the kitchen. Basking in the afterglow of their lovemaking, Paris could hear running water, then the clanging of pots and pans as Camron went about the business of preparing a morning meal.

He's so sweet, she thought. *It's too bad he can't cook much of anything beyond breakfast that well. But he loves me, and I think I love him too.*

Such thoughts made her heart sail. But her heart was also heavy. Heavy with concern for her mother, alone now in Chicago.

A week later, Camron and Paris were at Dixies, a St. Paul restaurant on Grand Avenue that offered samplings of Louisiana cuisine.

"So when should we take that trip to Montego Bay?" Camron asked of their excursion that was canceled due to her father's death.

"I don't know," Paris answered.

"The plane tickets are nonrefundable, but they can be rescheduled anytime for up to a year. And, considering how much vacation you used when you were in Chicago, we might have to wait nearly that long before we take it."

"I didn't have to use too much vacation time," Paris said. "My job gave me three bereavement days, so I used those plus two sick days and two vacation days."

"That's good."

"Yeah, it worked out well."

"Well, since you still have plenty of vacation, we'll go next week then," Camron joked.

Paris smiled, shook her head, and took a sip of Merlot from an oversized wineglass.

"So what is it you wanted to talk with me about?" Camron asked.

Paris had told him two days earlier that she needed to discuss something with him, and he'd been curious as to what was on her mind ever since. Paris's facial expression went from the relaxed smile she was sporting to a look that suggested she had just been reminded of something unpleasant. She averted her eyes down toward her bowl of gumbo, then back to him.

"I don't know how to tell you this," she said. Her eyes were focused on his now, and even seemed to be looking beyond them. And in her eyes, Camron thought he detected something akin to pain.

He tried to lighten a mood that had suddenly become heavy. "If you don't want to tell me face-to-face, we could always go on a talk show and you could spring it on me there."

Paris forced a barely discernable smile. Camron was about to speak again, if only to once more break the stiff silence, but she spoke before he had the chance. "Camron, I'm moving back to Chicago."

Camron's heart, like a scratched CD, lost its rhythm for a second.

Back to Chicago? he thought. *What the hell?*

"Oh," he said struggling to conceal a sudden rush of anxiety. "When did you decide to do that?"

"Last week. I'm just so worried about my mother being there at that house all by herself."

"Your brother's there, right? Right there in Chicago, I mean."

"Yeah, he's around. But he's hardly someone she can rely on."

Camron couldn't dispute that. Certainly not based on what information Paris had shared with him about her brother: two drug related arrests, parole violations, and three out of the last seven years in prison. *Irresponsible, drugged-out, punk-ass mothafucka.*

"That's big news," he said, then thought, *Damn.*

"Yes it is," Paris said. "I've been thinking about it since I first got back to St. Paul. Deanna and I have been talking about it and I ... I don't know. I just feel Momma needs somebody to be there for her right now."

Shit. Why can't Deanna and Jake and Cicely move to Chicago?

Paris responded to his thoughts: "And, of course, it's more difficult for Deanna to do something like that because she's there in Kansas City with a family and whatnot."

But what about us? In another year or two, who knows? Maybe we could have a family too.

"You'd live with your mom?" Camron asked.

"Yeah. For a while anyway."

I can't believe this is happening. The first woman I've truly cared about since I separated from Mara, and now she's about to skip town. God damn it.

"Paris, I don't want to seem insensitive, but where does that leave us?"

Paris deliberated his question, then said, "I don't know."

Giving in to his feelings, Camron asked, "Were we even a consideration when you were deciding this?"

Paris didn't say anything, and, in a flash, Camron realized he couldn't let his emotions get the best of him; allow him to be selfish.

"You know what? I shouldn't say that," he admitted. "I'm sorry. You need to do what you need to do. And I need to be supportive of that."

"I'm sorry, Camron. I don't know what else to do right now."

"There's nothing to be sorry about, sweetheart. You didn't create this situation. It's just one of those things. One of those ... unexpected things in life."

Paris, perhaps wanting to console, said, "Chicago's not too far away."

"No, it's not."

Camron knew, though—he knew right at that moment—it was far *enough* away that time could creep in between them and cool the emotions and desires they had for each other.

"When are you leaving?" he asked.

"At the end of the month."

There were two weeks left in the month of March. Two more weeks, Camron felt, before their relationship would fall from the clouds on which it had been floating, and land in a desert: a nether land of broken dreams and promises. A place where there was little hope of finding an oasis.

29

Separation

THE LAST FEW MONTHS OF MY LIFE as a husband to Mara were dominated by a sense of relief and liberation. To be sure, there were challenges involved with being estranged under the same roof. But there was always this overriding feeling that our self-imposed misery would soon be over.

We had scheduled our separation to begin in January. *Scheduled.* Ridiculous, isn't it? As if the commencement of a separation is something one pencils into their personal calendar like a woman's hair appointment. But that was how P referred to it in an e-mail he had sent to me in early November. *"When is the separation scheduled to start?"* he had written. It struck me as such a bizarre way of putting it that I laughed out loud.

Anyway, January was the month we had decided upon for our separation (exactly when in January we didn't discuss). However, Mara was a die-hard sentimentalist when it came to holidays, and a few days after Thanksgiving she concluded that it would be less wringing emotionally if we parted before the next holiday season.

"Camron, I don't know if I want to go through Christmas like this," she said to me after we had gotten into bed one night. "I talked with Kay last week"—Kay was her supervisor at NorWest—"and I'll be taking the last three weeks of the year off. I was thinking that spending that time at home in North Carolina would be good. I've called a few apartment complexes too, so having a place lined up when I get back right after New Year's shouldn't be a problem. I'll need some of the money that you were going to be giving me though."

The money she was referring to was the crux of what would essentially become our divorce agreement: I give her $20,000 and we call it a day. No lawyers, no mess.

"All right. I can give you half in a couple of weeks, and the rest later on in January," I said.

I had made that $20,000 offer to Mara in late October. By that time, the concept of separating, and—the logical next step—divorcing, had marinated to the point of becoming less surreal and abstract. As a result, our conversation on the matter was not as emotion-laden.

"Mara, I'd like to avoid as much rigamarole as possible with this separation," I had said to her over the phone on that October evening. She was working and in Miami at the time. I had planned to talk with her when she returned home, but the issue was beginning to weigh too heavily on my mind.

"Rigamarole? How do we avoid rigamarole with a situation like this?" Mara asked in amazement.

"I'm not talking about emotionally. I'm talking about the legal aspects. If possible, I'd like to avoid getting lawyers involved."

"Right," she said. There was caution in her tone.

"So what I'm proposing is this: Once we're separated, I give you $20,000. Then, however or whenever a divorce is finalized, we just sign whatever legal documents we need to sign, and that's it. That way we can do this without a lot of haggling."

For a moment, only silence could be heard across the telephone lines that joined us. Then Mara said, "That sounds fine."

I borrowed half of the money from my 401(k). The rest I got through an increase in an equity line of credit. Considering that, when all was said and done, we would end up being married for not much more than two years, and with no kids involved, I felt I was being more than fair. And while that settlement would later put a serious crimp in my cash flow, the most serious challenge for me during those last few months of us being together was, without a doubt, sex. Or more precisely, the lack of it.

Before there had been any talk of separating, our sex life had already been reduced to sporadic, stiff exercises void of affection. But with plans for the termination of our union taking shape, sex became nonexistent. So it was in this environment—as the final leaves of fall fell from the trees, and October became November—I slipped into an affair.

Her name was Nena, a big-eyed, light-skinned cutie with luxuriously wavy, shoulder-length, chemical-free hair. I had run into her several times at the clubs, and we had developed a friendly, teasing rapport.

She knew I was married. She also knew I wasn't happy. And when I told her one evening, over the beat of the DJ's music, that I was separating from my wife, she showered me with the obligatory condolences: "That's terrible" and "I'm so sorry to hear that." But I also noticed a twinkle in her eye.

We danced and further loosened our inhibitions with MGDs and Alizés. Soon after midnight, I said to her, "You should take me home with you tonight."

With a smile on her face, she pondered my suggestion for about three seconds. "All right."

Later that night in her bedroom, with slivers of moonlight slicing through the openings in her horizontal blinds, it was nice to finally fuck with some passion. But having broken my vows, I was a hypocrite. Nevertheless, I did not feel guilty because once Mara and I had agreed to separate, the marriage, for all practical purposes, was over. All that was left to officially end the relationship was the technicality of a six-month separation, followed by some paperwork.

Nena and I saw each other regularly well into the Spring of 2000. Eventually, though, she got caught up in the wake of my exuberance at being single again, and, over the summer months, the relationship faded.

When Mara left during that second week in December for North Carolina, I expected to see her when she returned a few days into the New Year. However, she called me the day after Christmas, which was also Umoja, the first day of Kwanzaa.

"Camron, it's me," she said after I answered the phone.

I was taken aback when I heard her voice because she had called the day before to wish me a Merry Christmas. "Hey. What's up?"

"Nothing much."

"How was Christmas?" I asked.

"Christmas was wonderful. Everyone was here."

"Even your sister from Jersey?"

"Yeah, Bobbi finally made it."

Bobbi was Mara's oldest sister. Her given name was Barbara, but everyone called her Bobbi.

"Good. So what's up?" I repeated.

"I needed to talk with you about something. I was going to mention it yesterday, but then thought it might be better to discuss it later."

"Later meaning now?" I asked.

"Yeah."

"Okay. What is it?"

"You know when you said you wanted us to transition into this separation as smoothly as possible?" Mara said.

"Yes."

"I do too. And right now I'm still needing some time to adjust to this."

"Right," I said, wondering what she was trying to get at.

"So I need you to give me the space I feel I need."

"Okay," I said. I still couldn't fathom what she was talking about. A separation, by definition, should fulfill one's need for space. And as far as literal space was concerned, she had already signed a lease on a one-bedroom apartment in a downtown Minneapolis high-rise that she and Patrice (who was seven months pregnant with her and Donnell's second child) had discovered before she left for North Carolina.

Mara continued. "I'll be getting back in town next Tuesday."

"January 4th?"

"Yes. So I was planning on coming to the house and getting a few things packed that afternoon, and I was wondering … if you would mind not being there."

That was it? That was what she needed to talk with me about?

"That's fine, Mara. How much time do you need?"

"Probably until seven o'clock."

"All right. I'll be sure not to be here."

And I wasn't. When I did return home on that evening around seven-forty-five, all of Mara's things were gone: her clothes and shoes (which suddenly left me with more closet space than I knew what to do with), dishes, and the few pieces of furniture she had brought with her when she had moved into my home twenty-eight months earlier. The fact that all of her stuff was gone suggested to me that she had used a moving company. After the $10,000 check I had given her a couple of weeks earlier, she could certainly afford it.

I walked into the kitchen and saw that Mara had also left some items on the table: two silver keys—one for each of the house door locks—and the garage door opener.

After Mara moved out, nearly three weeks passed before I heard anything from her. She called late one weekday afternoon, told me she was doing okay, and gave me her mailing address, presumably so

I'd have somewhere to send the remainder of the $20,000 I owed her. The next time we talked was in mid-February, a phone conversation as well. She wished me a belated happy birthday, told me Patrice and Donnell had had another baby boy, and that she had decided to move back to North Carolina. I suggested we get together before she left. She agreed, and, three weeks later, we met at a dingy but quaint corner coffee shop a block down the street from her new place.

I was there before her, right at the appointed time of four o'clock. Mara arrived ten minutes later, walking in from what was an unusually mild, but gray, March Sunday afternoon. She looked delectable in a purple and black three-quarter-length skirt, purple top, and long black trench coat. Her face was framed by the dark brown coils of hair she had taken a liking to some months earlier.

I stood as she approached the table. "Hey," I said and gave her a light hug.

"Sorry I'm late," she said. "You haven't been here too long, have you?"

"No."

She seemed to be in good spirits, with a vim about her that I hadn't seen in a long time.

"How do you like living downtown?" I asked.

"I love it. Everything's within walking distance of my apartment. And the drive from here to the airport isn't too bad either."

"And now you're moving again."

"Yep," she said.

"What made you decide to move back to North Carolina?" I asked.

"This cold place just isn't home to me. It doesn't *feel* like home. You know? And now that we're no longer together, there's no reason for me to stay."

I nodded.

"At the time that we met at Patrice's reception, I was seriously considering moving then," she added. "But, of course, we *did* meet, and the rest is history."

"That's one way to put it," I responded. "So are you moving to Raleigh?"

"No. Charlotte. That way I'll have more options at NorWest."

"You want to stay with NorWest?"

"Yeah. For now."

"Cool."

Our chocolate brown eyes locked for a second.

"So what happened to us, Dickerson?" Mara asked.

"Can I get you something to drink?" That was the waitress, a petite, youngish-looking brunette, busting into the middle of our conversation.

Mara looked up at the waitress and smiled. "Can I get a mocha *au lait*? Large."

"All right. Anything else for you, sir?"

"No, I'm fine," I said, touching the glass that contained the lemonade I had ordered two minutes after my arrival.

"You need menus?" the waitress asked, continuing with her intrusion.

"You want something?" I asked Mara. She shook her head. I told the waitress, "No, just the drinks," who then turned and walked away.

"What happened to us?" Mara asked again. The sincerity with which she asked the question surprised me.

"I've asked myself that question too. I don't know."

"We loved each other, didn't we?"

"Yes we did," I assured her. "But sometimes, love's not enough."

Mara shook her head again. "You know it's funny, but problems in my first marriage started in the same exact way."

"What do you mean?" I asked.

"With me finding a phone number in his pocket."

"Mara, I never even talked with that girl again."

"I know. He denied any involvement too," she said of her first husband. "Denied, denied, denied. Denied everything. Right up until I caught 'em in bed together."

My face crinkled a bit. "You never told me that. Mara, why didn't you tell me?"

"Because I was too busy trying to keep myself from being paranoid. But I knew you were going out when I was out of town, so it was hard for me *not* to be paranoid."

"I wasn't going out that much in the beginning of our marriage," I reminded her. "And as far as that phone number goes, we were having problems long before you found that."

"I know, I know," she said scoldingly. "We weren't screwing enough for your tastes."

"That was one thing, yeah."

"Camron, do you know how tired I would be sometimes when I'd get home from work? Especially at night."

"Of course. But you know what, Mara? Sometimes—no, a lot of times—you would use sex as a weapon. Withhold it if we happened to have had an argument that day, or if you were upset at me about something."

The waitress returned with Mara's drink, and, perhaps sensing we didn't care to be interrupted again, sat it before her and left without a word.

"I didn't use it as a weapon. But I'm like any other woman. If there's no love in the room, how am I supposed to be in the mood to *make* love?"

The conversation was beginning to take on a feeling of familiarity.

"Listen," I said. "I don't want to rehash all the issues we had in our marriage right here."

"Nor do I," Mara agreed.

"Good," I said. "So let's just drink and be merry."

"Let's."

We both smiled at our sudden turn to silliness.

"Seriously, I just wanted to wish you well in your move back to North Carolina," I said.

"Thank you. I won't be moving until the end of June."

"Oh. I thought you were moving at the end of the month?"

"I was hoping I could," Mara said. "But the apartment people won't let me out of my lease, which won't expire till then."

"Good. That gives us plenty of time to go back to your place for some hot, passionate, monkey love."

"Camron, you're so silly. And after all that passion died down, then what?"

"I don't know. Do it again."

Mara smiled and shook her head.

When we left the pub, the sky was grayer, and a cold, drizzling rain was falling. I ran to my car while Mara stood on the sidewalk just outside the front door of the establishment, sheltered from the water by an overhead canopy. I pulled around, she hopped in, and I drove her the short distance to her complex.

"Thank you for the mocha," she said sweetly as we rolled to a stop on a semicircular drive near the entrance of her building.

"You're welcome. Thank you for coming. And since I now know you'll be here until June, I'm sure we'll talk more than once between now and then."

"I'm sure we will," she said.

"Okay. Well, you take care, Mara."

"You too, Dickerson."

Mara opened the car door and was about to step out.

"Hey!" I said, causing her to look back in my direction and freeze in place. "Are you keeping the name?"

"What name?" she asked.

"Dickerson."

"I suppose. At least until I find my next Prince Charming."

I chuckled. "Bye."

"Bye," she said, and slammed the car door shut. I watched her as she ran into her building, and out of the rain.

Mara and I would see each other three more times before she moved back down South. And now as I lie here staring at this empty ring box, remembering her and me, I still wonder exactly what tore us apart and forced us into separate lives. I wonder because I truly thought she was that special someone. My soul mate. But, of course, that turned out not to be true. And now she's gone. No longer a part, for better or worse, of the ebb and flow of my daily routine.

Sometimes I believe, albeit insincerely, my chance for a lifetime love is over. Time and space can permit a man only so many opportunities for that kind of happiness.

So let the young souls take their shot at love. They're still full of hope!; yet able to dream that true love will find them.

As for me, I still *hope* for love. Now and then, late at night, I even ache for it. But with the innocence of my younger days behind me, love is something of which I no longer dream.

30

Resolution

AS CAMRON DROVE TOWARD THE DARK St. Paul skyline during the wee hours of a Saturday morning, he could clearly see the silhouette of Paris's former high-rise home. It evoked memories of dinners, laughter, and passion-filled nights.

Three weeks had passed since Paris's move back to the Windy City, and Camron was more convinced now than then of the fatal path their relationship was on. They had spoken several times by phone since her departure, but each exchange seemed more and more like a dress rehearsal for that final conversation when one or the other would express their desire to end the relationship. Indeed, things had come close to ending during their last conversation the previous Wednesday.

"So when do you want to come see me?" Paris had asked.

"Sweetie, you know I don't have a free Saturday for another four weekends," Camron said. He was referring to the Java class he was taking that ran all day on Saturdays. "You should come see *me*."

"Yeah. That's an option too. This weekend won't work though. Nor next."

"So we'll see each other in two or three weeks. And then what? We wait six more?"

"No," Paris said. "We'll figure something out."

"I hope so. Otherwise this is going to get difficult."

"Why do you say that?" she asked.

"Paris. We haven't seen each other in three weeks, and probably won't see each other for that many more. That's no way to run a relationship, baby."

"So what do you want to do?"

"I don't know," he told her. "I don't know. We got to do something though."

Despite that declaration, the conversation ended with no resolution.

As the highways brought Camron closer to his neighborhood, he thought about what the next step should be for them. Perhaps he should call her tomorrow and put a stop to this foolish notion that they could sustain a romance with nearly four hundred miles between them. That way they could confront the inevitability of the end of their relationship directly, and avoid the elongated pain of a gradual breakup. Because what were they to each other if they only saw one another every six weeks? Certainly not, by Camron's estimation, boyfriend and girlfriend. At best, he figured, they would be friends who got together every few weeks to screw.

Arriving home, Camron walked into the dark silence of his house, kicked off his shoes, and trudged upstairs. He tuned the TV to a constant satellite stream of light jazz, then went mechanically about the business of preparing for bed. Halfway through the process, he decided a late-night soak in the Jacuzzi was more appetizing than his waterbed, and began filling the oversized tub with water. He lit some candles, switched the bathroom lights off, peeled out of his underwear, and climbed into the comfortable, warm water. He added some bubble bath, and turned on the Jacuzzi's jets to make suds. He laid his head back onto the inflatable pillow and closed his eyes.

"Ah ... this feels good," he said out loud, barely able to hear himself over the hum of the swirling water. Four minutes later, his body was covered with foamy bubbles. The froth had climbed close to the top of the tub before Camron turned off the water jets and the noise that accompanied their operation.

The relaxing sounds of Najee's "Tokyo Blue" were drifting from his bedroom, and Camron began to float toward sleep. The ring of the phone, however, awakened him. He considered hopping from the tub and running into the bedroom to answer it, but decided he wouldn't be able to reach the receiver before it turned over to his messaging service. Or maybe he could reach it, he thought, but not without leaving a trail of water and bubbles from the bathroom to the bedroom. Not to mention the chill he'd have to endure. He brought his left arm up from the water and brushed away the foam from his wrist. His watch showed 2:17 A.M.

Who'd be calling this late? he thought. *Hope nothing's wrong back home.*

Camron soaked in the warm bath for a few more minutes, then, curious as to who had just called, stood up, brushed away as many of the soapy bubbles from his body as he could, climbed out of the tub, and began toweling himself dry. He walked into the bedroom and to the base on which the cordless phone rested. He picked up the receiver, scrolled to the call log, and quickly saw the number that had just rang his phone belonged to Paris. His anxiety that something may be awry in North Carolina was immediately replaced with concern for Paris. He added a "1" to the beginning of her number and pressed redial. She answered on the second ring.

"Hello," Paris said.

"Paris. Did you just call?"

"Mm-hmm. Did I wake you?"

"No. I was in the Jacuzzi."

"Oh, I'm sorry."

"No, that's okay," Camron said as he reclined on the bed. "Is everything all right?"

"Everything's fine. I couldn't sleep, that's all."

"Why not?"

"Couldn't get something off my mind."

"What?" Camron asked.

Paris hesitated before speaking. "Us."

"What about us?"

"Our conversation on Wednesday bothered me for some reason. It felt like things were ending."

"What gave you that impression?" he asked.

"Your frustration. I could hear it in your voice."

"That obvious, huh?"

"Yes," Paris said. "And I'm frustrated too."

"How so?"

"I'm frustrated by the same thing you're frustrated with. That we haven't been able to see each other, and just be together."

"True. But you're there providing as much support as you can to your mom, and I'm here in this class all day on Saturdays. And that, for at least the next three weeks, is our situation."

Paris hinted at something. "Maybe we won't have to wait that long."

"What do you mean?" Camron asked.

"Maybe I can come see you next week."

"Next week? I thought you said that wouldn't work."

"It didn't, but my mom and I had a long talk."

"About what?" he wondered.

"Everything," Paris said. "We talked about everything. From things that happened when I was a little girl, to all that's been going on in the last few weeks."

"That must have been a long conversation."

"It was," Paris said. "And of course we talked about you and I. I told her I was afraid of what all this distance would do to us."

"And what did she say?"

"She asked me if I loved you. I told her yes. And then she said, 'Does he love *you*?' I said, 'Yes. That's what he tells me.' And she said, 'If that's true then, together, you'll figure out a way to make it work.' "

A soft smile spread over Camron's face. "Sounds like good motherly insight to me."

"I thought so too. So since it's up to us whether this thing will work or not, I figured—given that your class lasts for a few more weeks—I'll just come see you next weekend. Then, when your class is over, you can come see me. Then I'll come see you, then you can come see me, and on and on like that."

"Sounds like you got it all figured out."

"Mm-hmm. So is that all right? Me coming to see you next weekend?"

"Of course, sweetie," Camron said. "And I know exactly what we can do."

"What?"

"No, never mind," he said, reconsidering his thought. "Bad idea."

"Why?"

"We'd need a little more time than just a weekend. We'd need four days, minimum."

"A four-day weekend? That might be doable too."

"Wait wait wait. Why is it that, suddenly, you have all this extra time on your hands?" Camron asked.

"During our talk, Momma told me that I have to stop worrying so much about her. That I have to live my own life. And she made me promise I'd do that."

"Moms are so wise," Camron said.

"So tell me your idea about what we can do next weekend?"

"Well ... we do still have those tickets to Montego Bay."

"Oh, that's right," Paris recalled. "You think they'd let us use them on such short notice?"

"Probably. If not, we could just get two more."

"What about your class?"

"That class won't miss me for one Saturday."

"That would be so much fun," Paris said, elated by the prospect of a Caribbean weekend together. "But that was supposed to be our escape from winter. There isn't much winter to escape from now."

"True. But we could avoid the last few showers of April," Camron said.

Paris chuckled. "I guess that's as good an excuse as any."

*For reading group discussion questions
and order information,
please visit the author's website at*

www.dcdouglass.com